...agency. And
with Christmas just around the corner they're
gearing up for their busiest period yet!

But as the snowflakes begin to fall these
Christmas Cinderellas are about to be swept
off their feet by romantic heroes of their own...

Don't miss the first book in our
Maids Under the Mistletoe quartet

A Countess for Christmas
by Christy McKellen
October 2016

Also in this series

Greek Tycoon's Mistletoe Proposal
by Kandy Shepherd
November 2016

Christmas in the Boss's Castle
by Scarlet Wilson
December 2016

Her New Year Baby
Secret by Jessica Gilmore
January 2017

A COUNTESS
FOR CHRISTMAS

BY
CHRISTY MCKELLEN

MILLS & BOON

First Published in Great Britain 2016
By Mills & Boon, an imprint of HarperCollins*Publishers*
1 London Bridge Street, London, SE1 9GF

© 2016 Harlequin Books S.A.

Special thanks and acknowledgement are given to Christy McKellen for her contribution to the Maids Under the Mistletoe series.

ISBN: 978-0-263-92024-6

23-1016

Our policy is to use papers that are natural, renewable and recyclable products and made from wood grown in sustainable forests. The logging and manufacturing processes conform to the legal environmental regulations of the country of origin.

Printed and bound in Spain
by CPI, Barcelona

Formerly a video and radio producer, **Christy McKellen** now spends her time writing fun, impassioned and emotive romance with an undercurrent of sensual tension. When she's not writing she can be found enjoying life with her husband and three children, walking for pleasure and researching other people's deepest secrets and desires.

Christy loves to hear from readers. You can get hold of her at www.christymckellen.com.

This one's for all my wonderful friends,
especially Alice, Karen and Sophie, my best buddies
since our school days, and for the fabulous ladies
writing this continuity with me, Kandy, Scarlet and
Jessica, who I'm also privileged to call my friends.

CHAPTER ONE

THIS HAD TO be the most challenging party that Emma Carmichael had ever worked at.

As fabulous as the setting was—a grand Chelsea town house that had been interior designed to within an inch of its life, presiding over the genteel glamour of Sloane Square—the party itself felt stilted and lifeless.

The trouble was, Emma mused as she glided inconspicuously through the throng, handing out drinks to the primped and polished partygoers, it was full of people who attended parties for a living rather than for pleasure, in an attempt to rub shoulders with London's great and good.

She knew all about that type of party after being invited to a glut of them in her late teens, either with her parents or with friends from her private girls' school in Cambridge. But she'd been a very different person then, pampered and carefree. Those privileged days were long gone now though, along with her darling late father's reputation and all their family's money.

As if her thoughts had conjured up the demons that had plagued her for the six years following his death, her phone vibrated in her pocket and she discreetly slipped it out and glanced at it, only to see it was another text message from her last remaining creditor reminding her she was late with her final repayment. Stomach sinking, she shoved the phone back into her pocket and desperately tried to reinstate the cheerful smile that her boss, Jolyon Fitzherbert, expected his staff to wear at all times.

'Emma, a word! Over here!' came the peremptory tones of the man himself from the other side of the room.

Darn. Busted.

Turning, she met her boss's narrowed eyes and swallowed hard as he beckoned her over to where he stood holding court to a small group of guests with one elbow propped jauntily against the vulgar marble fireplace.

Emma had encountered the bunch of reprobates he was with a number of times since she'd begun working for Jolyon two months ago so she was well used to their contemptuous gazes that slid over her face as she approached now. They didn't believe in fraternising with the hired help.

If only Jolyon felt the same.

It was becoming harder and harder to avoid his wandering hands and suggestive gaze, especially when she found herself alone with him. So far she'd been politely cool and it seemed to have held him at bay, but as soon as he got a couple of drinks into him dodging his advances became a whole lot harder.

Fighting down her apprehension, she gave Jolyon a respectful nod and smile as she came to a halt in front of him.

'Can I be of service?'

Jolyon's eyes seemed to bulge with menace in his flushed face. 'I do hope I didn't just see you playing with your mobile phone when you're supposed to be serving these good people, Emma, because that would be rude and unprofessional, would it not?' he drawled.

Emma's stomach rolled with unease. 'Er—yes. I mean no, I wasn't—' She could feel heat creeping up her neck as the whole group stared at her with ill-disguised disdain. 'I was just checking—'

'I'm sure you think you're too good to be serving drinks to the likes of us—' Jolyon said loudly over the top of her, layering his voice with haughty sarcasm.

'No, of course not—'

The expression on his face was now half leer, half snarl. '—but since I'm paying you to be here, I expect to have your full attention.'

'Yes, of course, Jolyon. You absolutely have it,' Emma said, somehow managing to dredge up a smile, despite the sickening pull of humiliation dragging her spirits down towards the floor.

He eyed her with an unnerving twinkle of malice in his expression, as if he was getting a thrill out of embarrassing her. 'In that case I'll have a large whisky.'

Emma opened her mouth to ask whether anyone else in the group required anything, but before the words could emerge Jolyon flapped a dismissive hand in her face and barked, 'Go on, fetch!'

Stumbling backwards, stupefied by his rudeness, she gave him a jerky nod and turned away, mortification flooding her whole body with unwelcome heat.

Twisting the chain she always wore around her neck to remind her of better times—before everything in her life had gone to hell in a hand basket—

she took a deep, calming breath as she walked stiffly over to where Jolyon kept his whisky decanter in an antique burr walnut drinks cabinet. Pouring his regular measure of two fingers of the dark amber liquid into a cut-glass tumbler with a shaking hand, she managed to slosh a little over the rim and had to surreptitiously wipe it off the wood with her apron so she didn't get shouted at for not treating his furniture with due respect.

That was the most frustrating thing about working for Jolyon; he treated *her* with less respect than an inanimate object and all she could do was bite her lip and get on with it.

Clio Caldwell, who ran the high-end agency Maids in Chelsea that had found her this housekeeping position, had warned her that Jolyon was a difficult character when she'd offered her the job, but since he also paid extremely well Emma had decided she was prepared to handle his irascible outbursts and overly tactile ways if she was well remunerated for it. If she could just stick it out here for a little while longer she'd be in the position to pay off the last of her father's debts and be able to put this whole sordid business to bed, then she could finally move on with her life.

What a relief that would be.

Out of nowhere the old familiar grief hit her hard in the chest.

Some days she missed her father so much her heart throbbed with pain. What she wouldn't give to have him back again, enveloping her in a great big bear hug and telling her that everything was going to be okay, that she was loved and that he wouldn't let anything hurt her.

But she knew she was being naïve. All the years he'd been telling her that, he'd actually been racking up astronomical debts. The life that she'd once believed was real and safe had evaporated into thin air the moment she'd lost him to a sudden heart attack and her mother had promptly fallen apart, leaving her to deal with a world of grief and uncertainty on her own.

Gripping the tumbler so hard her knuckles cracked, she returned to where her boss stood. 'Here you go, Jolyon,' she said calmly.

He didn't even look at her, just took the glass from her outstretched hand and turned his back on her, murmuring something to the man next to him, who let out a low guffaw and gave Emma the most fleeting of glances.

It reminded her all too keenly of the time right after her father's funeral when she couldn't go anywhere without being gossiped about and stared at with a mixture of pity and condescension.

Forcing herself to ignore the old familiar sting of angry defensiveness, she plastered a nonchalant smile onto her face and dashed back to the kitchen, and sanctuary.

Stumbling in through the door, she let out a sigh of relief, taking a moment to survey the scene and to centre herself, feeling her heart rate begin to slow down now that she was back in friendly company.

She didn't want anyone in here to see how shaken up she was, not when she was supposed to be the one in charge of running the party. After years of handling difficult situations on her own she was damned if she was going to fall apart now.

Fortunately, Clio at the agency had come up trumps

with the additional waiting staff for the party today. Two of the girls, Sophie and Grace, had become firm friends of hers after they'd all found themselves working at a lot of the same events throughout the last year. Before meeting these two it had been a long time since Emma had had friends that she could laugh with so easily. The very public scandal surrounding her father's enormous debts had put paid to a lot of what she'd thought were solid friendships in the past—owing someone's family an obscene amount of money would do that to a relationship, it seemed, especially within the censorious societal set in which she used to circulate.

Sophie, a bubbly blonde with a generous smile and a quick wit, had brought along an old school friend of hers tonight too, a cute-as-a-button Australian who was visiting England for a few months called Ashleigh, whose glossy mane of chestnut-red hair shone so radiantly under the glaring kitchen lights it was impossible to look away from her.

During short breaks in serving the partygoers that evening, the four of them had bonded while having a good giggle at some of the entitled behaviour they'd witnessed.

Emma's mirth had been somewhat tainted though, by the memory of how she'd acted much the same way when she was younger and how ashamed she felt now about taking her formerly privileged life so much for granted.

'Hey, lovely ladies,' she said, joining them at the kitchen counter where they were all busying about, filling fresh glasses with pink champagne and mojitos for the demanding guests.

'Hey, Emma, I was just telling Ashleigh how much fun it was, working at the Snowflake Ball last New Year's Eve,' Sophie said, making her eyebrows dance with delight. 'Are you working there again this year? Please say yes!'

'I hope so, as long as Jolyon agrees to give me the time off. He's supposed to be going skiing in Banff, so I should be free for it,' Emma said, shooting her friend a hopeful smile.

The annual New Year's Snowflake Ball was a glittering and awe-inspiring event that the whole of Chelsea society turned out for. Last year she and the girls had enjoyed themselves immensely from the wings after serving the guests with the most delectable— and eye-wateringly expensive—food and drink that London had to offer. Caught up in the romance of it all, Emma had even allowed herself to fantasise along with the others about how perhaps they'd end up attending as guests one day, instead of as waiting staff.

Not that there was a snowflake's chance in hell of that happening any time soon, not with her finances in their current state.

'Are you ladies working there too?' Emma asked, bouncing her gaze from Sophie to Grace, then on to Ashleigh.

Grace, a willowy, strikingly pretty woman who wore a perpetual air of no-nonsense purpose like a warm but practical coat, flashed her a grin. 'Wouldn't miss it for the world. You should definitely let Clio know if you're interested, Ashleigh.' She turned to give the bright-eyed redhead an earnest look. 'I know she's looking for smart, dedicated people to work at that event. She'd snap you up in a second.'

'Yeah, I might. I'm supposed to be going back to Australia to spend Christmas with my folks, but I don't know if I can face it,' Ashleigh said, self-consciously smoothing a strand of hair behind her ear. 'It's not going to be much of a celebratory atmosphere if I'm constantly trying to avoid being in the same room as my ex-fiancé the whole time.'

'He's going to be at your parents' house for Christmas?' Grace asked, aghast. 'Wow. Awkward.'

'Yeah, just a bit,' Ashleigh said, shuffling on the spot. 'If I do stay here I'm going to have to find another place to live though. I'm only booked into the B and B until the beginning of December, which means I've got less than a month to find new digs.' She glanced at them all, her eyes wide with hope. 'Anyone looking for a roomie by any chance? I'll take a floor, a sofa, whatever you've got!'

'Sorry, sweetheart,' Sophie said, shaking her head so her long sleek hair swished across her shoulders. 'As you know, my tiny bedroom's barely big enough for the single mattress I have in it and with my living area doubling as my dressmaking studio I can't even see the sofa under all the boxes of cloth and sewing materials.' She smiled grimly. 'And even if I could, it's on its last legs and not exactly comfortable.'

The other girls shook their heads too.

'I can't help either, Ashleigh, I'm afraid,' Emma said. 'My mother's staying with me on and off at the minute while her place in France is being damp proofed and redecorated and I don't think her nerves would take having someone she doesn't know kipping on the sofa. She's a little highly strung like that.'

'No worries,' Ashleigh said, batting a hand even

though her shoulders remained tense, 'I'm sure something will turn up.'

One of the other waitresses came banging into the kitchen then, looking harassed.

'Emma, the guests are starting to complain about running out of drinks out there.'

'On it,' Emma said, picking up a tray filled with the drinks that Grace had been diligently pouring throughout their conversation and backing out through the swinging kitchen door with it.

'Later, babes.'

Turning round to face the party, readying herself to put on her best and most professional smile again, her gaze alighted on a tall male figure that she'd not noticed before on the other side of the room. There was an intense familiarity about him that shot an unsettling feeling straight to her stomach.

It was something about the breadth of his back and the way his hair curled a little at his nape that set her senses on high alert. The perfect triangle of his body, which led her gaze down to long, long legs, was her idea of the perfect male body shape.

A shape she knew as well as her own and a body she'd once loved very, very much.

Blood began to pump wildly through her veins.

The shape and body of Jack Westwood, Earl of Redminster.

The man in question turned to speak to someone next to him, revealing his profile and confirming her instincts.

It was him.

Prickly heat cascaded over her skin as she stared

with a mixture of shock and nervous excitement at the man she'd not set eyes on for six years.

Ever since her life had fallen apart around her.

Taking a step backwards, she looked wildly around her for some kind of cover to give her a moment to pull herself together, but other than dashing back to the kitchen, which she couldn't do without drawing attention to herself, there wasn't any.

What was he doing here? He was supposed to be living in the States heading up the billion-dollar global electronics empire he'd left England to set up six years ago.

At the age of twenty-one he'd been dead set on making a name for himself outside the aristocratic life he'd been born into and had been determined not to trade on the family name but to make a success of himself through hard work and being the best in his field. From what she'd read in the press it seemed he'd been very successful at it too. But then she'd always known he would be. The man positively exuded power and intelligence from every pore.

After reading in the papers that his grandfather had died recently she'd wondered whether he'd come back to England.

It looked as if she had her answer.

He was surrounded, as ever, by a gaggle of beautiful women, all looking at him as if he was the most desirable man on earth. It had always been that way with him; he drew women to him like bees to a honeypot. The first time she'd ever laid eyes on him, at the tender age of twelve, he'd been surrounded by girls desperate for his attention. His sister, Clare—her best friend from her exclusive day school—had laughed and rolled her eyes about it, but Emma knew she loved her brother deeply and was in awe of his charisma.

Emma, on the other hand, had spent years feeling rattled and annoyed by his unjustified judgemental sniping at her and for a long time she'd thought he truly disliked her. Her greatest frustration at that point in her life was not being able to work out why.

As she watched, still frozen to the spot, one of the women in his group leaned towards him, laying a possessive hand on his arm as she murmured something into his ear, and Emma's heart gave an extra-hard squeeze.

Was he with her?

The thought made her stomach roll with nausea.

Feeling as though she'd stepped into the middle of one of her nightmares, she took a tentative pace sideways, hoping to goodness he wouldn't choose that exact moment to turn around and see her standing there wearing her Maids in Chelsea apron, holding a tray of drinks.

'Hey, you, don't just stand there gawping, missy, bring me one of those drinks. I'm parched!' one of Jolyon's most obstreperous acquaintances shouted over to her.

Face flaming, Emma sidestepped towards him, keeping Jack's broad back in her peripheral vision, hoping, *praying*, he wouldn't spot her.

Unfortunately, because she wasn't paying full attention to where she was stepping, she managed to stand on the toe of the woman talking with Mr Shouty, who then gave out a loud squeal of protest, flinging her arms out and catching the underside of the tray Emma was holding. Before she had a chance to save it, the entire tray filled with fine crystal glasses and their lurid contents flipped up into the air, then rained down onto the beige carpet that Jolyon had had laid only the week before.

Gaudy-coloured alcohol splattered the legs of the man standing nearby and a deathly silence fell, swiftly followed by a wave of amused chatter and tittering in its wake.

Emma dropped to her knees, desperately trying to save the fine crystal glasses from being trampled underfoot, feeling the sticky drinks that now coated the carpet soak into her skirt and tights.

All she needed now was for Jolyon to start shouting at her in front of Jack and her humiliation would be complete.

Glancing up through the sea of legs, desperate to catch the eye of a friendly face so she could escape quickly, her stomach flipped as her gaze connected with a pair of the most striking eyes she'd ever known.

Jack Westwood was staring at her, his brow creased into a deep frown and the expression on his face as shocked as she suspected hers had been to see him only moments ago.

Heart thumping, she tore her gaze away from his, somehow managing to pile the glasses haphazardly back onto the tray with shaking hands, then stand up and push her way through the agitated crowd, back to the safety of the kitchen.

'Sorry! Sorry!' she muttered as she shuffled past people. 'I'll be back in a moment to clean up the mess. Please mind your feet in case there's any broken glass.'

Her voice shook so much she wouldn't have been surprised if nobody had understood a word she'd said.

Please let him think he just imagined it was me. Please, please!

As she stumbled into the kitchen the first person she saw was Grace.

'Oh, my goodness, Emma! What happened?'

Her friend darted towards her, relieving her of the drinks tray with its precariously balanced glasses.

Grabbing the worktop for support, Emma took a couple of deep breaths before turning to face her friend's worried expression.

'Emma? Are you okay? You're as white as a sheet,' Sophie gasped, also alerted by her dramatic entrance. 'Did someone say something to you? Did they hurt you?' From the mixture of fear and anger on Sophie's face, Emma suspected her friend had some experience in that domain.

'No, no, it's nothing like that.' She swallowed hard, desperately grasping for some semblance of cool, but all her carefully crafted control seemed to have deserted her the moment she'd spotted Jack.

'There's someone here—someone I haven't seen for a very long time,' she said, her voice wobbling with emotion.

He'd always had this effect on her, turning her brain to jelly and her heart to goo, and after six long years without hearing the deep rumble of his voice or catching sight of his breathtaking smile or breathing in his heady, utterly beguiling scent her body seemed to have gone into a frenzy of longing for him.

'I wasn't expecting to see him, that's all. It took me by surprise,' she finished, forcing a smile onto her face.

The girls didn't look convinced by her attempt at

upbeat nonchalance, which wasn't surprising considering she was still visibly trembling.

'So when you say "him",' Ashleigh said, with a shrewd look in her eye, 'I'm guessing we're talking about an ex here?'

Emma nodded and looked away, not wanting to be drawn into giving them the painful details about what had happened between her and Jack. She needed to be able to do her job here tonight, or risk being fired, and if she talked about him now there was a good chance she'd lose her grip on her very last thread of calm.

'It's okay, I can handle it, but I managed to drop a whole tray of drinks out there. The carpet's absolutely covered in booze right by the camel-coloured sofa and I managed to spray the legs of a partygoer as well. He didn't seem entirely pleased to be showered in pink champagne.' She let out a shaky laugh.

'Don't worry, Emma, we'll cover it,' Grace said, putting a reassuring hand on her arm. 'Sophie, find a cloth to mop up as much of the liquid as possible, will you?'

'Will do,' Sophie said, swivelling on the spot and heading over to the broom cupboard where all the cleaning materials were kept.

'Ashleigh—'

'I'll get another tray of drinks out there right now and go and flirt with the guy you splattered with booze,' Ashleigh cut in with a smile, first at Emma, then at Grace.

'Great,' Grace said, grinning back. 'Emma, go and sit down with your head between your knees until your colour returns.'

'But—' Emma started to protest, but Grace put her

hands on her shoulders and gently pushed her back towards one of the kitchen chairs.

Emma sat down gratefully, relieved that everything was being taken care of but experiencing a rush of embarrassment at causing so much trouble for her friends.

After a moment of sitting quietly, her heart rate had almost returned to normal and the feeling that she was about to pass out had receded.

She was just about to stand up and get back out there, determined not to shy away from this, but to deal with Jack's reappearance head-on, when Sophie came striding back into the kitchen.

'You look better,' she said, giving Emma an assessing once-over.

'Yeah, I'm okay now. Ready to get back out there.'

'You know, you could stay in the kitchen and orchestrate things from here if you want. We can handle keeping all the guests happy out there.'

Emma sighed, grateful to her friend for the offer, but knowing that hiding wasn't an option.

'Thanks, but I can't stay in here all evening. Jolyon expects me to be out there charming his guests and keeping a general eye on things.' Rubbing a hand over her forehead, she gave her friend a smile, which she hoped came across with more confidence than she felt.

'Okay, well, let's fix your hair a bit, then,' Sophie said, moving towards her with her hands outstretched. 'We'll get it out of that restricting band and you can use it to shield your face if you need to hide for a second.'

Grateful for her friend's concern, Emma let Sophie gently pull out the band that was holding her up-do neatly away from her face so that her long sheet of hair swung down to cover each side of her face.

'It's such a beautiful colour—baby blonde,' Sophie said appreciatively, her gaze sweeping from one side of Emma's face to the other. 'Is it natural?'

Emma nodded, feeling gratified warmth flood her cheeks. 'Yes, thank goodness. I'd never be able to afford the hairdressing bills.' Her thoughts flew back to how much money she used to waste on expensive haircuts in her pampered youth and she cringed as she considered what she could do with that money now—things like putting it towards the cost of more night classes and studying materials.

The kitchen door banged open, making them both jump, and Emma's gaze zeroed in on the puce-coloured face of Jolyon Fitzherbert as he advanced towards her.

'Emma! What's going on? Why are you skulking in here when you should be out there making sure my party's running smoothly? And what the hell was that, throwing a tray of drinks all over my new carpet?'

She put up a placating hand, realising her mistake when his scowl only deepened. Jolyon hated it when people tried to soothe him.

'I was just checking on the stores of alcohol in here. I'm going back out there right now,' she said, plastering a benevolent smile onto her face.

Jolyon's eyes narrowed. 'Come with me,' he ground out, turning clumsily on the spot and giving away just how drunk he was.

Sophie put a hand on Emma's arm, but she brushed her off gently. 'It's okay, I can handle him. You make sure everything runs smoothly here while I'm dealing with this, okay?' She gave her friend a beseeching look, pleading for her support, and was rewarded with a firm nod.

'No problem.'

Running to catch up with Jolyon, Emma saw him unlocking the door to his study and the lump in her throat thickened. This couldn't be good. She was only ever summoned to his study when he felt something had gone badly wrong. He liked to sit behind his big oak desk in his puffy leather armchair as if he were lord of the manor and she were his serving wench being given a severe dressing-down.

Deciding to pre-empt his lecture, she put out both hands in a gesture of apology. 'Jolyon, I'm very sorry about dropping those drinks. It was a genuine accident and I promise it won't ever happen again.'

Stopping before he reached the desk, he turned to regard her through red-rimmed eyes, his gaze a little unfocussed due to the enormous amount of whisky he'd drunk throughout the evening.

'What are you going to do to make it up to me?' he asked.

She didn't like the expression in his eyes. Not one little bit.

'I'll pay to have the carpet professionally cleaned. None of the glasses broke, so it's just the stain that needs taking care of.'

He shook his head slowly. 'I don't think that's apology enough. You ruined my party!'

Despite knowing it would be unwise to push him when he was in this kind of mood, she couldn't help but fold her arms and tilt up her chin in defiance. She might have made a bit of a mess, but, if anything, her little accident had livened the party up.

'Jolyon, everyone's having a great time. You've thrown a wonderful party here today,' she said carefully. What she actually wanted to do was suggest where he could shove his job, but she bit her lip, mentally picturing the meagre numbers in her bank balance rapidly ticking down if she let her anger get the better of her.

As she'd predicted, her boldness only seemed to exacerbate his determination to have his pound of flesh and he took a deliberate step towards her and, lifting his hand, he slid it roughly under her jaw and into her hair. His grip was decisive and strong and she acknowledged a twinge of unease in the pit of her stomach as she realised how alone they were in here, away from the rest of the party.

He began to stroke his thumb along her jaw, grazing the bottom of her lip. Waves of revulsion flooded through her at his touch, but she didn't move. She needed to brazen this out. She knew exactly what he was like—if you showed any sign of weakness that was it, you were fired on the spot.

'Well, you ruined it for me,' he growled, moving even closer so she could smell the sharp tang of whisky on his breath. 'But perhaps we can figure out a satisfactory way for you to make it up to me,' he said, his gaze roving lasciviously over her face and halting on her mouth.

She clamped her lips together, racking her brains for a way out of this without making the situation worse.

'Jolyon, let go of me,' she said, forcing as much authority into her voice as she could summon, which wasn't a lot. 'I need to get back to the party and serve your guests and they'll be missing you, wondering where you are,' she said, grasping for something— anything—to aid her getaway. Appealing to his ego had worked well before, but she could tell from the look in his eyes that it wasn't going to fly this time. He wanted much more than a verbal apology from her.

The thought made her shudder.

Taking a sudden step backwards, she managed to break his hold on her. 'I need to get back. Let's talk about this tomorrow, shall we?' Before he could react, she turned and walked swiftly out of the door and back towards the noisy hubbub of the party, her heart thumping hard against her ribcage and the erratic pulse of her blood spurring her on.

She heard him come after her, his breath rasping in his throat as his movements picked up into a drunken jog. She'd just made it to the living-room doorway when he caught up with her, grabbing hold of her arm and spinning her around to face him.

'Jolyon, please—' she gasped, then froze in horror as his lips came crashing down onto hers, his arms wrapping around her like a vice. She couldn't breathe, couldn't move, her heart hammering hard in her ears as she struggled to get away from him—

Then suddenly he seemed to let go of her—or was he being dragged away? The loud *ooof!* sound he made in the back of his throat made her think that perhaps he *had* been and she spun around only to come face to face with Jack.

His mesmerising eyes bore into hers, blazing with anger as a muscle ticced in his clenched jaw, and her stomach did a slow somersault. His gaze swept over her face for the merest of seconds before moving to lock onto Jolyon instead, who was now leaning against the doorjamb, gasping as if he'd been winded.

'What do you want, Westwood?' Jolyon snapped at Jack, flashing him a look of fear-tinged contempt.

Jack glared back, his whole body radiating tension as if he was having to physically restrain himself from landing a punch right on Jolyon's pudgy jaw.

He took a purposeful step towards the cowering man and leaned one strong arm on the jamb above Jolyon's head, forming a formidable six-foot-three enclosure of angry, powerful man around him.

'I want you to keep your hands off my wife!'

CHAPTER TWO

JACK WESTWOOD KNEW he'd made a monumental mistake the moment he heard the collective gasp of the crowd in the room behind him.

What the hell had he just done?

It wasn't like him to lose his head, in fact he was famous in the business circles in which he presided for being a cool customer and impossible to intimidate, but seeing Emma again like this had shaken him to his very soul.

It occurred to him with a sick twist of irony that the last time he'd acted so rashly was when he'd asked her to marry him. She'd always had this effect on him, messing with his head and undermining his control until he didn't know which way was up.

Logically he knew he should have stayed away from her tonight, just until he was mentally prepared to see her again, but after finding he couldn't concentrate on a word anyone had said to him after he'd spotted her earlier his instinct had been to search her out, then jump in to defend her when he'd seen Fitzherbert trying to kiss her.

She was still his wife after all, even if they hadn't had any contact for the last few years—that was what had prompted him to do it. That and the fact he hated any kind of violence towards women.

The searing anger he'd felt at seeing this idiot being so rough with her still buzzed through his veins. Who did he think he was, forcing himself on a woman who clearly wasn't interested in him? And it was obvious that Emma wasn't. He knew her too well not to be able to read her body language and interpret her facial expressions, even when she was trying to hide her true feelings.

'Emma, are you okay?' he asked, turning to check her face for bruises. But it seemed all that was bruised was her pride. At least that was what the flash of discomfiture in her eyes led him to believe.

'I'm fine, thank you, Jack. I can handle this,' she said, laying a gentle hand on his arm and giving him a supplicatory smile.

Unnerved by the prickle of sensation that rushed across his skin where she touched him, he shook the feeling off, putting it down to his shock at seeing her again mixed in with the tension of the situation. Nodding, he took a couple of steps backwards, allowing Jolyon to push himself upright, and watched with bitter distaste as the man brushed himself down with shaking hands and rolled back his portly shoulders.

'I'd like you both to leave,' Fitzherbert said, his voice firm, even if it did resonate with a top note of panic.

Jack turned to see Emma looking at Fitzherbert with a pleading expression, making him think that leaving was the last thing she wanted to do. Why on earth would she want to stay? Unless they were together as a couple?

The thought of that made him shudder. Surely she couldn't have stooped so low as to have attached herself to a playboy like Fitzherbert. He knew she'd been brought up living the high life, was used to being taken care of by other people, but this was beyond the pale.

'Jolyon, please, this is just a misunderstanding. Can we talk about it—?'

Fitzherbert held up a hand to halt her speech and shook his head slowly, his piggy eyes squinty and mean.

'I don't want to hear it, Emma. I want you to leave. Right now. The other girls can cover for you. From what I've seen tonight that's already been happening anyway. Whenever I've looked for you, you've been skulking in the kitchen.'

'I've been orchestrating the party from there, Jolyon—'

He held up his hand higher, his palm only inches away from her face.

Jack experienced a low throb of anger at the condescension of the act, but he kept his mouth shut. He didn't think Emma would appreciate him butting in right now. He'd let her handle this.

For now.

'Didn't you hear me, Emma? You're fired!' There was no mistaking Fitzherbert's tone now. Even though he was drunk, his conviction was clear.

Fired? So she was working for him? Jack found this revelation even more shocking than the idea that they'd been a couple.

She went to argue, but Fitzherbert shouted over her.

'I specifically requested the agency find me a

housekeeper that wasn't married so there wouldn't be any difficulties with priorities. I need someone who can work late into the evening or on short notice without having to check with a partner first. I've been burned by problems like that before.'

He glanced at Jack now, his expression full of reproach. 'A *decent* chap doesn't want his *wife* working for a bachelor such as myself.'

By that, Jack assumed what Fitzherbert actually meant was that he'd wanted the option to pursue more than just housekeeping duties with his employees without the fear of a husband turning up to spoil his fun, or, worse, send him to the hospital.

A prickle of pure disgust shot up his spine at the thought.

'You said in your application that you were unmarried,' Fitzherbert went on, apparently choosing to ignore Jack's balled fists and tense stance now.

'You lied. So I'm terminating our contract forthwith. I don't want a liar as well as the daughter of a wastrel working in my house.'

Shock clouded Emma's face at this low jibe and Fitzherbert smiled and leaned closer to her, clearly relishing the fact that he'd hit a nerve. 'Yes, that's right, I know all about your father's reputation for spending other people's money. I make sure to look up everyone I employ in order to protect myself.'

He jabbed a finger at her. 'I gave you the benefit of the doubt because you're a hard worker and easy on the eye…' his snarl increased '…but who knows what could have gone missing in the time you've been here?'

That did it.

'Don't you dare speak to her like that!' Jack ground out.

Emma turned to him with frustration in her eyes and held up a hand. 'Jack, I said I can handle this. Please keep out of it!'

'No wonder you've kept your marriage to her a secret if that's the way she speaks to you,' Fitzherbert muttered, slanting Jack a sly glance.

'Oh, go to hell, Jolyon,' Emma shot back, with a vehemence that both surprised and impressed Jack. 'You know what, you can keep your measly job. I was going to leave at the end of the month anyway. Your wandering hands had got a bit too adventurous for my liking.'

And with that, she pulled an apron that Jack had not noticed she was wearing before from around her middle and dropped it on the floor at Fitzherbert's feet, then spun on her heel and strode towards the front door.

Glancing back into the room, Jack saw that a large crowd of partygoers had gathered to watch their tawdry little show and every one of them was now staring at him in curious anticipation.

It suddenly occurred to him that they were waiting for him to chase after his *wife*.

Damn it.

Now the secret was out, he was going to have to find a way to handle this situation without causing more problems for himself. The last thing he needed was to catch the attention of the gutter press when he was just finding his feet again here in England. Knowing Emma as he did, he was aware that it would be down to him to handle the fallout from this, which was fine, he was used to dealing with complex situations in his role as CEO so this shouldn't be much of a stretch, but he could really do without an added complication like this right now.

Throwing Fitzherbert one last disgusted glance, Jack turned his back on the man then went to grab his overcoat from the peg by the door. Following Emma out, he caught her up as she exited into the cold mid-November night air.

She didn't turn round as she hopped down the marble steps of the town house and out into the square.

'Emma, wait!' Jack shouted, worried she might jump into a cab and he'd lose her before he had a chance to figure out what he was going to do about all this.

'Why did you have to get involved, Jack?' she asked, swinging round to face him, her cheeks pink and her eyes wild with a mixture of embarrassment and anxiety.

The sight of it stopped him in his tracks. Even in his state of agitation he was acutely aware that she was still a heart-stoppingly beautiful woman. If anything she was even more beautiful now than when he'd last seen her six years ago, with those full wide lips that used to haunt his dreams and those bright, intelligent green eyes that had always glowed with spirit and an innate joy of life.

Not that she looked particularly joyful right now.

Shaking off the unwelcome rush of feelings this brought, he folded his arms and raised an eyebrow at her.

'I wasn't going to just stand by and watch Fitzherbert manhandle you like that,' he said, aiming for a cool, reasonable tone. There was no way he was going to have a public row in the middle of Sloane Square with her. What if there were paparazzi lurking behind one of the trees nearby?

He shifted on the spot. 'I would have done the same for any woman in that position.'

There was a flash of hurt in her eyes. 'Well, for future reference, I can take care of myself, thanks. It wasn't your place to get involved, Jack.'

The muscles in his shoulders tensed instinctively. 'I'm your husband. Of course it was my place.'

She sighed, kicking awkwardly at the ground. 'Technically, maybe, but nobody knew that. I certainly haven't told anyone.'

He was annoyed by how riled he felt by her saying that, as if he was a dirty secret she'd been keeping.

It was on the tip of his tongue to start demanding answers of her—about what had happened in the intervening years to make it necessary for her to work for a man like Fitzherbert and why she hadn't contacted him once in the six years they'd been estranged, even just to let him know that she was okay.

But he didn't, because this wasn't the time or place to discuss things like that.

'Why did you shout about us being married in front of all those people?' she asked, her voice wobbling a little now.

He took a deep breath, rubbing a hand over his forehead in agitation. 'I reacted without thinking in the heat of the moment.'

That had always been his problem when she was around. For some reason she shook him up, made him lose control, like no one else in the world could.

To his surprise the corner of her mouth quirked

into a reluctant smile. 'Well, it's going to be round Chelsea society like wildfire now. That crowd loves a bit of salacious gossip.'

Sighing, he batted a hand at her. 'Don't worry, people will talk for a while, then it'll become old news. I'll handle it.'

She looked at him for a moment, her eyes searching his face as if checking for reassurance.

Jack stared back at her, trying not to let a sudden feeling of edginess get to him. As much as he'd love to be able to brush the problem of them still being married under the carpet he knew it would be a foolish thing to do. There was no point in letting it drag on any more now he was back. It needed to be faced head-on so they could resolve it quickly and with as little pain as possible.

Because, inevitably, it would still be painful for them, even after all this time.

Emma tore her gaze away from him, frowning down at the pavement now and letting out a growl of frustration. 'I could have done with keeping that job. It paid really well,' she muttered. 'And who knows what the knock-on effect of embarrassing Jolyon like that is going to be?'

He balled his fists, trying to keep a resurgence of temper under control at the memory of Fitzherbert's treatment of her. 'He won't do anything—the man's a coward.'

'Jolyon's an influential man around here,' she pointed out, biting her lip. 'He has the ear of a lot of powerful people.'

She stared off into the distance, her breath coming rapidly now, streaking the dark night air with clouds of white. 'Hopefully Clio at the agency will believe my side of the story and still put me forward for other jobs, but people might not want to take me on if Jolyon gets to them first.'

'Surely you don't need a job that badly?' he asked, completely bemused by her anxiety about not being able to land another waitressing role. What had happened to her plans to go to university? She couldn't have been working in the service industry all this time, could she?

The rueful smile she flashed him made something twang in his chest.

'Unfortunately I do, Jack. We can't all be CEO of our own company,' she said with a teasing glint in her eye now.

He huffed out a mirthless laugh and shook his head, recalling how it had been through Emma's encouragement that he'd accepted the prodigious offer for a highly sought-after job at an electronics company in the States right after graduating from university, which had enabled him to chase his dream of setting up his own company.

It had been an incredible opportunity and one he'd been required to act on quickly. Emma had understood how important it had been to him to become financially independent on his own merits, rather than trading on his family name as his father had, and had urged him to go. In a burst of youthful optimism, he'd asked her to marry him so she could go with him. She'd been all he could think about when he was twenty-one. He'd been obsessed with her—every second away from her had felt empty—and the mere suggestion of leaving her behind in England had filled him with dismay.

In retrospect it had been ridiculous for them to tie the knot so young; with him only just graduated from Cambridge University and she only eighteen years old.

They'd practically been children then: closeted and naïve.

She coughed and took an awkward step backwards and he realised with a start that he'd been scowling at her while these unsettling memories had flitted through his mind.

'It's good to see you again, Jack, despite the less than ideal circumstances,' she said softly, her expression guarded and her voice holding a slight tremor now, 'but I guess I should get going.'

She seemed to fold in on herself and he realised with a jolt that she was shivering.

'Where's your coat?' he asked, perhaps a little more sharply than was necessary.

'It's back in the house, along with my handbag,' she muttered. 'I can't go back in there for them now though. I'll give one of the girls a ring when I get home and ask her to drop them over to me tomorrow.' She paused as a sheepish look crossed her face. 'I don't suppose you could lend me a couple of pounds for my bus fare, could you?'

The tension in her voice touched something deep inside him, making him suddenly conscious of what a rough night she was having.

'Yes, of course.' Taking off his overcoat, he wrapped it around her shoulders. 'Here, take my coat. There's money in the pocket.'

She looked up at him with wide, grateful eyes. 'Are you sure?'

'Yes,' he clipped out, a little unnerved by how his body was responding to the way she was looking at him.

He cleared his throat. 'Will you be able to get into your—er—flat?' he asked. He wasn't sure where she was living now. He'd heard that she'd moved to London after they'd sold the family home in Cambridge, but other than that his information about her was a black hole. He'd deliberately kept it that way, needing to emotionally distance himself from her after what had happened between them.

He'd told himself he'd find out where she was once he'd had time to get settled in London but he'd had a lot on his plate up till now. His business back in the States still needed a close eye kept on it until the chap he'd chosen to take over the CEO role in his absence was up to speed and he was keenly aware of his new familial duties here.

'My mother's staying with me at the moment so she'll be able to let me in,' Emma replied with a smile that didn't quite reach her eyes.

He nodded slowly, his brain whirring now. It occurred to him with a jolt of unease that he couldn't let her just skip off home. If she disappeared on him he'd end up looking a fool if the press came to call and he said something about their relationship that she contradicted later when they caught up with her. Which they would eventually.

And after not having seen her for nearly six years he had a thousand and one questions he wanted to ask her, which would continue to haunt him if she vanished on him again.

No, he couldn't let her leave.

'Look, why don't we go back to my house to talk? It's only a couple of streets away,' he said, wishing he hadn't dismissed his driver for the night. He hadn't intended to go out this evening but had been chivvied along at the last minute by an old friend from his university days who was a business acquaintance of Fitzherbert's.

'We need to figure out what we're going to do about this,' he said, registering her slight hesitation. 'You know what the gutter press are like in this country. We need to be able to give them a plausible answer if they come calling. If they think there's any kind of mystery about it they'll hound us for ever. I don't know about you, but I'm not prepared to have the red tops digging into my past.'

That seemed to get through to her and he saw a chink of acceptance in her expression. And trepidation.

He moved closer to her, then regretted it when he caught the sweet, intoxicating scent of her in the air. 'All I'm asking is that you come back to my house for an hour so we can talk. It's been a long time. I want to know how you are, Em.'

She looked at him steadily, her expression closed now, giving nothing away. He recognised it as a look she'd perfected after the news of her father's sudden death. He'd been a victim of it before, right after the tragedy had struck, and then repeatedly in the time that had followed—the longest and most painful days of his life.

'Okay,' she said finally, letting out a rush of breath.

Nodding stiffly, he pointed in the direction they needed to go. 'It's this way,' he said, steeling himself to endure the tense walk home with his wife at his side for the first time in six years.

CHAPTER THREE

IT WAS A blessing that Jack's house was only two streets away because Emma didn't think she'd be able to cope with wearing his heavy wool coat so close to her skin for much longer, having to breathe in the poignantly familiar scent of him and feel the residual warmth of his body against her own.

It had been a huge struggle to maintain her act of upbeat nonchalance in front of him outside Jolyon's house and she knew she'd lost her fight the moment she'd seen the look in his eyes when he'd realised how cold she was. It was the same look he used to give her when they were younger—a kind of intense concern for her well-being, which reached right into the heart of her and twisted her insides into knots.

Gesturing for her to follow him, Jack led her up the stone steps of the elegant town house and in through a tall black front door that was so shiny she could see her reflection in it.

The house was incredible, of course, but with a dated, rather rundown interior, overfilled with old-fashioned antique furniture in looming, dark mahogany and with a dull, oppressively dark colour scheme covering the walls and floors.

Jack's family had a huge amount of wealth behind them and owned a number of houses around the country, including the Cambridge town house overlooking Jesus Green and the River Cam that Jack and his sister, Clare, had grown up in. She'd never been to this property before though. They'd not been together long enough for her to see inside the entire portfolio of his life.

'What a—er—lovely place,' she said, cringing at the insincerity in her voice.

'Thank you,' he replied coolly, ignoring her accidental rudeness and walking straight through to the sitting room.

She followed him in, noticing that the décor was just as unpleasantly depressing in here.

'Was this place your grandfather's?'

'Yes,' he said. There was tension in his face, and a flash of sorrow. 'He left me this house and Clare the one in Edinburgh.'

Emma recalled how Jack had loved spending time with his grandfather, a shrewd businessman and a greatly respected peer of the realm. He'd always had an easy smile and kind word for her—unlike Jack's parents—and she'd got on well with him the few times she'd met him. Jack had notably inherited the man's good looks, as well as his business acumen.

'I was sorry to read about him passing, Jack,' she said, wanting to try and soothe the glimmer of pain she saw there, but knowing there wasn't any way to do that without overstepping the mark. He'd been very careful up until this point not to touch her and, judging by his tense body language, would probably reject any attempt she made to reach out to him.

She needed to keep her head here. This wasn't going to be an easy ride for either of them, so rising above the emotion of it was probably the best thing they could do. In fact they really ought to treat this whole mess like a business transaction, nothing more, if they were going to get through it with their hearts intact.

The mere thought of what they had ahead of them made her spirits plummet and she dropped into the nearest heavily brocaded sofa, sinking back against the comforting softness of the cushions and pulling her legs up under her.

'Have you seen Clare recently?' she asked, for want of a topic to move them on from the tense atmosphere that now stretched between them.

'Not since Grandfather's funeral,' he replied, his brow drawn into a frown. 'She's doing well though—settled in Edinburgh and happy.' He looked at her directly now, locking his gaze with hers. 'She misses you, you know.'

Sadness sank through her, right down to her toes. 'I miss her too. It's been a long time since we talked. I've been busy—'

She stopped herself from saying any more, embarrassed by how pathetic that weak justification sounded.

In truth, she'd deliberately let her friendship with Clare slip away from her.

A couple of months after Emma's father had passed away, Clare had gone off to university in Edinburgh and Emma had stayed at home, giving up her own place in an Art course there, which had made it easier to disassociate herself from her friend. Not that Clare hadn't put up a fight about being routinely ignored and pushed away, sounding more and more hurt and bewildered every time Emma made a lame excuse about why she couldn't go up to Scotland and visit her.

There had been a good reason for letting their friendship lapse as she had though. Clare hadn't known about her and Jack's whirlwind relationship. Emma hadn't known quite how to tell her friend about it at the time—in her youthful innocence she hadn't even known how to feel about it all herself—and she'd been sure Clare wouldn't have responded well to hearing how she'd snuck around with her brother behind her back, then how much she'd hurt Jack by walking away from their marriage.

Emma couldn't have borne being around her friend, whose smile struck such an unnerving resemblance to Jack's own it had caused Emma physical pain to see it, and not being able to talk about him to her. It would have been lying by omission. So instead she'd cut her friend out of her life.

The thought of it now made her hot with shame.

'How's your mother?' Jack asked stiffly, breaking into her thoughts.

She realised she was worrying at her nail, a habit she'd picked up after her father had died, and forced herself to lay her hands back in her lap.

'She's fine, thanks,' she said, deciding not to go into how fragile her mother had become after losing her wealth, good standing and her husband in one fell swoop. She liked to pretend none of it had happened now and had banned Emma from talking about it. 'She's living in France with her new husband, except for this week—she's staying with me while Philippe's away and the house is being damp proofed and re-decorated.'

Jack let out a sudden huff of agitation, apparently frustrated with their diversion into small talk. 'Do you want a drink?' Jack asked brusquely.

Clearly *he* did.

'Er, yes. Thanks. I'll have a whisky if you have it, neat.' A strong shot of alcohol would be most welcome right now. It was supposed to be good for shock, wasn't it?

Jack got up and moved restlessly around the room, gathering glasses and splashing large measures of whisky into them.

The low-level tension in the pit of her stomach intensified. She'd thought she'd be able to cope with being around him here, but his cool distantness towards her was making her nerves twang.

'So how's the electronics business in the good old US of A?' she asked, wiggling her eyebrows at him in an attempt to lighten the atmosphere.

'Profitable,' was all he said, striding over to her and handing her a heavy cut-glass tumbler with a good two fingers of whisky in it.

'Are you trying to get me drunk?' she asked, shooting him a wry smile.

He didn't smile back, just turned away and paced towards the window to stare out at the dark evening.

Her heart sank. Where had the impassioned, playful Jack she'd once known gone? He'd been replaced with this tightly controlled automaton of a man. There was no longer any sign of the wit and charm she'd loved him so much for.

Knocking back a good gulp of whisky, she turned

in her seat to face him, determined not to let her discouragement get to her. 'So you decided to come back and take on your social responsibilities as an earl, then?' She rolled the glass between her hands, feeling the pattern of the cut glass press into her palms.

He turned his head to look at her, his gaze unnervingly piercing in the gloomy room.

'Yes, well, after being responsible for running my own company for the last five years it's made me realise how important it is to uphold a legacy,' he said, folding his arms and leaning back against the window sill. 'How much blood, sweat and tears goes into building a heritage. My ancestors put a lot of hard work into maintaining the estate they'd inherited and it'd be arrogant and short-sighted of me to turn my back on everything they strove so hard to preserve.'

She was surprised to hear him saying this. She'd expected him to be reluctant to return to take on his aristocratic responsibilities after working so hard to achieve such a powerful position in his industry.

But then for Jack it had always been about doing things on his own terms. From the sounds of it *he'd* made the decision to come back here; no one had forced him to do it.

She gave an involuntary shiver as a draught of cool air from somewhere blew across her skin.

Frowning, Jack left his vantage point at the window and paced over to the other side of the room, bending down and grabbing a pack of matches by the fireplace to light the tinder in the grate.

'So you're going to be living in England now?' she asked, her voice trembling as she realised what that would mean. There was a very good chance they'd see each other again, especially as Jack would be fraternising with the type of people they'd just left at the party. The worst of it was that she'd probably find herself serving him drinks and nibbles as a waitress at the society events he was bound to be invited to now.

'Yes, I'll be based in England from now on.' He sat back on his heels and watched the tinder catch alight, before reaching for a couple of logs from a basket next to him and laying them carefully over the growing flames.

Turning back to face her, he fixed her with a serious stare. 'So I guess we should talk about what we're going to do about still being married.'

Divorce.

That was what he meant by that.

She knew it was high time they got around to officially ending their marriage, but the thought of it still chafed. Dealing with getting divorced from Jack was never going to be easy, that was why she'd not made any effort to get in contact with him over the years, but the mere thought of it now made her stomach turn.

They'd been so happy once, so in love and full of excitement for the future.

She wanted to cry for what they'd lost.

'Yes. I suppose we should start talking to lawyers about drawing up the paperwork,' she said, desperately trying to keep her voice even so he wouldn't see how much the subject upset her. 'If that's what you want?'

He didn't say anything, just looked at her with hooded eyes.

'Are you—' she could barely form the words '—getting married again?'

To her relief he shook his head. 'No, but it's time to get my affairs straight now I'm back in England.'

'Before the press interest in you becomes even more intense, you mean?'

She saw him swallow. 'Speaking of which, we need to work out what we're prepared to say to reporters about our relationship if they come calling.' He stood up and came to sit on the sofa opposite her. He was suddenly all business now, his back straight and his expression blank.

She took a shaky breath. 'Should we tell them we were married but we got divorced and we're just friends now?' The uncertainty in her voice gave away the fact that she knew deep down that that would never work.

He shook his head. 'They'll go and look for the decree absolute and see that we're lying. It'll only make things worse.'

Sighing, she pushed her hair away from her face. 'So what do we say? That our marriage broke down six years ago after you moved to the States, but we're only just getting round to finalising a divorce?'

'They'll want to know why you didn't go to America with me,' he pointed out.

'We could just say that I needed to stay here for family reasons,' she suggested, feeling a rush of uncomfortable heat swamp her as it occurred to her that they might go after her mother too.

'Well, at least that would be pretty close to the truth and it's better to keep things simple,' Jack said, seeming not to notice her sudden panic.

'It doesn't sound great though, does it?' she said, aware of her heart thumping hard against her chest.

'In fact it's probably going to pique their interest even more. They'll want to know what was so important here to make me stay and that'll mean dragging up my father's debts all over again.'

And if they did that Jack would find out she'd been keeping the true extent of them a secret from him for all these years.

After he'd left for the States she'd become increasingly overwhelmed by what she'd had to deal with and had eventually become so buried by it all she'd ended up shutting out everything except for dealing with her new responsibilities in order to just get through the day. Which meant, to her shame, that she'd shut Jack out too.

She'd been so young when it had happened though, only eighteen, and incredibly naïve about the way the world worked and how people's cruelty and selfishness kicked in when it came to protecting their wealth.

Not that there was any point in trying to explain all that to him now. Jack liked to feel he was in control of everything all the time and he'd probably only get angry with her for having kept him in the dark.

And anyway, there was no point getting into it if they were going to get a divorce.

She sighed heavily and put her head in her hands, massaging her throbbing temples. 'I don't know if I could bear having the press camped out on my doorstep, documenting my every move. And I know my mother certainly can't.'

'That might not happen,' Jack said softly. 'They may not even get wind of this. It depends on who overheard us at that party. But if they do find out about us I'll deal with it. If the question is asked we'll just say we got married on a whim when we were young and it didn't work out, but that we've always been on friendly terms and have decided to get a divorce now I'm back in England.'

She nodded her acceptance, feeling a great surge of sadness at how such a happy event could now be causing such problems for them.

Fatigue, chased on by the heavyweight alcohol, suddenly overwhelmed her and she hid a large yawn behind her hand, thinking wistfully of her bed.

The problem was, she was a long way from home and would need to take two different buses to get there. The thought of facing her mother's inquisitive gaze when she walked in made her stomach sink. She'd know immediately that something was wrong; the woman was particularly sensitive to changes in moods now after suffering with depression for years after her first husband's death.

Jack must have seen the worry in her face because he frowned and got up and came to sit down next to her.

'You're exhausted,' he said, the unexpected concern in his voice making the hairs stand up on her arms.

She shrugged, trying to make light of it. She didn't want him to think he had to mollycoddle her; she was perfectly capable of looking after herself. 'That's what happens when you work for a man like Jolyon Fitzherbert. He expects perfection from his employees. I've been up since five a.m. preparing for that party.'

Jack continued to look at her, his gaze searching her face.

Her stomach jumped with nerves as she forced herself to maintain eye contact with him, not wanting him to know just how fragile she was right now. He could probably blow her into dust if he breathed on her hard enough.

'Where do you live?' he asked.

She shifted in her seat. 'Tottenham.'

Not her first choice of places to live, but it was cheap.

'How were you planning on getting home?'

'We mere mortals take the bus.'

He ignored her wry joke. 'You can't take a bus all the way to Tottenham now. Stay here tonight, then we can talk again in the morning when we've both had a good rest and a chance to get over the shock of seeing each other again.'

She hesitated, on the brink of refusing his suggestion, but also keenly aware that if she left now she'd only have to psych herself up to see him again anyway, and probably somewhere much less convivial than here. Despite the terrible décor the house had the comforting atmosphere of a family home.

She realised with a shock that she'd missed the feeling of belonging somewhere, having lost her own family home and all the happy memories that went along with it when they'd been forced to sell it to pay off some of the debts.

So many memories had been tarnished by finding out the truth about her father.

She shook the sadness off, not wanting to dwell on it right now.

'Okay, thank you. I'll stay tonight and leave first thing in the morning,' she said.

He nodded, standing up. 'Good. The first bedroom

you come to at the top of the stairs is made up for guests. Feel free to make yourself at home there.'

Make yourself at home. That wasn't something that was ever going to happen here, Emma reflected with another swell of sadness.

It was such a shame too. This house had the potential to be amazing if only someone showed it some love.

Not that she should be thinking things like that right now.

Pushing the rogue thought away, she stood up and brushed self-consciously at her skirt, trying to smooth out the still-sticky wrinkles. She must look such a mess, especially compared to Jack in his pristine designer shirt and trousers.

'Thank you,' she said stiffly. 'Could I use your phone? I'll need to let my mother know I won't be home tonight or she'll worry.'

'The landline's in the hall,' Jack said.

She gave him a stilted nod—how had things become so formal between them? They were acting like strangers with each other now—and made her way out to the hallway to find the phone.

It was telling that he hadn't lent her his mobile. Perhaps he didn't want her scrolling through his contacts or messages, nosing into his life. Was he trying to hide something from her? Or someone?

She didn't want to consider that eventuality right now; it would only increase the painful tightness she was experiencing in her chest and she needed all her composure if she was going to sound normal on the phone and not worry her mother.

It took a few rings before the line at home was

picked up. From the sounds of her mother's voice she'd woken her up, so Emma quickly reeled off a story about Jolyon wanting her to work late and told her she was going to stay with a friend because she'd finish too late to get the last bus home.

At one point during the conversation, she heard Jack come out of the living room and mount the stairs, presumably going up to his room, and a layer of tension peeled away, making it easier to breathe.

From the tone of her mother's voice she could tell she wasn't convinced by the lie, but seemed to think Emma was ensconced in some clandestine affair instead. Which ironically wasn't far from the truth.

What would her mother say once she knew the truth? She'd be hurt, of course, that Emma hadn't felt she could confide in her, but the last thing she'd wanted to do right after her father's shocking death was add more stress to the situation by admitting to getting married to Jack without her mother's knowledge. And then when things had calmed down a little there had been no point in saying anything about it because things had fallen apart with Jack by then and she hadn't been able to see any way to fix them.

So she'd kept mum. In every sense of the word.

After saying goodbye to her mother, she made her way wearily up the stairs, turning onto the landing to find Jack standing outside the door of the bedroom she was meant to be staying in.

She came to a stop and stared at him in confusion. Why was he waiting for her here?

Unless…

'Were you listening to my phone call?' she asked, unable to keep the reproachful tone out of her voice.

'I was waiting to show you which room was yours,' he said, but she could tell from a slight falter in his voice that he was lying.

'You were checking that I wasn't calling a boy-friend, weren't you?' she said, narrowing her eyes.

He raised an eyebrow, refusing to be intimidated by her pointed accusation. 'I am still your husband, Emma.'

She folded her arms. 'Well, don't worry, you don't need to set the dogs on anyone. I haven't had a boy-friend since you left.'

There was a heavy pause where he looked at her with a muscle flicking in his clenched jaw. 'Since you decided not to follow me, you mean,' he corrected.

She sighed, feeling the weight of his resentment pressing in on her. 'I really don't want to argue with you right now, Jack. Can we discuss my failings to-morrow? It's been a very long day.' She forced herself to smile at him and went to walk past him, but he put an arm out, barring her way.

'Have you really not had another partner since we split up?'

Taking a breath, she turned to face him, feeling a small shiver run up her spine at the dark intensity she saw in his gaze. 'Well, my mother needed me for a long time after my father died and I've been working all the hours of the day to fit in both full-time work and night classes since then. So no. There hasn't been a lot of space for romance in my life.' She was aware of the bitter bite to her voice now and couldn't stop herself from adding, 'From what I've read in the press, it hasn't been the same for you though.'

When she'd first seen the articles about the high-profile relationship he'd had with the daughter of a famous hotelier six months after he'd moved to the States she'd had to rush to the toilet to be sick. She suspected it had been a deliberate move on his part to let her know that he'd moved on and that she hadn't broken his heart.

Even though she knew she had.

She'd heard the pain in his voice the last time they'd spoken to each other. The desperation, the frustration. But she'd had to harden herself to it.

They were never meant to be. The universe had made that very clear to her when it had killed her father.

Jack's eyes flashed with anger. 'Our relationship was over by then, Emma. You'd made that perfectly clear when you decided to stay in England with your mother instead of joining me, your *husband*, in the States.'

She took a calming breath, knowing that now wasn't the time to have a conversation about this when they were both stressed and still in shock from seeing each other again. 'I never meant to hurt you, Jack. Please believe that.'

He leant in towards her, his expression hard. 'I waited for you, Emma, like a fool, thinking you'd finally put us first once you'd had time to grieve for your father, but you never did.'

His gaze burnt into hers, his eyes dark with frustration.

'I know you took it all very personally, Jack, and I can't blame you for that, but I promise you it wasn't because I didn't love you. It was just the wrong time for us.'

He didn't respond to that, just kept looking at her with that unsettling, intense gaze of his.

'Goodnight, Jack,' she forced herself to say, moderating her tone so he wouldn't hear the pain this was causing her in her voice, and without waiting for his response she walked past him and shut the door.

Staggering into the room, her legs suddenly weak and shaky, she flopped down onto the large four-poster bed, its heavy mahogany frame squeaking with the movement, and curled into a ball, taking deep, calming breaths through her nose to stop herself from crying.

She understood why he was still upset with her. In his eyes she'd betrayed him, and Jack was not a man to easily forgive people who had hurt him. And she really couldn't blame him for so publicly cutting off their association at the knees, instead of letting it limp on painfully when there had been nowhere left for it to go.

Uncurling herself, she turned onto her back and stared up at the dark burgundy canopy above her.

Seeing him again, after all these years apart, made her heart heavy with a sorrowful nostalgia for the past. She'd grieved for Jack the same way she'd mourned her father at the time, only it had been a different kind of pain—with a sharp edge that constantly sliced into her well-being, reminding her that it had been her decision to end things with him and that there could be no going back from it. The damage had been done.

It had left a residual raw ache deep inside her that she'd never been able to shake.

Too tired now to even get undressed, she crawled

beneath the sheets and let her mind run over the events of the evening. Her heart beat forcefully in her chest as she finally accepted that Jack was back in her life, although for how long she had no idea. He was obviously keen to get their 'situation' resolved so he could cut her completely out of his life and become available to marry someone more fitting of his position when the need arose.

She lay there with her thoughts spinning, suddenly wide awake.

In the first year after they'd parted she'd regularly tossed and turned in her bed like this, feeling so painfully alone that she'd given in to the tears, physically aching for Jack to be there with her, to hold her and whisper that everything would be okay, that she was doing a good job of dealing with the fallout from her father's death and that he was proud of her.

That he was there for her.

But he hadn't been.

Because she hadn't let him be.

A while after they'd split she'd considered moving on from him, finding someone new to love, but what with her intense working schedule and the mental rigor of taking care of her emotionally delicate mother there hadn't been room for anyone else in her life.

So she'd been on her own since Jack left for the States, and perhaps that had been for the best. She hadn't wanted to rely on someone else for emotional support after her father had let her down so badly, because that would have left her exposed and vulnerable again, something she'd been careful to put up walls against over the last few years.

At least on her own she felt some semblance of control. She was the one who would make things better.

She turned over in bed and snuggled down further into the covers, hoping that fatigue would pull her under soon.

She'd find a way to deal with having Jack back in her life again. It would all be okay.

Or so she thought.

Waking early the next morning, her head fuzzy from a night of broken sleep and disturbingly intense dreams, Emma heaved herself groggily out of bed, wrinkling her nose at the smell of old booze on her crumpled clothes, and went to the window to see what sort of weather they had in store for them today, hoping for a bit of late autumn sunshine to give her the boost of optimism she needed before facing Jack again.

But it seemed that bad weather was to be the least of her problems.

Peering down at the street below her window, Emma realised with a sickening lurch that the pavement in front of Jack's house was swarming with people, some of whom were gazing up at the window she was looking out of as if waiting to see something. When they spotted her, almost as one, they raised a bank of long-lens cameras to point right at her. Even from this distance she could see the press of their fingers on the shutter buttons and practically hear the ominous clicking of hundreds of pictures being taken of her standing at Jack's window looking as if she'd just climbed out of his bed.

Leaping away from the window, she hastily yanked the curtains together again.

Someone at the party must have blabbed about what they saw and heard last night.

The press had found out about them.

CHAPTER FOUR

JACK HAD WOKEN EARLY, feeling uneasy about what he'd said to Emma the night before. He was annoyed with himself for losing his temper as he had, but hearing her practically accusing him of cheating on her had caused something to snap inside him.

He'd waited for *months* after moving to the States for word from her to let him know she was finally going to join him there, months of loneliness and uncertainty, only to finally be told, in the most painful conversation of his life, that she wasn't coming after all.

She'd given up on their marriage before it had even started.

He'd understood in theory that he'd been asking too much of her, expecting her to walk away from her life in England at such a difficult time, but he'd also been left with a niggling feeing that she'd chosen her mother over him and that she hadn't loved him enough to put him first.

After taking a quick shower and pulling on some clothes he strode down to the kitchen to set the coffee maker up, waiting impatiently for the liquid to filter through.

He was determined to stay in control today. There was no point in rehashing the past. It was time to move on.

Lifting a mug out of the cupboard, he banged it down on the counter. What was he thinking? He *had* moved on. Years ago.

But seeing Emma again had apparently brought back those feelings of frustration and inadequacy that had haunted him after he'd finally accepted she wasn't interested in being married to him any longer.

Sighing, he rubbed a hand over his face. He needed to get a grip on himself if he was going to get through this unscathed. The last thing he needed right now was Emma's reappearance in his life messing with his carefully constructed plan for the future.

He'd just sat down at the kitchen table with a mug of very strong coffee when she came hurrying into the kitchen, her eyes wide with worry and her hair dishevelled.

'What's wrong?' he asked, standing up on instinct, his heart racing in response to the sense of panic she brought in with her.

'The press—they must have found out about you being married because they're swarming around outside like a pack of locusts trying to get pictures.' She frowned and shook her head vigorously, as if trying to shake out the words she needed. 'They just got one of me peering out of my bedroom window at them—make that *your* bedroom window. I don't know whether they'll be able to tell exactly who I am, but their lenses were about a foot long, so they'll probably be pretty sharp images.'

He watched her start to pace the floor, adrenaline humming through his veins as he took in her distress.

Damn it! This was his fault for announcing their marriage to the whole of Fitzherbert's party last night. He'd been a fool to think they might get away with hiding from it. There was always going to be someone in a crowd like that that could be trusted to go to the papers for a bit of a backhander or the promise of future positive exposure for themselves.

'Okay. Don't panic, it might not be as bad as we think,' he said, reaching for his laptop, which he'd left on the table. Opening it up, he typed a web address into the browser and brought up the biggest of the English gossip sites.

He stared at the headline two down from the top of the list, feeling his spirits plummet.

The Earl of Redminster's Secret Waitress Wife! the link shouted back at him from the page.

He scanned the article, but there was no mention of Emma's name. 'Well, it can't have been Fitzherbert who tipped them off because they don't seem to know who you are. I guess he's kept his mouth shut out of embarrassment about the way he acted last night. Despite his drunken bluster, he won't want to get on the wrong side of the Westwood family in the cold light of day.'

He shut the laptop with a decisive *click*. 'Still, it looks like neither of us are going anywhere today. We can't risk going out there and having more photos taken of us until we've spoken to our parents and briefed them about what to say if any reporters contact them.'

She flopped into the chair opposite and raised a

teasing eyebrow. 'What exactly do you intend to tell them, Jack? Funny story, Mum and Dad. You know how you thought your son was the most eligible bachelor in England? Well, guess what...?'

He tried and failed to stop his lips from twitching, gratified to see she wasn't going to let this beat her. Even so, he needed to keep this conversation on a practical level because this was a serious business they were dealing with.

'We can't hide from this, Emma, it'll only make things worse.'

She frowned at his admonishing tone. 'You think I don't know that? It took years for the papers to stop rehashing the story about my father's debts. Any time high society or bankruptcy was mentioned in a story, they always seemed to find a way to drag his name and his "misdemeanours" into it.'

She sighed and ran a hand through her rumpled hair, wincing as her fingers caught in the tangles.

He stared at her in shock. 'Really? I had no idea they'd gone after your family like that,' he said, guilt tugging at his conscience. 'I didn't keep up with news in the UK once I'd moved to the States.'

What he didn't add was that after leaving England he'd shut himself off from anything that would remind him of her and embraced his new life in America instead. It seemed that by doing that he'd missed quite a lot more than he'd realised.

'Look, why don't you take a shower and I'll go and find you some fresh clothes to put on,' he suggested in an attempt to relieve the self-reproach now sinking through him. 'I'm pretty sure Clare keeps a couple of outfits here for when she visits London—

they'll fit you, right? You were always a similar shape and height.'

The grateful smile she gave him made his stomach twist. 'That would be great. Yes, I'm sure Clare's stuff would fit me fine. Don't tell her I've borrowed it though, will you? She always hated me stealing her stuff.' Her eyes glazed over as she seemed to recall something from the past. 'I really do miss her, you know. I was an idiot to let our friendship fizzle out.' She paused and took a breath. 'But she reminded me too much of you,' she blurted, her eyes glinting with tears.

The painful honesty of her statement broke through the tension in his chest and he leant forward, making sure he had her full attention before he spoke. 'You should tell her that yourself. I'm sure she'd love to hear from you, even after all this time.'

Emma's gaze flicked away and she nodded down at the table, clearly embarrassed that he'd seen her flash of weakness. 'Yeah, maybe I'll do that.'

Standing up quickly, she clapped her hands together as if using the momentum to move herself. 'Right. A shower.'

He felt a sudden urge to do something to cheer her up. There was no need for them to be at each other's throats after all—what was done was done. In fact, thinking about it practically, it would make the divorce proceedings easier to handle if they were on amicable terms.

'When you come back down I'll make you some breakfast. Bacon and eggs okay with you?'

'You cook now?' Her expression was so incredulous he couldn't help but smile.

'I've been known to dabble in the culinary arts.'

She grinned back and he felt something lift a little in his chest.

'Well, in that case, I'd love some artistic bacon and eggs.'

'Great,' he said, watching her walk away, exuding her usual elegance, despite her crumpled clothes.

Out of nowhere, an acute awareness that she was still the most beautiful woman he'd ever known—even with her hair a mess and a face clean of make-up—hit him right in the solar plexus, stealing his breath away.

He thumped the table in frustration. How did she do this to him? Shake him up and make him lose his cool? No one else could, not even the bullying business people he'd battled with on a daily basis for the last few years.

Ever since the day he'd met her she'd been able to addle his brain like this, by simply smiling in his direction. As a teenager he'd been angry with her for it at first and to his enduring shame he'd treated her appallingly, picking at her life choices, her manners, the boyfriends she chose. Particularly her boyfriends.

The way she used to glide through life had bothered him on a visceral level. She was poised and prepossessing, and, according to his sister, the girl most likely to be voted the winner of any popularity contest at the eminent private girls' school they'd both attended in Cambridge. She'd seemed to him at the time to accept her charmed position in life as if it was her God-given right. He, on the other hand, had always prided himself on being subversive, bucking the trends and eschewing the norm and the fact she epitomised what others considered to be the perfect woman frustrated him. He hadn't wanted to be attracted to her. But he had been. Intensely and without reprieve.

What would it be like to hold her in his arms again, he wondered now, to feel her soft, pliant body pressed up against his just one more time, to kiss those sultry lips and taste that distinctive sweetness he remembered so well?

He pushed the thoughts from his mind.

The last thing they both needed now was to slip back into their old ways.

It could only end in disaster.

Even after a bracingly cool shower, Emma still felt prickly and hot with nervous tension.

Being here, in such close proximity to Jack, was playing havoc with her composure.

She knew it was necessary and practical to stay here today, but she had no idea how she was going to get through the day without doing or saying something she might regret—just as she had a few minutes ago in the kitchen when she'd blurted out why she'd deliberately cut contact with his sister.

Not wanting to dwell on that misstep right now, she dried herself and put on the clothes Jack had found for her and left out on her bed while she was in the en-suite bathroom.

The thought of him being in her room while she was naked next door gave her a twinge of nerves. He could so easily have come in when she was in there. Walked into the shower and joined her. If he'd wanted.

But clearly he didn't. And that was for the best.

It would be ridiculous to even contemplate the idea of anything developing between them again.

They'd be fools to think they could breach the chasm that had grown between them over the years. They were different people now. Wiser, older—harder, perhaps. More set in their ways. Certainly not young and carefree and full of excitement for the future as they had been right before they got married.

Twisting the necklace that had her wedding ring looped through it—something she'd never taken off, not in all the years they'd been apart—she gave it a sharp tug, feeling it digging into the back of her neck, reminding herself that any connection they'd once had was lost now and that she'd do well to remember that.

They would get a divorce and that would be the end of it. Then they could move on with their lives.

Trying to ignore the tension in her chest that this thought triggered, she turned on her heel and went downstairs to eat the breakfast Jack had promised her.

Passing through the hallway, she noticed that the handset had been left off the phone and it occurred to her that the press must have started calling by now to try and find out who she was and to hound them for details about their clandestine marriage.

It seemed Jack's plan was to ignore them for as long as possible.

Just as she thought this, the doorbell rang and continued to ring as if someone was leaning on it, determined not to stop until someone answered the door.

Damn press. They'd been the same way right after her father's death, hounding her and her mother for weeks, trying to get titillating sound bites or pictures that they could use in their repellent articles.

Hurrying out of the hall, she went straight to the kitchen to find Jack standing at the large range cooker, frying delicious-smelling bacon in a cast-iron pan.

It was such an anachronistic scene it made her tummy flip.

This was not how she'd pictured Jack whenever she'd allowed herself to think about him over the years.

Not that she'd allowed herself to do that too often.

When they'd been young and in love she'd thought of nothing but him: how it felt to be held in his arms, to be loved and worshipped by him. Then how it would be to live with him. Laugh with him every day. Grow old with him.

He was just as handsome now as he'd been when they'd got married, more so if anything. He'd grown into his looks, his face more angular, showing off that amazing bone structure of his, and his body harder and leaner than it had been in his youth.

She guessed he must have done regular power-gyming along with his power-businessing in the States. Wasn't that what all executives did now? Strong body, strong mind and all that.

'Something smells wonderful,' she said, walking over to where he was busy cracking eggs into the pan.

'It's my natural scent. I call it Eau de Charisma,' he said with a quirked brow as she came level with where he was standing.

She was so surprised that he'd made a joke, she instinctively slapped him gently on the arm in jest and just like that she was transported back in time, into a memory of Jack making her laugh like this the morning before they'd skipped off to the register office.

She'd been trying to fix his tie and their fake squabbling had almost escalated into a rough and lustful lovemaking session on the kitchen table.

The memory of it hit her hard, chasing the breath from her body so that she had to back away from him quickly and sit down at the table, her legs suddenly shaky and weak.

What was wrong with her?

Couldn't she even eat breakfast without going to pieces?

Jack didn't seem to notice though and, after tipping their food onto bone-china plates, each one probably worth more than her entire stock of crockery at home, he brought them over to the table, placing hers in front of her without a word and sitting down opposite.

'Thank you,' she managed to murmur, and he nodded back, immediately tucking into his food.

Her appetite had totally deserted her, but she couldn't leave the food he'd so generously made for her, so she struggled through it, taking a lot of sips of tea to wash it past the large lump that had formed in her throat.

Neither of them spoke until their plates were clean.

Jack leant back in his chair and studied her, only making the jitters in her stomach worse.

Clearing her throat hard, she looked down and concentrated on straightening her knife and fork on the table until she'd got the feeling under control.

'Let's go and sit in the living room where it's more comfortable,' he suggested, and she nodded and got up gratefully, feeling a twang of nerves playing deep inside her.

* * *

Jack took the armchair near the fireplace and watched Emma as she fussed around the sofa she'd chosen to sit on, fluffing cushions and straightening the covers.

He felt stressed just watching her.

'Emma, why don't you sit down? I don't think that cushion's going to get any fluffier.'

Giving the offending article one last pat, she plonked herself onto the sofa opposite him and let out a low groan.

'I'm so full! There's a good chance I won't be able to move off this sofa now I've sat down, which is a worry because the view from here is giving me a headache.' She flashed him a speculative smile.

'Who decorated this place anyway? Please tell me it wasn't you,' she said with a glint in her eye. 'I really can't be associated with a man that thinks that aubergine and mustard yellow are good colour choices for what's meant to be a relaxing environment.'

He snorted in amusement. 'It was chosen by my grandfather's assistant—who he was not so secretly bedding—and I haven't had time to change it since I've been back in England.'

She tipped her head to one side and studied him. 'I bet your place in the States was all cool chrome and marble without a speck of colour to be seen.'

He shrugged, a little stung by her pointed attack on his taste. 'I like my surroundings to feel clean and calming.' Despite his attempt not to sound defensive he could see from her expression that he hadn't managed it.

'Sterile, you mean.' She wrinkled her nose.

'Okay, Miss I-Have-Better-Taste-Than-You, what would you do to improve this place?'

'All sorts of things.' She got up again and walked around the room, peering around at the décor. 'Get rid of the awful dark wood furniture for a start. Put some warm heritage colours in here and some furniture to reflect the era in which the house was built, but with a modern twist.'

'A *modern twist*?'

She folded her arms and raised a brow. 'Yes. What's wrong with that?'

He grinned, amused by her pseudo outrage. 'Nothing. Nothing at all. I'm just not sure what a *modern twist* is. Do you mean you want to fill it with chrome and plastic?'

'No!' She slanted him a wry glance. 'Well, maybe a little of both, but only as accents.'

'Right,' he said, 'accents. Uh-huh.'

He realised with a shock that his earlier joke in the kitchen had brokered an unspoken truce between them and he was actually enjoying teasing her like this. It had been such a long time since they'd had a conversation that didn't end in one or both of them getting overly emotional, and it was comfortingly familiar to have a sparky back and forth with her again. He'd forgotten how fun it was to banter with her.

How? How had he forgotten so much? The gulf between them had been more than just a physical ocean, he realised; it had been a metaphorical minefield too, filled with piranhas. And quicksand. At least a galaxy wide.

They were both quiet for a minute, each seemingly lost in their thoughts.

Emma walked over to the mantelpiece and straightened the ugly carriage clock in the centre. 'Sorry,' she said when he glanced at her with an eyebrow raised. 'This is what stress does to me. It makes me want to tidy and clean things.'

'I know. I remember Clare telling me that you'd blitzed your whole house from top to bottom, including the attic, during your exams when you were seventeen.'

That had been about the time he was most struggling with his feelings for her. He'd been half relieved, half frantic when she'd failed to come over to their house to see Clare for two weeks during that time. It had made him realise just how strong his feelings for her were, which had only made him step up his condescension of her when she'd finally turned up again, looking fresh faced and so exquisitely beautiful it had taken his breath away. He also remembered the look of abject hurt on her face when he'd snapped at her for something totally inconsequential. And then what had happened as a direct result of it.

He was suddenly aware that he'd been staring at her while she stood there with a puzzled smile playing around her lips. 'You look awfully serious all of a sudden. What are you thinking about?' she asked, her voice soft and a little husky as if she'd read his thoughts.

He cleared his throat, which suddenly felt a little strained. 'Actually I was thinking about what happened after you came back to our house after going AWOL for those two weeks after your exams.'

She visibly swallowed as she seemed to grasp what he was talking about.

'You mean when you laid into me about how I'd supposedly flirted with the guy that was painting your parents' house and I decided to finally confront you about why you hated me so much?'

'Yes,' he said, remembering how she'd stormed up to his room after him and hammered on the door until he'd been forced to let her in. How she'd shoved him hard in the chest in her anger, the force of it pushing him against the wall, and how something inside him had snapped and he'd grabbed her and kissed her hard, sliding his hands into her silky hair and plundering her mouth, wanting to show her what she did to him and how much he hated it.

That was what he'd *actually* hated: his inability to control his feelings for her.

But instead of pushing him away, she'd let out a deep breathy moan that he'd felt all the way down to his toes and kissed him back, just as fiercely.

It had been as if a dam had broken. They couldn't get enough of each other's touch. He'd thought in those seconds that he'd go crazy from the feel of her cool hands on him. He'd wanted her so much, he'd ached for her. Desperate to get closer, he'd tugged at the thin T-shirt she'd been wearing, yanking it over her head until they were skin to skin. It had electrified him. He'd never felt anything like it before. Or since.

Getting up from the armchair, he went over to the fireplace to prod at a piece of charred wood that had fallen out of the grate, feeling adrenaline buzz through his veins from the intense mix of emotions the memories had conjured up.

'Jack? Are you okay?' She looked worried now and he mentally shook himself, angry for letting himself think about the past, something he'd been fighting not to do. For so, so long now.

'I'm fine,' he said tersely.

She recoiled a little at his sharp tone, looking at him with an expression of such hurt and confusion he had a crazy urge to drag her into his arms and soothe her worries away.

Fighting past the inappropriate instinct, he went over to the window to peer through a crack in the drawn curtains at the world outside to try and distract himself. The press were still milling around the front of the house, chatting and smoking and laughing as if they didn't have a care in the world.

Vultures.

'You know it won't be long until they find out who I am,' Emma said behind him. She'd walked over to where he was standing and as he turned to face her the sweet, familiar scent of her overwhelmed him, making his senses reel.

He struggled past it, taking a couple of paces away from her and folding his arms.

Obviously a little stung by his withdrawal, she frowned and mirrored his stance, crossing her own arms in front of her.

'You're right. We should go to see our parents right away. I don't want to do it all over the phone—it's too delicate a situation. I'll call the car and we'll go to Cambridgeshire to see my parents this afternoon, then we can both go and see your mother together when we get back to London. We owe them that consideration at least.'

As if the mere mention of them had conjured them

up, Jack's mobile rang and he glanced at the screen to see his parents' home phone number flash up.

A heavy feeling sank through his gut. This didn't bode well. His parents rarely contacted him unless they needed something from him.

He pressed to receive the call. 'Father.'

'Jack? What the hell's going on? Apparently the press have got it into their heads that you're married to some down-and-out waitress! I've had a number of them already call the house this morning asking us to comment on it. Please tell me this ludicrous bit of gossip is unfounded!'

Judging by the strain in his voice, Jack could tell his father was not a happy man. This was the epitome of a disaster as far as Charles Westwood was concerned.

Jack took a steadying breath before answering. 'I am married. To Emma Carmichael. You remember her, she's Clare's best friend from school.'

There was a shocked silence on the other end of the line.

'Is this a joke?'

'No joke, Father. We got married six years ago, just before I moved to the States. We didn't tell anyone at the time because we thought both you and Emma's parents might try to stop us, thinking we were too young to know what we wanted.'

He actually heard his father swallow.

'Well, if she's Duncan Carmichael's offspring that makes total sense. That family was always good at wheedling what they needed out of people.'

Jack felt rage begin to build from the pit of his

stomach. 'Emma can't be held responsible for her father's actions.'

His father let out a grunt of disdainful laughter. 'I'm surprised at you, Jack. I thought you were more savvy than to be taken in by a gold-digger.'

'I'll thank you not to speak like that about my wife,' Jack ground out.

'I'll speak any way I choose when it comes to the reputation of my family name,' his father said, his voice full of angry bluster. 'You need to come to the house *today* and explain yourself.'

'We were already planning on doing that,' Jack said coldly, barely hanging onto the last thread of his cool. 'We'll be with you just after lunchtime.'

'Good. I hope for everyone's sake you're not letting this woman manipulate you. She could take a large part of your fortune if she decides to divorce you and we can't have our family's name brought into disrepute by having it dragged through the courts!' Before Jack could answer there was a click on the line as his father cut the call.

Jack stuffed his phone back in his pocket and turned to face Emma, who was staring at him with dismay on her face.

'They're expecting us,' he said unnecessarily. Clearly she'd heard the whole conversation judging by her expression.

'He thinks I married you for your money and that I'm going to take you for every penny you've got in the divorce,' she whispered, her voice raw with dismay.

Instinctively, he put a steadying hand on her arm, feeling the heat of her skin warm his palm. 'It'll be fine. I'll deal with him and my mother. They're just in shock at the moment and don't know how to handle what little they've been told.'

She blinked and gave her head a little shake as if trying to pull herself together.

'Okay,' she said on a breathy exhalation, lifting her hands to smooth her already perfect hair down against her head. 'Well, I guess we'd better get ready to leave pretty soon if we're going to make it over there for after lunch. I'll call my friend Sophie now and ask her to bring my bag and coat here, then.'

Once again he found himself impressed with her cool handling of the situation. He hadn't expected her to be so composed about it all.

'Okay, you do that. I'll see you back down here in an hour and we'll hit the road.'

She gave him one last assertive nod and turned away.

He watched her go. Despite her fortitude he was unable to shake the feeling that exposing Emma to his parents was tantamount to taking a lamb to the slaughter.

CHAPTER FIVE

THE THOUGHT OF seeing Jack's parents again fired adrenaline through Emma's veins as she walked out of the room to get herself ready to face them.

It had been years since she'd had any contact with the marquess and marchioness. They'd been quick to cut ties with her family the moment the news of her father's debts had broken, not even sending a card of condolence at his passing, and a little part of her hated them for that.

They'd known her quite well when she was a child, after all. She'd spent a lot of time at their house visiting Clare, but as soon as there was a hint of scandal attached to her she'd become persona non grata in their eyes.

And she was absolutely certain their opinion of her wasn't going to change any time soon.

Not that she particularly cared what they thought about her any more.

Unfortunately though, their interference still had the potential to make things very difficult for her if they decided she was a threat to them and their family's assets.

She was going to have to watch her back around them.

Shaking off the twinge of worry, she took a deep breath and went over to the phone in the hallway. She wouldn't worry about that now. There were more important things to give headspace to before they left for Cambridge.

The first thing she needed to do was call her boss, Clio, and let her know what had happened last night at Jolyon's house.

Clio picked up after a couple of rings and before she had a chance to say much, Emma launched into an abbreviated story of last night's debacle, quickly filling her boss in on the state of her and Jack's relationship and the complicated situation she found herself in now.

There was a pause on the line as Clio took a moment to digest all that Emma had told her before she spoke.

'It sounds like you had quite a night, Emma. Are you okay?'

Her boss's concern for her well-being above all else reminded Emma of why she loved working for her so much.

Even though she hadn't expected Clio to be angry with her it was still a relief to actually hear that she wasn't.

'I'm okay. Sort of. I'm not quite sure how this is all going to play out, but there's a good chance I won't be available to work for at least a week or two.'

'Don't worry about that,' Clio reassured her in soothing tones. 'I'll be able to find another job for you as soon as you're ready, Emma. You're one of my best girls; all the other clients you've worked for have sung your praises to me.'

Emma let out an involuntary sigh of relief. 'That's good to hear, Clio. Thank you.'

There was a pause on the line before her boss spoke again. 'You know, Emma, if you ever need to talk you give me a ring, okay? I'm always here if you need a listening ear.' She paused again. 'I had a similar experience myself a few years ago so I understand what you're going through.'

'Really?'

Emma was shocked to hear this. Her boss seemed so together, so focussed on her business. It was comforting to hear that someone she respected and looked up to so much wasn't infallible either.

'Are you secretly married too?' she asked tentatively.

Clio made a wryly amused sound in the back of her throat. 'Unfortunately it's not as straight forward as that.'

'When are relationships ever straight forward?' Emma said with a sigh.

'A good point,' Clio agreed.

There was a short pause. 'Listen, Emma,' Clio said carefully, 'for what it's worth, my advice is to keep in mind that just because the marriage wasn't right for you then, it doesn't mean it isn't right for you now. Both of you have had a lot of time to grow and learn things about yourself since then. That's worth considering.'

Emma's first reaction was one of scepticism that Jack would be at all interested in a reconciliation based on his angry outburst last night, but maybe Clio had a point. Sure, they'd grown apart over the years, each finding their own way forwards, but neither of them had gone so far as to ask the other for a divorce. And surely he never would have lost his cool with Jolyon if he didn't still care about her, at least in some small way?

Her heartbeat picked up as she cautiously entertained the idea of it. Even though he'd been standoffish around her since then, she couldn't help but wonder whether the more time they spent together, the more chance there was she'd spot a chink in his armour.

That there might still be hope for them.

But she'd be a fool to get too excited about the idea of it. There was probably too much water under the bridge now for them to turn things around.

Wasn't there?

'Anyway,' Clio said, breaking into her racing thoughts, 'like I said, don't worry about anything. Just let me know when you're in a position to take on another job and I'll make sure to find you something. In the meantime you take care of yourself, okay?'

'I will, Clio. And thanks. I really appreciate the support.'

She became aware of an achy tension building at the back of her throat and she concluded the call quickly so that her boss wouldn't hear the emotion in her voice.

She felt so confused all of a sudden.

After putting down the phone to Clio she took a moment to compose herself before calling Sophie, whose number she'd memorised because they'd worked so frequently together for the agency.

After giving her the same quick summary that she'd given Clio, she asked her friend to drop her missing bag and coat over to Jack's house, as she couldn't risk picking them up in person in case the press took more photos of her leaving.

Sophie's mixture of earnest concern and soothing support nearly set Emma's tears off again, but she managed to hold it together until they'd arranged how to get the missing items back to her.

Twenty minutes after she'd put the phone down to her friend there was a discreet knock at the back door where they'd agreed to rendezvous. Emma opened it to find Sophie waiting there with a look of worried anticipation on her face.

'One handbag, one coat,' Sophie said, holding the items up for her to grab as she dashed inside before any press noticed that she'd vaulted over the back wall and snuck through Jack's garden to gain entry.

'You're a lifesaver,' Emma said, giving her a tight hug.

'Are you okay?' Sophie asked, her voice muffled by Emma's hair.

It took Emma a moment before she was able to let go of her friend—the comfort of the hug seemed to be releasing some of the straining tension in her—and they drew away from each other.

Emma nodded, tried to smile, failed, then shook her head. 'Not really.'

'You poor thing. What a mess,' Sophie cooed.

'I know, and it's all of my own making. I should have contacted Jack before now…' she sighed and tugged a hand through her hair '…but I never seemed to find the strength to do it.'

'It must be a horrible thing to have to deal with. I don't blame you one little bit for letting it slide.'

'Well, there's no sliding out of it now. We're leaving to see his parents at their massive stately pile in Cambridgeshire in about ten minutes. I'll certainly be facing the firing squad there. They're very uptight about how their family is portrayed in the media and I'm not exactly the daughter-in-law they were hoping for.'

'Emma, how can they not love you? You're an amazing woman, kind, compassionate, smart. They'd be lucky to have you as part of their family.'

Emma managed to dredge up a droll smile. 'Try telling Jack that.'

Sophie gave her a discerning look. 'You still have feelings for him, don't you?'

Emma sighed and rubbed a hand across her aching forehead. 'To be honest I don't know how I feel about him right now. He can be the most frustrating man in the world, but he does something to me on a visceral level, you know?'

'I do,' Sophie said, watching her with a worried frown. 'You can't help who you fall in love with.'

'No.'

They were both silent for a moment, each of them lost in their own personal reverie.

'Hey, do you have something knockout to wear to meet his parents?' Sophie asked, breaking Emma out of her thoughts about how she was going to deal with spending more up-close-and-personal time with Jack when she was feeling so mixed up about him.

She glanced up at her friend. 'Jack's sister left some of her clothes here, which I can wear. They're a bit casual for a meeting with a marquess and marchioness, but they'll have to do. I haven't got time to go home now. Not that I've got anything suitable there either.'

'Okay, well in that case I'm glad I brought these with me.' Sophie slipped the strap of a suit carrier off her shoulder and held it out towards her.

'They're dresses I've just finished sewing for a charity catwalk show. You're so lovely and slim I think they'll fit you perfectly.'

The kindness of the act brought tears straight to Emma's eyes and she blinked hard, knowing that if she let as much as one of them fall she was a goner.

'That's so sweet of you, thanks,' she said, pulling Sophie in for another hug and holding onto her tightly until she'd got herself under control.

After disentangling herself, Sophie smoothed down her hair and gave her a warm smile. 'You're welcome. Knock their socks off, Emma! And call me as soon as you can to let me know that you're okay, all right. The girls and I were really worried about you when you disappeared like you did last night and they'll want to know you're in good hands.'

'I will. And thanks again, you're a good friend.'

'My pleasure, sweetheart.'

Blowing her one final kiss, Sophie nipped out of the door and hared back off across the garden before the paps got a chance to get a good look at her.

Shutting the door firmly behind her friend, Emma smiled and took a deep fortifying breath, thanking her lucky stars for such good friends.

It was so good to know that she wasn't completely on her own with this.

Jack was pacing the hall when Emma walked down the stairs to meet him looking a little pale, though still her poised, beautiful self. She was wearing a stunning dress, the structured soft grey material framing her curves in a way that made it impossible for him to drag his eyes away from her. There was something sharply stylish about the cut of it, even though the design was simple, giving the impression of confidence and effortless style. He had to hand it to her, she was a class act, even in the face of such a challenging situation.

In fact after what he'd witnessed in the last twenty-four hours it seemed he'd done her a disservice by assuming he'd have to handle the fallout from this all by himself. Instead of shying away from it, she'd stepped right up when it had become clear he needed her in this with him, and without one murmur of protest.

'My friend Sophie loaned it to me,' she said, following his gaze and fluttering her hands across the front of the dress. The strap of the handbag she was wearing over her shoulder slipped down her arm at the movement and dropped to the floor before she could catch it. As she bent down to pick it up something slipped out of the neck of her dress and flashed in the light as it twisted and swung around. He stared at the slim sliver chain. And the ring that was looped through it.

With a lurch of astonishment he realised he recognised it.

Her wedding ring.

She still wore it. Close to her heart.

Following his gaze, Emma looked down to see what he was staring at and when she realised what it was, she tried to stuff the necklace hastily back inside her dress again.

'You still have it,' he said, the words sounding broken and raw as he forced them past his throat.

'Of course.' She was frowning now and wouldn't meet his eye.

'Why—?' He walked to where she was standing with her hand gripping her handbag so hard her knuckles were white.

'I'm not very good at letting go of the past,' she said, shrugging and tilting up her chin to look him straight in the eye, as if to dare him to challenge her about it. 'I don't have a lot left from my old life and I couldn't bear to get rid of this ring. It reminds me of a happier time in my life. A simpler time, which I don't want to forget about.'

She blinked hard and clenched her jaw together and it suddenly occurred to him that she was struggling with being around him as much as he was with her.

The atmosphere hung heavy and tense between them, with only the sound of their breathing breaking the silence.

His throat felt tight with tension and his pulse had picked up so he felt the heavy beat of it in his chest.

Why was it so important to him that she hadn't completely eschewed their past?

He didn't know, but it was.

Taking a step towards her, he slid his fingers under the thin silver chain around her neck, feeling the heat of her soft skin as he brushed the backs of his fingers over it, and drew the ring out of her dress again to look at it.

He remembered picking this out with her. They'd been so happy then, so full of excitement and love for each other.

He heard her ragged intake of breath as the chain slid against the back of her neck and looked up to see confusion in her eyes, and something else. Regret, perhaps, or sorrow for what they'd lost.

Something seemed to be tugging hard inside him, drawing him closer to her.

Her lips parted and he found he couldn't drag his gaze away from her mouth. That beautiful, sensual mouth that used to haunt his dreams all those years ago.

A lifetime ago.

'Jack?' she murmured and he frowned and shut his eyes, taking a step away from her, letting go of the chain so that the ring thumped back against her chest, breaking the strange sensuous connection between them. This was crazy; he shouldn't be giving in to his body's primal urges, not with her. Not now.

It was too late for them. They were different people now. There was no point trying to rehash the past.

'We should go,' he said, giving her a reassuring smile, which faltered when he caught the look of pained confusion on her face. 'We don't want to be late.'

Jack had arranged for his driver to pull up right outside the house and he and Emma—who had hidden her face behind a pair of Clare's old sunglasses and the brim of a baseball cap—practically sprinted to the car and flung themselves inside, determinedly ignoring the questions that were hurled at them from all sides.

Once safely in the back seat, Jack shouted for his driver to hit the gas and they left the pack of journalists behind them, scrambling for their own transport. Luckily his driver was able to shake them all off by taking a convoluted route through some back streets and when Jack checked behind them ten minutes later, there still wasn't anyone obviously tailing them.

They sat quietly, not speaking for the first part of the journey, and Jack took the opportunity to check work emails and calls. After he'd satisfied himself that everything was running smoothly without him, he sat back and looked out of the window, finally allowing his mind to dwell on the situation with Emma again, his thoughts whirring relentlessly.

Something had been bothering him since the phone call with his father, and it suddenly struck him what it was.

They'd be fools to think that trying to get divorced quickly would make all their problems go away. The press would be far more interested in them if they suddenly announced they were splitting up after their marriage had only just become news. His father would be sure to drag Emma's troubled past into the spotlight again, especially if he thought it would add weight to the Westwood's side of the claim in the divorce settlement. The man was capable of doing whatever it took to protect the family's estate.

He hated the idea of Emma having to go through the torture of being hounded by photographers again, having them hiding in her bushes and jumping out at the most inopportune moments. It would be incredibly stressful, especially if she had to cope with it on her own. At least when she was with him he could protect her from the majority of it, using the vast resources he had to hand.

The more he thought about it, the more an idea began to take shape in his mind. What if they stayed married, at least for the time being, and made out to the world that they were happy together? The press would soon grow bored with that—there wouldn't be any conflict in the story to get excited about. His father would be forced to leave her alone too if she retained the Westwood name.

Surely they could deal with being around each other for a while longer, just until the interest in them had died down.

'Emma?'

'Hmm?' She turned to look at him with an unfocussed gaze as if she too had been deep in thought.

'What if we stayed married?'

Her gaze sharpened up pretty quickly at that.

'What do you mean?'

'I mean what if we pretend our marriage is solid? To everyone. Including our parents. That would give them time to get used to it and for the press interest in us to die down, then we could get divorced quietly and without anyone noticing in a few months' time.'

'A few months?' she repeated, as if she couldn't believe what she'd just heard and was a little unnerved by it.

'We'd only have to project a happy marriage in public—in private we could completely ignore each other if you like.' He knew he sounded defensive, but her sceptical response had rattled him.

Surely they could get past any awkwardness about being around each other again if it meant they'd be left alone to deal with this mess in a private and dignified manner. On their terms.

She seemed to be mulling the idea over now that she'd got over the initial shock of his suggestion, and she turned to face him again with a small pinch in her brow.

'You mean we'd live together in the same house?'

He took a breath. 'Yes, I guess that would make sense. To make it seem plausible that we're a happy couple, madly in love.' He was aware of tension building in his throat as he talked. 'You could move into my house. Just for those months. You'd be able to hide out there more easily than your flat and use my driver to get where you wanted to go.'

Turning away, she stared out of the window, her shoulders slightly hunched and her hands clasped in her lap.

'Okay,' she said so quietly he wasn't sure if he'd heard her correctly.

'Did you say okay?'

'Yes.' She swivelled to face him. 'I said okay. It makes sense to do that.' She paused to swallow, the look in her eyes a little circumspect. 'Just to be clear, you are talking about just being housemates, nothing more?'

He clamped his jaw together and nodded. 'Yes, that's what I meant.'

They'd be fools not to keep things strictly platonic between them; it would only complicate things if they didn't.

Sex hadn't even been on his mind when he'd made the suggestion. He'd been more concerned with protecting her from the press and keeping his own family out of the limelight.

He was thinking about sex now though.

That dress she was wearing was doing something unnerving to his senses. It accentuated her body in all the right places, making his blood race and his skin prickle as an urge to run his hands down it and trace her soft curves with his fingertips tugged at him.

Giving a small cough to clear the sudden tension in his throat, he gripped the handle of the door more tightly.

'I'm sure we can outwardly project the image that we're madly in love if we try hard enough,' she said quietly.

He twisted to look at her again, but she was staring out of the window again, her face turned away from him.

Sighing, he sat back in his seat and watched the countryside whizzing past, wondering exactly what they were letting themselves in for here.

The Westwood ducal estate was one of the most impressive in the country. Emma had heard that whenever the family opened their doors to the public, which wasn't often, they were so inundated with eager visitors there was gridlock in the roads around the estate for miles.

She would have been excited to have been invited to visit here under less stressful conditions, but as it was her stomach rolled with nerves as Jack's driver drove the car up the oak-tree-lined road to the front of the formidable-looking gothic stately home, with its geometric towers interspersed with harsh spires of grey stone, and came to halt in front of the grand entrance.

Jack's suggestion that they live together for the next couple of months had both terrified and electrified her.

The tense standoff at the bottom of the stairs earlier when he'd discovered that she wore her wedding ring around her neck seemed to have changed something between them. In that moment when he'd lifted it from around her neck she'd thought for a second he was going to kiss her. Her whole body had responded on a primitive level, her blood rushing through her veins and heating her skin in anticipation of the feel of his mouth on hers again after all this time.

The scary thing was, she'd wanted him to. So much.

Because then she'd know once and for all whether there was any way they could rekindle what they'd once had.

But he'd pulled away from her and the moment had disintegrated around them, taking any hope she might have had with it.

Until he'd just made the suggestion that they stay married, at least for a little while longer.

She could see that he was coming at it from a practical point of view, but, even so, she didn't think he would have suggested it if he didn't still care about her, at least a little bit.

Jack got out of the car and walked round to her side, opening her door and holding out his hand to her.

'Shall we?' Jack asked, his voice tinged with tension. Hearing that he wasn't entirely comfortable with being here either gave her that little bit of determination she needed to swing her legs out of the car, put her hand into his and stand up with a grace and dignity that she summoned from the depths of her soul.

They were in this together now.

He squeezed her fingers gently, as if hearing her thoughts, sending goose bumps rushing up her arm from where his warm skin made contact with hers.

'Okay. Are you ready?' he asked.

'As I'll ever be,' she said, dredging up a tense smile for him.

'Good. Remember, we're the ones in control here, not them.'

She let out a nervous laugh. 'If you say so.'

He nodded, his mouth twisting into a grim smile, and tugged gently on her hand, asking her to walk with him.

They'd barely made it halfway up the wide stone steps when the door was flung open and Jack's mother appeared on the doorstep, her perfectly coiffed chignon wobbling a little in her haste to get to them.

'Jack! Darling!' She tripped nimbly down the steps to meet them, the pearls around her neck swinging merrily from side to side. 'I'm so glad you're here.' Taking his face in her hands, she drew him towards her for a kiss on each cheek, then turned to Emma, giving her an assessing glance. 'It's good to see you again, Emma, dear.' The wary expression in the marchioness's eyes made Emma think she wasn't being entirely truthful about the 'good' part.

'Come on in, we're all in the drawing room.'

All? Emma mouthed at Jack with a worried frown as his mother walked regally back up the steps, leaving them to follow in her wake.

Jack just shrugged, looking as confused as she felt.

Emma had never been in this house before. It had

belonged to Jack and Clare's grandfather when she'd known them and she'd never been invited here. It was a breathtakingly impressive seat, with wide corridors filled with ancient paintings and artwork, leaning heavily on gold and marble to propagate the ridiculous wealth of the family.

'We're just through here,' the marchioness called over her shoulder, her voice sounding a little more strained now they were about to walk into what was bound to be the close equivalent of the Spanish Inquisition.

The room they walked into, with their hands still tightly entwined and their postures stiff, was positively cavernous, with a soaring ceiling painted with gaudy frescos of angels frolicking in the clouds. Emma held her breath, her eyes scanning the room quickly to take it all in before she was forced to concentrate solely on the people that sat stiffly on the sofas positioned around the grand gothic fireplace in the centre of the room.

Which was why it took her a good few seconds to realise that there was at least one other friendly face in the room.

'Clare!' she gasped, dropping Jack's hand in her shock at seeing the woman she'd considered to be her best friend for most of the formative years of her life.

Clare stood up and walked towards them, her face breaking into a huge smile, a smile that flipped Emma's stomach with the warm familiarity of it.

'What are you doing here?'

'I happened to be visiting the olds and thought I'd stick around to greet my new sister-in-law. Or apparently not so new,' her friend said, her lips twisting into a wry, quizzical smile.

'It's so good to see you,' Emma said, burying her face in her friend's curly auburn hair and breathing in the comfortingly floral scent of her. 'I've missed you,' she whispered fiercely into Clare's ear, pulling back to look into her face so her friend could see just how sincerely she meant that.

'I've missed you too, Em,' Clare said, her eyes glinting with tears.

'Well, Jack,' Clare said, turning to give her brother the same perplexed smile, 'you've pulled some crazy stunts in your life, but I never thought getting secretly married to my best friend would be one of them.'

Jack smiled at her with a pinch in his brow as if trying to figure out how best to frame his answer.

'How—? I mean, when—?' Clare shook her head and took a breath. 'I mean *how* did I not know about this? I'm beginning to worry I've been abducted by aliens and had six years' worth of memories erased or something.'

A lead weight of guilt dropped into Emma's stomach.

Jack advanced towards his sister and pulled her into a tight hug before releasing her to look her in the eye.

'I'm sorry we didn't tell you, Clare. I feel terrible about keeping you in the dark all this time.'

Emma put her hand on Clare's other shoulder. 'I'm sorry too, sweetie. I should have told you when it happened, but I—' She looked down at the floor and shook her head. 'I guess I got a bit carried away with the romance of it all and I had no idea how to explain my feelings for Jack to you. To be honest, I was terrified you'd hate me for falling for your brother. The last thing I meant to do was hurt you.'

'Yes, yes, this is all very touching, but I'd like to hear how this all came about,' said a deep, penetrating voice from the corner of the room.

Emma turned to see Jack's father, Charles Westwood, Marquess of Harmiston, advancing towards her.

'Emma,' he said, giving her a curt nod.

She wondered for a second whether he expected her to drop into a curtsey.

Well, he could expect all he wanted, there was no way she was going to pander to him.

'My Lord,' she said, keeping her chin up and her back straight. 'Thank you for welcoming me here today. I can imagine how upsetting it must have been for you to hear about Jack and I being married the way you did, and I apologise for that.'

Something flickered in the man's eyes, but his expression remained impassive.

'Are you going to tell us why it's been kept such a secret for all this time?' he asked, his tone strident now.

Before she could speak, Jack stepped up next to her to address his father.

'As I mentioned on the phone, we started a relationship when Emma was seventeen and I was twenty, but we decided to keep it quiet at the time because we wanted time to explore it without our families sticking their noses into our business.'

Jack let that hang in the air for a moment before continuing.

'Then when I got the offer from the States to go and work out there I decided I wanted Emma to go with me and the easiest way to make that happen was for us to get married.'

His father raised a censorious eyebrow and looked as though he was about to say something, but Jack ignored him and carried on speaking.

'Unfortunately Emma's father passed away right after the wedding ceremony so it became impossible for her to follow me out there and I'm sad to say our relationship drifted after that. In retrospect we realise we weren't emotionally mature enough at the time to make it work then.'

She felt his arm slide around her shoulders and forced herself to relax into his hold, as a woman who felt loved would, despite the awareness that Jack must be struggling not to add that he actually believed she'd abandoned him.

'We've stayed in contact over the years and since I've been back in England we've decided to reconcile our marriage,' Jack continued, still not looking at her. Even though he looked outwardly relaxed she would swear she could feel the underlying tension in his hold on her.

To her surprise, Clare moved quickly towards them and wrapped her arms around her and Jack, dragging them all into an awkward group hug.

'Well, I couldn't be happier for you both. Honestly. I always thought you'd make a great couple. You were always so sparky together. And now there's definitive proof that I'm *always right*,' Clare said, grinning at them both.

Emma forced herself to grin back, her scalp feeling hot and tight as her friend's misplaced enthusiasm caused a stream of discomfort to trickle through her.

She pushed the feeling away. Now wasn't the time to feel guilty about what they were doing.

'Well, now that's all straightened out I suppose we can relax a little,' the marchioness said in a rather brusque voice.

Clearly she didn't share Clare's joy at the news that she now had a waitress with a tarnished reputation for a daughter-in-law for the foreseeable future.

Jack's father didn't say anything, just looked at them with a disconcerting smile playing about his lips, as if he suspected there was more to it than they were telling him.

Shrewd man.

And a dangerous one. Emma could see now why Jack had wanted them to show a united front. Judging by the look of cold distrust in the marquess's eyes, Emma imagined the man would happily feed her to the wolves, given half a chance.

Well, at least it was over with now and they could go back to London without the fear of Jack's parents interfering in their relationship.

A loud ring of the doorbell made them all start in surprise.

'Ah, that will be Perdita,' the marchioness said, rising from her chair.

A moment later a deathly pale woman with a shock of white-blonde hair and the palest eyes Emma had ever seen was shown into the room by a butler, followed by a man with a camera slung around his neck.

'Perdita is our good friend and a journalist from *Babbler* magazine,' Jack's mother announced to them all with a cool smile. 'She's going to do a lovely feature for us showing how invested we all are in your marriage and how excited we are about welcoming you into your place in our family, Emma.'

CHAPTER SIX

'WHAT THE HELL is this?' Emma heard Jack growl under his breath to his father as his mother tripped over to greet her friend with an exaggerated air kiss.

Emma knew exactly why he was so angry. The more fuss they made about being a happily married couple, the harder it would be to let the relationship dissolve without a lot more press attention.

'Surely you don't mind having people know how happy you are to be married to each other?' his father said loudly with a glint of devilry in his eyes.

He had them trapped. There was no way they could refuse to do this without it looking suspect. Clearly Jack knew that too because he gave her an extra hard squeeze as if asking her to play along.

She turned to smile at him. 'Of course we don't mind, do we, darling?' she said, hoping her expression relayed her understanding of the situation to him and her acceptance of it.

A whole conversation passed between them in that look and Jack finally nodded curtly and turned to the new additions to their group and said, 'What exactly did you have in mind?'

'We only have time for a couple of photos today

if we're going to squeeze you into the next issue, but I'll come over to your house in a week or so and do a more in-depth interview for an *"At home with the Earl and Countess of Redminster"* feature,' Perdita said in a gush of fawning enthusiasm. 'For starters I'd like to get some lovely shots of the happy family together.'

Reluctantly, they allowed themselves to be herded into a tight group in front of the looming marble fireplace in the centre of the room and Emma found herself standing between the marquess and marchioness, pressed up tightly to Jack, with her back flat against his broad chest and his arms wrapped around her waist.

'Love's young dream!' Perdita gushed, giving them an insipid smile that made Emma squirm inside.

Heat rushed through her as she felt Jack shift behind her, his arms tightening infinitesimally to press a little harder into her pelvis, only increasing the heavy pounding of her heart. The fresh, exotic scent of his aftershave mixed with his own unique scent enveloped her, making her head swim.

He'd always smelled good. More than good. In fact in her younger days after being with him she used to hold the clothes she'd been wearing up to her nose and breathe in his lingering scent. She'd not been able to get enough of it.

She still had one of his old sweaters at home that he'd loaned to her one day when they'd gone on a cold walk together, just days before they were married, which she'd deliberately not given back so she could sniff it at home like some kind of Jack junkie.

She remembered with a twang of nostalgia how full of hope she'd been that day, how excited about their future together. The intensity of her love for him had taken her breath away, robbed her of all common sense, made her dopey with happiness.

The day she'd married him had been the best day of her life—and the worst.

She could still remember the feeling of absolute horror and helplessness when she'd arrived home after their clandestine marriage—her one and only rebellion in a life of respectful rule-following—ready to tell her parents that she was going to move to America to build a life with Jack there, only to find her mother prostrate on the sofa, her face a sickly white and her eyes wild with grief. She'd rushed to her, panicked by the look on her face, and her mother had told her in a broken voice filled with tears that her father was dead.

She'd spent the next few hours desperately trying to hold herself together for the sake of her mother, who had totally fallen apart by then, as if Emma's appearance had released her from the responsibilities of dealing with her husband's death.

In her state of shock she'd ignored the calls on her mobile from Jack, who had been waiting impatiently for her to meet him in the hotel room they'd booked, where they had been going to celebrate their wedding night together.

Eventually she'd called him, finding him in a state of frantic worry, and explained what had happened, feeling as though she was looking down at herself from above. Jack had wanted to come over and be with her, to help in some way, but she'd told him no, that it would only distress her mother more to have him in the house and that she didn't want to have to explain his presence there. She wasn't going to tell her they were married, it wasn't the right time.

That moment was the point at which their relationship had begun to unravel. She recognised it now, in a flash of clarity. She'd pushed him away, rejecting his love and support, and it had hurt him more deeply than she'd realised at the time.

So it was absolute torture, standing there enfolded in his arms once again, but this time having to fake their love for the camera so that strangers could gawp at their lives as if it was entertainment.

If only her father hadn't died, maybe they would have still been blissfully happy together today.

If only...

But there was no point in wishing she could change the past. It was futile and a waste of energy. Instead she needed to look to the future with positivity and have faith that she'd find happiness again there.

'Ooh, that's a lovely one,' Perdita purred from the other side of the room as her photographer snapped another shot and it appeared on the screen of a laptop Emma had seen him toying with earlier.

'Let's just have one of the happy couple on their own now, shall we?' Perdita said with a cajoling lilt to her voice. Emma thought she and Jack had been doing a convincing job of looking comfortable with each other, but there was a strange gleam in the journalist's eye that she didn't like the look of. Did she suspect all wasn't quite as it seemed? Probably. It was her job to see past people's façades and get to the heart of a story, after all.

Emma swallowed hard, but managed to keep her smile in place.

The rest of Jack's family moved away from the stiff tableau they'd formed for the photo and went to perch on the nearby sofas to watch the rest of the show.

'When will the next issue of the magazine come out, Perdie?' Jack's mother asked, her eyes glued to the way Jack's arms were still wrapped around Emma's middle as if she was looking for something to criticise.

'In a couple of days. We'll just be able to squeak them into the next issue along with some upbeat captions about them renewing their vows.'

Jack's arms tightened around her and her heart jumped in her chest in response.

'What makes you think we're going to renew our vows?' he snapped.

'I told Perdita that's what was going to happen, dear,' Jack's mother broke in. 'It's such a *prudent* course of action, what with being so suddenly reconciled after all this time. And it means all your friends and family will be able to celebrate your union with you this time.' Despite the cajoling note in her voice Emma clearly heard the undertone of steel in her mother-in-law's words.

Jack didn't say anything more, but she could practically feel the waves of frustration rolling off him.

'The full interview will be in the next issue because there just isn't room for it in this one and we'll want to do a nice big spread,' Perdita went on gaily, apparently enjoying the drama that was unfolding in front of her. Emma guessed she could see a whole career's worth of titillating stories in the offing.

'I had a fight on my hands finding some room for these pictures, to be honest,' Perdita went on. 'We had to bump a spread on Fenella Fenwicke's third wedding.'

Tripping over to where she and Jack stood shifting uncomfortably on their feet, she put a cool hand onto Emma's wrist.

Emma had to work hard not to whip her arm away from the clingy covetousness of the woman's grip.

'Now then. Shall we have one of the two of you looking adoringly into each other's eyes? That should play well with our readers.'

Emma's heart sank. She was going to have to look into Jack's eyes with the same insipid expression she'd been struggling to maintain for the past twenty minutes and still hold it together.

What if he saw past her nonchalant façade and noticed how she was desperately trying to hide how much she still cared for him? And what if he didn't actually care about her any more and she saw it there clearly in his face? How would she cope when all these people were watching them?

Taking a breath, she steeled herself against her trepidation and turned around to look at him.

Jack looked back at her, his green-flecked hazel eyes filled with an unnerving intensity behind his long dark lashes.

Emma's heart thumped hard against her chest as she forced herself not to break eye contact with him.

He was so outrageously handsome it dragged the breath from her lungs.

But handsome didn't keep her warm at night, she reminded herself. It didn't make her feel secure and loved, wanted and treasured.

Safe.

Falling in love was a precarious business, full of hidden dangers and potential heartbreak, and she didn't know if she could bear the idea of being that vulnerable again. Not when she'd already experienced how quickly and catastrophically things could go wrong.

After a few more seconds of torture, Jack and Emma holding the same pseudo loving pose for the camera, Perdita finally clapped her hands together and gave a tinkling little laugh.

'That's it! Perfect. I think we have all we need for now.' She turned to Jack's mother. 'I'll let you know when the issue with the pictures is out, Miranda.'

'Thank you, Perdie. You're a good friend.'

And a shrewd businesswoman, Emma thought with a twinge of distaste. Those pictures would probably be worth a fortune if she leaked them to the papers, not to mention the career-enhancing glory of getting the scoop for her magazine.

'I'll call you about setting up that *at home* interview in a couple of days,' she shouted across to Jack and Emma as she bustled about, gathering up her bag and laptop.

After another minute of fussing and gushing pleasantries with the marquess and marchioness, Perdita finally left in a flurry of kisses and a blast of expensive perfume and the atmosphere in the room settled into an unnerving hum of prickly discontent.

Jack had had enough of his parents' intrusion into his affairs.

'Right, well, now this circus is over we'll be leaving,' he said to them.

'Wait, Jack, why don't you stay a little longer so we can get to know our new daughter-in-law a bit better?' his mother said in an appeasing tone, bustling over to where he and Emma stood.

He didn't like the glint of mischief in her eyes. No doubt she would spend the time grilling Emma in the hope of getting her to admit to something they could use against her later.

There was no way he was letting that happen.

'You got what you wanted. We put on a good show for the sake of your image as invested parents-in-law, so now you can leave us alone,' he snapped.

'Jack, we just want what's best for the family—' his father began.

'No, you don't,' Jack broke in angrily, 'you want what's best for you. Well, I'm doing what's best for *us* and that means getting the hell away from this toxic atmosphere. Come on, Emma.' He held out his hand to her.

She took it, wrapping her fingers tightly around his, and he was alarmed to feel how much she was trembling.

She'd projected such an outwardly cool exterior throughout the whole debacle he was surprised to discover she seemed to be suffering just as much as he was.

'I'm sorry to leave so suddenly, Clare,' he said, turning to his sister.

He was grateful that she'd stuck around to be here today. It had been good to have another ally for Emma in a strained situation like this.

And he was glad for the opportunity to see his sister again; he'd missed her open smile and level-headed, easy company while he'd been living away in the States.

Clare gave them both an understanding smile. 'You must both come up to Edinburgh soon,' she said, her expression telling him there was no way she was letting them get away without seeing her for that long again.

He just nodded at her, uncomfortably aware that he and Emma might not be together for very much longer so there was no point in trying to arrange anything with his sister for the future.

He'd work out how to handle all that later though.

Right now he wanted to get Emma out of there and as far away from his parents as possible.

They left without another word, Jack aware of his parents' disgruntled gazes on his back but not giving a fig how they felt about him laying down the law to them. No way was he going to let them try to run his life.

Back outside he opened the passenger door for Emma and watched her slide into the car, as graceful as ever—struck by how even in the most difficult situations she still managed to maintain her poise—then went round to the other side of the car and got in next to her.

They drove away in silence, Emma watching out of the window as the car made its way down the long driveway, glancing back to look at the house as if concerned that his parents might come out and hotfoot it after them.

She caught his eye and he gave her a tight smile, which she returned.

'Are you okay?' he asked her, half expecting her

to shout at him now for putting her through that. 'I'm sorry about them landing a journalist on us like that. I know how you must hate them after what they did to your family when your father died.'

'It wasn't your fault, Jack. It's fine,' she said, but he was sure he saw a glimmer of reproach in her eyes.

For some reason her controlled restraint bothered him. He realised he actually wanted her to rage at him, so he could rage back at her. To get all the pain and anger out in the open, instead of all this polite pussy-footing around they were doing.

Instead, he took a deep breath and told himself to calm down. His parents' meddling was no fault of hers. Or his.

But as he stared out of the window the memory of having to stand in full view of his family and look lovingly into Emma's eyes came back to haunt him, crushing the air from his lungs. He could have sworn he'd seen something in her gaze, something that made his heart beat faster and his blood soar through his veins.

It had made him nervous.

He still felt twitchy and wound up from it now and a sudden urge to get out of the confines of the car and walk around for a minute to get rid of his restless energy overwhelmed him.

'We should stop and get a drink somewhere before we head back to London,' he muttered, and before Emma could protest he leant forwards and asked John to stop at the country pub that was coming up on their left.

Once they'd pulled into the car park he said, 'Let's

take a quick break here,' getting out before she had chance to answer him.

The temperature was cool, but the sun was out and Jack felt it warm the skin of his face as they walked towards the pub. It was a relief to be outside again. Despite the impressive dimensions of the rooms in his parents' house he'd felt claustrophobic there and had been hugely relieved to leave its austere atmosphere.

The exterior of the pub had already been decorated for Christmas and strings of fairy lights winked merrily at them as they walked up to the front of the building.

'Let's sit out in the beer garden,' he suggested as they came to a halt at the front door. He could already imagine how the dark cosy interior would press in on him. He needed air right now.

'Sure, okay,' Emma said, slanting him a quizzical glance.

'I just need to be outside for a while.'

She nodded. 'Okay, I understand. I'll go and get the drinks. What would you like?'

He frowned. 'No, I'll get them.'

Putting up a hand, she fixed him with a determined stare. 'Jack, I can stretch to buying us a couple of drinks. Let me get them.'

Knowing how stubborn she could be when she put her mind to it, he conceded defeat. 'Okay, thanks. I'll have an orange and soda,' he said, aware he needed to keep his wits about him, despite an almost overwhelming craving for a large shot of whisky to calm his frazzled nerves.

'Okay, you go and find us a good table in the sun.

I'll see you out there,' she said, already heading into the pub.

He found a bench right by a small brook in the garden and sat down to wait for her to return, watching the fairy lights twinkling in the distance. Barely a minute later he spotted her striding over the grass to join him, a drink in each hand. It looked as though she'd gone for the soft option as well.

He was surprised. He'd expected her to come back with something much stronger after having to deal with the nonsense his parents had subjected her to.

A sudden and savage anger rose from somewhere deep inside him—at his parents, at her, at the world for the twisted carnage it had thrown at them both.

She put the drinks carefully down on the table like the good little server she'd become.

It burned him that she hadn't done anything worthwhile with her life when there had been so much potential for her to do great things with it.

Instead she'd given up her life with him in the States for what? To become a *waitress*. At this last thought his temper finally snapped.

'Why the hell are you wasting your time working in the service industry? I thought your plan was to go to university to study art and design,' he said roughly, no longer able to hold back from asking the question that had been burning a hole in his brain since he'd first seen her again.

Her initial shock at his abrasive tone quickly flipped to indignation.

'Because I've had to work to pay off my father's debts, Jack,' she blurted, sitting down heavily oppo-

site him, clearly regretting her loss of control as soon
as the words were out.

He stared at her in shock. *'What?'*

She swallowed visibly but didn't break eye contact. 'They were rather more substantial than I told
you they were, but I was finally on track to pay off the
last of them—until I lost my job yesterday.'

Guilt-fuelled horror hit him hard in the chest. 'Why
didn't you tell me? You said the money from the sale
of your family house had taken care of the debts your
father left.'

Frustration burned through him. If she'd told him
she needed money he would have offered to help. Not
that she would have taken it from him at that point,
he was sure. After her father's death she'd sunk into
herself, pushing everyone she'd loved away from her.
Including him.

'It wasn't just the banks he owed money to,' she
said with a sigh. 'He'd taken loans from friends and
relatives too, who all came out of the woodwork to call
the debts in as soon as they'd heard he'd passed away.'

Jack frowned and shook his head in frustration.
'Emma, your father's debts weren't yours to reconcile all by yourself.'

She shrugged and took a sip of her drink before
responding. 'I didn't want to be known for ever as the
poor little rich girl whose daddy had to borrow money
from his friends in order to keep her in the lifestyle
to which she'd become accustomed, who then ran to
her rich husband to sort out her problems.'

The pain in her eyes made his stomach burn. He
went to put a reassuring hand on her arm but stopped
himself. He couldn't touch her again. It might undo

something in him that he was hanging onto by a mere thread.

'I didn't want you to have to deal with being hounded by the press too,' she added in a small voice. 'You had enough on your plate what with starting at your new job.'

He thought again about how he'd avoided seeking out any news from the UK after moving to the States. The cruel irony of it was, if he hadn't done that he'd have been more aware of how her father's name had been dragged through the press and what she'd been put through after he'd left. And ultimately that would have helped him understand why she'd shut him out of her life once he'd moved away.

'I'm sorry I didn't tell you the whole truth, Jack, but I was overwhelmed by it all at the time. I guess I was too young and naïve to deal with it properly. It felt easier just to shut you out of it,' she said suddenly, shocking him out of his torment.

He felt a sting of conscience as he remembered his angry rant at her the other night.

'I know I promised I'd put us first once things had settled down but sorting out the carnage that my father had left us to deal with took up my every waking second, my every ounce of energy. I felt adrift and panicky most of the time, lost and alone, and I couldn't see past it. There didn't ever seem to be an end in sight.'

She took another sip of her drink but her hand was shaking so much some of the liquid sloshed over the edge of the glass and onto the table.

'Every day after you'd gone I told myself that I'd

call you tomorrow, that once things had settled down I'd get on a plane and go and find you, but they never did.'

She mopped absently at the spillage with a tissue that she'd pulled out of her bag.

'Months bled into each other until suddenly a whole year had passed and by that time it felt too late. I'm sorry I let things drag on the way I did, but I didn't want to have to face the reality that there couldn't be any *us* any more. That my life with you was over. You were everything I'd ever wanted but I had to let you go. I didn't feel I had any choice.'

She rubbed a hand across her forehead and blew out a calming sigh. 'The other problem was that my mother wasn't well after my father died. She became very depressed and couldn't get out of bed for a long time. I needed to be there for her twenty-four hours a day. To check she wasn't going to do anything—' She paused, clearly reliving the terror that she might come back home to find herself an orphan if she left her mother alone for too long.

Jack nodded and closed his eyes, trying to make it clear he understood what she was telling him without her needing to spell it out.

Dragging in a breath, she gave him a sad smile. 'So it was left to me to organise the funeral, arrange the quick sale of the home I'd lived in since I was a little girl and face the angry creditors on my own while my mother lay in bed staring at the wall.'

'I could have helped you, Emma, if you'd let me,' he broke in, feeling angry frustration flare in his chest.

'I didn't want you involved, Jack. I was hollowed

out, a ghost of my former self, and I didn't want you to see me like that. You would have hated it. I wanted to be sparkling and bright for you but my father's death drained it all away.' She sighed. 'Anyway, it was my family's mess, not yours.'

He leaned in towards her. 'I was your family too, Emma. Not by blood, but in every other way. But you pushed me away.'

She took a shaky-sounding breath. 'I know my decision to stay in England hurt you terribly at the time, but my mother needed me more than you did. She would have had no one left if I'd slunk off to America and there was no way I could just leave her. There was no one else to look after her. All her friends—and I use the word in the loosest of terms—abandoned her so they didn't find themselves tainted by our scandal.'

Her voice was wobbling now with the effort not to cry. 'I know that my father would have expected me to look after my mother. He would have expected us to stick together. I didn't want to dishonour his memory by running away from our family as if I was ashamed to be a part of it.'

She held up a hand, palm facing him. 'I accept that he made mistakes, borrowing all that money, but I believe he did it in order to make his family happy. So I've spent the last six years working hard to pay off his debts. To finally clear our name—'

Her voice caught on the last word and Jack shifted in his seat, distraught to hear how much she'd suffered in silence, but he didn't speak, letting her keep the floor, sensing how much she needed to let it all out now.

'I didn't want you to be dragged down by the mistakes my father made too. It wouldn't have been fair on you when you were so excited about taking that amazing job offer in America. I knew it was a once in a lifetime opportunity, and how determined you were to shun the unfair advantage of your family name and do something great with your life on your own merits. It would have been cruel of me to take that chance away from you, Jack.'

'There would have been other opportunities though, Emma. I was more concerned about the two of us making a new life for ourselves *together*,' he broke in, before he could stop himself.

She sighed and rubbed at her brow. 'I wasn't the same flighty, naïve girl you'd fallen in love with by then though. My father's death changed me. The girl you knew died the moment he did. The last thing you needed was an emotionally crippled wife pulling at your attention while you were trying to build a successful future for us. You would have only resented me for it.' She frowned. 'And I loved you too much at the time to put you through all that.'

At the time.

Those three words said it all. She *had* loved him, but apparently she didn't feel the same way any more.

His chest felt hollow with sadness, the desolation of it spreading out from the centre of him, eating away at his insides.

Her voice had become increasingly shaky as she'd gone on with her speech and she stood up now and brushed a tear away from under her eye.

'Will you excuse me? I'm just going to visit the bathroom before we get back into the car,' she said, giving him a wobbly smile.

'Yes, of course,' he said, grateful for a break from the intense atmosphere so he could mull over everything she'd just told him.

He sat staring into space after she'd walked away, acutely aware of the bizarre normality of the sounds in the garden all around them while he desperately tried to make sense of the heavy weight of emotion pressing in on him.

Emma's painful confession had pierced him to the core.

He was in awe of her courage and her strength in the face of such a humbling experience, but he still couldn't shake the painful awareness that she'd chosen her mother over him.

Frustration bit at him. If she'd only let him know what was going on at the time, how bad things had got for her, he could have helped her. But she'd chosen to shut him out and handle it all without him. She hadn't trusted him or his love for her enough to let him be the husband he'd wanted to be.

Though, to be fair to her, he had to give her credit for showing such strength of character in stepping up and taking on her responsibilities, even though it had meant giving up a life with him—an easy, wrapped-in-cotton-wool existence.

If she'd been a more fragile person she could have asked him to pay off her family's debts and saddled him with a reputation for having a gold-digging wife, but she hadn't wanted that for him. Or for herself.

She had more integrity than that.

She returned a minute later and he stood up to meet her, frustration, hurt and sorrow for what they'd lost still warring in his mind.

Just as she reached the table her phone rang and she plucked it out of her bag, giving him an apologetic smile at the interruption and muttering, 'It's my mother, I'd better get this,' before answering the call.

She sounded worried at first, which made his heart thump with concern that there was more bad news to deal with, but then her voice softened into a soothing coo as she listened to a tale of woe that her mother had called to impart to her. From what he could glean from Emma's responses it sounded as if her mother's new husband, Philippe, had broken something while skiing off-piste with friends and her mother was going to have to rush back to France to see him. Emma assured her that that was fine and that she'd fly over very soon to see them both.

After cutting the call she confirmed the news, assuring him that it was better if her mother didn't hear about what was going on with them right now as she was already upset and worried about Philippe.

He wanted to say something to her about how it wasn't right for her to feel she still had to protect her mother and that it should be the other way around, but he didn't. Because it wasn't really any of his business.

For some reason that simple truth filled him with despair.

Sliding her phone back into her bag, she gave him a grateful nod for waiting and started walking back to the car. He stood rooted to the spot for a moment, watching her go, and as she reached the edge of the garden he had an overwhelming urge to try and reassure her that everything would be okay.

'Emma.'

She stopped under a large tree strung with twinkling fairy lights and turned back to face him, her expression one of open interest.

He walked quickly up to where she stood. 'I wanted to say thank you,' he said, taking another step towards her, closing more of the gap between them.

'What for?' Her brow crinkled in confusion.

'For being so honest with me just now. It's obviously still hard for you to talk about.'

She glanced away, then back at him with a small smile of gratitude.

He took another step towards her, standing so close now he could smell the intoxicating, floral scent of her.

She looked up at him, her eyes wide and bright with unshed tears.

'I also wanted to say thank you for what you did today, standing up in front of my parents like that,' he said, putting a hand on her arm, his breath hitching as he felt her tremble under his touch. 'It was brave of you.'

Glancing up, he realised there was a sprig of mistletoe hanging from a branch above them, tied in amongst the glimmering lights.

Without thinking about what he was doing, he lifted his hand and slid his fingers along her jaw, cupping her face and rubbing his thumb across the flawless skin of her cheek.

Her eyes flickered closed for a second and she drew in a small, sharp breath as if his touch had burnt her.

'Emma?' he murmured, dropping his gaze to her beautiful, Cupid's-bow-shaped mouth. A mouth that he had a sudden mad urge to kiss.

His insides felt tangled, as if she'd reached inside him and twisted them in her hands.

He wanted to do something to take away the pain and uncertainty he saw in her eyes, but intellectually he knew that kissing her now would only make things more complicated between them.

Clearly she was feeling vulnerable and there was no way he was going to consciously make that worse.

So he dropped his hand to his side and took a step away from her. Then another.

'We should get back on the road so we miss the rush-hour traffic,' he said gruffly, concerned at how wild the look in her eyes was and how flushed her cheeks were.

The stress of their situation must be getting to her too.

'Okay,' she said roughly, nodding and glancing away towards where John, their driver, stood leaning against the car, his face turned towards the late autumn sunshine.

When she looked back her eyes seemed to have taken on a glazed look.

Perhaps she was just tired.

Giving her a nod and a smile, which he hoped would go some way towards reassuring her that he was with her in this, he gestured for her to lead the way.

He watched her walk back towards the car, stumbling a little on the uneven gravel.

If they were going to get through this without getting hurt again he was going to have to be very strict with himself about how close he let himself get to her again. From this point on he would do everything in his power to make her life easier and make sure that she was as secure and happy as she deserved to be.

But he'd be doing it from a distance.

CHAPTER SEVEN

WHEN EMMA WOKE up the next morning she felt as if she hadn't slept a wink.

The memory of the way Jack had looked at her with such warmth and understanding yesterday, after she'd opened up about what she'd gone through after her father died, had haunted her dreams.

Standing under that mistletoe outside the pub, she'd thought for one heart-stopping moment that he was going to kiss her. It had actually scared her how much she'd wanted him to, but judging by his swift withdrawal apparently she'd been crazy to imagine that he'd wanted it too.

But she could have sworn…

Ugh! This was all so confusing.

She was better off on her own anyway—at least that way she could keep full control over her life and keep her heart in one piece.

Rolling out of bed, she went over to the window and peered out at the street below, this time making sure to keep well hidden behind the curtain. There were still a few photographers lurking down on the street, but the majority of journalists seemed to have gone.

They must have grown bored with trying to get information about her. That was a relief.

After taking a quick shower and pulling on another one of the beautiful dresses that Sophie had brought over for her, this time in a flattering, draped soft green fabric that swished around her legs and clung gently to her torso, she clomped downstairs, steeling herself to face Jack again.

She had absolutely no idea what to expect from him today. What she did know was that she sure as heck wasn't going to hide from whatever was going on between them.

Walking into the kitchen, she spotted him sitting at the table with his broad back to her looking at something on his laptop.

The worry about how they were going to be with each other this morning evaporated the moment he looked round and she saw the flash of panic on his face.

'Emma, I didn't hear you come in.'

'What are you looking at?' she asked, already knowing she wasn't going to like the answer.

Snapping the laptop shut, he gave what she suspected was meant to be a diffident shrug. 'Nothing of any consequence.'

Folding her arms, she gave him a hard stare. 'Jack, there's no point in trying to hide anything from me. I'll see it sooner or later.'

He swallowed, then nodded towards the computer in front of him. 'The press found out who you are,' he said, rubbing a hand over his eyes.

Sitting down next to him, she slid the laptop towards her and opened it up to look at what he'd been reading.

All the blood seemed to drain from her head as she saw numerous links on the screen, all with her family name slashed across them with a variation on the theme of her family's money scandal and their exile from high society as well as Jack's name and title.

Gold-digger seemed to be the most commonly used term.

It was inevitable, she supposed. Once the press had that photo of her there must have been a race on to discover as much as they could about her in order to get their stories filed for this morning's news. The public seemed to be captivated by the lives of the upper-class gentry and apparently theirs were no exception.

Feeling sick, she leant back against the chair and covered her face with her hands, letting out a long low breath and concentrating hard on getting her raging heartbeat back under control.

'Are you okay?' Jack asked gently.

'I'm fine,' she said, dismissing his concern with the flip of her hand. She wasn't going to fall apart in front of him now. She still had her pride.

Getting up from the table, she smoothed her hands down her dress. 'Well, I guess if I'm going to be living here for a while I'll need to go to my flat to pick up some of my things,' she managed to say, amazed at how calm she sounded when her heart was thumping so hard she thought it might explode in her chest.

Jack looked surprised for a moment, then smiled and nodded. 'Take the car. In fact, I'll give you John's number now, then you can call him whenever you need to go somewhere.'

She frowned in surprise. 'Won't you need him?'

'I have another driver I can use.'

She must have still looked a little uncertain because he said, 'It's fine, Emma, and it's only until the press get bored and leave us alone. It'll be much less stressful for both of us.'

'Well, okay. If it's not going to cause any trouble.'

'No trouble,' he said, giving her a reassuring smile, which made something flip in her tummy.

His phone rang then, and he turned away to answer it with a curt, 'Westwood.'

She could tell from the look on his face that it wasn't someone he was keen to speak to.

He confirmed this by mouthing, 'It's Perdita,' and putting the phone on speaker so they could both hear the conversation.

'I'm calling to set up a good time to come and do that *"At home with the Earl and Countess of Redminster"* piece for the magazine,' came the journalist's crooning tones down the line.

Emma's heart sank. She'd hoped the woman would leave them alone for a little while, at least until they'd had a bit more time to practise playing the happily married couple, but apparently it was not to be.

'I was thinking a week on Friday,' Perdita continued, not giving either of them the chance to even draw breath, let alone answer. 'I'll pop over at about nine in the morning, which should mean we have plenty of light to get everything shot. Now the nights are drawing in, we have to start our days that bit earlier. Okay?' she finished finally, the uplift in her voice making the word sound more like a command than a question.

'Yes, fine,' Jack bit out. 'We'll see you then, Perdita.'

'Lovely!' Perdita breathed, then cut the call.

Jack scowled at his phone, looking as though he'd quite like to fling it across the room.

When he turned to look at her with a raised brow she matched his frustrated expression. 'So she's set on doing that interview, then,' she said, keenly aware of the tension in her voice.

'Sounds like it. We ought to do it though, just to keep my parents off our back.'

'I agree.'

He nodded. 'Thank you for understanding, Em.'

'No problem,' she said, forcing herself to smile back, feeling a little panicky about what exactly they were going to say to Perdita that would satisfy her curiosity about their relationship. They didn't even know what the state of it was themselves, for goodness' sake.

She got up from the table and went into the living room to peek out at the photographers still milling about outside.

Jack had followed her in and he flopped onto one of the sagging armchairs near the fireplace, wincing as it gave a groan of protest.

She walked over to where he sat and perched on the edge of the arm. 'You know, Perdita might think it's strange that we're living in a house like this,' she said, sweeping her hand around to encompass the nineteen seventies throwback décor. 'She'll never buy that a young couple plan to live here, and the readers certainly won't.'

He frowned. 'Good point.'

'Can you get it updated in time?' she asked hesitantly.

He ran a hand through his hair, messing up the neat

waves and making her long to smooth it back down for him. 'I don't have time to arrange it right now. I'm snowed under at work.'

'I can do it,' she said before she could check herself. 'If you like,' she added less forcefully, pulling her arms tightly across her middle. 'I can't work at the moment anyway, so I may as well make myself useful.'

He looked up at her with a smile of relief. 'That would be great, if you wouldn't mind. Spend whatever you think necessary—'

She gave an involuntary grimace at that and he frowned as if realising what a tactless thing that was to say to her.

'I'll transfer some money to you to get started and if you need any more, just let me know.'

'Okay. Should I give you my account details now?' she asked, feeling incredibly awkward about discussing money with him, especially with the word *golddigger* still floating around her mind.

'Sure. Go ahead,' he said, opening up an app on his phone and tapping in the numbers she gave him. 'I'll do a transfer as soon as I get to my desk. 'I've got a meeting in Belgravia now so I'll get out of your way.'

Emma was frustrated that they were dancing so politely around each other like this, with neither of them making any mention of their moment under the mistletoe yesterday. But then what was there to say? Nothing had actually happened.

They'd not talked at all on the journey back from Cambridge because Jack had been on the phone to his colleagues in America the whole time dealing with a crisis that had arisen, then he'd excused himself the moment they'd walked into the house, citing the need to do more work. She suspected he'd actually been avoiding having to talk about what was hanging in the air between them.

She followed him into the hallway, where Jack grabbed his coat from the cloakroom.

It can't have meant as much to him as it had to her, she decided with a sting of sadness.

It had probably just been a moment of camaraderie to him after a long and stressful day. But that was all. It hadn't meant anything more than that.

Disappointment was doing something funny to her insides, but she squashed the feeling quickly.

'Have a good day. I'll see you later,' Jack said, sliding his arms into his overcoat and giving her a tight smile.

She nodded solemnly, not wanting to give away how disconcerted she felt about being left alone with the press still hanging around the front of the building. Not that she'd ever admit that to Jack. She didn't want him thinking he had to mollycoddle her.

'Are you sure you trust me to redecorate your house?' she blurted in a moment of nervousness, belatedly adding a twinkle of mirth to her expression so he'd see she was only joking. The idea of being let loose on this place—to have such a fun project to get immersed in—filled her with utter joy.

Flashing her a wry smile back, he leant his arm against the wall next to her and regarded her with a mock stern stare. 'If I find you've kitted the whole house out in rubber and woodchip I will not be pleased. Other than that, go for your life. I'll be interested to see what you do with the place. It's crying out for a make over and you've always had great taste.'

'You think so?' she said, surprised by the out-of-left-field compliment.

He shot her a grin. 'You married me, didn't you?'

She couldn't stop her mouth from twisting with amusement. 'You just can't help yourself, can you?'

'I never could with you, my darling.' He leaned in a bit closer to her, capturing her gaze, and the mood changed in a second, the air seeming to crackle between them, the quiet in the hallway suddenly sounding too loud, the colours around them too bright.

Clearing his throat with a rough cough, Jack stepped back, snapping the mood, and Emma found she was digging her nails into her palms.

'I'll see you later,' he said, turning on the spot and striding away to pull the door open, then slamming it shut behind him.

The sound of him leaving reverberated around the hallway, making her suddenly feel very, very alone in the big empty house.

It took Emma a good twenty minutes to come down from her jittery high after Jack left.

Crikey, it was going to be hard, living here with him and having to get through those moments when they both became uncomfortably aware of how happy they'd once been together, but how much had come between them since.

Despite her body telling her she wanted him, more desperately than she could believe, she knew deep down that hoping things would get physical between them was foolish when their feelings about each other were so tangled. It would only make living together more problematic than it already was.

Sighing, she made her way to the kitchen to put the kettle on for a much-needed cup of tea.

At least throwing herself into redecorating the house would give her something to distract herself from thinking about him all the time.

Her thoughts were interrupted by the sound of her phone ringing in her back pocket. Plucking it out, she was pleased to see Grace's name flash up on the screen.

'Hello, you, how's it going?'

'I was going to ask you the same thing. I hope you don't mind, but Sophie filled me in on what happened after Jolyon's party and I read about the rest of it in the papers. Nice photo of you and your husband on the *Babbler* website by the way.'

'Er—thanks.' Was the picture out already? She hadn't expected it to appear for another few days. Thank goodness her mother never looked at the internet and was unlikely to see any of the news articles over in France.

'Are you okay, Emma? You must be having a rough time with the press camped out on your doorstep,' Grace asked in her usual no-nonsense manner.

There was a long pause where Emma tried to form a coherent sentence about how she felt about it all.

Where to begin?

'Yes, I'm fine. It all feels like a dream, to be honest, but we're handling it.'

'So you really are married to an earl?' There was a note of gleeful fascination in her friend's voice now.

'I am.' She swallowed, feeling her earlier nervousness returning. 'Although for how much longer I don't know,' she blurted.

There was a pause on the line. 'Really? Are things difficult between you?'

Emma sighed, annoyed with herself for losing her cool like that. She didn't want Grace to worry about her; her friend had enough on her plate. 'No, no, it's fine, ignore me. I'm just a bit stressed at the minute. I'm supposed to be interior designing the downstairs of the house we're living in for a photo shoot a week on Friday and I have absolutely no idea where to start.'

There was another small pause on the line before Grace spoke again. 'You know, I worked in a lovely boutique hotel in Chelsea called Daphne's a while ago. It has every bedroom decorated in a style from a different time period and the communal rooms are done out in a really cool and quirky way. It would be a great place to get some inspiration.'

'Ooh, I think I know it,' Emma said, feeling excitement begin to bubble in her stomach. 'I read an article about it a while ago. I've been meaning to go and have a peek at it. It looked like a fascinating place.'

'You should,' Grace said. 'I'm sure the manager would jump at the chance to show you around if you suggested that you were thinking about hiring the place for your vow-renewal ceremony.'

Emma tried to ignore the twist of unease that the mention of renewing their vows provoked.

'It would be great publicity for them if they could boast about having the famous Earl and Countess of Redminster as patrons,' Grace added with a smile in her voice.

'That's a fantastic idea,' Emma said, feeling a real buzz of excitement now. It was exactly what she needed today: a chance to escape from the house and take her mind off Jack for a while.

'I don't suppose you're free today to come with me, are you?' she asked her friend. 'We could go for a coffee afterwards.'

It would be lovely to spend some time in Grace's easy company. She desperately needed to do something *normal* feeling after the craziness of the last couple of days.

'I'd love to,' Grace said. 'I've just finished work so I can meet you there in half an hour.'

'Fantastic,' Emma said with a grateful sigh. 'I'll see you there.'

They spent a happy half-hour looking around the hotel, with Emma making copious notes on things that inspired her, then chatting it all over with Grace over large mugs of cream-topped hot chocolate in a nearby café afterwards, sitting next to a large Scandinavian-style Christmas tree hung with silvery white snowflakes, quirky wooden reindeer and red felt hearts.

It was lovely spending time with just Grace on her own for once and they discovered to their delight just how much their tastes aligned. It turned out Grace wasn't a fan of the pure white and chrome interior look that Emma had teased Jack about either.

'That must be tough,' she said, as her friend finished a diatribe about the hotel where she was currently working, which felt so clinical she was continually transported back to the months she'd spent visiting her grandmother in hospital before cancer finally took her from her.

'Your house is going to look wonderful when you're

finished,' Grace said, changing the subject and shaking off the air of sadness that had fallen over her at the mention of her beloved grandmother—the woman, Emma knew, who had been more like a mother to Grace.

She was perpetually impressed by the strength and tenacity that Grace showed to the world, despite having had such a tough start in life.

'What a fantastic opportunity to showcase your skills as a designer too,' her friend said. 'Hey, do you think it's something you'd be interested in pursuing as a career?'

Giving Grace a smile, she shrugged non-committally, but felt a tug of something akin to excitement deep in her belly. She'd always loved art and design at school and had done both a graphic design and business night class recently in the hope she'd be able to apply her artistic bent to a job in the future. Fortuitously, the classes had given her a set of skills to be able to make up mood boards on a computer, put together cost sheets and even do some technical drawing, which would no doubt prove very useful for this project.

While she'd been paying off her father's debts she hadn't allowed herself to think about what else she could be doing with her life, but now she was getting so close to reconciling them it really was time to think about the next steps. As much as she loved working for Clio at the Maids in Chelsea agency, she'd be very happy for her long-term career to take another direction. One that didn't involve toadying to people who made an art form of peering down their noses at the hired help. She'd probably have to go to college and get proper qualifications if she wanted to pursue something like interior design, which she'd need to save up for, but it was a worthy goal to aim for.

It would be a good way to safeguard a more settled future for herself.

After losing everything she had once already, she never wanted to be in a position where she was at risk of that happening again. No way was she going to rely on someone else to keep her afloat.

Pushing away a concern about how this fed into her muddled feelings regarding her relationship with Jack, she turned her attention back to her friend.

'Thanks so much for today, Grace, it's been really useful. Now all I have to do is get out there and make it happen.'

CHAPTER EIGHT

To HER DISAPPOINTMENT, Emma didn't see much of Jack over the next ten days. For the first couple of them his work took him into his office in the City at a totally unreasonable hour in the morning and kept him there until well after Emma had dragged herself to bed in the evenings. Though to be fair, she *was* crashing out early after long, intense days of researching and planning the new design scheme for the downstairs of the house.

On the odd occasion when she did see him their conversations were stilted and tended to focus on the practicalities of living together, with him excusing himself before she had chance to ask him anything of a personal nature.

Seeing the place in total disarray on Friday night when he returned from work, Jack had then suddenly announced he was flying off to Italy for a few days to meet with a business acquaintance, though she suspected he was deliberately making himself scarce—partly to avoid having to live in what felt very much like a building site, but mostly to avoid having to be around her all weekend.

This thought made her stomach twist with a mixture of sadness and dejection. She'd really hoped that her confession in the pub garden would bring them closer, but instead it seemed to have driven even more of a wedge between them, crushing any hope she'd once had of a reconciliation.

So it was actually a relief in a way to have this huge project to take her mind off things.

With the contacts that she and her friends from the agency had managed to scrape together between them, she'd hired a talented, hard-working team and less than two weeks on she barely recognised the place. Luckily it had only needed cosmetic changes—though old, the house had been kept in good condition—and they'd been achieved with the minimum of fuss.

She'd not had so much fun at work in a very long time.

The new furniture was sourced from a couple of funky little independent shops on Columbia Road, which suited the brighter, more contemporary palette of colours she'd chosen for the walls and flooring. While it wasn't up to Daphne's standards of wow factor, she was delighted with the end result.

It was a much more relaxing, comfortable place to hang out in now.

When Jack returned a couple of days before they were due to do the interview with Perdita she stood nervously in the living room with him, crossing her fingers as he stared around him with an expression of pure amazement on his face.

'Well, Em, I think you've found your calling. This is fantastic!' he said finally, turning to give her a wide, genuine smile.

Her heart lurched at the sight of his pleasure, the tension in her shoulders fading away.

'Not a woodchip to be seen,' she joked, feeling her tummy flip when he grinned back at her.

'You've done an amazing job, thank you,' he said, walking over to where she stood.

Seeing him here again, with his hair dishevelled and dark smudges under his eyes, had sent her senses into overdrive and she was having a hard time keeping her nerves under wraps.

'I'm glad you like it. I had a real blast working on it,' she said, having to force herself to maintain eye contact so he wouldn't see how jittery she was feeling in his charismatic presence.

'I can tell. It shows,' he said, looking at her with a strange expression now. Was that pride she could see in his eyes?

Prickly heat rushed over her skin as they both stared at each other for a long, tension-filled moment.

Jack broke the atmosphere by clearing his throat. 'Well, I'm going to go and check in with the US office then head off to bed,' he said, running a hand over his tousled hair. He looked so exhausted she had a mad urge to spring into full-on wife mode and start fussing around him, telling him not to bother with work, but to go straight to bed and get some rest.

She didn't though.

Because she knew that it wasn't her place to do that. She was only his wife in name after all.

Sadness swamped her as she accepted the painful reality that she'd forfeited the right to have a say in how he lived his life six years ago.

He wasn't hers to care for any more.

* * *

The next morning, just one day before Perdita and her crew were due to sweep in and dissect their lives for the entertainment of the general public like some kind of twisted anthropology project, she was surprised to see Jack striding into the kitchen at nine o'clock in the morning.

She was in the process of stuffing her mouth with a croissant she'd rewarded herself with for all her hard work over the last few days, so it took her a moment to comment on his remarkable appearance.

'What are you doing here?' she muttered through a mouthful of buttery pastry, her heart racing at the sight of him looking all fresh and clean from the shower and, oh, so strikingly handsome in a dark grey, sharply tailored Italian suit.

'I happen to live here,' he replied, with one eyebrow raised.

'I know that. I'm just surprised to see you here so late in the day. You've always been up and out with the lark before now.'

'Some of us don't have the good fortune of having regular lie-ins,' he said, the twinkle in his eye letting her know he was only teasing her.

She turned back to her plate and chewed the last of the croissant hard, feeling heat rise to her cheeks. She hadn't even brushed her hair this morning and was still in her scruffy old brushed-cotton pyjamas, assuming he'd already left for the office when she'd got up to a quiet house.

Hearing the kettle begin to boil, she turned to look towards where he now stood, dropping a teabag into a mug. The ends of his hair were curling around the collar of his pristine white shirt and without thinking she said, 'You need a haircut.'

Swivelling to face her, he shot her an amused grin. 'Are you nagging me, wife?'

The heat in her cheeks increased. 'No!' She cleared her throat, distracted by the sudden lump she found there. 'I don't know why I said that. I just noticed, that's all.'

Turning back to her croissant again, she tried to ignore his rueful chuckle and the clinking and clanking noises as he made his breakfast. Grace and economy of movement had never been his more dominant traits.

He sat down opposite her, bringing with him his fresh, clean scent, and her stomach did a little dance.

Trying to smooth out some of the tangles in her hair, she gave him a sheepish smile.

Not that she should worry about what Jack thought of her looking such a mess. He'd always liked seeing her in disarray and had often commented on how sexy he found it after they'd made love in the good old days.

The rogue memory of it only made her face flame even hotter.

'How come you're not in the office already?' she asked, concentrating on brushing her fingers together to knock off the remaining flaky crumbs so she didn't have to look him in the eye.

'I have a meeting in Chelsea at nine-thirty so I'm having a slow start to the morning for once.' He shifted in his chair so he could pick up his mug of tea and take a swig from it, peering at her from over the top of the rim.

'And I have a favour to ask of you,' he said, once he'd had a good swallow of tea.

She looked at him in surprise. 'A favour?'

'Yes.'

'What is it?'

He shifted in his chair again, only this time looking a little discomfited.

'We've been invited to a party tonight, by a business acquaintance of mine. I could do with turning up and doing some schmoozing. The guy might be interested in having me buy out his company and I wanted to work on him in a more relaxed environment.'

'Okay,' she said slowly, her pulse picking up at the thought of spending the evening at his side. 'This is tonight, did you say?'

'Yes. It's in a house a couple of streets away.'

'And you want me to go with you as your *wife*?' Saying the words made her ache a little inside.

'You've got it in one.' He flashed her a grin, which she struggled to return.

Splaying his hands on the table, he looked her directly in the eye now. 'Look, I know it's probably the last thing you feel like doing, what with our lives and relationship being so complicated at the moment, but I wouldn't ask if it wasn't really important.'

She glanced down at the table where his hands still lay spread on the solid oak top, her eyes snagging on the second finger of his left hand as she noticed something glinting there.

He was wearing his wedding ring.

Her blood began to pound through her veins. Even though she knew it was all for show, the sight of the gold ring that she'd touched with such wonder and awe after she'd slid it onto his finger at their simple wedding ceremony, back there on his finger, made her body buzz with elation.

'Yes, okay, I'll go,' she blurted, buoyed by the fact that he'd asked for her help. She would happily do whatever it took to make things easier between them. She owed him that. And she'd missed him while he'd been away and liked the idea of spending time with him this evening.

His look of gratified surprise made her think he'd been expecting her to refuse.

'Thank you, Emma, I really appreciate it.'

'You're welcome.'

His full mouth widened into a smile, the lines at the corners of his eyes deepening, reviving the look of boyish charm that had swept her off her feet all those years ago, stealing her breath away.

She loved his face, especially when he let down that façade of cool that he wore for the rest of the world. It had taken a long time for him to trust her enough to let her see the real him, but when he had it had blown her away.

Was this the Jack she used to know finally peering out at her?

They stared at each other for another long, painful moment, where her traitorous brain decided to give her a Technicolor recap of the most blissful moments from their past, until she finally managed to tear her gaze away from his and stand up.

'What time do we need to get there?' she asked, making a big show of pushing her chair neatly under the table so she didn't have to look at him again in case her apprehension was written all over her face.

She needed to remember that this was just a business arrangement to him, not a date.

'We'll leave here at eight-thirty. It's a formal do, so if you have a little black dress or something it would be great if you could wear it.'

His voice sounded strained now and she wondered wistfully whether she'd somehow infected him with her own feelings of poignant nostalgia.

'No problem,' she said, turning and walking away from him before she blurted out something she might regret later.

The party was in full swing when they arrived and Emma was surprised, but delighted, when Jack kept hold of her arm after helping her climb the smooth slate steps up to the house in her sky-high heels. He'd been very complimentary about how she looked this evening, and she'd had to forcefully remind herself that his noticing how she looked probably didn't mean the same thing to him as it did to her.

After greeting their hosts, they walked into the living room to mingle with the rest of the partygoers and he turned to give her a reassuring smile as she tightened her grip on him, feeling a little overawed at being a guest at a party like this again.

'Just relax, it's a friendly crowd,' he told her.

But unfortunately he couldn't have been more wrong.

'Oh, no!' she whispered, coming to a halt in the middle of the room as a horrible thump of recognition hit her in the chest at the sight of a group of people standing next to the large picture window.

Angry resentment rattled through her as she relived the whispered taunts and cruel asides she'd been the victim to from this very group of people after the scandalous news about her father came out.

'Vultures,' she whispered to Jack, 'who used to call themselves friends of my family, until they called in their loans and sold us out to the press.'

Looking up into his handsome face, she was a little afraid of what she might see there. Would he be sorry now that he'd brought her here tonight?

But instead of showing concern, his eyes darkened with anger. 'No one here will dare say a word to you, I promise you that,' he growled, putting her in mind of a wild animal defending its territory. 'If anyone so much as smirks in your general direction I'll make sure they regret it.'

Her heart leapt at his show of protectiveness, but she knew she couldn't really expect him to step in for her; this was her problem to deal with, not his. 'As heartening as this display of macho chest-beating is, I can't expect you to hang around by my side all night, ready to jump in and defend my honour,' she joked, trying to lighten the atmosphere. She didn't want this to have any kind of impact on his business deal.

'Yes, you can, Em. You're my wife and I'm staying right here next to you.'

The resolve in his eyes gave her goose bumps. She knew he meant every word he said—could feel it in the crackling atmosphere around him. He would look after her tonight, if she needed him to.

'Emma, look at me,' he said quietly, cupping her jaw in his hands and drawing her closer to him so she was forced to look him in the eye, her pulse playing a merry beat in her throat.

'You're the bravest person I know,' he said. 'You didn't slink away and give up when everything went to hell for you and I know you won't give these idiots the satisfaction of breaking you tonight either. This is an opportunity for you to show them just how incredibly strong you are and how much you've achieved despite the cards being stacked against you. You should be proud of yourself. I'm proud of you. Proud to call you my wife.'

The air beat a pulse between them, as she rolled his pep talk around in her mind. He was proud of her? Proud to be her husband? Hearing those words suddenly made her anger at the people here fade into the background. She could handle anything they said to her if she truly had Jack on her side. There wasn't anything they could do to hurt her any more.

Buoyed by that uplifting insight, she gave Jack a grateful nod and a smile.

'It means a lot to me to hear you say that, Jack.' She turned and took his arm again, wrapping her fingers tightly around his biceps, feeling him pull her more tightly against his body.

To her surprise, Jack then marched them straight up to the group, who were staring at them with a kind of cynical fascination.

'Do you have something you'd like to say to my wife?' Jack growled at them and she was both astonished and amused to see them all take a small step backwards and shake their heads as one.

'We were just saying what an impressive couple you make,' a red-faced man who used to go out shooting with her father said in a faltering voice. 'And that you're a very lucky man to have such a beautiful wife, Westwood.'

The whole group nodded in agreement, but Jack didn't move away from them, giving every last one of them that unnerving weighted stare that Emma knew from first-hand experience he was so good at employing.

'And that we're sorry we weren't more supportive about your situation after your father died, Emma,' a tall, moustached man with a slight stoop said hurriedly. 'It's good to see that you're happy and settled now though,' he added.

Emma coolly nodded her thanks, knowing he didn't mean a word of it.

Not that she cared one jot.

'It's all water under the bridge,' she said, smiling serenely to show them just how little they meant to her now.

After that, they strode confidently around the room, arm in arm in a show of solidarity, with Jack loudly and proudly introducing her to everyone as his wife, and her floating around on a cloud of happy contentment.

Jack's gaze followed Emma as she walked back towards him after getting her glass refilled at the makeshift bar that Rob, a prospective business partner, had set up in the corner of his grand living room.

She really was breathtaking to behold. Her head was held high and her body language confident, showcasing the natural elegance and poise he admired so much in her.

Emma had been brilliant with Rob, laughing at his

jokes and showing interest in his tales of his children and their schooling. She'd asked him intelligent questions and had clearly listened to the answers because she was able to comment on them with thoughtful insight. Even Rob's wife was charmed by her, which was an unexpected bonus. The woman was known for being standoffish with the wives of her husband's business acquaintances, but Emma had managed to break through her wall of cool and engage her in a conversation about interior design and the woman had even gone so far as to give Emma a quick tour of their newly decorated bedrooms.

He'd been intrigued to see how genuinely interested Emma was in talking about the redecoration she'd done to his house. Considering how little time she'd had to get it done, he was hugely impressed by what she'd achieved. And she really seemed to have enjoyed it too, judging by the gleam in her eye and the flush in her cheeks when they'd looked over the improvements together.

It seemed she was a natural.

And far too talented to be wasting her time serving drinks at parties.

He ran a hand over his hair, watching with a growing sense of impatience as she stopped to talk to a woman who pointed at the dress she was wearing and gave her a complimentary smile.

Even though he'd been flat out with work, he'd not been able to keep his mind off the knowledge that she'd be there in his house when he got home each evening—and, even more frustratingly, that he wouldn't be returning to one of her beguiling smiles and her soothing embrace.

After having time away from her for the last week or so, which had given him more of a chance to ruminate on what she'd revealed after they'd visited his parents' house, he realised that her heartfelt admission seemed to have broken the evil spell his pride had held over him since they'd parted ways.

He ached to be on friendlier terms with her, rather than having to step so carefully around her as he had been doing.

Hopefully the plan he'd put in place for when they were finally able to escape this party would set him on a path towards that.

'Did you manage to speak to Rob alone? Is it a done deal?' Emma murmured into his ear as she finally made it back to where he stood.

The soft caress of her breath on his skin chased shivers up his spine.

Taking a steadying breath, he turned to look her in the eye; hyperaware of his pulse beating an erratic rhythm through his veins as he looked into her beautiful face and saw only genuine interest and concern for him there.

Was there still something there between them? And could there be something again, even after all this time?

He pushed the thought away, knowing he was playing with fire even considering the idea.

'Yes, I'm all done here. It's time to go,' he told her, detecting a flash of relief on her face.

He made a mental note to pay her back tenfold for putting herself out for him like this. Her willingness to help him proved she was still the same big-hearted, generous person she'd always been. This travesty with her father hadn't broken her—in fact, like the age-old adage, it had only made her stronger.

Taking her hand, he gently led her towards the door, where their hosts were standing, chatting to a group of new people that had just arrived.

'Rob, we're going to make a move. Thanks for a good party,' he said to his future associate, shaking the man's hand.

'Glad the two of you could make it,' Rob said, returning the firm handshake and giving Emma a courteous nod. 'It was lovely to meet you, Emma. I hope we get to spend more time with you soon.'

He meant it too; Jack could tell by the conviction in the man's voice. It was one of the things that had him excited about amalgamating their companies. Rob was well known for his straight-talking attitude and ability to cut through the bull. They seemed to be very similar in the way they conducted business and he was going to be a most useful ally.

'Thank you for your kind hospitality,' Emma said graciously, returning Rob's smile and accepting a kiss on both cheeks from his apparently rather lovestruck wife, who was gazing at Emma with something akin to adoration in her eyes.

Not that he was surprised; she was such a genuine, warm person it was impossible not to fall under her spell.

The air was mercifully cool on his overheated skin as they walked carefully down the smooth slate steps of the Chelsea town house, making allowances for Emma's high heels.

His body twitched with nerves as he ran over what he had planned for them this evening. It had taken some doing—calling in favours from here, there and everywhere—but he was pleased with what he'd been able to pull together at the last second.

The idea had struck him earlier as he'd watched her walk away from the kitchen table looking adorably dishevelled in her baggy old pyjamas that had done absolutely nothing to dampen his body's desire for her.

She was the kind of woman that would look sexy in a hessian sack.

After the years of hard work she'd put into clearing her father's name, denying herself the kind of life that she ought to have been living as a young, driven and intelligent woman, it was time she was allowed to have some fun for once.

As they reached the pavement, right on cue his driver pulled up next to them in the car.

Emma turned to frown at him. 'You ordered the car to pick us up to drive us the two streets home? I know my heels are a bit high, but I think that's what you'd call overkill, Jack. I can make it a hundred yards in them without falling flat on my face, you know.'

He shot her a grin. 'I'm sure you can, but do you really want to take the chance? Especially if we have to make a run for it into the house.'

Shaking her long, sleek hair back over her shoulder, she gave an indifferent shrug. 'I've been managing fine all evening and I'm getting quite good at putting on a blithely bored face for any journos that cross my path now.'

He smiled as she treated him to a demonstration of the facial expression she'd just described.

'Actually, we're not going home,' he told her.

'Where are we going, then? We have the interview

with Perdita in the morning, remember, and I don't think she'll be too impressed to have to change her article's name to *"At home with two hungover zombies"*. It's not that kind of magazine.'

Flashing her a grin of wry amusement, he motioned for her to get into the car, holding the door open for her and raising a playful eyebrow when she frowned at him in confusion.

'Don't worry, Cinderella, I'll have you back before midnight. Well, maybe a *little* after midnight.'

'From *where*?' she asked pointedly.

'You'll see. It's a surprise. Trust me,' he added when she gave him the side-eye.

Muttering under her breath, she finally relented and slid into the back seat of the car, swinging her long legs in last so he was rewarded with a flash of her slender, creamy-skinned thighs before shutting the door for her.

The evocative image remained stubbornly planted in his mind until he managed to shake it out by determinedly replacing it with a vision of his plan for the evening.

The car drove them slowly out of Chelsea then along the tree-lined Embankment that ran next to the majestic expanse of the river Thames, the newly hung sparkling Christmas lights running parallel with their route. Taking a right, they travelled across Vauxhall Bridge then past the vibrant greenery of Lambeth Palace Gardens until their final destination was in sight.

Emma didn't utter a word throughout their whole journey, but repeatedly gave him searching looks as famous landmarks passed them by, which he gently rebuffed each time with a secretive smile.

By the time John pulled the car up a short walking distance from the South Bank promenade her brow was so crinkled and her eyes so wide with bafflement he couldn't help but laugh.

'We're here,' he said, and, not waiting for her reply, he got out to walk round the back of the car and open her door for her. 'I wanted to do something to say thank you for all the work you've put into making the house look so spectacular,' he said as he took her hand and helped her out of the car, holding onto her until she'd centred her balance on those preposterously high heels of hers.

Her fingers felt cool and fragile in his grip and he had a mad urge to wrap his arms around her and hold her close, to let her know he was there for her now and she didn't need to do it on her own any more.

He didn't though, afraid that he might wind up with both a sore shin and a profoundly bruised ego.

Not that he didn't deserve that.

'Are we going to see a film?' she asked with a hint of disappointment in her voice.

'Nope,' he said, looping his arm through hers and letting out a secret breath of relief when she didn't pull away from him.

Her body radiated heat next to him as they walked along the mercifully deserted riverside towards their destination, arm in arm, the culmination of his plan for the evening looming over them in all its grand spherical glory.

She stumbled a little and he tightened his grip to keep her upright.

'Okay, you're going to have to tell me where we're going so I know how far I have to make it in these *not made for hiking along the South Bank* heels,' she grumbled.

He smiled at her frustration, which of course only made her scowl back at him.

'Okay, we're here,' he said as they reached the entrance to the London Eye where a young woman was standing at the end of a plush red carpet, snuggled into a jacket branded with the attraction's logo.

Emma stared at him in surprise. 'The Eye? But I thought they closed it at night.'

'Not for us. They've made a special exception.'

She blinked twice. 'Why?'

'Because when I told them how much you deserved a chance to finally have something you wanted they had no choice but to say yes.'

She looked at him as if she couldn't quite believe this was happening, her nose adorably wrinkled.

'Let's get on,' he said, tugging gently on her arm.

She looked up at him and he smiled at the expression of awe on her face.

'I hope you're ready for the ride of your life, Em.'

CHAPTER NINE

EMMA SMILED IN stunned wonder at the woman who greeted them warmly by name and invited them to board one of the luxurious glass-domed pods that gradually travelled upwards to give the rider an unsurpassed view of the London skyline.

Tightening his grip on her arm, as if sensing she needed a little persuading to believe this was actually real, Jack guided her along the carpet and into the dimly lit interior of the pod, where the doors immediately swished closed behind them.

It hit her then exactly what this meant.

Jack had remembered how she'd once talked about wanting to commandeer the whole wheel for her own personal ride one day, so she could look down on the sprawling metropolis at midnight—how it was on her whimsical bucket list to gaze down at the city that had always held such excitement for her in her youth and feel like a goddess of all she surveyed.

He'd remembered that and gone out of his way to make it happen for her.

Her heart did a somersault in her chest at the thought.

In fact the only thing missing from her fantasy was—

'Champagne!'

Swivelling to face him, she was totally unable to keep the astonished grin off her face. 'You arranged for a bottle of champagne on ice for us to drink up there?'

'I did.' The look of deep gratification in his eyes at her excited response sent shivers down her spine.

Deftly popping the cork out of the bottle, he filled two flutes and handed one to her.

She took it with a trembling hand, first clinking it against his then taking a long sip in the hope the alcohol would help calm her raging pulse.

'Cheers,' he murmured, taking a sip from his own glass but keeping his gaze fixed firmly on hers.

Unable to maintain eye contact for fear of giving away her nervous excitement at what he'd done for her and what it could mean, she moved away from him, taking a long, low breath in an attempt to pull herself together. She shouldn't read too much into this. After all, he'd made sure to tell her it was a reward for helping him out, nothing more.

Walking further into the pod and taking another large gulp of fizz, she noticed that the large wooden bench in the middle had been covered in soft red velvet cushions for them to sit on.

'You know, for the want of a camping stove and some basic provisions I could probably live in here for the rest of my life,' she joked nervously, walking over to look out of the floor-to-ceiling glass windows as the pod continued its breathtaking ascent.

The hairs stood up on the back of her neck as she felt him come to stand behind her, so close that she could feel his warm breath tickling the skin of her cheek.

'Beautiful,' he murmured, and she wasn't sure whether he was talking about her or the view.

She was trembling all over now, unable to keep her nerves at being here alone with him from visibly showing. It *terrified* her how much she craved to feel his arms around her, holding her tightly as they enjoyed this experience together.

Taking another big gulp of champagne, she was surprised to find she'd finished the glassful.

'Here, let me refill that for you,' Jack said, taking the flute gently out of her fingers.

She stared sightlessly out at the view, her senses entirely diverted by the man moving purposefully around behind her.

He returned a moment later and she took the refilled glass gratefully from him, recognising a desperate need to maintain the bolstering buzz of courage that the alcohol gave her as it warmed her chest.

'Em? Are you okay?' she heard him murmur behind her, the power of his presence overwhelming her senses and making her head spin.

'I'm fine, Jack.'

He put a hand on her arm, urging her to turn and face him.

Swivelling reluctantly on the spot, she looked up into his captivating eyes.

'You were amazing tonight, you know,' he said, pushing a strand of hair away from her face and tucking it behind her ear, sending a rush of goose bumps across her skin where he touched her. 'You conducted yourself with such integrity, a quality a lot of the people there tonight would never be able to claim for themselves.'

'Thank you.' Her words came out sounding stilted and coarse due to a sudden constriction in her chest. 'Well, I'm glad I didn't let you down as your—' she swallowed '—wife.'

He snorted gently and glanced down, frowning. 'You've never let me down, Em.' When he looked back at her his eyes were full of regret. 'It was me that expected too much from you too fast after your father died, then gave up on you too quickly. I've been selfish and short-sighted.'

She blinked, shocked by his sudden confession and not sure how to respond to it.

He sighed, his shoulders slumping. Moving to stand next to her now at the floor-to-ceiling window, he rested his forehead against the glass and stared out across the vast, night-lit city. They were a good way up in the air now, much higher than any of the buildings that surrounded them.

Together, but alone, at the top of the world.

'I hate myself for the way I treated you back then. I don't know what made me think it was okay to expect you to jump, just because I asked you to. I was an arrogant, naïve fool who had no idea how a marriage really worked.'

Pushing away from the window, he turned to face her again, his expression fierce.

'I miss what we had, Emma.'

He took a small step towards her and her heart rate accelerated.

'I remember everything from our time together as if it was yesterday,' he murmured, his gaze sweeping her face. 'How beautiful you look when you wake up all tousled in the mornings, the way your laugh never fails to send a shiver down my spine, how kind and non-judgemental you are towards every single person you meet.' His gaze rested on her mouth, which tingled in response to his avid attention.

'You're a good person through and through, Emma Westwood.'

Adrenaline was making her heart leap about in her chest now and the pod, which had felt so spacious for two people only minutes ago, suddenly felt too small.

His dark gaze moved up to fix on hers. 'I've been punishing you for rejecting me—' he took a ragged breath '—because you broke my heart, Em.' His voice cracked on the words and on instinct she reached out to lay a hand against his chest, over his heart, as if she could somehow undo the damage she'd done to it.

He glanced down at where her hand lay before looking up to recapture her gaze with his. 'The way I responded was totally unfair. I know that now. And I'm sorry. Truly sorry, Emma.'

Her breath caught in her throat as she saw tears well in his eyes.

He was hurting as badly as she was.

This revelation finally broke through her restraint and an overwhelming urge to soothe him compelled her to close the gap between them. Wrapping her arms around him, she pressed her lips to his and immediately felt him respond by pulling her hard against his body and kissing her back with an intensity that took her breath away.

Opening her mouth to drag in a gasp of pleasure, she felt his tongue slide between her parted lips and skim against her own, bringing with it the heady familiar taste of him. She'd missed kissing him, so profoundly it made her physically ache with relief to finally be able to revel in its glorious return.

They moved against each other in an exquisitely sensual dance, their hands pushing under clothing, sliding over skin, reading each other's bodies with their fingertips.

Stumbling together, they moved to the centre of the pod and Jack carefully laid her down on the soft velvet cushions, not letting her go for a second, and she let him take control, forcing herself not to ruin this by questioning the wisdom of what they were doing—because she needed this right now, needed to blot out all the complications and responsibilities in her life and just sink into the safe familiarity of his strength.

To feel desired and happy and free again.

The sex was fast and desperate, as if they couldn't stop themselves even if they'd wanted to. Their hands and mouths were everywhere, their touch wild and unrestrained.

Alone, but together, at the top of the world.

Afterwards, after they'd come back down to earth and stumbled out of the pod, rumpled and high on champagne and emotion, they returned home and made love again, this time taking the opportunity to explore each other's bodies properly, relearning what they used to know and finding comfort and joy in the fact that being together again was as wonderful as they remembered—maybe even more so—until they finally fell asleep in each other's arms, both mentally and physically replete after their long-awaited wedding night.

* * *

Jack woke the next morning with a deep sense of satisfaction warming his body.

Memories of having Emma in his arms last night swam across his vision and he allowed himself to exult in them for a while before opening his eyes.

He hadn't intended to make love to her last night, the trip on the London Eye was meant to be an apology for the awful, cold way he'd been acting towards her, but she'd looked so wary to be there alone with him he'd known if he wanted to gain her trust again he was going to have to be totally honest with her about how he was feeling.

It had been incredibly hard saying those things to her after years of burying his feelings so deeply inside him, but he was intensely relieved that they were finally out in the open.

He knew now with agonising certainty that he'd never felt like this with anyone but her. The women he'd dated in the years they'd been apart had all been pale imitations of her. Mere tracing paper versions. Without substance. None of them had her grace and finesse, or her smart, sharp wit. Or her beauty.

After Emma had left him, he'd shut himself off from romantic emotion, not wanting to deal with the torment he'd been put through, but as soon as she'd reappeared in his life all those feelings had come rushing back. But it had been too painful to bear at first, like emotional pins and needles. So he'd numbed himself against her.

Until it wasn't possible to any more.

From the way she'd kept herself gently aloof from him since they'd met again he'd been afraid that she wasn't interested in renewing their connection—that she'd moved on from him—but judging by the passionate fervour of her lovemaking last night, it seemed she did still care about him after all.

Which led him to believe that there might be hope for them yet.

Excitement buzzed through his veins and he turned to look for the woman who had made him an intensely happy man last night, only to be disappointed when he found the space where she'd lain in bed next to him empty and cold.

Frowning, he grabbed his phone, glancing at the screen to see it was already eight-thirty. It wasn't like him to sleep in late, but after the intensity of the night before he guessed it wasn't entirely surprising.

At least he'd taken today off work to be available for the *Babbler* interview, so he and Emma would be able to spend the day in each other's company—hopefully most of it in bed.

Heart feeling lighter than it had in years, he got up and took a quick shower, then pulled on some fresh clothes.

It was a shame there wasn't time to lure her back to bed now. That damn interview! It was the very last thing he wanted to do today.

Still, perhaps once Perdita had cleared off he could take Emma out for a slap-up meal to apologise for forcing her to take part in his father's media circus, then drag her back to the house for a lot more personal attention and a chance for them to talk about their future together.

Taking the stairs two at a time, he went straight to

the kitchen to seek out Emma so they could start their life together again as soon as possible.

Emma had woken up in the dark to find Jack's arm lying heavily across her chest and his leg hooked over hers, trapping her within the cage of his body.

Her first thought was, *What have I done?*

She'd let her crazy romantic notions get the better of her, that was what.

She was suddenly terrified that she'd made a terrible mistake.

Heart pounding, she'd wriggled out of his covetous embrace and dashed into the en-suite bathroom, her forehead damp with sweat and her limbs twitchy with adrenaline.

After splashing some water on her face and feeling her heart rate begin to return to normal, she'd crept back out to the bedroom and stood looking at Jack as he slept. He'd looked so peaceful, lying there on his side, with his arm still outstretched as if he were holding onto the ghost of her presence.

Unable to bear the idea of getting back into bed with him when her feelings were in such chaos, she went to her own room to get dressed, then headed downstairs to make herself a soothing cup of tea. She sat with it at the table, staring into space and thinking, thinking, thinking...

Half an hour later, she was still sitting there with a cold cup of tea in front of her, her thoughts a blur of conflicting emotions.

She was so confused, so twisted into knots. In her haze of lust and alcohol last night she'd thought she'd be able to remain in control and keep her feelings safe.

What an idiot she'd been.

It hadn't taken much for him to break through the barriers she'd so carefully constructed over the last six years to keep her safe from any more emotional upheaval.

Just the thought of it made her go cold with fear.

What had she been thinking, imagining reconciliation with Jack was what she wanted? It was crazy to try and reinstate what they'd once had. Impossible! They couldn't just pick up where they'd left off and she couldn't put herself through the torment of wondering when it was all going to be ripped away from her again.

Because it would be.

She didn't get to keep the people she loved.

Anyway, he was still probably clinging on to a vision of her from when she was eighteen, all bright-eyed and full of naïve optimism. The Emma she'd been then was the perfect match for someone of his standing—a billionaire businessman and earl of the realm—but the Emma she was now was all wrong to be the wife of someone like that. Especially as his family put such store in appearances. They'd humoured the match up till now, but surely it would cause all sorts of friction for Jack in the future. It could tear his family apart, and, after having her own torn asunder, that was the last thing she'd wish on him.

He'd only end up hating her for it.

After already suffering through the turmoil of losing him once; she couldn't bear the thought of going through it again. It would break her in two.

She jumped in surprise as Jack came striding into

the kitchen looking all rumpled and sexy, with a wide smile on his face.

Her stomach did an almighty flip at the sight of him, but she dug her fingernails into the table top, reminding herself of all the reasons why it would be a bad idea to take things any further with him.

Striding over to where she sat, he bent down to kiss her and she steeled herself, flinching a little as his mouth made contact with hers.

As he pulled away she could tell from the look of wounded surprise in his eyes that he'd noticed her withdrawal.

'Emma? What's wrong?' he asked, his tone confirming his apprehension.

But before she could answer there was a long ring on the doorbell.

'That'll be Perdita,' Jack said, annoyance tingeing his voice. 'She's early.'

Jack paced the floor of the living room with a feeling of dread lying heavily in his gut while Emma went to let Perdita and the photographer in.

He didn't understand why she was suddenly acting so coldly towards him after what they'd shared last night. The way she'd flinched away from his kiss had completely rattled him.

A moment later she reappeared with Perdita hot on her heels, the journalist bringing with her a cloud of the same cloying perfume she'd worn the last time they'd seen her.

Jack's stomach rolled as it twisted up his nose.

'Jack, darling! How lovely to see you again!' Perdita shot him a quick smile before striding around the room, glancing around at the décor that Emma had so painstakingly instated.

'What a wonderful room! The lighting is perfect for taking some photos of the two of you in here. What do you think, David?'

David, the photographer, nodded his agreement, then carelessly dumped his camera bag and laptop onto the polished cherry-wood coffee table.

Jack saw Emma wince in his peripheral vision, but she didn't utter a word of reproach. Perhaps she thought she had no right to because this wasn't her house. The thought frustrated him, making his limbs twitchy and his head throb.

'It's good for me,' David said, nodding at a light metre he was now holding up. 'I'll get set up while you do the interview, Perdie.'

'Okey-dokey,' Perdita trilled, turning to Jack with a simpering smile, then looking towards where Emma still stood in the doorway. 'Let's get started, shall we?'

They all sat down, he and Emma on the sofa next to each other and Perdita in the armchair opposite.

As Jack sat back his leg pressed up against Emma's and he bristled as she shifted away from his touch. Perdita was never going to believe they were a happily married couple if it looked as if she couldn't even stand to sit next to him.

What was going on? Had he done or said something last night that had upset her? If he had, he had no idea what it could have been.

He took a breath and slung his arm around her shoulders. She tensed a little under his touch, but at least she didn't move away this time.

Looking over at Perdita, he steeled himself for

spending the next half an hour—that was all he was going to give her—fielding her impertinent questions about his and Emma's life together, while also trying to make their relationship sound real and exciting enough to titillate the readers of *Babbler* magazine.

'So, how are the plans for the renewal of your wedding vows going?' Perdita purred, after she'd set up her phone to record their conversation.

'Er…well, we're still talking about when and how we're going to do it—' Emma said quickly, her smile looking fixed and her eyes overly bright when he glanced round at her.

'Uh-huh,' Perdita intoned, looking between the two of them with a quizzical little pinch in her forehead.

'We're hoping it'll be some time in the new year. We'll let you know when we've made some firm plans,' Jack said brusquely, in an attempt to close that line of questioning down as quickly as possible. Emma shuffled in her seat beside him.

Luckily Perdita didn't press them on it.

'So are you planning on spending Christmas here? I see you already have your decorations up,' Perdita said brightly, sweeping her hands around to gesture at the strings of silver baubles that Emma had hung from the picture rails and the spicy scented Douglas fir she'd covered with tasteful vintage Victorian ornaments.

'Yes, I think we'll be here for Christmas this year,' Jack replied, glancing around him at the decorations. They lent the room such a cosy festive air, so much so he found he was actually enjoying sitting in his living room for once, despite having to answer Perdita's inane questions.

'It must be so lovely to have a family home again to spend Christmas Day in, Emma. I understand you had to sell the house you grew up in after your poor father passed on,' Perdita cooed, raising her brow in a shocking show of pseudo sympathy.

'That's right, Perdita, we did,' Emma answered, keeping her chin up and her gaze locked with the woman's though Jack was aware of her shoulders tensing ever so slightly. 'And yes, it'll be a lovely house to spend Christmas in.'

He was desperate to call a halt to this ridiculous debacle, but he didn't want to give the woman the satisfaction of seeing him riled.

'You know, Perdita, Emma did all the interior design in the house,' he said, leaning in to draw the journalist's unscrupulous attention away from his wife.

Perdita glanced around at him, quickly hiding a flash of irritation that he'd foiled her underhand pursuit of some juicy gossip with which to titillate her readers. 'Is that right?'

'Yes. She has a real talent for it, my wife. I'm incredibly proud of her. In fact, why don't you mention to your readers that she's available for consultation if they're looking for an interior designer? I can give them a personal guarantee that they'll be delighted with Emma's talent for making a house into a home.'

He picked up Emma's hand from her lap, giving it a reassuring squeeze. After a second's pause she gave him a squeeze back.

There was definitely something very wrong here. Was she feeling ill? Too tired from their night of passion to think straight? Just sick to death of being hounded for answers to questions that brought up painful memories from her past?

Perdita continued to fire tricky questions at them: about how they fell in love, how they came to be reconciled, what their plans were for their future together and even though Emma fielded the questions well with vague but upbeat answers he imagined he could feel her slipping further and further away from him with every second that passed.

By the time the interview finally concluded he was desperate to get Perdita out of the house so that he and Emma could talk again in private.

But unfortunately the journalist had other ideas.

'Well, I've got everything I need for the article. We just need to get some lovely snaps of the two of you together in this beautiful living room. You've done such a wonderful job on the décor, Emma. It'll make a lovely backdrop.'

She stood up from the armchair that she'd been perched on and Jack and Emma stood up awkwardly too.

Judging by the look on Emma's face, Jack was pretty sure she was as desperate for this to be over as he was.

'Are you ready for us, David?' Perdita called out to her photographer.

'As I'll ever be, Perdie,' David replied, shooting them all a wink.

They allowed Perdita to manhandle them into a 'loving' clinch on the sofa by the window, and Jack's spirits sank even lower as he felt Emma tense as he wrapped his arms around her.

'Okay, let's have a lovely kiss now, shall we?' Perdita purred, giving them a lascivious smile.

To his horror, he realised Emma was actually vibrating with tension now and when he turned his head to look at her, his gut twisted as he saw only a cool remoteness in her eyes.

Leaning forwards, he pressed his lips to hers, hoping he could somehow wake the Emma from last night, to remind her how good it had been between them, and how good it could be again, if only she'd let him back in.

Her mouth was cool and pliant beneath his, but he could feel the reluctance in her, taste it on her lips, sense it in the raggedness of her breathing—as if she was only tolerating his touch until she could get away from him without looking bad in front of Perdita.

The rejection tugged hard at him, causing pain in his chest as if she'd torn something loose inside him.

'Wonderful!' Perdita said, as they drew apart.

'Is that it?' Jack asked gruffly, at the very end of his patience with the woman now. He wanted her and her nauseating presence out of his house so he could be on his own with Emma again and finally be able to find out what was going on with her.

'We're done,' Perdita said, all businesslike now as David gathered up his equipment behind her.

'I'll let your mother know when to expect to see the article,' she said.

As soon as he shut the door on Perdita's designer-suited back, Jack returned to the living room to find Emma perched on the arm of the sofa, staring out of the window.

'Thank you for doing that,' he said, walking towards her. 'I'm sorry to put you through it.'

She shrugged, but didn't look at him.

'I guess it'll satisfy your parents. At least for a while.' She took a deep shaky-sounding breath. 'I'm going to go now, Jack,' she said quietly, still not turning around.

His heart turned over at her words. 'What are you talking about?'

She turned to face him, her expression shuttered. 'I need to get out of here.'

Emma took a deep breath, trying not to let Jack's incredulous glare stop her from saying what needed to be said.

'I don't need to stay here now the journalists have stopped prowling around the house and Perdita's got her pound of flesh from us,' she said, keeping her voice steady and emotionless, even though it nearly killed her to do it.

Jack stared at her in shock. 'But you don't need to go, Em. You should stay. I want you to.'

She shook her head. 'I can't stay here now, Jack, not now we've crossed an irreversible line by sleeping together, something we agreed not to do.'

Couldn't he see that they shouldn't risk putting themselves in a position where it might happen again, that it would only make things harder and more complicated later when they started the inevitable divorce proceedings?

'I thought it's what you wanted too,' he ground out, his troubled gaze boring into hers. 'It certainly seemed like it last night.'

She folded her arms across her chest, hugging them around her. 'You didn't really think that one night together would fix what's wrong with our relationship, did you?'

His steady gaze continued to bore into hers, his eyes dark with intent. Sitting down opposite her, he put his elbows on his knees and leaned forwards, his eyes not leaving hers. 'Emma, I want us to try and make this marriage work.'

Her mouth was suddenly so dry she found it hard to swallow and she was aware of a low level of panic beginning to grow in the pit of her stomach.

'We've been apart for too long, Jack. How can we expect to make a relationship work now?' Her voice shook with the effort of keeping her emotions at bay.

'But it does work, Emma, we proved that last night.'

'You didn't really think we could just pick up from where we left off, did you?'

He blinked at her in surprise, then opened his mouth as if to answer.

But she couldn't let him try and persuade her otherwise; this was hard enough as it was. She really couldn't bring herself to trust that it could all be okay with them this time. What guarantees did they have that it wouldn't all fall apart again?

'We shouldn't have let last night happen. Sex always messes things up,' she said, her voice wobbling with tension.

He cleared his throat uncomfortably. 'Are you telling me you regret what happened now?' A muscle was twitching in his jaw and his brow pinched into a disbelieving frown.

She was hurting him; she could see it in his eyes and it was tearing her apart.

'I—can't do this again, Jack.' But her voice held no conviction. She could see that he thought so too by the way he was looking at her.

As if he knew how very close she was to giving in.

He was still looking at her that way as he got up and walked towards her. Still looking as he pushed his hand gently into her hair and tilted her face towards him. Still looking as he brushed his lips against hers with a feather-light kiss that made her insides melt and fizz.

'Don't, Jack...' she murmured against his mouth, her willpower a frail and insubstantial thing that she was having trouble holding onto.

To her surprise he drew back, giving her the space she needed.

Finally acting as though he was *listening* to her.

Sliding his hand out of her hair, he took a deliberate step backwards, but didn't stop looking at her.

She felt the loss of his touch so keenly her body gave a throb of anguish.

'I want us to have another try at our marriage.' He took a breath. 'I need you.'

The passion and the absolute certainty she heard in his voice sent her heart into a slow dive, but she fought the feeling, still too afraid to believe what he was saying was true. 'You don't *need* me, Jack.'

'Yes, I do! There's this big hole in my life without you that I've never been able to fill. It's like part of me is hollow. A wound that just won't heal.'

'You're comparing me to a wound now? How romantic.' But despite her jibe she was aware of a warm glow of longing pulsing deep in her chest now.

She pushed it away, telling herself not to be a fool. It was dangerous to hope for this to work out after last time. Too much time and pain and heartache had come between them since those happier days. He was being naïve to think they could get back what they once had.

He locked his gaze with hers, his expression sincere. 'I'm going to be here for you this time, Em, every step of the way. I'll look after you, I promise.'

'Promises aren't enough, Jack.'

He ran a hand over his face, suddenly looking tired. 'Then what do you want from me? Tell me, Emma!'

'A divorce! Like we'd planned!' she shouted back in frustration.

He stared at her in shock. 'You want to get a divorce after what happened between us last night?'

'It was just sex, Jack. We were both a little tipsy and feeling lonely. It was inevitable, I suppose, after all the time we've been spending together. But it didn't mean anything to me.' She swallowed hard, forcing back a lash of anguish as he stared at her with pain in his eyes.

'Don't tell me last night didn't mean anything to you because I won't believe you, Emma. You're not that good an actress,' he shot at her.

She recoiled at the fury in his voice, resentment suddenly rising from the pit of her belly at the unfairness of it all. 'You want to bet?' she retorted in anger. 'I've had years to perfect my mask. Years of smiling and looking serene in the face of some very taxing situations.'

'Is that what our marriage is to you? A *taxing situation*?'

'It hasn't been a marriage for years, Jack, just an inconvenience,' she shouted in utter frustration, feeling a jab of shame at how cruel that sounded.

Unable to bear the look of hurt on his face any longer, she strode away from him, banging her shin hard on the coffee table in her haste. But she didn't stop to soothe the pain away. She had to get out of there. Away from his befuddling presence. He was making her crazy—bringing back all these feelings she didn't want to have again.

'Where are you going?' he said, trying to block her path with his body, but she pushed past him, dodging away from his outstretched hand.

'Emma, can we please talk some more about this?'

'It's not what I want, Jack. I've already explained that. There's no point trying to hold onto the past. We can never get back what we once had. Everything's different now.'

'It doesn't have to be, Em. Fundamentally we're still the same people. We can make this marriage work.'

Shaking her head, she backed away from him. 'No, I'm sorry, Jack.' She took a deep shaky breath and dug her nails into her palms. 'I don't want to be married to you any more.'

Jack felt as though his heart were being crushed in his chest.

'Don't leave, Emma. Please. Stay and we'll talk some more about it.' He put a hand on her arm, aware that he was vibrating with fear now. *'Please.'*

Shaking her head, she pulled away from his touch and stumbled backwards. 'I can't, Jack.'

Her gaze met his and all he saw there was a wild determination to get away from him.

Chest tight with sorrow, he tried one last time to get through to her. 'Emma, I love you, please don't leave me again.'

Putting up a hand as if to block his words, she took another step away, reinforcing the barrier between them, rebuffing his pleas.

'I have to go,' she said, her voice rough and broken. 'I can't be here any more. Don't follow me. I don't want you to.'

And with that, she turned on her heel and strode away from him.

Frozen with frustration, he remained standing where she'd left him, listening to her mount the stairs and a minute later come back down, hoping—praying—that she'd pause on her way out, to stop and look at him one last time. If she did that, he'd go to her. Hold and comfort her. Tell her she could trust him and he'd make everything okay.

If she did that, he'd know there was still a chance for them.

But she didn't.

Instead he saw a flash of colour as she walked quickly past the doorway to the living room, and a few seconds later he heard the front door open, then close with the resounding sound of her leaving.

Silence echoed around the room, taunting him, widening the hollow cavity that she'd punched into his chest with her words.

Picking up a vase that Emma had bought as part

of the house redecoration project, he hurled it against the wall with all his strength, drawing a crude satisfaction from seeing it smash into tiny little pieces and litter the floor.

He knew then that this was why he hadn't been back to see her in the six years since he moved to America. His heart had been so eviscerated the first time he hadn't wanted to risk damaging it again.

But the moment he'd seen her again at Fitzherbert's party he'd known in the deepest darkest recesses of his brain that he had to have her back. She was the only woman he'd ever loved and making himself vulnerable again for her would be worth the risk.

But it had all been for nothing.

Six years after she'd first broken his heart she'd done it to him all over again.

CHAPTER TEN

EMMA GOT OFF the plane in Bergerac, head-weary and heart-sore.

The very moment she saw her mother's anxious face in the crowd of people waiting to pick up the new arrivals at the airport, the swell of emotion that she'd been keeping firmly tamped down throughout the journey finally broke through. Tears flowed freely down her face as she ran into her mother's arms and held onto her tightly, burying her face in the soft wool of her jumper and breathing in her comforting scent.

'Darling, darling! What's wrong? I was so worried when I picked up your message. Is everything okay?' her mother muttered into her hair.

It took the whole of the thirty-minute journey to her mother's house in the tiny village of Sainte-Alvère for Emma to explain—in a halting monologue broken with tears—about the marriage and aborted elopement and all that had happened to her since Jack had made his shocking reappearance.

Her mother listened in silence. Only once Emma had finished did she reach out her hand to cover her daughter's in a show of understanding and solidarity.

It was such a relief to finally talk to her mother

about it all. She apologised profusely for keeping her in the dark for all this time, but, in a surprising show of self-awareness, her mother seemed more concerned with apologising to Emma for not being there to support her through such tough times.

A little while later they were ensconced on her mother's plant-pot-filled terrace sitting under thick woollen blankets, looking out over the fields behind the house with steaming cups of coffee cradled in their hands.

Philippe, her stepfather, had taken one look at her tear-stained face and promptly left the house so that she and her mother could talk on their own.

'Poor, Philippe, I hope he doesn't feel like I've chased him out of his own home,' Emma said, grimacing at her mother. 'He must still be in pain with his leg.'

'Don't be silly,' her mother said, flapping a hand. 'It's good for him to get out after being stuck here with just me for company for the last few days. He'll be much happier at the bar with Jean.'

Emma stared into the distance, watching the birds wheel in dizzying circles over a copse of trees as dusk fell, bathing the autumnal landscape in a soft, hazy glow.

'You know, I keep asking myself why Jack would want to be with a lowly waitress when he's a billionaire earl,' she said quietly, turning to flash her mother a crooked smile.

Her mother frowned and swatted her hand dismissively. 'He won't be with a *waitress*, he'll be with *you*,' she said fiercely. 'What you do for a living has no bearing whatsoever on you as a person. I'm sure he'll tell you the same.'

Emma sighed and pulled the blanket tighter around her. 'Yeah, I know that really. It's just—' She paused, then said in a rush, 'What if it all went wrong again?'

Her mother smiled sadly. 'That's the chance you take when you fall in love. It's terrifying to make yourself vulnerable like that, but you know what? I was more afraid of what would happen to me if I didn't allow myself to have a relationship with Philippe. It was a good instinct to trust in his love because he brought me alive again.'

She watched her mother smooth her hands over the blanket on her lap.

'I still had to take a leap of faith when he asked me to marry him though,' her mother said, glancing at her with a small frown.

Emma tried to smile, but the muscles around her mouth refused to work, so she stared down at her hands in her lap instead, trying to get herself under control.

'Imagine the alternative, Emma,' her mother said, obviously noticing her distress. 'Imagine what you'll lose if you turn him away because you've given in to your fear. Imagine how that will make you feel. It'll eat away at you, darling—the "What if?"'

When she looked up she was surprised to see tears in her mother's eyes.

'This is all my fault. I should have been stronger for you when your father passed away, Emma. You were too young to take on all that responsibility by yourself—you were just a baby.'

Emma frowned. 'You weren't well, Mum. It wasn't your fault.'

Her mother shook her head, her bottom lip trembling. Lifting a hand, she touched her fingers softly to Emma's cheek. 'You lost your youth and innocence too early and look what it's done to you. You can't even let yourself be loved by a man who's perfect for you. You should. Give him a chance to prove himself to you, Emma. You owe him that much at least. You owe it to yourself to be happy.'

The memory of the hurt on Jack's face suddenly flashed across her vision, causing the hollow ache in her chest to throb and intensify.

Poor Jack.

He'd opened his heart to her and she'd pushed him away.

Again.

It had to have been just as hard for him to let himself fall in love with her again after the way she'd let him down, but he'd trusted his heart to her anyway, making the ultimate sacrifice.

Could she really not do the same for him?

Taking a long, deep breath, she felt determination start to course through her veins.

After everything she'd been through, was she really going to deny herself the chance to carve out a happy and rewarding life for herself?

In that moment she knew deep down that she wanted to be with Jack, she loved him and it was worth risking her heart if it meant she got the chance to be with him again.

But would Jack still want her after all she'd put him through?

There was only one way to find out.

She was going to have to go home and ask him.

His house, which had come alive with the addition of Emma's vibrant presence, felt still and vacant without her.

Lying awake until the early hours, tossing and turning in his empty bed, Jack relived the way Emma had rebuffed his affection with such vehement dismissal over and over again.

His stomach ached with misery as he finally gave up on sleep and made his way to his office at three in the morning.

He spent the rest of the early hours working on a project that had taken second place in his attention ever since Emma had reappeared in his life. Keeping busy had helped him the last time she'd left him, for a while at least, but it didn't seem to hold the same restorative powers any more.

Where was his wife?

He pictured her sleeping on one of her friends' sofas, getting on with her life without him. Going back to work for some idiot like Fitzherbert again. Keeping him well and truly out of the picture, only to turn up one day with divorce papers in her hands.

Finally, giving up on the hope of concentrating on anything else, he went to lie on the sofa and put the television on, staring at the news channel with unseeing eyes until exhaustion finally overtook him and dragged him into a restless sleep.

He woke a few hours later with a start, blearily checking his phone to realise with a shock that it was lunchtime.

Pulling himself into a sitting position, he was just about to haul himself up and go and make some strong coffee in the kitchen when a movement in the corner of his eye made him start in surprise.

Jumping to his feet, he turned to see Emma standing in the doorway, looking at him with a hesitant smile.

'You came back,' was all he could utter past the huge lump in his throat, the unexpected sight of her standing there in front of him making him stupid with relief.

She walked tentatively into the room towards him, as if she wasn't sure what sort of reaction to expect. 'I'm so sorry I left, Jack.' She visibly swallowed. 'I was scared. Terrified to let myself love you again.' Breaking eye contact, she turned to glance out of the window, and let out a low laugh. 'Not that I ever really stopped.'

He stared at her, not sure whether to believe what he was hearing in case his addled brain was playing cruel tricks on him.

'Are you okay?' she asked shakily, turning back, her nose wrinkled with worry.

He continued to stare at her, only becoming aware that he was frowning when he noticed the anxiety in her expression.

Finally managing to pull himself together, he walked to meet her in the middle of the room and raised his hand to touch her soft cheek with his fingertips.

'Are you really here?' he murmured.

She laughed quietly and he saw relief in her face.

'It looks like I woke you. Did you sleep on the sofa all night?' she asked, her eyes clouding with concern.

He glanced back towards the rumpled cushions. 'Er…no. I couldn't sleep so I got up and worked, then I dozed off in here this morning.' He shook his head, trying to clear it. 'Where did you go?'

'To France. To see my mother.'

He nodded. 'Did you tell her about us?'

She smiled sheepishly. 'I did. She was really supportive. She basically told me to stop being such an idiot and to come back to the man I love.'

Emma couldn't help but smile at the almost comical look of relief on Jack's face.

'I guess I owe you an explanation about what got me so spooked,' she said, waiting until he'd nodded before continuing.

She played with a loose thread on the sleeve of her jumper, summoning the courage to speak.

'I think losing you and my father in such quick succession must have damaged me on a fundamental level.'

She rubbed a hand over her face, letting out a low sigh.

'Ever since then I've been terrified of putting myself in a position where I have to trust my heart to someone again.'

He looked down at her with a small pinch between his brows. 'I understand that, Emma. It makes total sense after everything you've been through.'

'When it looked like it might be possible to have you again I panicked,' she said with a sad smile. 'I wanted you so much it scared me. I think I was afraid to be happy in case it was all whipped away from me again.'

She took a deep shaky breath.

'You know, the day we got married I couldn't quite believe I could be so lucky as to have you. You were everything I'd ever wanted and when I looked at you I could see a bright shiny future shimmering in front of me. And then when it was whisked away from under my nose I sincerely wondered whether I was being punished for something. Up till then I'd led such a charmed life and just taken and taken without appreciating how much I had. Perhaps I was being penalised for my selfishness?'

'You weren't being selfish, you were living the life you'd been dealt and what happened was just really bad luck. It wasn't your fault. None of it was your fault.'

He sighed and frowned down at the floor, then looked up at her again with one eyebrow cocked.

'Pretending we were happily reconciled to everyone was a ridiculous thing to put ourselves through,' he said with a sigh. 'We should have been braver and talked about how we really felt, honestly and openly, instead of hiding and pretending there wasn't anything between us any more.'

He ran a hand through his hair, then scrubbed it across his face.

'I don't know what I was thinking, imagining I could have you living here, so close, without it driving me crazy with longing for you.'

Reaching out for her, he slid his hands around her waist and drew her nearer to him.

'Let's make a pact to deal with anything that comes

at us *together* from this point on. We can take things as slowly as you like—take time to get to know each other properly again. I'm more than prepared to do that, Em. I just want you back in my life.'

There was a heavy beat of silence where they stared into each other's eyes.

'I love you, Emma,' Jack murmured.

She smiled as joy flooded through her. 'You really still love me after what I've just put you through?'

'Are you kidding? I've never *not* loved you.'

He gave her a squeeze. 'I'm in awe of you and what you've achieved on your own—what you must have gone through to pay off those debts and what you've given up to do that. A lesser person would have thrown in the towel a long time ago. But you didn't and I have the utmost respect for you for that.'

She cupped his jaw in her hands, feeling his unshaven bristles tickling her palms. 'Thank you for saying that. It means a lot.'

She felt his chin slide beneath her touch as he turned his head until his lips came into contact with her palm. He kissed her there lightly, before turning back to look at her again.

'You know I'll support you in whatever you want to do, don't you?'

She flashed him a smile, excitement making her heart race. 'Actually, I've been wondering about training to be an interior designer. I'd have to go to college and become qualified for it, but I think it's something I'd love to do for a living.'

He nodded. 'If that's what you want I'll support you one hundred per cent with it. You can practise on this place if you like. As you've seen, it needs a lot more tender loving care upstairs, so perhaps you could fix the rest of it up as a practice project.'

'I would love that,' she said, a surge of joy lifting her onto her toes to kiss him.

His mouth was warm and firm and she sighed with relief as she felt his lips open under hers. And then he was kissing her fiercely, as if he never wanted to stop.

It felt so right, so absolutely *right* that it dragged all the breath from her lungs and the blood from her head, sending her dizzy with happiness. She knew with absolute certainty now that this was exactly where she was meant to be—in Jack's arms.

Finally, he drew away from her and she almost complained bitterly about the loss of his mouth on hers, until he pulled her tightly against his chest and held her there, safe in his embrace while they swayed gently together on the spot.

They stayed like that for a long time, feeling the beat of each other's hearts under their palms and listening to the gentle exhalation of their breath.

She knew then that she was never going to walk away from this man ever again.

On a sigh of satisfaction, Jack finally drew back and brought both hands up to cup her chin, gazing down into her eyes. 'I love you, Emma Westwood.'

Looking up into his handsome face, a face she knew as well as her own, she smiled at him with everything she had. 'I love you too.'

This admission seemed to galvanise something in him. Releasing his hold on her, he got down on one knee and looked up at her with resolution in his eyes.

'Well, in that case, will you renew your marriage vows with me?'

She looked down at the man she loved—had always loved—and knew in her heart that remaining married to him, fighting any battles she might encounter in the future with him there at her side, would make her the happiest woman on earth.

'I will!'

A wide smile of relief broke over Jack's face and he stood up and lifted her off the ground, hugging her fiercely to him.

'It looks like we've got another job to do, then—planning our vow renewal ceremony, which apparently is happening some time in the new year,' he said, pulling back to grin at her. 'Do you know anyone that can help us out with that?'

Emma smiled, imagining the looks of delight on Sophie, Grace and Ashleigh's faces when she asked for their assistance.

'I know exactly the right people to ask,' she said, bouncing up and down on the spot in her excitement. 'I can't wait to tell the girls our news. They're going to be thrilled!'

Jack smiled at her, his face alive with happiness, then drew her towards him, pressing his mouth to hers and sealing their future with a kiss to end all kisses.

* * * * *

"What are you staring at?"

"You." He thought of the feel of Elise in his arms, the scent of her that he would know anywhere—and it hit him like the proverbial bolt from the blue.

He was going about this all wrong. Staying away from her in order to keep her made no sense at all.

He needed to get closer.

Closer. Dear God. He would love that.

Too bad he was no good at all that love and romance crap. And if he went for it with Elise and it blew up in his face, where would he be then? Zero and two—and minus the assistant who made it all hang together.

"Jed." She'd reached the table and now stood over him, watching him, her smile indulgent, her eyes so bright. "What's going on in that big brain of yours?"

"Not a thing."

"Liar. You've got your scary face on—give me your plate. I'll warm it up."

He handed it over. He watched her walk away. Always a pleasure, watching Elise walk away.

What would it be like, him and Elise, living together, working together, sleeping in the same bed night after night? He was starting to think he really needed to find out.

* * *

The Bravos of Justice Creek:
Where bold hearts collide under Western skies

MS. BRAVO
AND THE BOSS

BY
CHRISTINE RIMMER

MILLS &
BOON

First Published in Great Britain 2016
By Mills & Boon, an imprint of HarperCollins*Publishers*
1 London Bridge Street, London, SE1 9GF

© 2016 Christine Rimmer

ISBN: 978-0-263-92024-6

23-1016

Printed and bound in Spain
by CPI, Barcelona

Christine Rimmer came to her profession the long way around. She tried everything from acting to teaching to telephone sales. Now she's finally found work that suits her perfectly. She insists she never had a problem keeping a job—she was merely gaining "life experience" for her future as a novelist. Christine lives with her family in Oregon. Visit her at www.christinerimmer.com.

For Nalria Wisdom Gaddy,
who knows the names of all the flowers
and never fails to brighten my day.
Nalria, this one's for you.

Chapter One

Elise Bravo wanted a bath. A long, relaxing one. With lots of bubbles. She longed to shed every stitch and pile her hair up on her head. To grab a juicy paperback romance and sink into her slipper tub, the one she'd had specially installed in the big master bath of her two-bedroom apartment above her catering shop in the gorgeous old brick building she co-owned with her best friend, Tracy.

Unfortunately, Elise's beautiful slipper tub was no more. Neither was her apartment. Her business? Gone, too. Three months ago, the historic building on Central Street in her hometown of Justice Creek, Colorado, had burned to the ground.

As for her lifelong best friend? Tracy had moved to Seattle to start a whole new life.

Now, Elise lived in a tiny rented studio apartment

over Deeliteful Donuts on the less attractive end of Creekside Drive. The studio had a postage stamp of a bathroom—with a shower, no tub.

And sometimes lately, as she raced through the lunch rush at her sister Clara's café, or manned the counter at her half sister Jody's flower shop, Elise could almost lose heart. She was deeply disappointed in herself.

Because it wasn't the fire that had ruined her life. She'd been in trouble long before the idiot tenants who leased a shop on the ground floor had disabled the fire alarms and then left a hot plate turned on in the back room when they slipped out to run errands. By then, bad choices had already brought Elise to the brink of ruin. The fire had only slathered a thick helping of frosting on her own personal disaster cake.

Elise was one of four siblings. She had five half siblings. Of the nine children of Franklin Bravo, Elise was the only one who'd blown through her very generous inheritance. Shame dogged her for every one of her stupid choices in life, in love and in business. She was circling the drain and she didn't really know what to do about it.

Except to hold her head high, work hard and keep moving forward.

After the lunch rush at the Library Café on that fateful day in June, Elise took off her waitress apron and transferred her tips to her purse. Her sister Clara waved at her as she went out the back door.

It was a warm, sunny day. Elise had walked to the café. Now, she set out on foot along Central Street headed for Jody's shop, Bloom. It was good exercise, walking. Not to mention, it saved on gas. Walking fast, she could reach Bloom in six minutes and be right on time to give Jody a break at two o'clock.

She made it with a minute to spare. Jody, at the counter with a customer, glanced over at the sound of the bell. "There you are."

"What? Am I late? I thought we said—"

"You're not late," said a voice to Elise's left. She whipped her head around in surprise as her other half sister popped out from behind a ficus tree and grabbed Elise's arm. "We need to talk."

"What the…?" Elise tried to jerk free. "Nell! Let me go."

But Nell, who worked in construction, had a grip like a sumo wrestler. "Come on in back."

Elise sent Jody a pleading look as Nell dragged her toward the swinging café doors on the far side of the counter. "Jody, will you tell her to let go of—"

"Hear her out," Jody interrupted. She was tucking a stunning arrangement of succulents and red anthuriums into one of Bloom's trademark green-and-pink boxes. "This could be good for you."

"This? What?" Elise huffed in frustration as Nell knocked the doors wide and dragged Elise into the back room. "Will someone please tell me what's going on?"

"This way." Nell pulled her into Jody's office and shut the door. "Sit."

Elise plunked her purse on Jody's desk. "This is ridiculous."

"Just sit down and listen."

"Fine." Elise dropped into the guest chair. "But Jody has errands to run and she needs me out front."

"Don't worry about Jody. She'll manage without

you." Nell braced a hip against the desk and crossed her arms over her spectacular breasts.

Actually, Nell was spectacular all over. She had legs for days and long, thick auburn hair and lips like Angelina Jolie. A half sleeve of gorgeous ink accentuated her shapely left arm. Elise, on the other hand, possessed neither the style nor the courage to get a tattoo. She had dark brown hair, ordinary lips and a body that was heavier than it used to be due to some serious stress eating since the fire. Really, how could she and the gorgeous creature in front of her possibly share half of the same genes?

Elise and Nell had a difficult history. Recently, they'd healed the old wounds. But Elise still felt guilty about the way she'd treated Nell when Nell's mother married their father. And lately, with all that had gone wrong in Elise's life, the guilt was worse than ever. Now, she looked back on her earlier sense of entitlement and verging-on-mean-girl behavior and couldn't help wondering if she deserved the hard knocks she kept taking.

Still. Nellie had no right to go dragging her all over the place.

Elise folded her own arms tight and hard to match her sister's pose and demanded, "All right, I'm listening. What do you just *have* to talk to me about?"

Nell tossed her glorious hair. "A job, that's what. A lot better job than busting your butt waiting tables for Clara and running the register for Jody."

"What job?" Elise tried to stay pissed off, mostly in order not to get her hopes up. But still, she could feel it. A sudden pulse of optimism, a lifting sensation under her ribs. She used to love it when she got that feeling. Not anymore. Lately, hope only led to disappointment.

She'd had way more than enough of that already, thank you very much.

Nell uncrossed her arms and hitched a long jean-clad leg up on the desk. "This is the deal. Jed Walsh is in need of another assistant." Jed Walsh, so the story went, had grown up in a one-room cabin on a mountain not far from Justice Creek. He'd moved away right out of high school, eventually becoming the world-famous author of a series of bestselling adventure novels. Several months ago, he'd come back to town.

And yep. There it was. The sinking sensation that came when each new hope was dashed. "Of course Jed Walsh needs a new assistant. He always needs a new assistant. How many has he been through now?" Since his return to town, Walsh's inability to keep an assistant had become downright legendary.

"Don't be negative," her sister muttered.

"Nellie. They run away screaming. He's that bad."

"Let me finish. I was at Walsh's house an hour ago switching out custom hardware and—"

"What are you doing switching out hardware?"

"Stop changing the subject." Nell worked with their brother Garrett running Bravo Construction. They'd built Walsh's new house.

"But switching out hardware is way below your pay grade."

"If you must know, when Jed Walsh wants a tweak or an upgrade, I handle it. He can be annoying and I don't want him giving our people any crap. And *because* I was just there at his house, I heard him fire the woman he hired a few days ago." She leaned toward Elise. "I know you can type, Leesie. I remember you took keyboarding class back in high school and Mrs. Clemo kissed your ass because you were so good at it."

"So what? I hate typing."

"Yeah, maybe. But you can do it and do it well. And that's what Jed Walsh needs. Someone to type his book while he dictates it. The man pays big bucks."

"Come on. No one ever lasts. They all say he's a slave driver. And just possibly borderline insane. I've heard the stories. He terrorizes them. Seriously, why would I last when no one else has?"

"Because it's a lot of money."

"Not if I run away screaming, it's not."

"You're not running anywhere. You'll be the one who lasts."

"And you say that because…?"

"You're motivated. And deep down, where it counts, you're as tough as they come."

"Thanks. But no thanks." Elise reached for her purse.

Nell got to it first. She shoved it away to the center of the desk.

"Enough now, I mean it." Elise rose. "Cut it out."

"Please stop." Nell looked straight in her eyes and spoke with heartfelt intensity. "Come on, Leesie. Give up the act. You need the money and you need it bad. Stop pretending you don't."

Elise realized her mouth was hanging open and snapped it shut. She'd been so sure that nobody knew the extent of her problem. She sank back into the chair and hung her head. "Just tell me. Please. Does everybody in the family know?" Silence from Nell. Elise made herself lift her head and pull her shoulders up straight. "Do they?"

Slowly, Nell nodded. "We love you and we are not

blind. You're working yourself into the ground. And if you had the money, you would have reopened Bravo Catering when the insurance paid out." She would have, it was true. But half of that money had been Tracy's and Tracy had finally admitted that the catering business wasn't for her. Plus, Elise had had all those debts to pay. In the end, they'd split the insurance money and sold the lot to a merchant next door who wanted to expand. Once Elise had paid off what she owed, there wasn't much left. Nell went on, "That's why you need to go see Jed Walsh. Leesie, we are talking thousands a week if you can last."

"Oh, come on. Thousands? For a secretary?"

"The woman he just fired said so. I asked her as she was stomping out the door."

"She must have been exaggerating. If he pays thousands, someone would have stayed."

"No. I think he's actually *that* bad. And he's evidently damn picky. Most of them he fires, so they can't stick no matter how much they want the money he's paying. But the good news is, he's really desperate now. I heard he's blown off his book deadline over and over. At some point he's got to keep an assistant and get the damn book done."

Elise sighed in defeat. "Be realistic. If none of the others can put up with him, what makes you think *I* can?"

"Because you're a Bravo and a Bravo gets out there and gets it done." Nell stood. "Jed Walsh is going to get the assistant he needs, which is you. And that means Jed Walsh is going to put *you* back in the black."

"Oh, I doubt that."

Nell braced her hands on her shapely hips. "You

know, Leesie… On second thought, you're right. You should just give up now. We all love you and we're all doing great financially. We can help and we will. No one's going to hold it against you if you let your family rescue you from the consequences of your own stupid pride and bad decision-making."

Elise rose again, slowly. She said in a low voice that sounded like a threatening growl, "No. Freaking. Way. I'll rescue myself, just you watch me."

A slow grin tipped the corners of Nell's impossibly sexy lips. "That's the spirit." She grabbed a square of paper from the pad on the desk and bent to scribble on it. Then she took Elise's hand and slapped the paper in it. "Here's the address. Now get over there and show Mr. Number One *New York Times* Bestselling Author that you're the assistant he's been looking for."

Walsh's new house was really something, Elise thought. Bravo Construction must be proud. Surrounded by giant pines and Douglas firs, the gorgeous, rustic, wood-and-stone home sprawled impressively on the crest of a hill.

I really, truly do not want to do this, Elise repeated to herself for the hundredth time as she parked her SUV in front of the slate walk that meandered upward toward the massive front door. Excuses scrolled through her mind: She really should at least have called first. Her typing was rusty. She hated to be shouted at and everyone said that Walsh was a yeller.

But then again, her family *knew*. She could no longer lie to herself that her abject failure to take care of herself and her future was her own little secret. They knew and they worried for her and if she didn't pull herself out of this hole she was in, they would do it for her.

Uh-uh. No way. Not going to happen. *She'd* dug this hole and then fallen into it. One way or another, she would get *herself* out of it. If there was any possibility that Jed Walsh might provide the solution she'd so desperately been seeking, she needed to convince the madman to hire her.

Elise smoothed her hair, straightened her white button-down shirt and put one foot in front of the other all the way up the winding stone walk. The front porch was really something, made of rough-hewn rock and thick unfinished planks cut from various exotic-looking woods. The studded door had copper sculptures of leaves and vines attached to the windows on either side. No doorbell, just a giant cast-iron boar's-head knocker.

Elise lifted the knocker and banged it three times against the door. The thing was loud. She could hear the sound echoing on the other side. She waited for a full count of twenty for someone to answer. When no one did, she lifted the ring through the boar's snout to knock again.

Before she could lower it, the big door swung inward.

And there stood Jed Walsh, a giant of a man in jeans and a black T-shirt with muscles on his muscles, a scruff of beard on his rocklike jaw and a phone at his ear.

He shouted into the phone, "I don't care about any of that, Holly. She didn't work out and I need someone else *now*." The person on the other end started talking. Walsh pulled the phone from his ear and looked Elise up and down with a way-too-observant pair of icy green eyes. "Who are you and what do you want?"

"I'm Elise Bravo and—"

"With the construction company?" he barked. "The hardware's great and I'm happy with the copper sink. No problems." He started to swing the door shut in her face.

Elise talked fast. "You need an assistant and I'm here for the job."

He grunted, swung the door wide once more and spoke into the phone again. "Never mind for now." Whoever Holly was, she was still talking as he disconnected the call. And Walsh was giving Elise another leisurely once-over, from the top of her head to the toes of her practical black shoes.

The look was way too assessing. Please. The last thing she needed right now was to have some man—any man, crazy or otherwise—looking her over. She was not at her best, all frazzled and tired, with the buttons down the front of her shirt on the verge of popping and her black pants clinging tighter than they ought to. She was an excellent cook, after all. Plus, there was the donut shop right downstairs from her cramped apartment. Food could offer great comfort when your world went up in flames.

And then again, so what if he ogled her? She hitched up her chin and ogled right back. Let him stare. She didn't have to be skinny to type.

Eventually, he stepped back and gestured her into his cavernous foyer. Against her better judgment, she went.

"Elise, you said?"

Ms. Bravo to you, she fervently wished she had the nerve to reply. "Elise. That's right."

"I'm Jed."

"I know."

"Who sent you?"

"My half sister Nell said she thought you might be looking for a new assistant today."

"Nell Bravo, you mean?"

"That's the one."

He frowned, considering. "That was enterprising of Nell."

Elise could easily lose patience with this guy. "Do you need a new assistant or not?"

Was that a smirk on his face? "Fair enough then, Elise." The smirk vanished to be replaced by an expression of utter boredom. And then he said in a tone that commanded and dismissed her simultaneously, "Let's see what you can do."

He really did piss her off—not that that was a bad thing. Her irritation made her determined to show him he'd be an idiot not to hire her. Because Nellie was right. She was a damn fine typist. But more important, she was a Bravo and a Bravo didn't let some big, grouchy butthead intimidate her.

"This way." He turned on his heel and started walking.

She went where he led her, through a fabulous three-story great room, down a hall at the back to a two-story home office with a breathtaking view of the mountains and one entire floor-to-ceiling wall filled with books. The opposite wall was padded, covered in burlap, had a number of bull's-eye targets hanging from it and was scarily studded with what appeared to be stab marks.

Okay, so maybe he played darts. But stab marks? Surely not...

"Sit here." He pulled back the high-end leather desk chair in front of a computer with a screen the size of Cleveland.

Her heart pounding wildly, she sat.

He stood way too close behind her. She swallowed hard and pressed her lips together to keep from ordering him to back off. When he reached over her shoulder, she had to steel herself not to flinch as she felt the heat of his big body.

So close, she could smell him. He smelled really good —like cinnamon. She stared at the ropy tendons in his muscled forearm, at the silky brown hair that dusted his tanned skin, at the sheer size of his big hand as he tapped on the keyboard.

A document popped onto the screen.

He withdrew his hand and backed off, moving over so that he stood in her line of sight. "Start a new paragraph." As the cursor blinked tauntingly at her, he explained, "I'll use your name as the signal to start and stop. When you hear 'Elise,' you will type the next word I say and keep typing every word I utter until I speak your name again. And so on. Are we clear?"

"Crystal."

He made a grunting sound, as though he doubted that. "Do not speak. Not one word." He paused, as if expecting her to say something and thus prove she was incapable of following instructions. *Fat chance, buddy.* When she only waited, he added, "Fake the punctuation. We'll clean it up in edits. Elise."

Did he think she wouldn't be ready? Ha.

He began, "It was a day for killing underlings." She typed each word as it fell from his mouth. "A day without mercy, the sky a gray wolf, crouched on the land, hungry and unforgiving. The man in the watch cap was waiting for him at the station as agreed Elise." He said her name so softly, without even a hint of a pause to signal it was coming.

But she was ready. She punched in a period after the word *agreed* and stopped typing. The room was suddenly totally silent. A strange, hot little shiver raced beneath her skin as she waited, fingers poised on the keyboard, for the sound of her name.

Finally, almost in a whisper, he said, "Not bad, Elise." And they were off and running again. "The man thought he was safe, thought he understood his place and his function. He assumed he would come through this in one piece as long as he did his job. But no one was safe. It was the nature of the game they played. Jack didn't want to kill the man. And maybe, if things went as planned, he wouldn't have to. Too bad things so rarely proceeded as planned…"

Jed went on, his deep voice rising and falling.

Breathing slowly and evenly, Elise had found that calm space she'd learned to inhabit back in Mrs. Clemo's second period keyboarding class. So few people took keyboarding, even back then. But Elise had, because you never knew when it might come in handy to actually be good at something so basic, something most people nowadays just fumbled their way through.

Elise let his words wash into her, through her, and then pushed them out her fingers as he kept on.

And on. Sometimes his voice was eerily soft—and sometimes he shouted.

She tuned out his unnerving changes in volume and tone and stayed with her task, typing the words as he spoke them, throwing in punctuation wherever his pace and phrasing seemed to indicate it, stopping when she heard her name, and then waiting—calm, ready, silent—until he said her name again.

There was something about typing that just worked for her, that was as effortless as drawing her next breath.

Not that she'd ever want to type for a living. Uh-uh. Too much sitting. For the long haul, she needed a job with variety, a job where she didn't have to spend all day on her butt.

But Nellie had mentioned a looming deadline, hadn't she? How long did he have? A few months at the most? Elise could be a typist for three months. If the money was good enough.

About twenty minutes after he started dictating, Jed said her name yet again—and after that, he was silent.

She cast him a quick, questioning glance.

With one big arm across his chest and the other elbow braced on it, he stroked the scruff of beard on his square jaw, a calculating gleam in his eyes. Finally, he spoke. "The typing test is over. Swivel that chair around." She turned her chair to face him. "Can you go on like that for hours?"

She took a minute to consider the question.

It was a minute too long, apparently, because he muttered impatiently, "You may speak now."

"Thank you," she replied with a sarcasm he either didn't notice or chose to ignore. "I would need a five-minute break every two hours, long enough to stand up and walk around a little."

"I can accept that."

"An hour for lunch."

He scowled as he continued to stroke his rocklike jaw. Apparently, in his world, typists shouldn't be allowed to waste precious time on food. But then he conceded, "All right. An hour. But you'll need to be flexible as to *which* hour. If the story's flowing, you might have to wait a while to eat."

"Even with regular five-minute breaks, there have to be limits. No more than five hours at a stretch without an hour-long break."

A grunt of disapproval escaped him. But then he agreed, "Five hours. All right. The work will be intense and you'll need to roll with that. I have to get a book out fast and I'll need you when I need you—which will be ten to twelve hours a day. You will have to live here and you will work six days a week, with Sundays off."

Live here in his house? God, it sounded awful. But in the end, it was all about the money. If the money was good enough, she could bear a whole boatload of awful.

And wait. What about Mr. Wiggles? He would have to come with her. "I have a cat. My cat will be moving in with me."

Dead silence from Walsh. He stopped stroking his jaw and moved to the windows. For several seconds, he stared out at the mountains.

It appeared that Mr. Wiggles was going to be a deal-killer. Well, so be it. She'd barely gotten the big sweetie out alive during the fire. If she had to live with this strange, grumpy man, Wigs was coming with her. Or she wouldn't come at all.

Jed turned those intense eyes on her again. "Fine. Bring the damn cat." She felt equal parts triumphant that she'd won her demand and let down that she was one step closer to being Jed Walsh's typing slave for she still didn't know how long. She was about to ask him how long the job would last when he said flatly, "Unfortunately, I find you sexually attractive. That *could* be a problem." Did he actually just say that? Another of those odd shivers swept through her as he added thoughtfully, "But then there's the cat. I hate cats. That should help." Frowning, he kept those cold eyes steadily on her. "You're thinking I shouldn't have told you that I'm attracted to you. But *I* think it's better if we're on the same page."

She probably shouldn't ask, but she couldn't resist. "What page is that, Jed?"

He didn't miss a beat. "The one where you know that I'm aware of you as a woman, but we both know that work is the focus here and we will be keeping it strictly professional."

Elise said nothing. Really, what was there to say? The less the better, clearly. She shouldn't be flattered. But she was, a little. Apparently the extra pounds she'd put on since the fire didn't look so bad on her, after all.

"My deadline is November first and it will not be extended."

"Four and a half months." She mentally calculated the money that might be hers.

"It's likely you'll be finished by mid-October, but I need you to commit till November first, just in case I run into trouble. I do most of my rewriting while composing the first draft of the manuscript. So essentially, the book is finished when I get to the last page. Then I clean it up, but that I usually can do on my own in a couple of weeks, max."

"All right. Four to four and a half months, then."

"Yes. If you last, the position will become permanent. It's a grind when I'm on a project. But as I said, I type my own rewrites, so as soon as I've made it to the end of the first draft, I probably won't need you until I start the next book. You'll have weeks and sometimes months off at a time between books."

Elise thought of all those thousands he supposedly would pay. She could almost let him think she might be willing to type his novels long-term to get a chance at that money.

But she *wasn't* willing, no way. And it was only right to let him know up front. "I'm sorry, Jed. If we can come to terms, I'll do this one project. But as of November first, I'll be moving on."

His scowl deepened. "I pay well."

"So I've heard."

"If you work out, I'll need you to stay on."

"Sorry, not happening. I'm done the first of November. If you can't accept that, then—"

He cut her off with a grunting sound. "All right. Have it your way. Even if you make it through the trial period, you're done when I finish this book. If it turns out we work well together, I'm not gonna like it, but I need someone ASAP. Let's move on to the money. You'll be an independent contractor. You pay your own insurance and deal with your own taxes."

"Not a problem if the money's right."

"Three thousand a week."

Amazing! When this ordeal was over, she could have enough to get Bravo Catering up and running again. Her heart raced in excitement and her palms started sweating at the prospect. But really, why stop there?

She wiped all signs of greedy glee from her face and manufactured a serene smile. "Four thousand a week."

His cold stare went subzero. She was dead certain they were done here and she knew a moment of stark regret. No, she didn't want to sit in a chair all day typing her fingers to the bone, but she did want that money.

And then at last, wonder of wonders, he nodded. "All right. Four." She was just breaking into her mental happy dance when he added, "*If* you last. We'll start with a three-day trial at five hundred a day."

She opened her mouth to shout out a *yes*. But some contrary creature within her spoke up first. "I'll have my own room, correct?"

He looked down his blade of a nose at her. "Of course."

"Just to be clear, I will need my own bathroom, en suite."

"There are six bedrooms in this house." He was wearing his bored face again. "Each has its own bath."

"I want to see the one where I'll be staying, please."

He asked wearily, "Would you prefer the ground floor or upstairs?"

Choices. She loved those. Lately, there had been so few. "Where is your room?"

Green eyes narrowed. "And that matters, why?"

"I need my space."

He made a humphing sound. "I have half of the upper floor."

"Ground floor, then." She really did need a place to go where he wasn't. "Show me, please."

Jed's expression asked why she insisted on wasting his precious time. But all he said was, "Follow me."

She rose and went after him, back through the great room and down another hallway. He stopped at a door and pushed it inward.

The room on the other side was larger than her apartment over the donut shop. It had a king-size bed and its own sitting area, with a big-screen TV above the modern gas fireplace. The wide windows revealed another beautiful mountain view. There was even a set of French doors leading out to a small private patio. She could hardly wait to settle in.

"Walk-in closet there." He pointed at one of the two interior doors. "I hope this will do," he said, heavy on the irony.

She had one more question. The most important one. "May I see the bathroom?"

"Be my guest." He gestured at that other door.

Elise marched over and pushed it open.

Pure luxury waited on the other side. She'd never been much for the rustic look. But in this case, she could definitely make an exception.

The woodwork was dark and oversize, breathtaking. Travertine tiles in cream and bronze covered the floor and climbed halfway up the walls. The long vanity had two sinks and copper fixtures. There were separate stalls for the toilet and the open shower, which had side jets and a rain showerhead.

Very faintly, she smelled cinnamon. Jed had come to stand behind her in the doorway. "The towel racks have warmers, of course," he said. "And the floor is heated."

"Of course," she said softly, transfixed by the glorious sight of the giant jetted tub tucked into its own windowed alcove. The tub windows had center-mounted cellular shades that could be raised to the top to block glare, or lowered to the bottom for privacy. She could stretch out in bubbly splendor and stare at the sky.

"Well?" Jed demanded.

She turned and met his eyes. "When do you want me to start?"

Chapter Two

Elise Bravo was a find.

Jed knew she was going to last.

He'd known it the minute he'd let her in his house. She wasn't like the never-ending string of hopeless cases he'd hired and fired in the past year. She could type like nobody's business while keeping her mouth shut and not getting frazzled or riled. There was something downright soothing about her, something receptive. She was exactly what he'd been afraid he would never find again. At last.

And he liked looking at her. He could go for her, definitely. She was so soft and pretty, round-faced and bright-eyed, with just enough junk in the trunk. She smelled good, as well. Fresh. Like clean sheets.

She also had attitude. Jed liked a woman with attitude. He liked a woman who could hold her own.

Not that he'd ever make a move on her. Any woman could provide sex. But a skilled assistant was a pearl beyond price. He'd learned that the hard way during the past god-awful year after Anna deserted him.

So yeah, he'd resigned himself to the fact that he wasn't going to be seeing Elise naked. It was going to be all about the work. He'd taken his last extension on this book. With Elise at the keyboard, he would knock the damn thing out.

"I need to get to work immediately," he said.

"I understand. But first I have to get my cat, move my things and settle in a little."

The cat. For a moment, he'd almost succeeded in forgetting the cat. "We'll start tomorrow morning, then," he said grudgingly.

"Yes. All right, tomorrow." She cast a glance over her shoulder at the bathroom behind her, as if to reassure herself that it was actually there. She really seemed to like the bathroom. *Whatever floats your boat, Elise.* She could spend every free moment in there for all he cared. Just as long as she performed during the long working hours. "What about meals?" she asked. "I'll need to have the use of the kitchen while I'm staying here."

"No problem. I have a cook-housekeeper, Deirdre, who comes in five days a week. She'll make plenty for both of us. But if you want to cook, knock yourself out. You can consider the kitchen and any food and drinks you find in it yours."

"Works for me." She looked up at him expectantly. Probably because he was blocking her path. "I should get going…"

He felt a definite reluctance to let her out of his sight. Anything could happen. What if she changed her mind about working for him? Got hit by lightning? Got in an accident bringing over her stuff and her damn cat? He warned, "We start work at zero-eight-three-zero hours sharp."

"That's eight thirty, right?"

"Correct."

"No problem. I'll be here and I'll be ready."

He reconciled himself to letting her go. Turning for the outer door, he doled out necessary info as he led her along the hall to the front of the house. "It's a four-car garage. You can have the bay on the far left. Before you go, I'll get you a garage-door remote, a house key and the code for the alarm system…"

At her apartment, Elise parked in her space by the Dumpster and entered the building through the back door. The hallway and the stairwell smelled of donuts from the donut shop in front. She'd grown to hate that smell, mostly because it tempted her constantly. There was something so perfect about a donut, after all. Flour and fat and sugar, deep-fried and glazed or frosted. The purest sort of comfort to a desperate woman's soul.

Well, bye bye, temptation and hello, jetted tub. So what if she had to type Jed Marsh's book for a living? She'd have a bath every night and make buckets of money. Life was looking up.

Mr. Wiggles was waiting when she opened the door. "Mrow?" he asked.

"Wigs!" She scooped him up, all twenty-plus super-fluffy pounds of him. He was orange, with a huge, thick tail and a deep, loud purr. She buried her face against his lionlike ruff. "We are moving today," she told him.

"We'll keep this dump for now, I think. And reevaluate our crappy living situation once the job is over."

"Mrow, mrow," Wigs replied, as though he understood every word she said. He butted his big head against her cheek to let her know how much he loved her. She gave him one more kiss for good measure and then set him down to start packing.

Her cell rang as she was piling clothes into three suitcases spread open on the lumpy bed.

It was Nellie. "Well?"

"Nailed it."

"You got the job! I knew you would."

"I have to live there, in his house."

"I built that house and Chloe designed the interiors." Chloe was their brother Quinn's wife. "You're gonna love it."

She thought of the bathtub, of the king-size bed. "Oh, yes, I will. And the money is good. Really good."

"That's what I wanted to hear. What about Jed? Seriously, you think you can put up with him?"

"He's not so bad. A little weird. A lot intense."

"Sexy, though, right? In a club-you-senseless-and-drag-you-to-his-cave sort of way."

For some unknown reason, Elise felt a hot flush rush upward over her cheeks. "Don't even go there. He's my boss now and we're keeping it strictly professional."

Nell's naughty laugh echoed in her ear. "You have way more scruples than can possibly be necessary—and we have to celebrate. I'm buying the drinks."

"Rain check. I need to get moved in over there tonight. The job starts early tomorrow morning."

"He gives you crap you can't handle, you call me."

Elise's cheeks were still burning. She could almost

smell cinnamon. And what about that crazy thing he'd said? *Unfortunately, I find you sexually attractive.* "Oh, I think I can handle him."

Nell laughed. "There. That's what I've been missing. You've got your attitude back."

She felt all misty-eyed suddenly. "Thank you, Nellie."

"Hey. What's a sister for?"

"We, um…we're all right now, you and me. Aren't we? I mean, I know I was a total bitch to you back in the day…"

"Back in the day? You and Tracy treated me like crap right up until Clara's almost-wedding to Ryan." That was nearly two years ago now. Clara hadn't married her best friend, Ryan McKellan, but she had somehow succeeded in healing the lifelong breach between Elise and Nell—*and* Nell and Tracy.

Elise defended her absent bestie. "Don't be too hard on Tracy. She always just followed my lead." But not anymore. Tracy was forging her own way now.

Nell laughed again. "You're right. It was all your fault. But I did get my licks in, too. Remember that time I put bubblegum on your breakfast-nook chair?"

Elise started laughing, too. "I loved those yellow shorts. They were never the same."

"It's what you get for messing with me."

"I know. You're so scary."

"Oh, yes, I am. And don't you forget it."

"Never. And I guess what I'm asking is, do you forgive me for all the mean things I did?"

Nell gave a soft sigh. "You know I do."

"I'm so glad."

"Leesie? You're not getting sappy on me, are you?"

Elise swiped at her damp eyes. "No way. Gotta go."

They said goodbye and Elise made quick calls to Clara and Jody, to tell them she had a job typing Jed Walsh's newest book and wouldn't be in at the café or Bloom the next day.

Then she finished packing and dragged her suitcases down to her car, followed by all the cat gear and, last but not least, Mr. Wiggles. He rode in the front seat, sitting up tall beside her, watching the world go by and making those cute little chirping sounds, his own personal brand of kitty conversation. He loved the car and he never got in the way of her driving, so she'd given up on making him ride in his carrier.

She took the space in the garage that Jed had assigned to her and carried Mr. Wiggles in first, pausing in the utility room to check the alarm. As it turned out, Jed hadn't armed it when she left, so she didn't have to mess with it right then. She went on down a hallway and then through the kitchen and great room and down that other hall to her bedroom suite, finding no sign of her employer along the way.

Which was just fine. She had a lot to do and she didn't need the distraction of dealing with her big, crabby boss.

In her room, she put Wigs down in front of the window, promised him she would be right back and went out to start hauling everything in, taking care to shut the door as she left so he wouldn't get out. Jed had said he hated cats. No reason to test his patience right off the bat.

By seven, she had everything put away and her stomach was growling. Wigs, meanwhile, alternately circled his empty food bowl, chased the cleaning robot she'd started up a few minutes before and made a big show of scratching at his three-level activity center.

"Okay, okay. I'm on it." She'd stored his food in the utility room, which had seemed the most logical place for it. She scooped up his food bowls—for wet and for dry—and went out the door again.

The hallways and great room and kitchen were empty. Very odd. Her first night in his house and Jed had vanished into thin air.

She considered peeking into his office, or even looking for him upstairs.

But the thought of wandering through the unfamiliar house trying to track him down made her even more uncomfortable than not having a clue as to where he'd gone. So she went ahead to the utility room to dish up Wigs's dinner. She was pulling the top off a can when she heard music.

She shouldn't snoop.

But really. Where *was* he? And, no, wait… A better question was why did she care?

Well, she cared because…

Okay, fine. She had no idea why she cared.

She set the opened can on the counter and stuck her head out into the hall. Yep. Music.

She followed the faint sound back out into the great room, to the wide central staircase that switched up and back from the lower level to the top floor. It was coming from downstairs, the basement level. She leaned over the railing, listening. It was something with a hard beat, but the sound remained muffled, indistinct. Maybe there was a TV room down there. Her curiosity increased. She left the railing and started down the stairs, catching herself on the second step.

No, she told herself sternly. *Bad idea. Mind your own business.*

So she turned and retraced her steps back to the utility room, where she dished up the food and took it to her hungry cat.

"Mrow?" Wigs left off stalking the cleaning robot to get to work on his dinner.

Now what?

Her stomach growled again. Jed had said that she should make herself at home in the kitchen. She'd grab something to eat and then get up close and intimate with that glorious tub.

It was weird, raiding the refrigerator of the stranger she now worked for—and lived with, essentially. But the food looked good. She heated up a plate of roast chicken, mashed potatoes and mixed veggies and set herself a place at the table that would have looked just right in the castle of a medieval king. She even poured a glass of the pinot grigio she found in the door of the fridge—hey, the bottle was open. Why not? Pulling back one of the big, studded leather chairs, she sat down and smoothed her napkin in her lap.

Definitely weird. Just her, all alone at the massive slab of a table in the giant great room.

She'd just lifted her glass and taken a nice, big gulp of wine when Jed asked from behind her, "You all set up, then?"

Startled, she choked. Wine sprayed out her nose. Coughing and gagging, she shoved back her chair and pressed her napkin to her face. It wasn't pretty. Ragged, hacking sounds alternated with desperate wheezing as she tried to catch her breath.

"Breathe," he commanded. He was at her back by then, pounding on it with his enormous hand, instructing, "Slow, easy. That's the way."

After a terrifying minute or two wherein she wondered if she would ever breathe again, her throat loosened up. She sucked in a decent breath of air at last.

"Okay?" he asked warily.

After wiping the last of the wine from her cheeks, she turned to faced him—and almost choked all over again at the sight of him. Shirtless, he had on a pair of low-riding training shorts that displayed the sculpted tops of sharply cut V lines. His big, chiseled chest was dusted with manly hair and dripping sweat. He had a towel slung around his neck, one end of which he was using to wipe more sweat from his forehead.

Mystery solved: there was a gym in the basement. She'd heard his workout music.

Somehow, she managed to croak out accusingly, "Don't you ever sneak up on me like that again."

For that she got a lifted eyebrow and a disdainful "I never sneak." And then he asked again, "You okay?"

"Splendid. Thank you."

And just like that, he turned and walked away. She stared at his broad, sweaty back as he strode to the staircase. He went up, pausing to look down at her just before he reached the first landing. "Zero-eight-three-zero hours tomorrow. Be ready to work."

Like she was some scatterbrained child incapable of remembering the simplest instructions.

Four thousand a week, she reminded herself. Four thousand and a jetted tub. She nodded, sat back down, picked up her fork and did not glance toward the stairs again.

The next day was just as Elise had expected it to be. Endless.

She typed and she typed some more while Jed al-

ternately paced and loomed over her, sometimes shouting loud enough that she winced at the sound, now and
then murmuring so softly she could barely make out the
words. Luckily, she had excellent hearing and managed
to get down every whispered word he said. Already, it
was something of a point of pride for her that she could
keep up with him and never have to speak while at the
keyboard, not even to ask him what he'd just said.

He finished the scene he'd tested her with the day before. Jack McCannon, Jed's ongoing main character—
and, Elise suspected, his alter ego—ended up killing
the man at the station, whose name was Gray. Elise
felt a moment's pity for Gray, whom Jack eliminated
through the clever use of a ballpoint pen to the throat.
Jack, apparently, was quite creative vis-à-vis weaponry.
He killed Gray with a Bic and kept fishing line in his
pocket. Because who knew when he might need to tie
someone up or strangle them with a makeshift garrote?

After Gray met his end, Jack evaded a pursuer and
then met a contact at a café. They drank espresso and
Jack received critical information stored in a minichip
invisible to the naked eye. The contact, Lilias, caressed
his face and transferred the minichip to his cheek. Lilias
was gorgeous. Jack had history with her. Intimate history. Jack considered having sex with her again, but
decided against it due to time constraints and the fact
that he really didn't trust her. The men Lilias slept with
often turned up dead.

There was a scene at a shooting range. Jack was a
crack shot. Who knew, right?

And, yes, already Elise found herself keeping up a
snarky mental commentary on Jed's work-in-progress
as she typed away. The typing really was like breath-

ing. She didn't have to think about it. Even with the
yelling alternating with growls and rumbles, she found
Jed's voice easy to sink into, as if she'd been listening
to him all her life, as though some part of her mind
knew what he would say before he formed the words.
It left her the mental space to have a little fun at Jack
McCannon's expense.

Not that Jed wasn't good at what he did. Now and
then she got so involved she almost stopped typing to
enjoy the story. The action scenes were spectacular—
really edge-of-your-seat.

How many books had Jed written? Four or five, she
thought she'd heard. Maybe she'd have to try the first
one just for the heck of it. It wouldn't hurt to have a little background on the job.

They worked until six thirty that evening. When Jed
finally dismissed her, he stayed behind in the office
to look over the day's pages. She fed Wigs his dinner,
raided the refrigerator and called Tracy in Seattle to
see how she was settling in and report on her new job
with Jed.

Tracy knew her too well. "But you hate typing," she
pointed out. "What is going on? I really don't get this."

"It's amazing money and it's only for four months."

"But what about Bravo Catering?"

As she'd been doing for weeks now whenever she
and Tracy talked, Elise evaded the question. "I'm getting there. This came up, is all. And I thought, for this
much money, why not?"

Tracy wasn't buying. "Just how broke are you? I can
lend you—"

"Trace. Stop. It's tight, but I'm managing."

"I never should have left you."

"Yes, you absolutely should have. It was time and you know it." They'd grown up together, literally. Their mothers had been best friends. She and Tracy had shared the same playpen as babies. Then when Tracy's parents died in a house fire, Tracy had moved in with the Bravos. In every way that counted, Elise and Tracy were sisters, bonded in the deepest way.

They'd gone to CU together and had come home to open their catering business and live in adjoining apartments. But Tracy had always been a science nerd and what she'd never told Elise was that her real dream had nothing to do with planning weddings, designing perfect dinner parties or creating tasty menus that stayed fresh on a steam table. Not until after the fire had Tracy finally confessed that she dreamed of a career in molecular biology.

Well, Tracy was getting her dream now. She'd enrolled in a master's program at the University of Washington.

"I should come home, at least for a few weeks. The semester doesn't start until mid-August."

"Come home for what? Not to see me. I'll be working six days a week, ten hours a day."

"That's insane."

"Yeah, it is, a little. It's also what I want. And I have to tell you, I'm damn good at it, too."

Tracy laughed. "I thought you said this was your first day."

"I have a talent for it. He went through a whole bunch of assistants before I came along. They couldn't handle it. I can."

"What's he like?"

"Jed? Antisocial. Hates cats. Seems to know a lot about deadly weapons."

"He sounds awful."

"I'll say this. He's buff. Looks amazing without his shirt."

"I'm not even going to ask."

"A wise decision."

"You said he hates cats. How's Mr. Wiggles taking that?"

"So far, I've managed to keep the two of them apart."

"Leesie, I just feel bad about deserting you."

"Don't. I mean it. You didn't desert me. I'm doing just fine. Now, tell me what's going on with *you*."

Tracy hesitated, but then she did confess that she'd met a guy she liked. On Friday they were going out to a great Greek restaurant and then to hear some hot Seattle band. She had her fall schedule worked out around the TA and lab-assistant jobs she'd found. She loved Seattle. It was her kind of city.

Elise hung up feeling good about her friend. Yes, she missed her. A lot. But it was about time Tracy came in to her own.

And so far, working with Jed wasn't as bad as she'd thought it would be. She grabbed a sexy paperback and headed for the jetted tub.

Elise was waiting at the keyboard when Jed entered his office at 0830 the next morning. He felt a deep satisfaction just at the sight of her there, in knit pants that hugged her fine butt and curvy legs and a pale blue shirt that clung to her round breasts. They got right to work.

At a little before ten, the cat appeared. The thing was huge. It came and sat in the doorway to the office and watched him with unblinking eyes. Elise had her back to it and had no idea that the creature was there.

Well, fine. Let the cat stare. Jed went right ahead with the scene they were working on.

Eventually, the cat yawned, stretched and wandered off down the hall, its long, hairy tale twitching. Jed waited until they broke for lunch to tell Elise that the animal had gotten out.

She gasped. "Why didn't you say anything?"

"We were working," he replied, though it should have been patently obvious to her.

"But I don't get it. I'm sure I closed my door. How did he get out?"

"Why ask me? You think *I* left your door open?"

For that, he got a snippy little glare. She ran out calling, "Wigs! Come here, baby!"

The damn cat actually answered her. "Mrow? Mrow-mrow?"

He stepped over into the open doorway in time to watch it bound up the hallway to meet her. She scooped it up and buried her face in its hairy belly. "Bad, bad boy," she said in a tone that communicated zero displeasure. Jed felt a stab of actual jealousy. He wished she'd bury her nose in his belly like that. "Come on now," she cooed at the fur ball. "Back to our room…" She slung it over her shoulder and carried it off. The cat, its big hairy paws hanging down her back, watched him smugly through sharp golden eyes, until she turned the corner at the great room and they both disappeared from sight.

The annoying cat aside, that day went even better than the first, Jed thought. He got twelve usable pages by the time they packed it in at 1815 hours. There was just something about Elise Bravo, something soothing and stimulating simultaneously.

The woman was smart. She strictly observed his initial instructions and never spoke while he was writing. With her, as with Anna, he could concentrate fully on the next sentence, on the way the story was coming together.

Plus, every time she got up to stretch, he got to watch. He could write poems to her backside. And those breasts. He would love to get his hands on them. There was something about her, the softness of her, that he wanted to sink into, the way she bit the inside left corner of her mouth when he picked up the pace and the words were flying, her fingers dancing so fast over the keys.

He liked to move in close and suck in that clean-sheet scent of hers. And he got a kick out of the way she talked to him, sharp and snippy, but somehow with patience, too.

Elise did it for him in a big way. She wasn't beautiful. She was so much better than beautiful. She was... the exact definition of what a quality woman should be.

No, nothing was going to happen between them. They both understood that.

But that didn't stop him from enjoying the view, whether she was sitting, stretching or walking away. And he saw no reason he shouldn't take pleasure in imagining the lusty things he was never going to do to her.

The next day, the final day of her trial period, he introduced the knives.

Chapter Three

Jed found his knives both soothing and stimulating. In that sense, they reminded him of Elise. For him, there were few experiences as calming as a well-thrown knife. He often threw them while he worked. The knives were an integral part of his process. They increased his focus. He liked to send them sailing. And he liked the sound they made when they hit the padded wall that Bravo Construction had installed precisely to his specifications.

He'd put off introducing the knives to Elise. He dreaded the possibility that she might freak—or worse, walk out and not come back. And there he would be again, with no assistant, his deadline looming.

Not being all that nice of a guy, he'd often used the knives to get rid of typists who weren't working out. No, not by stabbing them, but by simply hurling a sleek *kunai* or a combat bowie knife without warning. More than one unsatisfactory keyboarder had screamed good and loud when surprised in that way.

But he wanted to keep Elise, so he prepped her.

When she entered the office for work that day, he was waiting for her, an assortment of knives laid out on the credenza next to the door.

She said, "Deirdre is here. She says good morning."

He grunted. Deirdre Keller was a perfectly acceptable cook and housekeeper. Beyond that, he had nothing to say to her. He certainly didn't require her to tell him "good morning."

And Elise had spotted the knives. She caught on immediately. "Okay, I get it now. The padded wall, right?"

Feeling strangely sheepish, he confessed, "I like to throw while I'm working. It clears my mind."

She glanced at the array of knives, then at the wall in question. "What about all the targets? Do you throw darts, too?"

"Just knives." She seemed puzzled. So he elaborated, "I throw the knives at the targets sometimes. And sometimes I just send them flying at the wall. It depends."

"On…?"

He hadn't expected all these questions. But he was willing to indulge her if answering her would keep her happy. "I honestly don't know what it depends on, why sometimes I want to hit a target and sometimes I just want to throw—the scene I'm writing, I guess. Or the mood I'm in."

"Have you ever missed the wall and hit your assistant?"

"Not once." He couldn't resist adding, "Though now and then, I've been tempted."

A burst of laughter escaped her. He found the happy sound way too charming.

"Oh, you're just so scary, Jed."

"Yes, I am," he replied darkly. "And you should remember that." She had that look, as though she was purposely *not* rolling her eyes. He added, "And as you can see, your desk is over there." He gestured in that direction. "And the wall is there." He indicated the wall. "You won't be in the path of a throw unless you get up and put yourself between me and the wall."

"What about if you get tempted?"

"I won't." *Not to throw a knife at you, anyway.*

"Hmm," she said, as though still suspecting she might end up a target one of these days. And then she asked, "Is this it, then?"

"Define *it*."

"Will there be more potentially life-threatening activities you're going to want to do while I'm in this room with you?"

He admitted, "Sometimes I clean my firearms. Handguns. Machine guns. Assault rifles. That kind of thing. I find cleaning weapons—"

"Let me guess. Soothing."

"Yes. Exactly."

Those fine dark eyes gleamed. "You find the strangest things soothing."

He almost allowed his gaze to stray downward to her breasts. "You have no idea."

"I'm going to assume that when you clean your guns, you make sure they aren't loaded first."

"You assume correctly."

Her gaze narrowed. "Anything else you find soothing while you work? Archery, maybe?"

"I haven't used a bow and arrow in years, but it's a thought."

"So I should be prepared for that?"

"No. Knife throwing is my impalement art of choice."

She hummed again, low in her throat. "That's a real thing? Impalement art?"

"It's usually referred to in the plural. Impalement *arts*. Strictly defined, impalement arts entail throwing dangerously sharp objects at a human target."

She considered. He loved to watch her think. "Like at the circus."

"That's right. A circus knife-thrower is in the impalement arts. A circus archer, too. Hatchet- and spear-throwers, as well." She reached out and brushed her fingers over the stacked leather washer handle of a full-size USMC KA-BAR straight edge. "That's the most famous fixed blade knife in the world," he said. "It was first used by our troops in World War Two."

She slanted him a glance. He couldn't tell if he'd amused her or she found the knives fascinating, or what. For a moment, neither of them spoke. He wasn't big on extended eye contact as a rule. But he didn't mind it so much with her.

She broke the connection first, her gaze sliding away.

He shook himself. "You ready, then?"

By way of an answer, she went to her desk and fired up the computer.

Jed threw a lot of knives that day. And he wrote a lot of pages. It was good. Really good. Elise took his knives in stride. She never turned a hair when he sent one flying. She just kept right on filling those blank screen pages with his words.

They worked until 1900, at which point he handed her a check for 2,832 dollars and told her she was officially hired.

She frowned at the check. "I thought we said fifteen hundred for the first three days."

"I included payment for tomorrow and Saturday at your full rate. And after this week, I'll pay you every Saturday at the end of the day."

She rose. "Works for me." She headed for the door to the hallway.

He caught himself with his mouth open, on the verge of calling her back and asking her to have dinner with him.

Not a good idea. She had her life. He had his. They met each morning for work and went their separate ways when the workday was through. He found her far too attractive to start sharing meals with her.

Fantasies involving her were fine—or rather, given that he was having them, he might as well roll with it. Fighting it too hard would only make him want her more.

But hanging around with her after hours?

Bad idea.

She lived in his house. It would be so easy to get more than professional. That would be stupid. Because when the heat between them burned out, the work would get strained. She would end up leaving.

And that couldn't happen.

He was keeping her. She just didn't know it yet. She thought she was quitting when this book was through. But she was wrong.

Before she had knocked on his door Monday, he'd been increasingly sure that his big-deal writing career was headed straight for the crapper. He'd spent way too many sleepless nights sweating bullets over his dawning realization that Anna had been a lucky fluke and he would never find the right assistant again. Now that he *had* found her, he would simply have to convince her to stay. So what if she seemed determined to go?

One way or another, whatever he had to offer her to keep her happy, he *was* keeping her.

And the best way to lose her was if they had a thing and then it ended—which it would. He'd never been any good at relationships. Sooner or later, most women wanted more than he knew how to give. Maybe Elise was different. Maybe she could have a good time and then have it be over and still sit down at the computer and type his words for him every day.

But he couldn't afford to take a chance on finding out.

So he kept his damn mouth shut as she disappeared down the hall.

As they'd agreed when he hired her, Elise had Sunday off.

That Sunday, she left the house at 0905 hours. Jed knew the time exactly because he was standing on the balcony outside the master suite when she backed her car out of the garage.

Unlike the previous Monday, when she took off to get her cat and her clothes, he was okay with watching her go. Today, he felt zero anxiety as she drove away. They were getting on well together, after all, and he was paying her an arm and a leg. No reason she wouldn't return.

Plus, he hadn't seen the cat in the car. And if the cat was still here, she would have to come back.

An hour later, he headed for the shooting range, where he remained until lunchtime. He had a burger at a truck stop out on the state highway and got back to the house at 1400 hours.

Elise was still gone.

He put on workout gear and went down to the basement to use the StairMaster and then pump iron for a couple of hours. After his workout, he had a shower and found something to eat in the fridge. Then he went to his office and researched poisons until past 1900 hours. He had a lot of book left to write and that meant a lot of characters to kill.

Elise still hadn't returned.

He wasn't concerned. No reason to be. As long as she showed up at her desk on time in the morning, he couldn't care less where she went or how long she stayed there.

But for some completely crazy reason, he was kind of worried about the damn cat. Had she taken the animal with her, after all? Or had she just left the poor thing alone in her room?

Yeah, he hated cats. But she shouldn't just leave it locked up like that all day. Wasn't that cat abuse?

Sure seemed like it to him.

An hour after he left his office, he wandered down the hallway that led to her room. He stood there in front of her door for several minutes and debated the acceptability of trying the handle, maybe letting the fur ball out—if it was in there and if she'd left the door unlocked.

But opening her door without her permission seemed like a really bad idea. She might get mad if he did that. And getting her mad was no way to keep her working for him.

In the end, he settled on putting his ear to her door, just to listen for the possibility of plaintive meowing.

"What are you doing, Jed?"

Luckily he had nerves of steel. He didn't so much as flinch at the sound of her voice—even though he felt like a bad child caught with his grubby hand in the candy box.

Slowly, he pulled his ear away from her door and stood to his full height, turning to face her as he did it. She watched him from the far end of the hallway, a stack of boxes in her arms. "Well?"

The best defense is always an offense. "Your damn cat. I was getting worried about it." He strode toward her. "Here. Let me help you with those."

She allowed him to take the boxes. "But you hate cats."

"Open the door."

She eased around him and did just that. It wasn't locked.

The cat was there waiting. It didn't look any the worse for wear. "Mrow? Mrow-mrow?"

"Wigs!" She scooped it up, scratched its big head and kissed it on its whiskered cheek. "How's my big sweetie?"

"Mrow-mrow." It started purring, the sound very deep. Rumbly. Like an outboard motor heard from across a misty lake.

Elise said...to Jed this time, "Just set those down inside the door. Thanks."

He set the boxes where she wanted them and then turned to leave, figuring he'd escape before she asked him any more questions about why she'd come home to find him with his ear pressed to her door.

No such luck. "Why where you worried about Wigs?"

Resigned, he stopped and faced her again. "You left the cat locked in there all day. That can't be good."

"Well, that's kind of sweet of you." She seemed bemused.

He hastened to disabuse her. "I am never sweet."

She actually giggled. He despised gigglers—or at least, he always had until this moment. She held up the cat. It hung from her hands, totally relaxed, and big enough that its rear paws dangled at the height of her knees. "See? He's fine. I left him plenty of food and water. He doesn't mind a little alone time."

"A little? You've been gone for eleven hours."

Her soft mouth pursed up. "It's my day off. How is it any of your business how long I've been gone?"

It wasn't and they both knew it, which meant there was absolutely no point in answering her. So he didn't.

Eventually, she got tired of waiting for him to defend himself and informed him icily, "I have one day off a week and I had a lot to do."

Yeah, he felt like a jackass. But somehow, he couldn't just apologize for invading her private space and move on. "That's a big cat."

Her mouth got tighter. "Thank you, Captain Obvious."

He narrowed his eyes and flattened his lips. "That cat needs space."

"He's fine in my room. My apartment is a studio, smaller than my room here. He was perfectly happy there."

Smaller than her room here? That was way too small. And she was a Bravo. He'd grown up in the area and he knew of her family. The Bravos had always had enough money to be comfortable, at least. The Bravos didn't live in cramped one-room apartments. He wanted to ask her how she'd ended up in one.

But that would be a personal question and they were

not getting personal. "Next time leave your door open, that's all I'm saying."

She blinked as that statement sank in. "You mean, let Wigs have the run of the house?"

Suddenly, his throat had a tickle in it. What was that about? He never got a ticklish throat. He coughed impatiently into his hand. "Yeah. And come to think of it, don't lock that cat up in there at all. Let it have the house to roam in."

A tiny gasp escaped her. "You mean, all the time?"

"Isn't that what I just said?"

"But what about how you hate cats?"

"I'm making an exception in this case," he growled at her. She looked at him with distinctly dewy eyes, so he commanded, "Don't make a big deal out of it."

"I...well, okay. I won't."

"Good," he said, scowling as hard as he could. And then he turned on his heel again and started walking away fast.

"Jed?"

He stopped. But he didn't turn. "What?" he grumbled at the great room in front of him.

"Thanks."

He almost said *You're welcome*, but caught himself just in time.

In the next week, the work continued to go well. Very well. Elise just kept typing, never dropping a word or making a sound, no matter how loud and aggressive he became while acting out the voices of his characters.

On Thursday, he cleaned three of his rifles and a couple of Glocks as they worked. She seemed to take that in stride—didn't even bother to comment when she saw the weapons, gun oil, cleaning rags and brushes laid out that morning on a folding worktable.

Jed had never been a happy man. He found the concept of happiness more than a little silly. A man did what he had to do in life and what he had to do was rarely that much fun.

But with Elise working out so well, the pressure was off in terms of his deadline and hopefully his career. He was getting more work done, faster, than when he had Anna. It was a hell of a relief. Maybe this was happiness.

If it was, it wasn't half bad.

The damn cat had free rein of the house. The animal talked too much and had a tendency to climb up on tall cabinets and drape its giant body on the wide-beam staircase railings and along the backs of couches. But so what?

Jed had told Elise that the cat could roam free and he wasn't a man who reneged on his word. He ignored the creature. It wasn't that hard.

Another week went by, as smooth and productive as the previous one. Jed dared to feel confident that he was out of the woods at last. He was going to make it. He would have the book turned in by the final deadline— or maybe even before, at the rate they were going. Elise was a damn treasure.

His only concern now was her plan to leave once this project was finished. He really needed to do something to keep that from happening.

Fortunately, he had until November 1 to figure out what.

Two and a half weeks after he hired Elise, Jed woke at 0200 to a rumbling sound.

He'd been dreaming of a misty lake and the soft roar

of a motorboat coming toward him through the fog. Shaking off sleep, he pulled himself to a sitting position and peered blearily into the darkness.

Gold eyes gleamed at him from down by his feet and the strange rumbling sound continued. The motorboat had followed him right out of his dream.

But it wasn't a motorboat.

It was the damn cat.

"Out!" he commanded, sweeping an arm toward the door for good measure.

But the cat was not impressed. It just watched him and continued to purr.

He stared it down for several seconds and then ordered, "Get!" good and loud.

No effect whatsoever. In time with the purring, it kneaded his comforter with its big paws.

Jed gave up glaring and growling and took action. Shoving back the covers, he scooped up the animal into his arms. Unconcerned, the cat kept purring as Jed carried it to the upper hallway, set it on the floor and firmly shut the door on it.

The next morning, he purposely went down to the kitchen early, when he knew Elise would be there.

And she was. He found her at the counter near the six-burner range with eggs, butter, a golden loaf of homemade bread, milk and several spices spread out in front of her.

The staircase met the ground floor just beyond the open-plan kitchen. She glanced over her shoulder and spotted him as he descended the last few steps. That wide mouth bloomed in a smile of greeting.

Strange. It was only a smile, yet it caused a distinct and disorienting stab of pleasure right to his chest.

"Jed. What a surprise." She turned to face him fully. She looked good, fresh and well rested in curve-hugging jeans and a big, white shirt of some silky material that clung to her tasty breasts.

He kept the corners of his mouth turned down and spoke with great severity. "I need a word."

Her smile vanished. He missed it the second it was gone and regretted being the reason it went away.

What was she doing to him? He wasn't sure he wanted to know. He entered the kitchen area. Her dark brown eyes were wary now. "Of course," she said. "Coffee?"

Why not? He grabbed a mug and poured himself a cup. She waited for him to say what was on his mind, her breakfast preparations suspended. "Your cat was in my room last night. I woke up and found the thing purring on the end of my bed."

"I'm sorry."

"Don't be sorry. Get control of it."

"No problem. I'll go back to keeping him in my room."

"No." He turned to lean against the counter. "I didn't ask you to lock the thing up. I just want you to keep it out of my room when I'm sleeping. I like leaving my door open at night, but I don't like waking up to a giant purring cat on my bed."

"I understand. I'll take care of it."

"Fair enough, then." He started for the stairs.

He'd taken a single step when she offered, "Care to join me? I'm making French toast."

Something good happened in his chest right then, a warm feeling. Kind of...cozy.

He did want to join her, he realized.

He really did.

But he *should* refuse her. Sharing meals was getting too friendly, stepping over the line.

But then again, maybe he was going about this all wrong. Maybe he didn't need to stay away from her to keep her.

Maybe he needed to get closer—no, not in a man-woman way. He had sense enough to see that getting into a sexual relationship with her was too risky in the long run.

But what about buddying up to her? That should be safer. And if they were friends, he'd have a better chance of convincing her to stay.

Then again, buddying up? Who was he kidding? He wasn't one of those guys that women made friends with. He got that, knew that he would never win any prizes in the personality department.

But she seemed a social sort of creature. If she had to be alone with him in his house day after day, shouldn't he put a little effort into making the experience a positive one for her?

"Stay," she said again, and she did seem to mean it. "Let me give you a delicious breakfast to make up for Mr. Wiggles messing with your sleep."

She was being nice to him. Come to think of it, she'd been nice to him often lately. Because of the cat? Probably. After that first Sunday, when he'd told her she should let the cat free in the house, she'd seemed to loosen up around him.

He'd come to like it when she was nice to him. He wouldn't mind if she was nice to him all the time.

"With bacon?" he asked hopefully.

And she smiled at him again. "Bacon, too. Absolutely."

"Well, then, yeah. I'll take you up on that."

So he set the table for both of them. He poured himself more coffee and settled into his chair as the wonderful smells of frying bacon and sweet spices filled the air.

When the food was ready, she brought him his plate, the silky sleeve of her white shirt brushing his shoulder as she set down the meal in front of him. He felt the slight pressure of her arm beneath the fabric. It was nothing, an accidental touch.

But it didn't feel like nothing. To him, that touch was a thunderbolt straight to the heart—and lower down, too. All at once, he was acutely aware that he hadn't been with a woman in almost a year.

He reacted on instinct, grabbing her wrist as she put down the plate. "What are you doing?" The words rumbled up from the depths of him.

"I... Nothing." Her wrist bones felt fragile in his grip, the skin over them far too soft. "Really, Jed. Not a thing." She was shaking a little.

Was he scaring her? He hadn't meant to scare her. "Don't brush up against me." He released her. "It's not a good idea."

Her stomach was flip-flopping and her mouth had gone dry, so Elise straightened and stepped back from him.

What had just happened?

Oh, please. She knew what had happened.

She'd gotten too close and he wanted to scare her off. Because he'd really meant what he said that first day. He was attracted to her and he didn't want to be. She shouldn't let that please her so much.

But it did.

She set down her own plate, pulled back her chair

and sat. Smoothing her napkin on her lap, she hid a
sly smile and remembered the way he'd looked at her
when he came downstairs this morning, a burning sort
of look, a look that could almost have her imagining
that he found her irresistible—which was totally crazy.
She was so not the irresistible type. Men never gave her
burning looks. They looked at her fondly or indulgently
or sometimes like maybe they wished she would quit
talking, but never as though she might be driving them
wild with desire.

Just the possibility that she might have that kind of
effect on Jed gave her a lovely little thrill. Because Jed
was…well, if a woman could go for the strong, scary,
noncommunicative type, he was hot. Way hot. And
lately, in the past week or so, as she soaked in her bubble bath at night or caught a glimpse of him on the way
upstairs, bare-chested and sweaty after a workout, she
found herself thinking that she *could* get interested.

Not that she would. Uh-uh. That would be seriously
unprofessional. Not to mention, hadn't she made enough
bad life decisions in the past few years? She finally had
a job that could put her back on track. No way would she
mess up this chance by falling into bed with the boss.

Jed let out a groan.

She slid him a glance. He had his eyes closed and
he was chewing slowly. Pure pleasure showed on his
hard face.

Her French toast?

Sure looked like it.

She hid another smile. Her French toast was quite
excellent if she did say so herself.

He swallowed. "Damn it to hell. On top of everything else, you cook."

Did those rough words make her feel lovely and desirable and talented? Oh, yes they did. Talk about a boost to her battered ego. Impossible macho madman Jed Walsh saw her as capable and sexy and maybe even slightly irreplaceable. He was a tough critic, yet he found her exceptional—at work, in the kitchen and as a woman.

She hadn't realized how much she needed that, how much she yearned for a little admiration, for some honest appreciation.

After all those endless months and months of doubt and fear and awfulness, Jed's reluctant approval was a vindication. As he groaned over her French toast, Elise felt strong. Indestructible. A superheroine.

But only for a moment. The surge of powerful emotion was just too much. She was the queen of the world—and then her fragile equilibrium snapped.

Hot tears welled, pushing at the back of her throat. Her cheeks burned and her heart set up a wild, out-of-rhythm tattoo. In the space of an instant, she hurt so much and she hated herself for it.

Just a moment of confidence. A flash of womanly power.

And she was completely undone.

She had to get out of there before Jed saw her like this and knew she was not the unflappable super-assistant he believed her to be.

Shoving back the heavy studded chair, she tossed her napkin on the table.

Jed looked up, startled, a slice of crispy bacon halfway to his open mouth. "Elise? What's the matter?"

Clapping her fingers over her mouth to hold back the sobs, she whirled and raced for the sanctuary of her room.

Chapter Four

Bewildered, Jed called after her, "What the hell, Elise?" But she was already gone.

As she vanished into the hallway that led to her room, Jed set down the slice of bacon without taking a bite of it. What had just happened? He could have sworn those were tears he'd seen in her eyes.

Tears? Elise?

Not possible. She was far too tough for tears.

"Mrow-mrow?" The fur ball trotted toward him across the great room.

"Not a clue," he answered, as though the cat had actually asked him a question.

Was he losing it?

Quite possibly.

The cat bounded to him, plopped down at his feet and stared up at him expectantly. "Mrow?"

"Yeah." He stood and tossed his napkin onto his chair. "You're right. We'd better go check on her." He headed for the hallway to her room, Mr. Wiggles in his wake.

When he got to her door, he tapped on it gently. "Elise?"

"Go away!" she shouted from the other side.

Going away was exactly what he wanted to do, but somehow he couldn't. What if she was sick and needed a doctor? What if she did something crazy in whatever strange state she was in?

He tried the door handle. Locked. "Elise, come on. Let me in."

"I said, go away!" She shouted it even louder that time. And then she sobbed—a short sound, swiftly muffled. But definitely a sob, no doubt about it.

"She's crying," he whispered uneasily to the cat. It returned his gaze steadily, but had nothing helpful to offer.

Jed decided to try coaxing, though God knew he was no good at that. "Elise." He tried to make his voice gentle. "Come on, now. Let me in…"

"Go away, Jed!"

He probably *should* go. She'd made it more than clear that she didn't want him there.

But that seemed plain wrong, somehow. He had decided to try and be her friend, hadn't he? Well, clearly, she needed a friend right now and he was the only one available—well, except for the cat. And what could a cat do at a time like this?

Carrie had always said he was hopeless when it came to understanding what went on in a woman's head and heart. He knew his ex-wife was right. What could he do to help right now?

Most likely nothing.

"I give up," he said glumly to the cat.

He turned and started back up the hall—at which point he heard the click of the lock disengaging behind him. Relieved and yet simultaneously terrified of the hundred ways he could screw this up, he turned back to the door as it slowly swung inward.

She looked so small. He hated that. The Elise he knew might not be all that tall, but she carried herself proudly, head back, shoulders straight.

She wasn't proud now. She hung her head and her shoulders sagged. And she was sniffling, her pretty eyes red and her nose even redder.

It hurt him to see her this way. "Aw, now. It can't be that bad."

"It can, Jed. It is." And with that, her face contorted and she burst into tears again.

This time, she didn't even try to hide them. She just stood there, clutching the door handle, her pretty face twisted, tears running down her cheeks. That was the worst, to see her so broken, to see her drooping and sobbing, stripped of her pride.

What should he do? He had no idea. But it turned out not to matter. His arms just kind of reached for her without conscious direction from his brain.

That was all she needed. With a hard sob, she threw herself against him. What could he do but gather her close?

"There now, there." He patted her back, feeling awkward. Inadequate. But she wasn't complaining. She scrunched in even closer, crying hard enough now that he felt the dampness of her tears through his shirt. "It's okay, it'll be okay," he promised, though he had nothing on which to base that assumption. "Come on. Sit down." He guided her into her room and over to the sitting area, where he pulled her down onto the sofa with him. Alternately patting her back and smoothing her hair, he held her and waited until she ran out of tears.

Eventually, she sniffled and asked, "Tissues?" into the soggy fabric of his shirt. Still curved tight against him she reached out a hand and groped for the box on the coffee table. He gave it to her.

"Thank you," she whimpered on a watery sob, pulling free of his hold and scooting away from him. Huddled against the sofa arm, she began whipping out tissues, dabbing at her wet cheeks and blowing her nose. Once she'd mopped up most of the tears, she let her hands fall to her lap and groaned, "God, I'm a mess."

"No," he lied.

"Yeah." She nodded glumly. "Yeah, I am." There was a long, heavy sigh. She tossed the wad of tissues toward the wastebasket in the corner and tugged at her shirt, straightening and smoothing as she squared her drooping shoulders.

The cat, which had jumped up and stretched out on the back of the couch during her meltdown, lifted its giant orange head from its paws and asked, "Mrow?"

"Fine, really," she replied. Then she looked directly at Jed for the first time since he'd pulled her into his arms. "Well." She tried for a brisk tone and mostly succeeded. "We should get to work, huh?"

He thought of his page goal for the day. Screw it. "What made you cry?"

A soggy little snort escaped her. She patted at her hair. "Believe me, my list of reasons is endless and you don't need to hear any of them."

"Sometimes it helps to talk about it." Did he actually just say that? Never in his life had he willingly offered to listen to a woman tell him her problems. But this was different. This was Elise, who kept her cool no matter how many knives he threw, who typed his words steadily, error-free and unflaggingly, two hours at a stretch, ten to twelve hours a day. Elise, who was simultaneously soothing and stimulating. And because it was Elise, he really wanted to know.

Elise studied his craggy face. Those jade eyes regarded her, unwavering.

She should ask him to leave now, say she would meet him in the office in fifteen minutes. And once he was gone, she should wash her face and comb her hair and get ready to work.

It had to be a bad idea to confide in a man whom everyone in town thought was crazy, a guy who cleaned his guns while he killed off bad guys and good guys alike, one by one. A guy who signed her paychecks, for crying out loud.

But, oh, he'd been wonderful just now. Gentle and caring and patient while she sobbed uncontrollably and dripped tears all down the front of his T-shirt. He'd been a complete sweetheart and she was so tired of holding her head up, of remembering her pride, of keeping it all inside.

For once, she would just like to tell *someone* all the things that had gone wrong in her life.

"You'll be sorry," she warned.

"Tell me," he said.

So she did. She told him about her trust fund that had matured when she was twenty-one, of the thousands of dollars she'd thrown away in the stock market because she'd been so sure she could figure out for herself which stocks were the best bets. About the bad boyfriend, Sean, a struggling artist who'd coaxed twenty thousand from her a year and a half before, supposedly as an investment in the Denver art gallery he was opening with several "world-famous" artist colleagues. As it turned out, there was no gallery and those colleagues didn't exist. Sean vanished with her money never to be seen or heard from again.

And Biff Townley, who'd been her friend forever. Biff's wife was a cheater who walked out on him and then took him to the cleaners in the divorce. Biff had only needed a little help, he said, to get back on his feet financially. Elise had lent him the money he needed so badly. Then he'd declared bankruptcy. "He said he was so sorry, but he couldn't pay me back my money because he'd been forced to discharge all his debts and he needed to start over with a clean slate."

And then there was the fire. "It took everything, including all our catering equipment. There was insurance money, of course, but my debts and bills had been piling up. I'd spent a whole bunch on renovating my apartment and I was paying it off in installments—small installments as the money got tighter, so I still owed a lot on that. I couldn't put off paying anymore. And my best friend, Tracy, was half owner of the building and the business. After the fire she finally admitted to me that she'd never really wanted to be a caterer, that her dream was to move to Seattle and study biology. That was the worst."

He frowned. "Which?"

"Tracy moving away." Her throat clutched. "That was the hardest blow of all."

"Elise?"

"Hmm?"

"Are you going to cry some more?" He looked kind of worried.

"You know, I just might—and aren't you sorry now you volunteered to listen to all this?"

He stuck out his hand. She watched his big, blunt fingers come toward her. He wrapped them around her arm. It felt really good, his touch, so warm and steady and more exciting than she would ever have admitted to anyone.

"Come here," he said roughly. She went where he pulled her, though she probably shouldn't have. He lifted her and turned her so she was leaning back against the rock-solid wall of his broad chest. Then he rested his chin on the crown of her head. "Continue."

Wigs, still stretched out along the sofa back, had started purring. She reached up and ran her palm along the warm, furry length of him.

"About your friend Tracy moving to Seattle…" Jed's deep voice rumbled in her ear.

She petted Wigs and leaned against Jed and realized she felt truly comforted for the first time in so long— comforted by Jed Walsh, of all people. "Tracy and I grew up together. She was the one person in the world I could tell anything to. She never judged me, though the awful truth is that I had some seriously bitchy years."

"What is a bitchy year?"

"Let's just say I wasn't always the nicest person in the world."

"But you are now?" He had the nerve to sound amused.

She would have elbowed him in his six-pack if only the angle had been right. "I still have attitude, I'll admit." He made a low sound. It just might have been a chuckle. She smiled to herself and continued, "But I used to be pretty certain that I knew everything. I was popular in high school."

"You mean all the boys were after you?"

"Hardly. I mean I was kind of bossy."

"Not possible."

"I'm going to pretend you meant that sincerely."

"Good idea. Continue."

She tried to think of something quelling to say to him. Nothing came, so she went on with her story. "I had a certain way of taking command of any given situation. I also treated some people like crap, like they were beneath me. I would snub them, you know? And say rude things behind their backs, even start rumors about them. So maybe it wasn't such a bad thing that I had it all and then threw it away. Maybe losing everything kind of showed me that I had a lot to learn."

He was silent, but his arms held her just a little tighter.

She forged on. "Anyway, Tracy was always the one person I could tell all my troubles to. But now she's gone. Now I can't just call her and unburden my heavy heart. If I did that, Tracy would only feel guilty and insist on coming home."

He rubbed his chin, very lightly, across the crown of her head. "Do you want her to come home?"

Her heart still cried yes. But she did know better now. "Tracy needed to go. It was time for us to find our own separate lives. So the answer is no. I want her to have what *she* wants, what she needs. I want that most of all."

"I asked you what *you* want, Elise. Do you want your friend to come back home?"

She drew a slow, shaky breath. "No. I don't think we *could* go back now, anyway. I think we're set on new paths and it wouldn't work to try to be what we were before."

That day, they had lunch together. Over sandwiches and chips, they talked about the scene he'd been working on when they broke to eat. She told him she thought Jack had too easily turned the tables on a mysterious woman with a scorpion tattoo who'd come after him with a syringe full of potassium chloride. Jed took the criticism well, she thought. And then he really surprised her by reworking the scene when they went back to the office, drawing out the tension before the scorpion lady got a deadly dose of her own medicine.

And that evening, he showed up when she was in the kitchen dishing up her dinner. He loaded up a plate for himself and they sat down together.

The next day was Saturday. He didn't eat with her at breakfast or lunch, but he showed up at dinnertime. They talked about it—about how they both kind of liked having meals together—but neither of them wanted to be locked into meeting up every time they ate.

So they agreed: no mealtime expectations. They spent so much time in the same space as it was, it would be easy to get sick and tired of each other.

But Elise wasn't getting sick and tired of Jed. Far from it. Every day she grew to like him more. She liked the way he listened to her, with such steady, serious attention, as though determined to absorb every word. And the way he treated Wigs—with a heavy dose of irony and grudging respect. He was kinder than he wanted anyone to know.

And goodness, he looked amazing without a shirt. He really got her lady parts humming. She could get interested in him in a big way.

But she wouldn't. They'd forged an excellent working relationship and that was nothing to fool around with. Sex would only mess with the program and she couldn't afford that. She was getting out of this with the nest egg she needed.

However, it couldn't hurt to know more about him. She would like to consider herself a friend of his. And she'd been meaning to read the McCannon books in order. It might give her insight into what made him tick. And it couldn't hurt on the job, to have more information about the stories that had preceded the current one.

There were five of them so far, she found out when she looked them up online. And all of them were available in audiobook. She downloaded the complete set for her iPhone so she could listen in the bathtub.

That Sunday, her sisters took her to the Sylvan Inn for lunch. The inn, on the highway a few miles from town, had excellent food and a homey, cozy atmosphere.

Elise joined not only Clara, Jody and Nell, but also Chloe, who had married their brother Quinn. Their cousin Rory McKellan came, too. And so did Ava Malloy, a Realtor who represented Bravo Construction whenever one of their houses went up for sale.

It was the first time they'd all been together since Elise started working for Jed. Sunday wasn't the best choice for a girls-only get-together, but it was the only day Elise had now and her sisters had put aside various family commitments to make it happen.

They sat down and ordered and then they all wanted to know how it was going with Jed.

"You've lasted how long with him now?" Nell sounded thoroughly pleased with the situation.

"On Tuesday, it will be three weeks," Elise replied with considerable pride. She raised her glass of white wine. "To you, Nellie. I can't thank you enough for finding me this job."

Nell laughed. "I love it when you're grateful." They all lifted their glasses and shared in the toast.

"I don't believe it." Ava, petite and adorable with long blond hair, looked pretty close to awestruck. "The way I heard it, nobody could last with that guy."

"He's not so bad." Elise set down her glass and reached for a fluffy, hot dinner roll.

"It's a triumph," Nell declared. "I knew you would be the one to tame that wild beast."

"I wouldn't call him tamed, exactly. But we get along."

Rory said, "I heard he was raised in the woods, just him and his reclusive survivalist father, that his mother died when he was really young." Elise had heard that, too. Most people in town knew the basic facts about the famous Jed Walsh.

Clara made a sympathetic sound. "That must have been hard for him."

Ava said, "And he was military, right? And married for a while."

"What's he like to work for, really?" Jody asked.

"Kind of scary at first." Elise described how he acted out the scenes. "He also throws knives while he's working."

Jody scoffed, "You're kidding, right?"

"Believe it." Nellie backed up Elise. "We built him a special padded wall to throw the knives at."

"He cleans weapons, too," Elise added. "It's part of his *process*, he says. And he demands absolute silence from me while he's dictating."

Chloe said, "It sounds awful."

"It took some getting used to. But believe me, the money is excellent and I find that very motivating. Plus, I guess I'm kind of getting used to Jed."

Jody was watching her a little too closely. "Ohmigod. You like him. I mean, you *really* like him…"

There were giggles and grins as Elise tried not to blush. "I told you. I've gotten used to him. And he's been kind to me, that's all."

"Kind, how?" demanded Nell.

Elise sipped more wine. "Long story. Not going into it today."

Nell gave her a too-knowing look. "Jody's right. You could go for him."

"But I won't," Elise replied with a lot more confidence than she felt.

Monday morning, Jed came into the kitchen as she was getting the oatmeal going. She offered to share and he accepted.

When they sat down to eat, she asked him, "So who typed your books before I came along?"

Was that almost a smile on his way-too-sensual lips? Sure looked like one. "Didn't you hear? I've had an endless chain of typist-assistants. I terrorize them and then they disappear, never to be heard from again—which reminds me, never enter the walk-in closet in my room."

"I see. It's where you keep the bodies, isn't it?"

"Just call me Bluebeard." He made a show of stroking the beard scruff on his chin.

But she wasn't letting it go that easily. "You've written five *New York Times* bestsellers. The last three made it to number one."

"Been reading my book jackets, haven't you?" He stirred brown sugar into his bowl.

She added raisins to hers. "Come on. You followed me to my room the other day and helped me through my meltdown. I'm grateful, Jed. And I would really like to know you just a little better."

He took a very slow, very careful sip of coffee. And then he shrugged. "Her name was Anna Stockard." He said the woman's name too quietly. Was he sad? Regretful? With Jed, it was difficult to tell.

But Elise thought she understood. "You were in love with her."

"Hardly." He was wearing that sardonic expression of his—the one that passed for amusement.

"What? That's funny?"

"Anna was calm. An excellent typist, like you. Unlike you, she was also a motherly woman in her fifties." *Motherly.* And his own mother had died when he was very small. "She typed my first book for me, which I started not that long after I left the service."

"Had you written before?"

"Fiction? Never."

"What made you decide to write a novel?"

He looked at her so patiently. "So. We digress?"

"You're right. I shouldn't have interrupted. I do want to know about Anna."

"But you also want to know what made some guy

raised in a one-room cabin by a half-crazy doomsday prepper imagine he could write bestselling thrillers."

"I wouldn't have put it exactly that way," she said gently.

"I know." He spoke as softly as she had. "My father was not only a paranoid survivalist who homeschooled me and taught me most of what I know about knives and firearms and living off the land, he was also a reader. He read everything he could get his hands on. He built a shed next to our cabin just to store the books, which he scrounged for free, showing up at the end of garage and estate sales when the sellers just wanted to get rid of what was left. He read to me. A lot. Those are my best memories growing up—him reading to me and later, as his eyesight failed, me reading to him. We got through all the great books of the western world, my father and me, before he died. And he loved a good thriller."

"Well. Now your brilliant career as the creator of Jack McCannon makes perfect sense. What did your dad die of?"

"A fall. He had cataracts and they just got worse and he hated doctors, so he never had the surgery that would have saved his sight. He fell from the front steps of our cabin and hit his head on a rock."

"I'm so sorry."

"Why do people always say that?"

"I don't know—because we feel sympathy and we don't know what else to say, I suppose. How old were you when he died?"

"Eighteen. I went straight into the service."

"And Anna? How did you meet her?"

"Anna was a widow. She rented the other half of the North Hollywood duplex I owned with my then-wife,

Carrie. I was in my late twenties by then. Anna was a great cook." *Like you.* He didn't say it, but she could see it in his eyes. "And Anna was lonely, I think. She was always dropping in with casseroles and cupcakes to share. I told her about the book I was trying to write and how I thought I needed to hire a typist, how I'd figured out that sitting at a computer didn't work for me. I needed to be up, moving around, saying the words out loud."

"So Anna volunteered?"

"That's right. Turned out she'd been a legal secretary for years. I hired her. And she was terrific. Carrie and I broke up when that first book, *McCannon's Way*, sold for seven figures at auction. Carrie got half the advance and her ticket out of a marriage that wasn't working."

Elise wanted to know what had happened with Carrie, but she was afraid he might clam up if she asked. Then again, he seemed relaxed, willing to tell her about his life. If he didn't want to get into it, he could just say so. "What went wrong there, with your wife?"

He made a low, amused sound. "I was wondering when you would get around to asking me that."

"You don't want to talk about it?"

"I'm fine with talking about it." He ate a spoonful of oatmeal. "I met Carrie when I was stationed in San Diego. We were kids, really. Both of us just twenty-one. I decided I was in love with her the first time I took her to bed. I proposed. She said yes. We got married and moved in together. And then we grew out of each other—or maybe we just slowly came to realize that we never had that much in common in the first place. And we never spent all that much time together, anyway. I kept re-upping, partly because I felt useful serving my country and partly because I didn't know what I would do with myself once I was a civilian again. Carrie got tired of waiting for me to come home. But she stuck. And then I finally left the service. I was home all the time and we had to face the fact that whatever we might have had once, it was gone. Divorce was the right thing for both of us."

"But Anna stayed with you when your marriage ended."

"Yeah. I bought a great house overlooking the ocean on the Oregon coast and Anna moved there with me. She worked with me through books two, three, four and five. She not only typed, she cooked meals and ran the house. It was all going so well."

"And then...?"

"Anna had two grandchildren in Phoenix and her daughter was going through a tough divorce. A year ago, Anna decided to move in with her daughter and take care of the kids. Exit Anna. Enter a bad case of writer's block. I started hiring typists. You know the rest. None of them worked out, not until you."

"What brought you back to Justice Creek?"

"After three months or so of getting nowhere on the book, I got this brilliant idea that going back to my roots would help me focus. It didn't." He was staring off toward the large oil painting of weathered barn doors on the wall opposite his seat at the table. But then he turned that green gaze on her. A shiver went through her, a lovely, warm one. He said, "What helped me focus was Anna. And now what helps me focus is you."

Jed felt good. Really good, for the first time in over a year. The book filled his mind. He had scenes all lined up, ready to be written.

He felt so good, he was even nice to his agent, Holly Prescott, when she called just as he and Elise were getting down to work.

"I need to take this," he said to Elise. "Fifteen minutes?"

"Good enough." She left him alone, pulling the door shut behind her.

He put his agent on speakerphone and dropped into Elise's chair. "What can I do for you, Holly?"

"Jed. You sound great."

"Thanks. And I'm working. What?"

"I have a surprise for you. We're in the process of getting you a spot on *NY at Night*. You'll hear from the publicist to set up the details for the trip."

The last thing he needed right now was to fly to New York to be on some talk show. "'In the process.' What does that mean?"

"It means it's going to happen and it will be sometime next month, though we're not confirmed on the date yet. I just wanted to tell you ahead. I knew you'd be pleased."

"Are *you* pleased, Holly?"

"Very."

"Then speak for yourself. I, personally, am on a deadline. You know about deadlines. They have to be met in order for books to get published."

"Jed, don't be a douche bag. It's *NY at Night*."

"So get me a slot in November—or better yet, during the next book tour."

"You know it doesn't work that way with a popular show. You've got to take it when they're willing to have you on. And next month Drew is running a whole series with top authors." Drew was Andrew Golden, the show's near-legendary host. "And can't you please be a *little* excited? Come on, Jed. *NY at Night.*"

"You keep saying that as though I'm suddenly going to have a different reaction."

"Once we get the date, the publicist will call with all the details."

"I don't have time for this."

"But you will *make* time—and the book?" she asked, switching subjects so fast he was lucky he didn't get conversational whiplash. "Going well?"

"It won't be if I have to break my rhythm to fly halfway across the country just to kiss some talk show host's ass."

"But it *is* going well?"

"I'm afraid to admit it to you," he grumbled. "You might put me on another talk show."

"I am really glad to hear this," Holly said fervently. He got that. She'd been just as worried as he was that his case of writer's block might never end.

He gave in and confessed, "Yeah, I'm relieved, too."

"You finally found an assistant." It wasn't a question. Holly understood his process. She'd been representing him from the first.

He thought of Elise and felt good about everything. "Yes, I did. Her name is Elise Bravo. She's just what I needed."

"Pay her a lot and never let her go."

The good feeling became less so. He didn't like being reminded that he still hadn't figured out exactly how he would convince Elise to stay. "Anything else, Holly?"

"As a matter of fact, yes. Carl's been worried about you." Carl Burgess was his editor and deserved to know that things were going well now.

He promised to call Carl and reassure him. There was more. Jed had turned down two film deals. A third had languished in "development." The option on that one had just expired. Holly had another film offer she wanted him to consider. And there were new foreign-rights contracts she was overnighting to him. Next, she started nagging him about social media. He had a brilliant virtual assistant who handled all that, but Holly wanted him to be more directly involved.

"I'm a recluse, Holly. It's what I do. My readers get that even if you don't."

"But if you'd only—"

"Work, Holly. I need to get down to it."

Finally, she let him go. He called his editor as promised. Carl picked up. They talked for maybe five minutes, Jed promising the other man that he was on top of it now and there would be no more deadline extensions. Then Carl had a meeting. He rang off.

Elise returned a couple of minutes later. The sight of her, so curvy and lush, in white jeans with rolled cuffs and a pretty pink shirt, her dark hair loose on her shoulders, had him realizing that even if his excellent agent drove him crazy and he hated making reassurance calls to his editor, it was a beautiful day.

She asked, "Ready to go?"

He got up from her chair and she took his place.

That day, he wrote double his page goal.

And that night, he had trouble sleeping. But for a good reason. The book filled his head. And when he finally did drop off to sleep, he dreamed plot points, tweaks for rough spots and clever ways to fit in boring exposition.

At some point, a motorboat started rumbling. He was dreaming of the misty lake again.

The cat.

He opened his eyes to find the fur ball curled up right beside him, making biscuits on the comforter, that motorboat purr vibrating against his thigh.

Elise must have left her door open again.

The golden eyes opened. The cat stared at Jed with a blissed-out expression.

It was kind of pleasant, to be truthful—the warmth of the animal against his leg, the rhythmic kneading, the soft, incessant purr. And Jed was still groggy, still half asleep. He had zero desire to get up from the comfort of his bed to put the creature out.

So fine. Let the damn thing stay. He punched at his pillow and settled back into sleep.

The cat was gone when he woke in the morning. He decided against mentioning the animal's nighttime visit to Elise. Let the cat roam free. If it ended up on his bed, so be it. Jed would simply roll over and pretend it wasn't there.

During the hour-long break for lunch, which Elise spent at the kitchen island chatting with Deirdre as the housekeeper prepared their dinner, Jed went downstairs for a quick session on the elliptical. When he came out of the gym into the open area at the base of the stairs, he saw the cat.

The animal sat staring out the French doors that led to a flagstone patio. Jed went over there and opened the doors for it. The cat glanced up at him as though puzzled.

"Well, go on then," Jed said. Mr. Wiggles went out. Jed shut the doors and ran upstairs to grab a quick shower before returning to work.

He didn't give the cat another thought until dinner-time, when Elise seemed preoccupied. They dished up

the food and sat down, all without a single word from
her. He was about to ask her what she had on her mind
when she glanced up from her untouched dinner with
a worried frown and asked, "Have you seen Wigs?"

"Not since lunchtime." He said it with a shrug. Inside,
however, he felt a definite stirring of alarm. It had suddenly occurred to him that not once in the weeks she'd
been living in his house had he seen her let the cat out.

Maybe he shouldn't have done that.

Elise set down her fork. "I keep trying to tell myself
he's just fallen asleep in a closet or something and he'll
be popping up out of nowhere any minute. But he didn't
come when I called him to eat. That never happens."

He stood. "Hold on." He headed for the stairs.

"Jed? What in the…? Where are you going?"

"Be right back," he called over his shoulder as he
started down.

On the lower floor, he went straight to the French
doors, hoping to find the cat waiting on the other side
of them.

No cat. Except for the fire pit and an empty circle of
Adirondack chairs waiting in the fading light of early
evening, the patio was empty.

If anything had happened to that fur ball, Elise would
never forgive him. How would he keep her then?

This was bad.

Plus, well, not that he would ever admit to such sil-
liness, but he'd started to grow rather fond of the creature. So beyond the possible loss of Elise, he would
really feel like crap if Mr. Wiggles met an untimely end.

He pushed the doors open and went out. Mr. Wiggles
was not anywhere on the patio. He made a quick tour
of the area near the house. Nothing.

So he set off at a jog to circle the building.

He called, "Mr. Wiggles? Where are you?" as he went, feeling ridiculous and guilty and increasingly aware that he'd made a serious mistake.

The cat failed to appear.

When he returned to the French doors, Elise was standing on the other side of them. Her big, sad eyes stayed locked with his as he entered. He couldn't bear her looking at him that way, so he turned around and shut the doors. He took a long time about it, far longer than necessary.

But eventually, he had to face her again.

And when he did, she asked the question he'd been dreading. "What's going on, Jed?"

Chapter Five

Bleak acceptance settled over him.

He couldn't put off the inevitable any longer. So he set about the grim task of confessing what he'd done. "At lunchtime, I saw the cat sitting right here, staring out the doors. I figured it wanted to go out."

Except for two bright red spots of color cresting her cheeks, her face went dead white. "You let Wigs out." She spoke at barely a whisper, but the accusation seemed to echo through the lower floor like a shout.

"Elise, I'm so sorry. I'm sure it's around. It'll be back."

"He's an indoor cat. He's never been outside, not once since I adopted him from the shelter when he was this big." She illustrated how small, holding her shaking hands just inches apart.

"Elise, really, I—"

"No. Stop." Her voice trembled like the rest of her. "I

don't even want to hear your excuses. I just don't. You saw him at a door, so you just…let him out? Who does that? Who in the wide world is that freaking oblivious?"

He felt he had to say something, so he muttered, "It's not an excuse. It's more of an explanation."

"Whatever you want to call it, I don't want to hear it."

"But I—"

"Uh-uh. No." Those big eyes glittered with tears. "I told you I lost everything and Wigs is all that's left. And it is *dangerous* out there." She threw out an arm in the direction of the patio. "Bears. Coyotes. Bobcats. Wolves. Who knows what all? Something could hurt him, something could *eat* him. If I never see him again, I don't know what I'll do."

Was she going to lose it right there in front of him? It certainly seemed so. "Elise. Please. I know you're upset, but there's no need to exaggerate."

She gritted her pretty teeth at him and let out an actual growl. "Oh, there damn well is a need. Anything could happen to him. Anything at all."

"Elise. Settle down. Nothing is going to happen to that cat."

She threw back her head and howled at the ceiling, after which she started peppering him with questions, each one louder and more hysterical than the last. "What is the matter with you? What were you thinking? What could possibly have been going through your mind?"

He strove for calmness. One of them had to. "I made a mistake, okay? A big one, apparently. But getting yourself all worked up isn't going to help us find your cat. You need to slow down, take a deep breath and—"

She cut him off with a wordless shout of fury and then commanded, "Get out of my way!" Dodging

around him, she threw open the French doors and ran
outside. "Wigs! Wigs, come here, baby. Wigs, here kitty,
kitty…" She headed for the trees that rimmed the property and called in a high, plaintive voice, "Wigs, here
kitty, come on, baby…"

"Elise, hold up…" He took off after her.

She ignored him and kept on going into the trees.

He didn't know whether to follow her into the woods
or not. Hesitating by an outcropping of decorative rock,
he tried to decide on his next move. She clearly wanted
nothing to do with his sorry ass at the moment. He got
that, loud and clear.

But given her emotional state, it seemed unwise to
let her wander off alone.

So he started moving again, trailing along behind her
as she searched the wooded area behind the house, calling for the cat as she went. After about fifteen minutes
of that, she led him into a clearing, a small meadow of
tall grass and wildflowers. Past the meadow, twin trails
wound upward into the trees.

In the middle of that clearing, she stopped at last.
Jed halted several yards away and waited to see what
she might do next.

But she only let her head drop back. For a good sixty
seconds, she just stood there, staring up at the slowly
darkening sky. And then, just as he was trying to figure out what his next move should be, she crumpled to
a sitting position on a boulder that stuck up through
the long grass.

He hesitated to approach. His nearness might just
set her off again.

But then she braced her elbow on her knee, plunked
her chin on her fist and looked straight at him across the

clearing. "It's okay, Jed." She sounded sane again. But how long would the sanity last? "I'm not going to kill you." He didn't find those words all that reassuring, but he started for her anyway as she added drily, "Though I probably should." He kept coming until he stood looking down at her. She tipped her face up to him.

When he offered his hand, she took it. Her slim, smooth fingers disappeared in his grip. He pulled her up and wrapped his arms around her, figuring the chances were about fifty-fifty that she'd shove him away.

But she didn't. With a sad little sigh, she rested her dark head against his chest. "I guess I kind of lost it."

He had to actively resist the need to stroke her silky hair. "It's understandable. You love the damn cat and I really screwed up." She felt good in his arms—too good and he knew it. Too soft, too sweet. He lowered his head and breathed in the scent of her.

She looked up at him then, eyes so bright, both scared and hopeful. "Tell me that he's going to be all right."

He tried not to stare at that wide mouth of hers, not to think about swooping down for a kiss, about how good it would feel if her lips parted, welcoming him. "He'll show up soon. He's going to be fine."

She gave him a slow, irresistible smile. "I think I'm having a moment."

"Why is that?"

"You just called Wigs a *he* instead of an *it*."

He admitted, "Yeah, Wigs and I are working things out. He showed up in my room again last night."

"Did he wake you?"

Jed nodded. "But then I realized he wasn't really bothering me, so I just went back to sleep."

"If he'll only come back, I promise to be more careful about letting him out of my room at night."

"*When* he comes back," he amended her gently.

"Right." Another shaky sigh escaped her. *"When."*

"And as I said, he doesn't bother me. Leave your door open anytime you want to." If he stared at her upturned mouth for one second longer, he was going to taste it. "Come on." He took her hand again and stepped back to a slightly safer distance. "Let's go."

She let him lead her across the meadow and into the trees. The walk back to the house didn't take long at all. When they reached the patio, she wanted to have a look out in front, too.

He said, "I checked there when I first went downstairs."

She turned those shining eyes on him. "Let's just look one more time."

So they circled around the house and walked up and down the winding paths in the steep front yard. They checked the far side of the garage and also the shed farther out. The cat was nowhere to be found.

He kept the front door locked and he hadn't stopped to grab a key on the way out, so they returned the way they'd come, to the French doors off the lower floor at the rear of the house.

Jed spotted the big orange cat when they rounded the corner to the backyard. Mr. Wiggles sat in front of the doors, staring straight at them. He appeared to be fine—alert, calm and uninjured. The relief Jed felt at the sight of the animal was a very fine thing.

"Look." Elise's soft voice vibrated with pure joy.

"Don't run at him," Jed warned quietly. "If he races off, we might lose him again."

"You're right. I'll go slow." She started forward at an easy pace. Jed fell in behind her. "Wigs," she chided in a soft, coaxing tone. "There you are. Where have you been?"

The cat replied with the usual "Mrow? Mrow-mrow."

Jed made out the small gray lump at Mr. Wiggles's feet about the same time Elise did. She asked the cat, "Baby, what's that you've got?"

"Mrow-mrow." Mr. Wiggles bent his leonine head and scooped up the object in question. About then, Jed saw the dangling pink tale.

Mr. Wiggles had brought home a mouse.

Elise gasped as she realized that her sweet baby boy had a dead rodent in his mouth.

Behind her, Jed warned softly in what she'd come to think of as his black ops voice, "Do not start screaming. The mouse is a gift."

She paused long enough to shoot him a dirty look over her shoulder. "Not all women start shrieking at the sight of a mouse."

"Unfair assumption. My bad." She knew he was trying to sound contrite. He just wasn't all that good at it.

And Wigs was what mattered. She focused back on him, moving steadily forward. When she stopped about a foot from him, he lowered the mouse to the flagstones again and then sat up tall. "Mrow."

"Say thank you," Jed instructed. It was actually kind of cute, him trying to school her on the psyche of her own cat.

"I'm on it." She reached down and scooped Wigs up into her yearning arms. "Thank you so much," she whispered, burying her nose in his thick fur, breathing in the unaccustomed smells of pine and dust on him. "I'm so grateful for that dead mouse. And I'm so, so glad you're home."

"Mrow." He'd started purring, the sound growing louder, making a pleasurable vibration against her chest.

She cuddled him closer. "You want your dinner, don't you?"

"Mrow, mrow-mrow." He definitely did.

She turned to Jed and asked, "Would you take care of my…gift?"

"Happy to." He actually smiled, a rarity for him. In the fading light, his eyes were the deepest, truest green. She watched them crinkle at the corners and thought that he was a good man. And also that she'd never been happier than she was right at this moment, with Wigs in her arms—and Jed at her side. "Go on in," he said.

Reluctantly, she broke the hold of his gaze and took Wigs inside.

Jed disposed of the mouse, washed his hands in the utility room and then returned to the table.

The food had gone cold. He grabbed a beer and waited for Elise, who was still off somewhere enjoying her reunion with the cat. Yeah, he could have just zapped his plate in the microwave and dug in.

But he enjoyed having her there with him while he ate, especially in the evenings. It kind of rounded out the day, the two of them together at the dining room table. It was something he looked forward to, something he'd quickly gotten accustomed to, something he fully expected to continue through the completion of his current book.

And every book after that.

She came toward him across the great room, her expression serene. "What are you staring at?"

"You." He thought of the feel of her in his arms, the scent of her that he would know anywhere—and it hit him like the proverbial bolt from the blue.

He was going about this all wrong. Staying away from her in order to keep her made no sense at all.

He needed to get even closer than friendship.

Closer. Dear God. He would love that.

Too bad he was no good at all that love and romance crap. He communicated through his books. Dealing with actual people had never been his strong suit. He'd been a rotten husband to Carrie, spending most of their marriage on a never-ending tour of duty, and not knowing what to say to her, exactly, on the rare occasions when he was home on leave. So far, he was zero and one in the forever department.

And if he went for it with Elise and it blew up in his face, where would he be then? Zero and two—*and* minus the assistant who made it all hang together.

Losing Anna had just about finished him.

Still, the differences between Elise and Anna needed considering. Elise was a woman of his own age, a woman he found desirable. Whereas Anna...

He had cared for Anna, absolutely. They'd been friends—remained friends, to this day. Anna had been good to him. She'd taken excellent care of him. But now, looking back on it, he saw that Anna was bound to leave, bound to go to her daughter and grandchildren eventually.

Family. It mattered. Even though he had no family left, Jed got that most people placed a high priority on having one.

If he managed to keep Elise in a business-only capacity, someday she would want a husband and children to call her own. As far as the books getting done, a husband and children didn't have to be a problem. Elise would meet some local guy, get married, have babies—and continue to make a boatload of money typing Jed's books.

Except Jed didn't even want to think about Elise with some nice, regular guy who would take good care of her and give her babies to love.

"Jed." She'd reached the table and now stood over him, watching him, her smile indulgent, her eyes so bright. "What's going on in that big brain of yours?"

"Not a thing."

"Liar. You've got your scary face on—give me your plate. I'll warm it up."

He handed it over. She took both plates to the kitchen area. He watched her walk away. Always a pleasure, watching Elise walk away.

She set the plates on the counter, got the vented plastic dome from the cupboard, covered one plate, heated it, covered the other and warmed it up, too. "How's your beer?" she asked, when she set his plate back in front of him.

"I'm good." What would it be like, him and Elise, living together, working together, sleeping in the same bed night after night? He was starting to think he really needed to find out. "So the fur ball's all right?"

She smoothed her napkin on her lap. "No thanks to you, Wigs is perfectly fine."

Jed enjoyed a bite of crab cake. "You know that he had a great time outside, right? He got to run free, hunt, bring home the bacon to the mistress he adores..."

"That was not bacon. That was a poor, dead little

mouse and I don't want to talk about it at the dinner table."

"But you can see that it wouldn't be such a bad idea to let Mr. Wiggles out now and then."

She set down her fork sharply. "Do not even *think* it. He's an indoor cat and he's staying that way. You should read the statistics. Outside cats get in fights and get injured. They eat diseased meat. They're targets for parasites and predators. Indoor cats live years longer than cats that are allowed outside." Her eyes flashed with heat and those telltale bright spots of pink stained her soft cheeks. He was tempted to say something else to provoke her, just because he liked to see her spitting fire.

But on the other hand, he didn't really want her pissed off at him. Especially not now that he was rethinking his own hard-and-fast rule against seducing his secretary. So he picked up his beer and saluted her with it. "I bow to your greater knowledge on this subject."

Her fire turned to sweetness. "Please never let him out again." Her wide mouth trembled. Her eyes held his.

Damn. She really did it for him. He'd been an idiot to try to tell himself he wouldn't end up in bed with her. "I won't let him out again. You have my word on that."

The next day during their lunch break, Jed found Mr. Wiggles waiting by the ground-floor French doors again. The cat stared out at the patio and the rim of trees beyond the yard with an expression that seemed to Jed to be very close to yearning. When a finch flitted down and pecked at the gravel between the flagstones, Mr. Wiggles made chirping, eager sounds. His whiskers quivered in anticipation of the hunt.

"Sorry, big guy. No can do." Jed turned for the stairs and didn't look back, though it did bother him that the fur ball had hunted his first, last and only mouse. All creatures deserved access to the great outdoors.

It wasn't until that night, when he woke to the sound of Mr. Wiggles's motorboat purr and opened his eyes to find the cat lying on the pillow next to him, that he knew what he had to do.

Jed spent a few hours Sunday researching the project. Monday, while Elise was taking her lunch break, he called Bravo Construction.

Nell Bravo was there and willing to take his call. For the past four months or so, he only ever dealt with Nell when he needed something from the builder. It was easier that way. She was smart, tough and direct and never accused him of hurting her feelings. In the past, he'd been brusque with the receptionist and yelled too loud at one of their carpenters. After that, Nell told him he was to deal with her and only her.

Nell didn't say hello. She opened with "You'd better be treating my sister right."

"She's still here. I think you can take that as a very good sign." He realized he needed to make nice. For giving him Elise, Nell deserved a thank-you. "Elise is just what I was looking for. Thanks for steering her my way."

"You're welcome, Jed. And what can I do for you today?"

"I have a project I need built. It's not exactly what you do. But I thought if you couldn't help me, you could refer me to someone who can."

"Happy to. Tell me what you need."

He described what he wanted and then elaborated

a little. "I was thinking a basic structure at first, with maybe add-ons, climbing runs, bump-outs, things like that later, after we see how it works out. I want it to look good, to fit with the landscaping and the house. High-end, you know?"

"I understand. But I didn't have a clue you had a cat."

"Of course I don't have a cat. Do I look like a man who would have a cat?"

"So it's for Wigs, then?"

"Why? Is that somehow a problem?"

"No. I'm surprised, that's all. This isn't exactly your style."

"You mean, because I'm such a hard-ass, I can't do something nice for Elise and her cat?"

"Pretty much. Tell me, Jed." He knew from her tone that he wouldn't like what came next. And he didn't. "Are you a secret softy?"

He had no idea what to say to that, so he demanded curtly, "Can you make it happen, or refer me to someone who can?"

"No way I'm referring you," she said with a low laugh.

"What the hell?" he growled. "Somehow, this is funny?"

"Well, yeah, it kind of is." He was just about to tell her thanks for nothing and hang up, when she asked, "So what time are you through yelling and throwing knives today?"

"When am I done *writing*, you mean? We knock off around nineteen hundred hours."

"Seven works for me. I'll draw up something basic and you can give me more details tonight to flesh it out."

"So you're telling you're going to build it for me and you'll be here at nineteen hundred hours?"

"Yes, I am."

"Excellent." He was relieved. Bravo Construction always did great work. They came in on time and gave him what he asked for, only better. Plus, if had to deal with other people, he preferred people he already knew, people who weren't the least bit afraid of him. The scared ones just never worked out. "When can you start on it?"

"Let me check the schedule before I commit, but I'm pretty sure once you approve the design we can get going within the week."

"The sooner the better."

She made a low, amused little sound. "I might even give you a special discount, being as how it's for Wigs and all."

"Money is no object. I want it to look good, like everything you build. And I want it roomy with lots of climbing, scratching and hiding options. Also, I want it as soon as possible."

"Of course you do, Jed. And at Bravo Construction, we make it our business to see that you get exactly what you want."

He wasn't sure he liked her tone. "You know, Nell. Sometimes I find your attitude humorous."

"How 'bout now?"

He wasn't touching that. "See you tonight. Join us for dinner?"

"Sure, thanks."

"Good, then." He hung up before she could give him more grief.

Besides the money and the jetted tub and the way she was getting to like her grouchy employer way more than she should, Elise appreciated being allowed to dress for comfort while working for Jed. If she had to spend the whole day sitting on her butt, at least she didn't have to do it in a pencil skirt.

Jed said he didn't mind what she wore as long as her clothes didn't constrain her or break her concentration in any way. So she wore leggings and roomy casual shirts. Now and then in the past couple of weeks as the summer turned hot, she even wore shorts. Jed didn't complain about the shorts.

On the contrary, she would often catch him looking at her bare legs with great interest, his eyes kind of glazing over. She loved that. Sometimes when she was typing and couldn't actually see him staring, she knew exactly what he was doing anyway, because he would pause in the middle of a sentence…and then catch himself with a throat-clearing sound. Then he would murmur, "Elise," so that she would stop typing, and follow it with a string of muttered swear words, at which point he would grumble out her name again and lurch back into the story.

That day, she'd started off in leggings and a lightweight tunic. But it was gorgeous out, and hot. At lunch, she'd changed to cutoffs, cowboy boots and a soft plaid shirt, and had taken her sandwich out on the deck off the great room to enjoy the sunshine.

When Jed joined her in the office after the break and she swung her chair around to greet him, he did a double take at the sight of her bare legs—and then instantly tried to pretend that he hadn't. She totally loved that.

He said, "Your sister Nell is coming tonight." He sounded furious. But she was on to him big-time. He often seemed angry when he was flustered. "She'll eat with us."

And wait a minute. Had she heard him right? Jed didn't make a habit of inviting her family members for dinner—he didn't make a habit of inviting *anyone* for dinner. "Okay. I'm just going to ask it. Why is my sister suddenly coming to dinner?"

"I invited her." He had on his scary face.

She rose from her chair. "That thunderous expression you're wearing? Doesn't faze me in the least. And let me put it this way. I'm not typing a word until you tell me what's going on."

He grabbed a bowie knife from the array on the credenza and whipped it toward the padded wall. It landed with a *thwack*. "Don't piss me off. It messes up my aim. You could get seriously hurt."

She sat on the edge of her desk, crossed her legs and thought how handsome he was when he tried to be intimidating. All testosterone and hunky grumpiness. "Are you trying to scare me? Because it's not really working."

He threw another knife. "You Bravo women. You're all about the attitude."

"You're saying Nell gave you attitude?" His answer to that was to send another knife flying at the wall. "I'm guessing that's a yes. What's going on, Jed?"

He had ninja stars, too. He picked one up and sent it spinning. Bull's-eye. Finally, he turned to her. "I wanted it to be a surprise. But then I knew you wouldn't like it if your sister just showed up out of nowhere. And I didn't want to spring it on you in front of her—just in case you don't take it well, you know?"

For a man who used words for a living, he was making a real hash of explaining himself now. "Take what well?"

Instead of answering her question, he scowled and added, "But I can't see why you wouldn't. It's a good thing and you should love it. I know the damn cat will."

"Jed. What in the world are you talking about?"

He picked up another knife and then set it down without throwing it. "Let's go for a walk."

This was a first. "But it's work time."

"Work can wait."

That was so totally not Jed that her mouth fell open. "Are you feeling all right?"

He held out his hand to her. "Get over here."

"You know you need to work."

"Fine. Grab a steno pad and a pencil."

"What for?"

"If I have an idea while we're walking, you can jot it down."

"But—"

"No buts. Think of it as working. Steno pad. Pencil."

She bent over the side of the desk, pulled open the pencil drawer and found both. "Fine." She waved the pad at him. "Got 'em."

"Good. Now, come here."

She got up from the desk. "You're the boss."

"And don't you forget it." He wiggled his big fingers at her impatiently.

She took her time strolling over there, partly because she loved baiting him. And partly to revel in how hard he was trying not to glance down at her legs. When she slipped her free hand in his, she gave him her sweetest smile. "Well, all right. I have to admit that a walk sounds really nice."

Downstairs, Wigs was sitting at the French doors staring longingly at the patio and the woods beyond, the way he'd been doing too often since last Wednesday when Jed had let him out.

"Sorry, sweetie. No can do." She scooped up the cat and set him safely out of the way.

They slipped through the doors and Jed shut them. Wigs stepped up to the other side and sat down to stare out again. He meowed at her, but softly enough that she couldn't hear him through the insulated glass. She got the message, though, loud and clear. He longed for the freedom of the great outdoors.

"Poor guy." Jed claimed her hand again.

She almost yanked it back. "No thanks to you."

"Come on." He said it gently, coaxingly even.

"What is going on with you?"

"Just walk." Pulling her with him, he set off across the patio and into the trees, where the shade made the air a little cooler.

They walked in silence to the meadow and across it. He took the winding trail on the left and they started upward into the forest again. Overhead, somewhere beyond the green canopy of the tall firs, she heard a hawk cry. Small creatures scrabbled in the underbrush. Elise breathed in the warm, pine-scented air and told herself to enjoy the moment.

A stroll in the woods with Jed. Who knew that was ever going to happen?

When the ground leveled out again and the trees opened up to a small, grassy space, he stopped suddenly and turned to her. She gazed up at him, admiring him though she probably shouldn't. His dark hair showed glints of bronze in the sunlight. And he had a little gray at the temples. It looked good on him.

"Might as well get on with it," he said bleakly.

She was all for that. "Great. Talk to me."

"It's like this. *I* want your damn cat to be able to go outside. Your damn *cat* wants to be able to go outside. But *you* want him safe. So I came up with a solution. It's called a 'catio'—get it? Cat patio. Which is too cute by half if you ask me. I want to enclose the back patio in wire fencing and rig one of the French doors with a cat door. Nell will build it for me, which is why she's coming over tonight, to agree on the plans and collect a deposit."

Elise stared up at him, into those green eyes she'd once seen as icy. This man.

Oh, God. This man.

Her arms ached to grab him close and hold him tight and never, ever let him go.

Except that grabbing him would be so stupid. She needed this job, needed to stick with it right through to the end of this book, as planned. She needed every penny he was paying her; she couldn't afford to take a chance on messing it all up. And falling into bed with the boss could definitely mess it all up.

Jed's mouth had a grim twist to it now. "You don't like it. You hate it."

She thought of last Wednesday, of Wigs and that poor, dead mouse. Of Jed warning her not to start screaming. *The mouse is a gift*, he'd said. At the time, she'd been offended that he assumed she would freak, but the point was, a gift mattered. A gift ought to be properly appreciated.

And this man had given her no end of gifts—not the least of which included a big boost to her self-image and self-confidence after the endless series of emotional and financial blows she'd sustained in recent months.

Yeah, there were plenty of reasons to say no to his catio plan. It would cost more than she ought to let Jed spend on *her* pet. And when this job ended, he'd just have to tear it down, wouldn't he? And how would Wigs react, to have a roomy outdoor space to roam in and then end up returning to the confinement of her dinky apartment over the donut shop?

It wasn't fair to Jed. It could be harder for Wigs in the end.

But wait just a second here. Why go negative? Why expect the worst?

She loved what he wanted to do. And maybe she needed to go with that. Go with the positive and focus on making sure he knew how grateful she was.

Moreover, just because this job with him would end didn't necessarily mean she and Jed had to be over, as well. Maybe they could have something good together, something that actually might last.

And a girl never got what she wanted by refusing to try for it, did she? Yes, she'd made a lot of mistakes. But the whole point was to learn from your mistakes, learn and move on, not let them paralyze you, not let them cut you off from the good things that might come your way.

Jed looked really worried now. "You're so quiet. That's not good, is it? Are you pissed at me? Just tell me."

How had this happened? She wasn't quite sure. But she could no longer deny the truth. She was falling for her crazy, knife-wielding, macho-man boss.

She stepped in closer to him. "I, um…"

He fell back. "What? Tell me. God, what?"

Go for it. Stop stalling.

And she did. She stepped right up to him again, lifted

her hands and laid them against his broad, hard chest. The pad and pencil were in the way, but not too much.

Heat flared in those beautiful eyes—and then he turned wary again. "Elise. What the hell?"

"I love it, Jed, that you're building Wigs a catio."

"You do?"

"It's a wonderful idea. Thank you."

"Ahem. Well, okay, then. You're welcome."

"And there's something else…"

"What?" The single word was weighted with suspicion.

Make your move, girl. Do it now.

She slid her hands up to clasp his neck and jumped, lifting her legs and wrapping them around him, hooking her booted feet at his back, letting out a silly "whoops" as she dropped the pad and pencil to the grass in the process.

"Elise!" He caught her automatically, big hands so warm and strong, cradling her thighs. "What in the…?"

She answered the question he couldn't quite seem to ask by threading her fingers up into his thick hair and guiding him down until his mouth finally crashed into hers.

Chapter Six

Jed wasn't sure exactly how this had happened.

He only knew he liked it. A lot.

Her mouth felt like heaven, soft and so willing. Exactly as he'd always imagined it might. He nudged at her parted lips until she opened wider on a sweet little moan. And he dipped his tongue deeper, into honeyed wetness, retreating only in order to catch her plump lower lip between his teeth.

Amazing.

He hadn't expected this. No way.

Apparently, the catio had been a very good idea.

She was grateful. And willing to show it—with that wide, sweet mouth of hers and those full, smooth thighs.

Elise, wrapped all around him. Talk about a red-letter day.

She tasted so good, like apples and honey, and she

smelled like clean cotton warmed by the sun. She moaned some more and wriggled against him, causing fine flares of heat to chase across his skin everywhere her curvy body rubbed his. He was already hard, aching. And it was good.

So good. Those full, soft breasts smashed against his chest, the hot notch between her thighs rubbing him right where he wanted her most.

Since the night the cat got out, he'd been considering how and when to make his move.

Leave it to Elise to make his move for him—and so enthusiastically, too.

Elise all over him. Did it get any better?

Yeah. Yeah, it did.

When he had her naked, that would be even better. And right now, judging by her kiss and her hot little sighs, he knew they would get there. He would have her in his bed minus all her clothes. He groaned at the thought of it.

Life was good. His book was coming together and Elise would be coming apart for him. Soon. Tonight.

He had no complaints. Not a one.

He had those pretty legs wrapped around him now, had her mouth fused to his as she rubbed herself against him.

Things were working out just right—or they were until she fisted her fingers in his hair and pulled her mouth away from his.

He let out a growl of protest. "Get back here."

She laughed, the sound low and way too damn sexy. "Let's not get carried away."

"Why not? Getting carried away sounds like a fine plan to me."

She kissed him again, a quick, hard press of her soft lips to his, the feeling so sweet—and over much too soon. "Let me down," she commanded.

Against his better judgment, he obeyed, another groan breaking from him as she slid along the front of him. Once she had boots on the ground, she offered that mouth again. He took it, hard and deep, kissing her for all he was worth, hoping that if he did a bang-up job of it, she wouldn't ever pull away.

But then she did. Damn it.

Dropping back onto her heels, she stared up at him dreamily. "We should get back. Nell is coming for dinner and your pages for the afternoon are not going to write themselves."

He touched her hair, because he could, because he'd wanted to for way too long and now was his chance. It was so warm under his hand. He couldn't wait to spear his fingers into it, rub the smooth strands against his mouth, his belly and even lower. "I want more. More of you. More of this…"

Those dark eyes were so serious. "Me, too." Her lips were flushed a deeper red from his kiss. He wanted to taste them again. "But we need to talk first."

What was it with women and talking first? "Talking's overrated."

Her smile bloomed—a little bit patient, a little bit tender and more than a little bit exasperated. "We would be changing everything up after you made it so painfully clear that first day. Strictly professional, wasn't that what you said?"

"I've rethought that."

"Jed. Are you sure?"

"Oh, hell, yes." He took her by the shoulders, pulled

her up tight against him and claimed that fine mouth one more time. He made this one last. But eventually, she pulled away again.

Sighing, she stared up at him, dreamier than ever, her red mouth still parted. "I can't think straight when you kiss me."

"Good. I like you like this—soft, unfocused. I like it a lot. You should be like this often, preferably while naked in my bed."

She blinked and her gaze sharpened. "I was so sure a few minutes ago."

"About...?"

"This. Us. But then it always comes back around to what if we go for it and it screws everything up?"

"There's no what-if about this. We're going for it. And nothing's getting screwed up. You're too tough and determined for that."

She hummed low in her throat. "I could say the same about you."

"Exactly. You want this job and I want you doing this job. That won't change."

He got a firm nod for that. "Until this book of yours is done."

And the next one. And the one after that. But she wasn't ready to go there yet.

So he offered her his hand. She bent and grabbed the pencil and steno pad from the tall grass. Then she slipped her fingers in his and they started back down the path.

Nell showed up right on time that night. She took a beer and she showed them the plans she'd drawn up. They looked great to Jed.

He suggested a few more catwalks, a cozy cat house
and a half roof projecting off the house instead of all
wire fencing overhead. "That way he can go out no matter what the weather's like."

"You got it." Nell made notes of the changes.

"It's fabulous," said Elise. Her cheeks were flushed
with pleasure. She was bent over the table admiring Nell's
sketches and she looked across at him and mouthed,
Thank you. She really did seem grateful.

Too bad he'd invited Nell to stay for dinner. He
wanted to hustle Elise's sister out the door and get on
with the evening, just the two of them alone.

But it turned out okay. Elise seemed really happy
to have her sister there. The two of them talked family
stuff. Their brother Carter was marrying his fiancée
and business partner, Paige Kettleman, on the second
Saturday in August. And their brother James's wife,
Addie, was expecting her first baby in October. The
Bravo women were planning a shower for her.

Nell asked him how the book was going.

"Great," he answered honestly. "Ever since your sister showed up at my door."

Nell left at 2100 hours. Elise walked her out. Jed had
just loaded the last dish and shut the dishwasher door
when she joined him in the kitchen.

She folded her arms across her beautiful breasts and
braced a hip against the granite counter. "Thanks. For
giving Wigs a designer-quality outdoor space. For inviting my sister to dinner."

He straightened to his height. "Just keep wearing
those little Daisy Duke cutoffs and whatever you want,
it's yours."

She glanced down at her cowboy boots and then back

up at him. And then she started in about his books, of all things. "As of last night, I've read all five Jack Mc-Cannon novels—well, actually, I listened to them in audiobook. In the bathtub."

Elise in the bathtub. Now there was an image to conjure with. He needed to be closer to her. It was a physical imperative. He left the dishwasher behind and joined her at the corner of the center island. "All five. Impressive."

"I enjoyed them." She tipped her face up to him. Like an offering, he decided. He was just about to take her mouth, when she said, "Jack is endlessly resourceful. Always coming up with new ways to kill people."

He raised a hand and brushed his fingers over the plump curve of her cheek. He needed more contact, so he smoothed a hand down her hair. It wasn't enough. So he lowered his mouth to hers.

The kiss was slow. Exploratory. She tasted of coffee and the raspberry gelato Deirdre had left them for dessert.

When he lifted his head, she said breathlessly, "Jack needs a real girlfriend."

"Oh, does he?"

"Mmm-hmm. He needs to get beyond the endless chain of gorgeous and potentially deadly hookups, you know?"

He slipped a hand under the warm fall of her hair and cupped the nape of her neck. "You're nervous."

"Yeah?" She made it a question. It was adorable.

He bent a little closer and whispered, "You don't really want to talk about work, do you?"

Her very kissable mouth trembled. "Why not? You love your work."

"At the moment—" he kissed one soft cheek "—work is the last thing on my mind." He kissed the other cheek. "But okay. You say Jack needs a girlfriend. I'm not completely averse to the idea. A man gets tired of bed-hopping after a while."

"And for Jack, it's worse."

"Because?"

"He's bed-hopping while the bullets are flying. He must be exhausted."

"You think you're cute." He kissed the tip of her nose. "It's okay. You are."

Her cheeks flushed the prettiest shade of pink. "She should be someone…unexpected. Someone who doesn't fit into his world. But maybe someone who turns out to be just as resourceful as he is in her own special way."

"I like that."

"I think it could be good. I think it could bring a whole new dimension to the, uh…" Her voice faded away as he ran the backs of his fingers down the side of her throat. He considered kissing her there, using his teeth a little, making a mark. "Jed?"

"Hmm?"

"How many women have you been with?"

"Several. And do you really want to talk about that now?"

"I don't know what happened. I was so confident this afternoon, but tonight…"

He bent close and brushed his lips against her hair just over her ear. "Tell me."

"Well, for some reason, now I just feel so…scared."

"Of me?" He bent and kissed that tempting spot on the side of her throat. A sweet shudder went through her. He scraped his teeth there, too—but very lightly. She shuddered again.

"Not really of you—but a *little* of you." Her voice had a slight tremor. "We have it all worked out, you know? It's all going so well. There's a…a balance of power. I'm afraid that you and me, like this, will put us all out of whack."

"It won't." He brushed his mouth up over her chin and settled his lips on hers again. "You taste so good." He breathed the words against her mouth.

"I've never been, well, particularly sexy, you know?"

He kissed one cheek and then the other and then her mouth again. "What idiot told you that?"

"Nobody had to tell me. I know exactly who I am, what I'm like. I'm…kind of fussy. Controlling. I like things a certain way. Men want me to take care of them when they're down. But nobody finds me especially exciting."

"They're blind. All of them. Luckily for you, you ran into me."

"Oh, don't be silly."

He caught her face between his hands and waited for her to look up at him. When she finally did, he said, "I am never silly."

She let out a gusty sigh. "I'm the kind of girl a guy comes to when he's in trouble, when he needs comfort. I'm the dependable type. A guy can come to my place—before it burned down, I mean—and I would cook him an excellent dinner. And until my recent financial crisis, I was always good for a loan if a guy was broke."

He nuzzled her hair aside and caught her earlobe between his teeth. "I don't need a loan, but you can cook for me anytime."

"And that's another thing…" She gasped as he took her by the waist and lifted her. "Jed!" She clutched at his shoulders. "What are you doing?"

He plunked her down on the island. "Getting eye-to-eye."

She shivered. "This granite is cold."

He nudged her thighs apart and stepped between them. "Let me heat you up." He got right to work on that, using his palms, rubbing her bare thighs in long, lingering strokes.

She laughed then, a sweet and nervous sound. "You never give up, do you?"

"Not a chance. What other thing?" When she frowned in puzzlement, he reminded her, "I said you can cook for me anytime, and you said 'that's another thing.'"

"Oh, right…" She chewed the corner of her lip, her eyes wide and anxious.

"Well?" He bent forward just enough to kiss the tip of her nose again.

"I probably shouldn't admit it…"

"Of course you should. Tell me."

"Well, speaking of food, the truth is I've put on some weight since I lost everything."

"Have you, now?"

"Sometimes it takes a lot of donuts to make a girl forget her troubles."

"And to that I have to say, thank God for donuts."

She wrinkled her nose at him. "What does that even mean?"

"It means the donuts look good on you and you should keep eating them."

"You don't really mean that."

"Elise. You ought to know me well enough by now

to realize that I don't bother to say things I don't mean. I like a woman to be womanly. Curvy. Soft."

"Well, I'm certainly that these days."

"Oh, yes you are." He cradled her face between his palms and stole yet another kiss. She sighed against his lips and then opened for him.

For a little while, except for the occasional soft, urgent moan, the kitchen was quiet. He unbuttoned her shirt, taking his time about it, working his way down, until the shirt was open and he could slip his hand inside, where she was so soft and perfect.

He cradled her breast, finding her nipple hidden under the lace. He flicked it with his thumb, enjoying the way it hardened into a tight little knot. At the same time, he trailed his mouth downward over her chin, her throat, to the two pretty points of her collarbone. He scraped his teeth against those.

She whispered his name then… "Jed…" It sounded so good, his name on her lips, a breathless, hungry little cry. The woman got him hard without even trying to. He took her lips again. "Jed…" She said it into his mouth that time. He drank it right down.

So good, the fresh, clean scent of her, turning musky and mouthwatering as he stroked her bare thighs and rubbed at her soft belly and then slipped his fingers around to unhook the clasp of her bra.

"Oh!" she cried. "I know what you're doing, Jed," she scolded as the clasp gave way.

He chuckled, something he didn't do every day. Then he eased her shirt off her plump shoulders and peeled off her bra. Now, he had her naked from the waist up and he felt really good about that.

Until she suddenly rediscovered the concept of modesty and brought up her arms to cover those round, ripe breasts he'd been waiting to see for weeks now. "Don't do it, Elise." He caught her wrists, one and then the other, and guided them back down. "Hold on to the counter."

She let out a low whimper of sound, but she did what he told her to.

He went to work on the cutoffs, undoing the metal button at the top, sliding the zipper down. Her little panties were pink. She wouldn't have them on for long.

"Lie back," he instructed.

"This is very unsanitary. Jed, we eat lunch here."

"Shh. Lie back."

"Oh, dear..." But she did it, went over onto her back. She stared up at the beamed ceiling and whispered, "This is so not me."

"Elise." He stroked both palms down one glorious thigh, over her knee and her calf to her boot. "Take my word for it." He pulled off the boot and dropped it to the floor. "It's you."

He took the other boot next, and then the little yellow socks she wore underneath them.

"So pretty." He moved in close again, bending over her where she was spread out on the counter, his own personal feast. He cupped both of her full breasts, one in either hand. All soft and white, they just happened to fit his palms exactly right. And then he spent a few minutes kissing her pretty pink nipples, taking turns on one and then the other, until she couldn't hold back her moans and she lifted her hips to him, rocking, begging him with that lush body of hers to give her more.

He had more for her.

He had lots and lots more.

The Daisy Duke cutoffs had to go next. He hooked his fingers under the waistband on either side. "Lift up."

She whimpered in protest. But she lifted. He whipped them down and tossed them away. He left her the panties, for the moment. They were so innocent and pink and he wanted to look at them, wanted to play with her through the cotton and lace.

He took her hips and pulled her right to the edge of the counter, moving in good and close, so his body opened her legs for him. And then he bent over her again.

"Jed, I…"

"Shh…" So much to enjoy. He hardly knew where to start.

He got to work, kissing. Touching. Biting a little, exploring the sweet, shadowed places—behind her ear, along the lush under curves of her breasts. And lower.

Her belly called his name. He answered with his lips, his tongue, the edges of his teeth, dipping into her navel, biting the beautiful rounded curve below it.

She wiggled and moaned and then whimpered, "Jed?"

"Hmm?"

"Do you have, you know, condoms?"

"I do."

"I keep thinking this is a bad idea."

"Thinking." He dropped a line of kisses along the lacy top edge of her panties. "That's your problem. You shouldn't be thinking. Stop."

"But I—"

"Shh…" He put his open mouth against her mound, right over the pink cotton that covered her from his sight.

"Oh, my goodness…"

He had to agree. The scent of her alone was pure heaven. A man could die happy with the smell of her around him. He drew in a big breath and he released it against the pink-covered core of her.

"I... Oh! Oh, my!"

"Baby, you are the hottest thing." He kept kissing her, breathing against her, heating her further through her little pink panties.

"But I'm not, I... Oh. My. Golly." She speared her fingers in his hair. "Oh, now that! Jed!"

"Hmm?"

"Yes! Please! That."

He chuckled again. Tonight he was a chuckling fool. He ached to have her, to just tear those panties right off, rip his fly wide and bury himself in her, hard and deep.

But half the fun was making it last, driving both of them crazy, making both of them burn. He slid his hand up her thigh again as she wriggled and moaned for him. "Wet," he whispered against her core, easing a finger in under the elastic, then nudging it aside farther with his nose. Silky. Hot. Dripping with need. "So wet, sweetheart. So fine..."

She clutched at his shoulders. "I never get like this..."

"You do now. And I like you like this. I like it a lot." And enough with the panties. Now they were just in his way. He used both hands, taking one side and then the other, tearing them at the seams, ripping them away.

With a sharp gasp, she lifted her head off the counter and accused, "You just ruined my panties."

"Sorry, beautiful." He tossed the torn pink scraps over his shoulder. "They had to go. Now, where was I?"

"Oh, my goodness..." She let her head fall back.

And he lifted her thighs, hooked them over his shoulders and bent to his work. She was so wet and open and ready, slick and eager, defenseless against him. He tasted her deeply, using his fingers, too, as she rocked and moaned and pulled at his hair. She was sweet and salty on his tongue, drenched and so willing now, opening her legs wider as he kissed her. She'd flown right past her own objections. She was no longer afraid.

She offered him everything, all of her.

He would definitely take that: all of Elise.

"Oh!" she cried again and pumped her hips faster, letting her thighs fall open even wider, bracing her feet on his back. He speared his tongue in, stroked her faster and deeper with his fingers and stuck with her as she climbed toward the finish.

When she shattered, he held on, riding it out with her, drinking her sweetness as she chanted his name.

Chapter Seven

Several minutes passed.

Elise was gone. Done. Finished. She felt as though she'd left her body behind, as though she floated near the ceiling, that she was nothing but a moonbeam, a thoroughly satisfied shimmer of pale, vibrant light.

Except, wait. No. She was very much in her body. She felt every inch of her own skin, every bit of her that Jed had stroked and kissed and driven to the kind of spinning, churning, mind-altering climax she'd only read about in books.

From some brave space within her, she gathered all her courage and lifted her head.

Jed, way down there between her still-open legs, looked up from the cradle of her thighs. His face was wet. From her. "So good," he said, and he bent close again to place three kisses—on her left thigh, then her right and finally on that place in the center where he'd just rocked her world. "Beard burn." He brushed more kisses on the scruff-red skin of her unabashedly open thighs. "Sorry…"

"Don't be." She reached down and touched his hair again, so thick and coarse against her fingertips. "It's kind of tingly. Feels good." Her legs were shaking a little. She eased them off his shoulders, put her arm across her eyes and indulged in a moan of total disbelief. "On the kitchen counter, no less. This can't be real."

"Sweetheart, take my word for it. This is as real as it gets." He rose from between her thighs and then bent over her. He pressed a kiss just below her navel. She lowered her arm to look at him again. "And we are not done yet," he said, his voice a low rumble, barely a whisper, deliciously rough. "Not by a long shot." He kissed his way upward along her body until they were face-to-face. "We're going up to my room now."

"Oh, I don't know if we really ought to do that."

"*I* know. We're going." He took her hand and pulled her to a sitting position. Then he clasped her waist and helped her down to the floor.

She looked around at her boots and her socks, her shirt, her cutoffs and her torn underpants all strewn across the floor. "I feel really, really bare right about now."

"It's a great look for you—and don't even think about trying to cover up."

"Let me at least pick up my—"

"Nope." He stopped her with a hand on her shoulder. "We're going upstairs and we're going now."

"Easy for you to say. You've still got all your clothes on, but I'm supposed to bounce through the house buck naked."

"I'm going to let go." He squeezed her shoulder. "Don't you dare move a muscle."

"I don't see why we have to—"

"Don't. Move." He said it in his master-of-the-universe voice.

And then he let go of her—and stripped. She stood there and stared with her mouth hanging open. He did it so fast, dropping everything to the floor where he stood.

And did he ever look good when he was done. There wasn't an inch of him that wasn't buff and hard and honed to perfection. He was fully erect. And large. Very large.

She gulped.

He said, "It's going to be fine, Elise. Better than fine. You do it for me in a big way and I'm not letting you out of my arms for the rest of the night." And then he grabbed her and scooped her high against his chest. He didn't even grunt at the effort.

She linked her hands behind his neck. "You'll probably get a hernia hauling me up the stairs."

"Shut up and enjoy the ride." He said it so tenderly, the way another, gentler man might declare undying love.

With a sigh of surprisingly happy surrender, she wrapped her arms around his neck and tucked her head under his chin.

His room was even bigger than hers. It took up half of the second floor and had tall windows on three walls. There was a sitting area the size of a giant living room, complete with a big-screen TV and a fireplace of volcanic-looking rock with an enormous rough-hewn slab of wood for a mantel. The bed was on the same grand scale as the rest of the suite, with a roughly carved headboard, the bedding in brown, black and bronze.

But they didn't make it to the bed.

Not right away, anyway. Jed carried her over the threshold, knocked the door shut with his heel and then let her down to the rug, which was thick and fur-like and covered most of the floor. She was barely on her feet before he was hauling her close again, kissing her deeply. She could feel him, every inch of him, hard and hot along the front of her, his erection pressing into her belly.

How did he do it? She'd never considered herself a particularly sexual person. Letting go wasn't easy for her. Her mind wouldn't stop working. She obsessed over really unsexy stuff—like what if they got fluids on the comforter and why hadn't she thought ahead to grab a towel?

But with Jed, it was different. With Jed, she'd just experienced the best climax of her life. Because he stayed with her; he refused to give up on her. When she'd fretted about the extra weight she'd put on, he called her perfect, soft and curvy and womanly. If she complained because he ripped her panties, he simply said those panties had to go and then put his mouth where she'd never liked any man to kiss her—and blew her mind.

The man had focus in all things.

Including having sex.

And somehow, he got her to focus, too, got her to center her mind down to her senses, to revel in the feel of his big, hard hands on her soft flesh, to glory in the wonder of his hot mouth opening on hers.

The kiss at the door went on and on, his tongue playing with hers, his teeth nipping at her lower lip.

He stroked those big hands along her back, tracing the bumps of her spine. He took a fistful of her hair and pulled on it slowly, insistently, until the kiss broke and she let her head fall back.

He growled low in his throat, a hungry sound, as though he wanted to take a big bite out of her. And then he did take a bite, more or less. He bent his head to her, latched on to the side of her neck and began sucking rhythmically.

Oh, my goodness gracious. She felt that sharp kiss so deep inside, as though a shimmering hot thread connected them, from his wet mouth through her eager flesh and down into the core of her. She ached with wanting. And what she wanted was for him never to stop.

She knew she would have a bruise there. So what? She loved it—loved the sting of his teeth, the warmth of his breath, the stroke of his tongue, soothing her and simultaneously stirring up sparks of sensation that made her shiver. And burn.

And when he clasped her shoulders and gently pushed her down, she didn't even hesitate. She went to her knees on the thick, fluffy rug, opened her eyes and gazed happily up over the thick, ready length of him.

Green eyes gleamed down at her. "Taste me."

Elise didn't hesitate. She made no excuses, didn't fall all over herself explaining that she wasn't any good at going down on a guy.

She didn't have to make excuses. Not with Jed. She just stuck out her tongue and licked him, a long, slow stroke, following the ridge of that thick, twisty vein from the base to the tip, where a pearl of moisture gleamed.

She licked that up, too. It tasted like the wind off the ocean, musky and fresh at the same time.

"Elise," he said. *Elise*, as though her name felt so good on his tongue he wanted to roll it around in his mouth for a while. His fingers grazed her cheek, wandered to her temple, combed through her hair. "More, sweetheart. Please."

So she gave him more. She reached up and wrapped her hand around him. He groaned at that. And then she opened her mouth and took him in.

He didn't fit. But she did her best and he wasn't complaining. He only said, "Harder. Tighter. That's it…"

She took him in and let him out, sucking him back again, using her hands to stroke him, to make him say her name like it was the only name he'd ever known, to wrap his big fingers around the back of her head, cradling her, guiding her…

Until he swore low and commanded, "Stop. Or I'll lose it," which sounded like a fine idea to her.

But he wasn't having that. He caught her face between his hands and his eyes were twin green flames burning down at her. "Come up here. Come on…"

She went, gathering her shaky legs under her and rising. He took her shoulders, steadying her. And then he kissed her, his tongue spearing in, tasting her so deeply, so thoroughly, that her knees grew weak again and threatened to give way.

Before they did, he lifted her and took her to the bed, where he laid her down so gently, you'd think she was fragile, some tender, young breakable thing.

She waited, gazing up at him, loving the sheer masculine beauty of him as he opened the bedside drawer, took out a condom, unwrapped it and rolled it down over his thick, hard length.

Sheathed, he just stood there, watching her as she

watched him. "Look at you," he said in that low voice that promised an endless array of impossible delights. "I could gobble you up, just start with your pretty pink-painted toes and keep going until I had every inch of you."

In her life, she'd felt attractive now and then. Kind of pretty, maybe, at times. But never had she felt truly beautiful.

Not until that moment. When Jed Walsh stared down at her spread out on his bed and said he could eat her right up.

He came down to her and took her in those hard, hot arms, kissing her, touching her, his hands gliding over her, both possessive and tender. Sliding a knee between her legs, he eased her thighs wider, making room to settle himself between them.

She took his weight with a willing sigh. And then he was reaching down, clasping her under her knees, guiding her legs up to wrap around him.

Once he had her as he wanted her, he levered up on his arms, framed her face between his hands and kissed her some more. Oh, she could feel him there, nudging her right where she wanted him.

"Jed. Jed, please…" And she reached down between them, wrapping her fingers around him to guide him in.

He didn't get far.

"Tight." He buried his head against her throat and groaned the word onto her skin. "And perfect. So hot and wet…"

She whispered, "Jed," and added a soft, pleading "yes" for good measure. It had been a long time for her, not since Sean, her last bad boyfriend, almost two years ago now. But she was burning—burning for Jed, wanting him, all of him, and wanting him now.

Still, he was careful. He took it slowly, by aching degrees, stretching her, filling her, stopping after each gentle thrust to give her body a chance to accept him, to make the transition from discomfort to fullness to outright pleasure.

At last, she had him all the way.

He was so still then, so still and so deep within her, filling her completely.

"Jed. Please…" She tried to move.

"Don't," he commanded. "Wait."

"I can't…"

"You will."

"I need…"

"I know."

She was breathing so hard, needing to move with every nerve in her body.

And then, at last, he did move; he withdrew. She moaned, frantic. Afraid she would lose him. But he gave one of those rare, rough chuckles of his and came back to her.

After that, it was so right, a rising wave of sensation. A river of it, flowing through her, into him and back to her again. It started slow and deep and then it was faster.

Harder.

He sat up, pulling her with him. And she was in his lap, her legs around his waist, her feet hooked at his back. She was moving on him, frantic and needful— then sighing and slow. He said things, raw things that only drove her higher, only made it better.

Hotter.

Deeper.

And then he said, "Now, Elise." Only that, only *now* and then her name.

It was all she needed. Her climax rolled through her, violent and beautiful. It lifted her so high and sent her tumbling. There was a shiver of hot light behind her eyes. She felt him go over, felt him pulsing inside her as she hit the peak and began the slow, weightless glide back into herself.

When she came back to the real world again, she was still sitting on his lap, her legs and arms twined around him.

He brushed his lips against her cheek. "Come on, now," he said and carefully guided her to stretch out with him, so they lay on their sides facing each other, her right leg draped across his thigh.

He was still inside her. She wondered how he'd managed to get them down to the pillows without slipping free. The guy kind of amazed her. He had more moves than his alter ego, Jack.

And speaking of moves, she needed to get going, get back to her own room. Maybe he would let her borrow a T-shirt or something. Really, she should have insisted on bringing her clothes when she let him carry her up here.

He put his big hand on the side of her head. "You still with me?"

"Of course." She tried on a smile. It only wobbled a little. "But I should get going, huh?"

"No, you shouldn't." He said it chidingly, and he stroked the hair back from her temple. "You're staying here with me tonight."

No, she wasn't. She needed to get back to her own room. She needed a little distance now, needed some time to herself to…regroup.

She chewed the corner of her lip as she tried to decide what to say.

But he spoke first. "I'm going to go and get rid of this condom." He bent close for a sweet little kiss. Her heart felt like a giant toothache, throbbing away in the cage of her chest. "Do not leave this bed while I'm gone."

"Look, Jed—"

"I'm going to need your word on that, Elise."

Well, okay. Now that she thought about it, she had to admit it would be beyond tacky to just get up and get the hell out the minute he left the room. She might be feeling a little bit shaky now that they'd done...all that they'd done. But she wouldn't just turn tail and run. Or at least, she wouldn't now that he'd gone and busted her on it ahead of time. "Okay. I'll be here."

"That's my girl."

It sounded way too good when he said that. But of course she wasn't really his girl. She needed *not* to make this more than it was.

He kissed her again and then rolled away from her. Rising, he eased off the condom, inspected it for damage and tied it off. Then he turned and started for the bathroom.

She watched him go. He looked so fine. There ought to be a law against a body like his. It really wasn't fair that just looking at that butt of his walking away had her longing to have sex with him all over again.

He disappeared into the other room. As soon as he shut the door, she jumped up, threw back the covers and climbed in between the white sheets. Plumping a couple of pillows at her back, she leaned against the headboard and breathed a sigh of relief as she covered herself.

She'd barely gotten settled when he came back.

He lifted the blankets and slid in beside her, his hard, hairy leg brushing hers as he sat against the headboard, too.

She waited a minute, thinking maybe he would say something first and then, whatever he said, she could just start arguing with it. Because she was not staying here all night. Yes, she was crazy for him. But she really shouldn't have let this happen. She needed this job too much.

And the silence was getting to her. She had to say something. "Look. What just happened was incredible. I, well, I really appreciate it."

"You're welcome," he said drily.

She made herself look at him then, all scruffy and muscled up. How had he gotten so incredibly good-looking? It just wasn't fair. "But seriously, Jed. I need to go back to my room and this can't be happening again."

He took her hand. "It can and it will. Stay."

She looked in those eyes of his and felt foolish. And also inexperienced with men, though she wasn't. She'd had boyfriends. She had experience. And experience had taught her that love didn't work out for her.

Not that this was love. It was way too early to call it anything like that. Yeah, she was falling for him, but how far and how deep remained to be seen.

And that scared the hell out of her. "I just, my life is a mess and this job means everything and I can't afford to be having sex with the boss."

He eased his big arm around her and drew her close to his side. She should pull away. But she didn't. It felt too good to have him hold her. It felt like she mattered to him. That what had happened—on the countertop, in this bed—was a good thing, a natural thing. Not just another stupid move in the never-ending chain of her own bad life decisions. "The boss really, really wants to have sex with you. And the boss sees your value. The last thing he would want to do is drive you away."

"Will you stop talking about yourself in the third person, please? It's kind of creeping me out."

He almost smiled. She could see a little twitch at the corner of that mouth she couldn't help wanting to kiss again. "You've got this job, no matter what happens between the two of us. I would be lost without you—I *was* lost without you. But then you came along and saved my sorry ass. Now Jack McCannon will have book number six and he can give up the endless chain of meaningless hookups and find a real girlfriend. All because of you. There is no way, no matter what happens, that I will ever want you to stop working for me."

She touched his beard-rough jaw in wonder. "Jed. That was beautiful."

He grunted. "I've been told I'm a caveman, but I try."

"I have to point out, though—"

"Of course you do."

She scowled at him. "This isn't funny."

He scowled back. "You're right. I am not laughing. Continue."

"It's just that if you go and break my heart, *I* will want to leave."

"I would never break your heart."

"Well, not that you would want to. But it does happen."

He leaned closer, nuzzled her cheek. "I have a suggestion."

"You are being much too wonderful. You know that, right?"

"It must be your civilizing influence."

"Okay, that's a little *too* wonderful. Dial it back or I'll start thinking you're trying to manipulate me."

"But I am trying to manipulate you—to stay here with me for the rest of the night."

She sighed and laid her head on his shoulder. "Well, guess what? I think it's working."

He pressed his lips into her hair. "Excellent. And how about this? Why don't we just play it by ear and not borrow trouble?"

"But I'm always seeing all the ways things could go wrong. I can't help it. Things *have* gone wrong for me and I just want to keep them from going wrong again."

He trailed his fingers up and down her bare arm. The slow caress soothed her. And excited her at the same time. "Stay with me," he whispered. "Please."

She took his hand, laced their fingers together and rested them against her heart. Because she did want to stay. And clearly, he still wanted her here. Shyly, she admitted, "You're amazingly convincing."

His fingers tightened on hers. "I'm going to consider that a yes."

She snuggled in a little closer. "So. I'm guessing you probably have your own bathtub in here..."

"Yours is bigger than mine," she said with a pout ten minutes later, when they sat in his jetted tub with bubbles all around them.

Jed sat behind her. He had her right where he wanted her, cradled between his legs. She'd piled her hair up and managed to twist it so it stayed on top of her head and she leaned back against him, so soft and sweet, every inch of her a blatant invitation to do more wicked things to her.

"Yes, my tub is bigger," he said. "And if you're very, very nice to me, I will share it with you often."

She wiggled against him. He tried not to groan. "I get the feeling you really do like having me here."

"And soon, I intend to show you how much."

"Um." She tipped her head back and looked up into his eyes. "A name came to me. For Jack's girlfriend? I don't expect you to use it, but I can't resist telling you, anyway."

"Go for it."

"Sadika. Sadika Niles."

He liked it. "It's good. I'm stealing it from you."

She giggled. "You can't steal it. I'm *giving* it to you."

"Thank you—and you're giving me ideas."

She wiggled again. "I can feel them."

"I'm talking about Sadika."

"Yeah. Sure you are."

He put his hands on her shoulders and stroked his way down her bubble-covered arms to her hands. "Sadika Niles is in her thirties. She's black, a surgeon. From a well-to-do family…or wait. A preacher." He wrapped his hands around the back of hers.

"She's a preacher? That's odd." She spread her fingers and he eased his between them.

"Not Sadika, her father. John Niles is a minister. In Biloxi, Mississippi. And Sadika is on duty in the ER at Manhattan General the night the one-handed man, whose name will turn out to be Vanko Tesler, is admitted, near death, after trying and failing to kill Jack. Sadika performs the extensive touch-and-go surgery that saves Tesler. But the next night, when she goes to check on her patient, she witnesses his execution by a hitman sent by K." The mysterious K, an international arms dealer and general scumbag, had appeared in four McCannon books so far.

"So the one-handed man dies?" Idly, she lifted their linked hands from the water. Bubbles slid off before she lowered their arms below the surface again.

He bent close to press a kiss against the side of her neck. "Elise. It's a Jack McCannon novel. A lot of people have to die."

"Mmm." She tipped her head to the side, allowing him better access. He took total advantage of that and nipped gently at her smooth, damp flesh. "Watch it," she warned, but in a low, throaty voice that contradicted her complaint. "I've already got one hickey. I don't need another. Deirdre will wonder what we get up to when she's not around."

He licked where he'd nipped her, caught a loose curl of dark hair and tugged on it with his teeth. "I don't care what Deirdre thinks."

"Well, I do." But then she turned her head enough that he could claim her mouth. They shared a long, lazy kiss, during which he eased his fingers from between hers and put his hands where they longed to be—over her wet, bubble-covered breasts.

"Where was I?" he asked when she turned back around and settled against him again.

She made a sweet little humming sound as he rubbed his thumbs across her hard little nipples. "Sadika witnesses the execution of the one-handed man in his hospital room."

"Right. And Jack finds out there's a witness and he's

there in her apartment when she gets home just before dawn. K's men come for her."

"Jack has to protect her." She laughed in delight. "And they're on the run together. You should have Jack get injured and she has to operate on him under less than optimal conditions."

"Absolutely."

"And maybe Sadika eventually has to kill that sexy assassin, Lilias, in order to protect Jack."

"Hold on. I'm kind of fond of Lilias."

"Well, I'm not. Especially if she goes after Jack, she really needs to die."

He wanted her facing him. So he took her shoulders and floated her around until those glorious breasts were pressed to his chest and his aching erection nudged her belly. "You are a bloodthirsty creature."

Her mouth was a soft O, her eyes low and lazy. "You make me...different. You make me feel things I've never felt before."

"I don't make you anything. You are what you are, Elise. Womanly. Sexy. Smart..." Beneath the bubbles and the cooling water, he traced a finger over the curve of her hip and inward, parting the soft, neatly trimmed hair between her lush thighs.

A moan escaped her. "Again?"

He dipped a finger inside. "Don't pretend you're surprised." And then he claimed that mouth he couldn't get enough of kissing.

A few minutes later, he pulled her out of the tub and licked off the bubbles that cascaded down her luscious wet curves, going to his knees for a while to enjoy the taste of her, then rising, sliding on a condom, backing

her to the wall and lifting her. She wrapped those beautiful legs around him and he eased her down onto him.

After that, he kind of lost touch with reality for a
while. Her soft heat surrounded him, her scent filled
his head and he drank her sweet cries off those lips that
whimpered his name as she reached her climax.

A little later, he carried her back to bed, turned off
the light and settled her in close to him, her round, soft
bottom tucked just right in the cradle of his thighs. He
waited until her breathing evened out in sleep before
he allowed himself to join her there.

Elise opened her eyes to darkness and the scent of
cinnamon: Jed. He was all around her, his huge, heavy
arm in the crook of her waist, his big hand cupping one
breast. She felt…engulfed by him.

It was far too pleasant a sensation. Arousing, somehow. Her whole body ached. But in a good way. A well-
used way.

She could too easily get accustomed to this—to Jed
holding her in sleep. To waking up beside him. To plot-
ting his stories while lazing around with him in that
giant tub of his.

And to the sex.

Oh, God. The sex. A pleasured flush swept through
her just thinking about the things they'd done.

Jed moved. His hand closed a little tighter on her
breast. It felt delicious. She almost arched her back to
press herself closer to his palm.

But then he let go. His arm left her waist. He rolled
away from her.

She lay very still and listened to his breathing. Even
and shallow. Sound asleep—and so far away now,

turned on his other side across the wide expanse of the bed.

The clock on the nightstand glowed at her—3:10 in the morning. She stared at it as a minute crawled by. And then another and another after that. As she watched the glowing numerals change, all the doubts he'd banished with his wonderfully flattering reassurances came creeping back.

Now, really. Did she honestly want to be here naked in this bed with him when daylight came?

It could be awkward. Awkward and strange and very likely embarrassing. And, well, she just didn't want to deal with that. There was no reason to deal with that. She had a perfectly lovely bed of her own downstairs. She could wake up in the morning in the privacy of her room and pull herself together before having to look in Jed Walsh's green eyes after he'd seen everything she had under her clothes. Seen it up close and from a whole lot of potentially unflattering angles.

Nope. Waking up to daylight in Jed's bed was not going to happen.

Moving at a snail's pace so as not to disturb him, she eased from under the covers, slid her feet to the floor and crept to the door. It opened for her without a sound.

Wigs sat waiting on the other side. "Mrow?"

"Shh, now." She shut the door behind her. Scooping up the cat, she headed for the stairs.

To get to her room, she had to pass the kitchen and the clothes all over the floor in there. Deirdre would be here tomorrow, sometime between eight and nine.

It should be fine. Elise would set the alarm for six and have everything picked up and put away long before the housekeeper arrived.

But after she and Wigs were safely in her room, well, those clothes just nagged at her. She kept flashing on images of Deirdre standing there in the kitchen, blinking in bewilderment at the bra tossed on the island counter, the torn panties on the floor.

So she put on her robe and went back out there. She gathered up Jed's clothes, folded them neatly and set them on the first step of the stairs, his boots beside them. Then she grabbed all of her stuff and took it back to her room.

By then it was twenty minutes to four. She put on some comfy sleep shorts and a frayed racer-back T-shirt, climbed into her bed, pulled the covers over her head and assumed there was no way she would get back to sleep.

But apparently, she dropped off rather quickly.

The next thing she knew Jed was bending over her. Even in the darkness, she could see enough to realize that he didn't have a stitch on. You'd think if he just *had* to break into her room in the middle of the night, he could have put some pants on first. "Elise. What the hell?"

She blinked at her bedside clock. Ten after four. And then she grumbled, "What are you doing in here?"

Apparently, Wigs didn't get it, either. "Mrow?" he asked from the foot of the bed.

Jed didn't bother to answer either her or her cat. He just tossed back the covers, gathered her into his arms and carried her back up the stairs with Wigs following happily along behind.

Chapter Eight

Elise slept in Jed's bed from that night on. Jed made it perfectly clear he wanted her with him. Why try to escape him when she only wanted the same thing?

She knew it wasn't wise or the least bit professional of her, to be the boss's plaything after working hours. She probably ought to be ashamed of herself.

But she wasn't.

She felt much too happy to be ashamed. She loved every minute she spent in his bed. As it turned out, it wasn't awkward or uncomfortable in the least to wake up beside him every morning. He made it crystal clear that he liked waking up with her there. Opening her eyes to morning light with Jed wrapped all around her? She'd never had it so good.

And making love with him just kept getting better. Every time she had sex with him, it was the best of her life.

So far.

With Jed, she shed her inhibitions along with her clothes. He made her feel like a goddess in bed. And after a lifetime of considering herself boring, fussy and repressed, seeing herself through Jed's eyes was pretty darn fabulous. Whatever happened in the end, how could she regret spending her nights with a smoking hot man's man who thought she was sex on a stick?

She worried a little in the initial few days of being his lover that his writing might suffer and he would rethink the wisdom of boinking his assistant, that he would tell her they had to go back to how it had been before.

But no. On the contrary, his book seemed to be going better than ever.

He said she inspired him, that the story just flowed. He claimed it was a lot because of Sadika, whom he'd introduced the morning after that first night. Sadika was turning out to be strong, sharp-tongued and capable, a woman even the great Jack McCannon didn't dare mess with. Jed thought Sadika brought out a whole other side of Jack—the dark side, where his heart lay hidden. Jed said he hadn't realized that Jack was getting a little stale until Sadika showed up and Jack had skin in the game again, someone who mattered, someone worth fighting for.

More than once in the two weeks after he first tore her panties off, Jed carried her upstairs during writing hours. She got lucky each time and Deirdre didn't spot them. Elise knew it was cowardly of her, to want to keep the personal side of their relationship strictly between them. But so what? She just wasn't ready for anyone else to know.

And sex during working hours? With Jed, it was

every bit as amazing as sex any other time. Just a little more urgent, somehow. They would make love hard and fast and then they would talk. About the story, about whatever element wasn't quite working. He said she was a great sounding board. He liked to bounce ideas off her, find out what she thought of them, get her take on how he might resolve any problems that cropped up.

She really liked hashing out story points. She could do that forever—unlike the typing, which she couldn't be finished with soon enough. When Jed completed this book, she would miss a lot about being involved in his writing process. But typing? If she never typed another sentence, it would be much too soon.

Nell and crew showed up the last Tuesday in July to begin construction on the catio. Elise took special care when her sister was there not to give Jed any smoldering looks, not to stand too close to him and definitely never to touch him. She did not want her sister to know that there was anything more than work going on between her and her boss. If Elise and Jed were still together when the book was through and she returned to her own life, that would be the time to let her family know that they were an item.

Bravo Construction did good work and they did it quickly. A week later, Mr. Wiggles had his own personal backyard. He loved it. He climbed the cat runs and hid in the hidey-holes, basked in the August sun and stalked the birds that flitted beyond the wire fencing.

Besides the fire pit and the Adirondack chairs, Jed had decided to add a comfy outdoor living room to the patio. He'd also had Nell install a fancy grill and a sink and counter space—essentially an outdoor kitchen. That way, after work, they could join Wigs outside.

The first Friday in August, Jed grilled chicken out there and Elise baked potatoes and whipped up a salad. They sat down to eat at the cast-iron table not far from the fire pit.

Elise was spooning sour cream onto her potato when he asked, "So what's on your mind?"

She plunked the spoon back in the tub of sour cream. "What do you mean?"

He shrugged. "Just now you were biting your lip. And you keep shooting me glances when you think I'm not looking. You're building up to hitting me with something and you're not sure how to go about it."

How did he do it? He read her like a billboard. Sometimes that made her feel special and important to him. Sometimes, like now, she had to tamp down annoyance that he found her so transparent. "My half brother Carter is getting married a week from Saturday."

"I know. You and Nell talked about the wedding that night she came for dinner."

"I need the afternoon off so that I can be there—and yes, when you hired me I agreed to work all day, every day, six days a week. I should have asked for my brother's wedding day then, but I had a lot on my mind and I just didn't think of it. Then, later, I kept putting off asking because I was afraid you'd say no and, given our agreement, you would be perfectly within your rights to say no and then I would have to decide whether or not to make some sort of stand about it. And then we made love and now I'm sleeping with you and I feel like I would be taking advantage of our intimate relationship to ask you—"

"Enough." He waved a chicken leg at her. "It's not

a problem. We're ahead on the book. Take the whole day off."

She picked up her fork and set it down without using it. "Seriously? I've got the whole day? Just like that?"

He nodded. She was about to leap up, run around the table and grab him in a grateful hug when he added, "Will I need to wear a tux, or what?" She sank back into her chair. Being Jed, he only had to look at her face to know what she was thinking. "So. You weren't planning on taking me."

"Well, Jed, it's only that I…" Ugh. Whatever she said next, it wouldn't sound good.

"I'm waiting, Elise. That sentence is never going to finish itself."

She let out a hard breath, sucked in another one and tried again. "If you go with me, my family will know that we're seeing each other—I mean, you know, dating, or whatever. That I'm not just your assistant, you know?"

"Yes, Elise. I do know. And you're *not* just my assistant. You're…" He let the word trail off as he drank from his water glass and set it back down with care. "What shall we call you? I don't especially like the word *girlfriend*. It's weak. *Lover* sounds vaguely reprehensible. And this isn't just an added-benefits situation, either. It's more."

"Well, yes, what we have is really good and I love it, Jed. I love being with you, I truly do, but—"

"What you are, Elise, is mine. My woman. And my woman does not go to her half brother's wedding—or anyone's wedding, for that matter—without me."

Her panties were suddenly wet. He went all caveman on her and she loved it. But still. She didn't want her family to know that she spent her nights in his arms. Not yet, anyway. It was much too soon to be anybody's business but hers and Jed's. "If my family knows that I'm more than just your assistant, they're going to worry about me. You know I've made bad choices. They know it, too. I just don't want to deal with that."

"Deal with what, exactly?"

"Oh, come on. Most of the time you read my mind, but now I have to draw you a picture?"

"Just say it, Elise."

"Fine. I can't deal with knowing that *they* know I'm sleeping with the boss."

"But you *are* sleeping with the boss. It's a fact. And you just said that it's damn good between us. It's nothing to be ashamed of."

She couldn't hold back a pained cry. "You don't know them. They're so protective—especially of me since I screwed up my life. At least one of my brothers is going to get you aside and tell you that you'd better treat me right, or else."

"Well, I do treat you right and I'm happy to tell your brothers that I do. No problem."

"And Nell. God, who knows what Nellie will do? I love her and I'm grateful for all the ways she's got my back. But she thinks she's big mama grizzly or something. She'll be threatening to kick your ass if you break my heart."

He waved a hand. "It's not a big deal. Nell has already threatened to kick my ass in regards to you. Twice."

She wanted to scream. "Excuse me? I didn't know that. Why don't I know that? You never said a word about it."

"I knew it would only freak you out and I was happy to reassure your sister. End of story."

"When?" she demanded.

"'When' what?"

"When did my sister threaten to kick your ass?"

"The first time was when I called her and asked her to make this cat patio."

"What? No, she didn't. We weren't even sleeping together then."

"Yes, she did. And no, we weren't. That time she only meant I'd better treat you right on the job."

"Oh, great. Fabulous."

"The second time was a week ago, after she and her crew had been working on the patio for three days. She called me outside under the pretense of approving some tweak she'd made to the outdoor kitchen layout. I joined her by the grill, at which point she grabbed my arm, dragged me into the trees and said she wasn't an idiot and it was crystal clear to her that you were doing more for me than typing my book."

Elise facepalmed. "Just shoot me now."

Jed went right on. "She threatened to make a eunuch of me if I ever made you cry. I reminded her that you were a hell of a woman and thus bound to cry now and then. I told her I planned always to be there to dry your tears."

Elise lifted her face from her hands. "You did? You do?" Now she definitely felt like crying.

"Yeah."

"How can you say such wonderful things?"

"One, I mean them. Two, I have a certain facility with words."

She blinked away the tears and sat up straighter.

"It's beautiful, what you just said. But I really think I need to remind you that it's much too early to be saying such things to other people, even my sister, about you and me."

His sexy mouth twitched at the corner. "I didn't know there was a schedule I was supposed to be following."

"It's only been two and a half weeks since that first time. We shouldn't rush into anything."

"I'm not rushing anywhere. I'm right where I want to be."

"And I'm glad." Her throat clutched with emotion. "I'm where I want to be, too." Her food was getting cold. She picked up a chicken thigh and had a bite, then she ate some of her potato.

"Elise." His voice had that tone. Absolute and unwavering. "You're not going to that wedding without me."

She wanted to cry again. "If Nell knows, Jody knows. And Clara, too, probably. And maybe my cousin Rory. And possibly Chloe, my half brother Quinn's wife. All my brothers probably know too, by now."

"So it's a done deal. Move on."

"Easy for you to say. You're not the family screwup."

"You're no screwup. Your family loves you and that makes them protective of you. And you're far too proud for your own good." He said it softly. Tenderly. And that made her want to go jump in his lap, wrap her arms good and tight around his neck and beg him to take her to bed right this minute. But then he added, "And you can look at it this way. If I don't go with you, they're all going to think you mean so little to me that I didn't even bother to take you to Carter's wedding. Your brothers will beat the crap out of me and Nell will cut off my—"

"Stop it. All right. I give."

He sent a glance heavenward. "Finally."

"You won't need a tux. A suit or a sport coat and slacks will be fine. It's outdoors. One of those scenic wedding venues not far out of town."

He gave her a look that smoldered and teased at the same time. "You haven't even asked me yet."

"Right. A minute ago I wasn't *allowed* to go without you. Now, suddenly, you need an invitation."

Those eyes of his swept over her, heating all her secret places. "I want you to ask me. Do it."

"You realize I have no privacy in my life. Somehow, my family always knows whatever's going on with me whether I want them to know or not. And *you* can read my mind."

He put his napkin by his plate and stood. She gazed across at him looming over her. Beneath her irritation that he couldn't just accept her defeat on this without rubbing it in, she felt that special shiver. It was glorious, that shiver.

Even if what he'd said a minute ago about always being there to dry her tears were only pretty words, she knew he wanted her more than any man had ever wanted her before. More than she'd ever dared to hope any guy ever would.

It meant so much, the beautiful, intense, complete way he wanted her. It meant everything. She'd thought she was falling for him the day he told her he would enclose this patio for Wigs. But she hadn't known what falling was. Every day she fell deeper. There seemed no end to how far she could go. And with Jed, she wasn't afraid of her feelings. With Jed, she gloried in the fall.

Wigs, sitting near his feet, looked up at him expectantly. "Mrow?"

He glanced down at the cat. "It's only right that she asks me."

Wigs tipped his head to the side and replied thoughtfully, "Mrow."

And then Jed's eyes were on her again. "Well?"

She surrendered a lot more willingly than she would ever let him know. "Jed, will you please take me to my brother's wedding a week from Saturday?"

He wrapped those muscled arms across his wide chest and studied her for a moment that went on forever. "Come here."

Her heart did the happy dance inside her chest. "Will you or won't you?"

"Come here first. And when you get here, I want you to kiss me nice and slow."

Like there was any way she could resist an order like that. She rose and circled the table. Taking his face between her hands, she went on tiptoe to claim his lips, so soft and warm. His beard scruff scratched a little. It felt absolutely delicious.

He kept his arms across his chest. But slowly, he opened to her, let his tongue spar with hers. She did love the taste of him: smoky sweet from the barbecue sauce, with the added promise of any number of intimate delights to come.

When she dropped to her heels again, she asked, "Please?"

He uncrossed his arms at last and put a finger under her chin. "So we're understood about this, then? We are together and we're proud to be together and we don't give a good damn who knows it or what they think about it."

"That's easy for you to say. You never care what anyone else thinks."

"And neither should you. Are we understood?"

She gave in. Because he was right and because she adored the big lug. "Yes. We're understood. Will you go to the wedding with me?"

"Yes, Elise. I will." And then he whipped out an arm, hauled her good and close and kissed her until her knees gave way.

Carter Bravo and Paige Kettleman were married at six in the evening on the terrace at Belle Montagne Chateau ten miles outside of Justice Creek.

After the ceremony, they all moved inside for the reception, including a sit-down dinner for eighty. Paige and Carter had originally planned to use Bravo Catering for their reception. But then the business burned down. Elise had helped them find another caterer.

She'd assumed she would feel low on entering the banquet area and seeing the beautifully set tables, the floral centerpieces that Jody had designed. She'd just known that it would break her heart a little to watch the staff, in black slacks and vests and crisp white shirts, serving another caterer's menu.

But she didn't feel bad in the least. The dinner was beautifully done and Elise knew now that, thanks to Jed, she would have Bravo Catering up and running again, maybe even before the year was out.

So it wasn't a sad time at all. As it turned out, she was having a ball. Carter and Paige looked so happy and Quinn's speech as best man brought several big laughs and also a tear or two.

Jed was amazing. He looked so good in a gray silk

suit that hugged his wide shoulders perfectly and fit just right over his lean hips and muscular legs. He actually visited with people. He was friendly and seemed genuinely interested in what the older lady seated on his other side had to say.

Elise realized she'd never seen him in a social gathering before. She supposed she should have known he'd be capable of holding up his end at a party, should have realized it wasn't that he *couldn't* say all the right things and put people at ease. It was only that most of the time he just didn't bother. He was Jed Walsh and he made his own rules.

But tonight, he was charming. He joked around with Nell and went off to smoke a cigar with two of her brothers—and returned to the table looking completely relaxed.

She leaned close to him when he folded his big frame back into the chair beside her. "Did they threaten you in any way?"

"Get over it, Elise," he replied. "Your brothers are good guys. There were no threats. Not a one—and who's that blond guy over there, the one who keeps staring at you?"

The guy in question gave her a wincing sort of smile and a limp wave. "He's an old friend, that's all."

"Does your old friend have a name?"

Jed was so protective of her, she hesitated to tell him. But if he wanted to know, he would find out one way or another. Like Jack McCannon, Jed was always on the case. "His name is Biff."

"The dirtbag who borrowed money from you and then declared bankruptcy so he 'couldn't' pay you back?"

"He's been my friend since we were children."

"Some friend."

"Jed, he had a very tough time of it."

"Lots of people have a tough time of it."

"He's not a dirtbag."

"He is from where I'm sitting."

She whispered, "Keep your opinions to yourself, please. At least until we're alone—and I can't believe you remember who Biff is. I only mentioned him to you that one time."

"I remember everything you tell me." Across the room, Biff had started moving. "And the dirtbag is coming this way."

Oh, dear God. Jed was right, Biff was coming over. Did he have no instinct for self-preservation? "You let me handle this, Jed." Jed made a low snorting sound much too reminiscent of a bull about to charge. "I mean it," she warned. "If you can't say something nice, you'd better not say anything at all." She turned to Biff as he kept coming—which meant she couldn't see Jed. But she could sure feel his seething silence behind her.

"Elise." Biff, blond hair tousled, blue eyes full of regrets, stopped beside her chair. "It's so good to see you."

"Biff." She got up and gave him a quick hug and an air kiss, though she knew it wouldn't go over well with the snorting beast behind her. "How've you been?"

"Not good."

"I'm sorry to hear that—Biff, this is Jed. Jed Walsh, Biff Townley." She turned and blasted a giant, threatening smile at Jed.

Biff's hand came out. "So great to meet you. I heard you'd moved back to town. I love your books."

"Thanks." Jed had not risen. His face had that Mount

Rushmore look: carved in stone. He did give a nod, but made no move to take Biff's offered hand.

After several painful seconds, Biff gave it up and lowered his arm. "Ahem, Elise, I wonder if I might have a minute alone?"

"Of course," she said pleasantly. And then she turned to Jed again. "I'll be right back."

"All right." He spoke without inflection. Then he looked straight at Biff. "I'll be waiting." Somehow, he made that sound like a warning.

Biff actually flinched. "Er, great to meet you."

Jed didn't even nod that time.

Elise brushed Biff's arm. "Come on out to the terrace." She glanced back at Jed as she hustled Biff toward the wide steps that led outside. Jed was watching her walk away, his gaze brooding and dark.

"I think your boyfriend hates me," Biff said once they were out on the terrace beneath the tall trees.

Elise perched on the rock wall that defined the giant circular stone space. She was about to pretend Jed's re-action was nothing. But that seemed wrong, somehow. Biff *had* treated her shoddily and she'd never had the guts to confront him about it. Jed did have the guts.

And she was with Jed now. If he could tell the truth, well, so could she. "Jed is protective of me. I told him about the money I lent you that you never paid back."

Now Biff looked crushed. "I *couldn't* pay you back. You know that."

"No, Biff, I don't. Not really. Are you telling me that when you borrowed that eight thousand dollars from me, you actually believed you were going to repay it?"

Biff raked his fingers back through his hair. "Look, Elise. I just wanted to say that I've missed you, okay?

I miss hanging out now and then. I miss that I could always count on you, on your level head and good advice, on the great dinners you would cook to make me feel better when my life was going all to hell."

Elise carefully smoothed her silk skirt. "You didn't answer my question."

"Well, I—I *wanted* to pay you back. Of course I did."

"When *will* you pay me back, Biff?"

He stared off toward a granite peak far in the distance. "Seriously? You want to get into this now, at your brother's wedding?"

"No time is a good time when you don't pay your debts." From where she sat, she could see the archway to the banquet room. Jed came through it. She met those green eyes and gave a slight shake of her head. He took her cue that she didn't need him—not yet, anyway. Moving to a tree-shaded spot on the outer edge of the archway, he waited.

And she knew why. Because she was his woman and he took care of what was his.

Her heart seemed to expand in her chest and great tenderness flooded her. Elise had known she was falling for him, and that she kept falling deeper. But it was not until that moment, when he came out on the terrace just in case she might need him, that she realized she had fallen all the way.

She loved Jed Walsh.

Chapter Nine

"I didn't come out here to be insulted," Biff huffed.

Elise hardly heard him. She was much too busy dealing with what had just happened in her heart.

I love him. I love Jed.

It was real. It was true. It was the most beautiful thing that had ever happened to her.

"Did you hear a word I just said?" Biff demanded.

"Not really." Elise kept her eyes on the big man standing in the sun-dappled shadows by the door to the banquet room. "I don't think we have much more to say to each other as of now, Biff. You have my cell number. Come up with a payment plan and give me a call."

"But I just *told* you—"

"You take care now." With a wave of her hand, she dismissed him. As she started toward Jed, he left his spot by the door and came for her. They met in the middle of the terrace. She needed to touch him, so she reached up and smoothed the lapel of his jacket.

He caught her hand. "I hope you put the dirtbag in his place."

"I think I did. More or less." She gave a half shrug. Biff Townley hardly mattered, not when every fiber of her being was vibrating with sheer happiness. Music had started up in the banquet room. "Will you dance with me, Jed?"

He kissed the tops of her knuckles and her heart felt bigger, her knees weaker in the sweetest sort of way. "Never was much of a dancer."

"Does that mean yes or no?"

"You want to dance with me, you got it." He wrapped her hand around his arm and led her back beneath the archway to where the music played.

That night, she told him she loved him—or rather, she shouted it good and loud as he pulsed inside her. A little later, when he turned off the lamp, held her close and stroked her hair, she wondered if it could be possible that he hadn't really noticed her yelling, "Oh, Jed, I love you!" minutes before.

He didn't say anything about it.

And she didn't ask. Let him chalk it up to one of those things a woman says in the heat of passion. She did love him, yes. With all of her heart. But she wasn't really ready to talk about what that might mean yet.

Monday morning, just as they were sitting down to a breakfast of poached eggs, toast and cantaloupe wedges, Jed's publicist called.

"It's official. A week from Friday, I'm on *NY at Night,*"

Jed said when he hung up the phone. "We'll fly in Thursday, returning Sunday."

Elise kind of wondered if she'd heard him right. "You're serious? You're going to meet Drew Golden and be on *NY at Night*?"

Wearing a look of great boredom, he sipped his coffee. "Isn't that what I just said? And it's damned inconvenient if you ask me. I hate a break in my rhythm when things are moving right along."

She chuckled at that. "You hate a break in your rhythm anytime and you know it."

"True. But it's a big freaking deal to get a spot on Golden's show, just ask my agent."

"Well, I have to say that *I'm* thoroughly impressed."

He drank more coffee, watching her face as he sipped and swallowed, his eyes low and lazy. "Hmm. I like you impressed, all pink-cheeked and adoring."

She spread jam on her toast. "*Adoring* might be carrying it a bit far."

"Maybe I should take you back to bed. You can show me just how impressed you are with me and my many accomplishments."

Okay, the plain fact was she did adore him and she would love nothing so much as to go straight back to bed with him. But then again, it was a lot of fun to give him a bad time. "I never said I was impressed with *you*, exactly."

He ate some cantaloupe. "But you are. Thoroughly. I'm an impressive guy."

"Egotistical much? And what's this *we*? I take it you think that I'm going with you to New York."

"Because you *are* going with me."

She was thrilled that she was going and she loved him more than life itself. But sometimes he needed reminding that he didn't actually rule the world. "I don't recall your inviting me."

"Ah. You need a special invitation, do you?"

"Yes, I do. Remember Carter's wedding?"

"As though I could forget. It was two days ago."

"I'm referring to how you insisted that I had to ask you to go with me."

"That was only right."

"Well then you should have no problem understanding how I might want you to ask me if would like to go to New York with you."

"You're my assistant. It's your job to be where I need you." He said it in that low, rough voice that sent little flares of excitement pulsing in her most secret places.

Still, she didn't give in. "So you're planning to write while you're there?"

"I just might."

"But you said we would be flying back on Sunday and Sunday is my day off."

He frowned. "Wait a minute. Are you saying that you really don't want to go?" He looked marginally worried.

And her heart melted. "Let me lay it out for you. I'm giving you grief because you just assumed I would do whatever you wanted me to."

"But you *are* coming with me?"

For such a brilliant man, he could be dense as a post. She said nothing, just gave him a moment to figure it out.

Finally, he did. "Elise."

"Yes, Jed?"

"Will you please go with me to New York next week?"

"Why, Jed. How lovely of you to ask. I would be delighted to go."

For that, she got one of his rare half smiles. "Excellent—
and I still think I need to take you back to bed."

"What for?"

He set down his spoon, pushed back his chair and
came for her, scooping her up in his arms the way he
loved to do. "Come on upstairs. I'll show you."

And he did, to their mutual delight.

A week and a half later, they left Wigs in Deirdre's
care and flew first class to JFK.

Elise tipped her roomy seat back, accepted a glass of
champagne and sipped it slowly. "I haven't flown first
class in forever."

Jed looked up from texting his social media assistant. "Ever been to New York?"

She had another sip of delicious bubbly. "Twice. Both
times first class, too. When I was eighteen, my great
aunt Agnes took Tracy and me to shop for our senior-
ball dresses. Aunt Agnes always flies first class. Then
in college, Tracy and I got one of those package deals—
hotel, dinners at a couple of nice restaurants, two Broad-
way shows and first-class flights. That was a great trip.
We walked all over Manhattan."

He watched her in that special way he had that made
her feel wanted and understood and totally fascinating.
"How long's it been since you've seen Tracy?"

"Not since mid-May, when she left for Seattle."

"When will she come back to Justice Creek again?"

"She'll be home for Thanksgiving—at least that's the
plan as of now. But you never know. She's mentioned
a guy she likes. If that goes somewhere she may want
to be with him for the holiday."

"You miss her."

"Yeah. But it's not as bad as it used to be." *Not since I fell for you—and kept on falling. Right into love.* "She's happy and I'm happy for her."

He tipped his head to the side, studying her. "So you're not secretly longing to hop a flight to Seattle?"

"No. I meant what I told you weeks ago. Tracy and I had years together. Great years. She'll always be a sister to me and we both know we can count on each other if things get too rough. But our lives have gone in different directions now and I'm good with that."

His gaze never left her face. "So are you saying that *you're* happy now?"

She leaned across the wide armrest to slip her arm through his. "Very. And I have a lot to be happy about. Thanks to you, my bank account is no longer on life support. The future looks bright in a number of ways. Plus, here I am on a first-class fight to New York—with you, which is the best part of all."

He leaned even closer and whispered in her ear, "You never know. You might decide to stay with me when the book's done, after all."

The way she felt right now, she never wanted to be anywhere else. But something in his expression had her wondering if he imagined she might remain his assistant, too.

Then again, no. She'd made it more than clear that this one book was the only one she would type for him.

So instead of reminding him of their original agreement, she whispered teasingly, "Stay with you? You'd better watch out. I just might never leave."

He had that look then, the one that melted her panties. "I was hoping you would say that."

And then he kissed her, slow and sweet.

* * *

They had a suite at the Knickerbocker right on Times Square, but with a beautiful view of Bryant Park. The rooms were all cool grays and misty blues. Very soothing. And the bathtub was waiting.

Yes, they got a little bit distracted and spent more time than they probably should have enjoying that tub together and also the very comfy king-size bed. Elise had to hustle to be ready in time to meet Jed's agent and editor for dinner. She'd brought a little black dress to wear and breathed a sigh of relief when the dress fit pretty well. True, it was snug where it had once flowed loosely over her waist and hips. And about her cleavage? She had a whole bunch more of that than before. It was kind of spilling out a little.

She turned to ask Jed if the dress made her look fat. One look in those smoldering jade eyes and she knew that if she *did* look fat, it totally worked for Jed. She faced the mirror again and grinned at her reflection. The dress would definitely do.

"Beautiful," he said in that gruff tone that told her he wouldn't mind getting that dress right off her again. He started toward her. She could see him coming over her shoulder.

She showed him the hand in the mirror. "Don't even think it. We have to go."

Jed's agent, his editor and a vice president from his publishing house were all waiting at their table when they entered the restaurant. The host seated Elise next to Jed, with his agent, Holly Prescott, on her other side.

Elise had a good time with Holly. The agent, who dressed like a fashion model and weighed maybe ninety pounds soaking wet, was a little like Jed—gruff and direct, smart and funny.

The men carried on their own conversation as Holly peppered Elise with questions on everything from her family and her previous occupations to how she liked working with Jed. Elise told the other woman that she was a caterer by profession. She said that she and Jed worked great together, but typing for a living wasn't her idea of a good time. "Which is why I only agreed to be his assistant for this one book."

Holly frowned. "But given that you two work so well together, maybe you'll reconsider, change your mind and stay on with him…"

Elise answered honestly. "No way. It's a great experience, working for Jed, and I'm enjoying it. But it's not forever. I'm not spending my life at a desk. Working for Jed now is going to make it possible for me to reopen my catering business, hopefully soon after this book's done."

In the meantime, she heard the vice president, Dan Short, describing Jed's bright future with his publisher. Carl Burgess, Jed's editor, got all excited when he heard that Jed was two thirds through the rough draft of the new book, which had the working title *McCannon's Fall*.

"So it's going well at last," Carl said with clear relief.

And Jed gave a dry chuckle. "Don't jinx me, Carl." He turned to Elise. "But yeah," he said, his eyes only for her at that moment. "I'm back on track and it feels really good."

Jed seemed happy and relaxed when they all walked out together after the long meal was through. Carl and the vice president hailed cabs and left. Holly said she needed a quick chat with Jed—nothing major but it would take a few minutes. At Jed's suggestion, Elise went back inside and ordered an Irish coffee at the cozy bar in the front of the restaurant.

From her corner stool, she could see Jed and Holly with their heads together standing under an awning not far from the entrance. Really, she had no clue what could have come up that Holly just had to share with Jed immediately…

Jed had been listening to Holly talk without really saying anything for close to ten minutes when he decided he needed to cut through the yadda-yadda and get back to Elise. "Stop trying to be subtle, Holly. It's not your style."

"Well, I hate to overstep my bounds, that's all."

"Oh, come on. When has a boundary ever slowed you down before?"

Holly narrowed her sharp eyes at him. "Don't be an ass. It pisses me off."

He let out a bark of laughter. "That's more like it. What's on your mind?"

"It's Elise."

His gut tightened. "On second thought, watch your mouth."

Holly raised a placating hand. "Stop. I like her. Carl and Dan liked her. And I can tell you like her, too—a lot more than you've ever liked anyone, if you ask me."

"Yes, I do. Get to the point."

"You're together, right? And I don't just mean during working hours."

"We are absolutely together. And we're staying that way."

"Which is great. I've never seen you this happy or this relaxed. And being happy and relaxed clearly works for you. Suddenly you're flying through the book you got nowhere on for a year."

"Whatever you're getting at, you're not there yet."

"Fine. Elise told me she's going back to catering as soon as you've finished the manuscript."

That had him falling back a step. "What did you say?"

"I said, Elise told me—"

"Never mind. I heard you." Okay, he knew Elise wasn't solid yet on continuing as his assistant. But on the plane, she'd said she was thinking about it. Didn't she? "*When* did she tell you she was going back to catering?"

"While Dan Short was describing all the big things they're going to be doing for you when *McCannon's Fall* comes out."

Crap.

How could he not have known this? How could he have read her so wrong when he could tell just by watching her face what she was thinking? He'd been so certain that he was making progress with her, that she was slowly realizing she wanted to stay.

Because she *had* to stay. Now that he'd found her, there was no way he could lose her. He'd never find another assistant like her.

She left even Anna in the dust. And it wasn't only her ability to type while he shouted and threw things. Elise had great instincts when it came to the story, to the characters. Yeah, he got advice and feedback on the books from Carl and Holly, from his virtual assistant and a number of copy editors and beta readers. But he'd never had anyone to bounce things off of day-to-day before. He didn't give his trust easily; critique groups and writing buddies weren't for him.

If he lost Elise...

But he wouldn't.

The woman loved him. He saw it when he looked in those dark eyes of hers. She'd even said it in bed the night of her brother's wedding. True, she'd been having an orgasm at the time. But he knew that she'd meant it by the nervous glances she'd sent him later, by the way she'd watched him the next morning at breakfast, shy and sweet. Hopeful, but not really ready to talk about it yet—or at least, that was how he'd read her signals that morning.

Had he read her all wrong about loving him, too?

He didn't think so. She cared for him. He knew she did. And she wanted to stay with him.

Now he just had to make her see that she should stay with him professionally as well as personally. He needed to get her to admit that there was no way throwing parties for strangers could beat what he had to offer her, financially speaking. And creatively, too.

"I just thought I ought to let you know," said Holly.

"Thanks."

"You've still got time to change her mind."

"Yes, I do."

"And, hey. Think of it this way. If it doesn't work out, you were looking for an assistant when you found her."

For that, Holly got his deadliest stare. "She's not going back to catering, don't worry."

Holly let out a slow breath. "Well, good. Because frankly, we've already learned the hard way that there aren't a whole lot of assistants who have what it takes to type your books for you."

Chapter Ten

When Jed slid onto the bar stool beside her, Elise leaned into his solid strength. Loving him was a revelation to her. All he had to do was move in close and the world got warmer and brighter.

She asked, "Everything all right with Holly?"

He wrapped an arm around her and pressed a kiss to her temple. "Fine. She had some suggestions for the interview tomorrow—how's the Irish coffee?"

"Delicious."

"Want another?"

When she shook her head, he grabbed her hand and pulled her out into the slightly sticky warmth of the August night.

It was a little after ten. They strolled around Times Square for a while. Elise enjoyed the lights and hurrying crowds.

But she liked it even more when he took her back to

the hotel, peeled off her tight black dress and showed her how glad he was that she'd come to New York with him.

The next day, they had room service for breakfast. Jed had a visit to his publisher's offices at eleven, followed by a working lunch with Holly, the publicity team and more publishing executives, so Elise had several hours on her own.

She spent some "me" time in the hotel spa, had a room-service lunch and then took a cab to Bloomingdale's, where she spent more of her recently hard-earned cash than she probably should have on a new flared skirt, silk top and sexy high-heeled shoes to wear to the *NY at Night* taping at five.

A limo took her to the studio, where she was ushered to a great seat on the aisle in the third row. Jed had the first guest slot after Drew Golden's monologue.

And Jed was good. Really good. He seemed totally relaxed, joking with Drew Golden as though the two of them were BFFs from birth. After a quick synopsis of Jed's personal history, from growing up as the only son of a bona fide survivalist, to a little about his years in the service, they talked about the first Jack McCannon book and how each one had sold better than the last.

Jed leaned back in his chair with one ankle hitched across his other knee and joked about the ways to kill people. "Because I have to tell you, Drew. Jack McCannon knows them all."

They talked about the potential for a series of Mc-Cannon movies. Jed said that he and his team were working on that. And then Golden had questions about the development of the McCannon character through the books so far, about what would change in Jack's life going forward.

Jed said, "Jack will be meeting a woman he can't walk away from, a woman who changes the direction of his life."

Drew Golden chuckled. "Is it possible that life is paralleling fiction here?"

Jed put it right out there. "Absolutely."

"Can you tell us about her?"

"Only that she's brilliant and beautiful, that nothing gets past her and I don't know how I ever got along without her. I even like her damn cat. And I hate cats."

That got a laugh and also a round of enthusiastic applause.

Blushing, Elise clapped, too. She felt like the heroine of her own personal romantic movie. Jed not only cared about her, but he was also willing to say so in front of a nationwide audience.

After the show, a production assistant came and led her backstage, where Jed was waiting. He put his arm around her and nuzzled her hair. "God, you're gorgeous."

She confessed, "I spent way too much money in Bloomingdale's."

He pulled her closer and whispered, "I like your new clothes, but I like what's under them even better."

She shook a finger at him. "Later for that." And then she smoothed the collar of his sport coat, feeling tender and fond and so very proud of him. "It went so well. You were really good."

"Did I say too much?" He sounded almost hesitant.

And she was blushing all over again. "Not too much. No way." She put a hand to her heart. "I'm keeping those words you said right here, storing them up, you know? To remember for all of my life." And then she couldn't resist a little teasing. "Especially the part about how you actually like Wigs."

He introduced her to the publicist and one of the *NY at Night* producers. Feeling dazed and happy and out of her element, but not really in a bad way, she smiled and said how great it was to meet them.

Finally, Jed took her out through a door backstage. The guy from the publicity department went with them, but then flagged down a cab and left.

Elise watched him go. "So…dinner with more publishing people?"

He shook his head. "Tonight and tomorrow, it's just you and me."

As it turned out, Jed didn't write a single word that weekend. He wanted a little time apart with Elise and he took it.

They had dinner that night at his favorite café in the Village. And Saturday, they visited the Arms and Armor collection at the Met, took the subway to the best pizzeria in Bedford-Stuyvesant and had dinner in a rooftop garden, the guests of a writer friend of his in Queens.

Saturday night, he kept her up very late. He couldn't get enough of her, really. Sexually, she managed to be shy and adventurous, funny and alluring all at the same time. They made love on just about every available surface in the hotel suite and when she finally fell asleep in his arms, he brushed the tangled hair off her forehead and tried to decide how to deal with what Holly had told him.

He still had two months until his deadline. Should

he bring it up now, ask Elise to reconsider their original agreement, to think about what would sweeten the pot enough to make her give up on the damn catering thing and stay on with him? Or should he play it out to the end and knock her socks off with some kind of terrific, irresistible offer she couldn't refuse? Whatever the hell that might be...

On the flight home to Justice Creek, he was still trying to decide which way to go.

Elise noticed. Which shouldn't have surprised him. It was one of the many things he loved about her. Nothing got by her for long.

He was staring off toward the door to the cockpit, endlessly considering his limited options, when she asked if something was bothering him.

It was a good opening. But he wasn't ready to make his move yet—mainly because he hadn't decided what that move should be. "Just working through a few plot points."

"I'm here if you need to talk about it."

I'm here...

Exactly. And she needed to stay here. With him, in every way. If only he could figure out how to make her see that.

The Thursday following the New York trip, when Elise checked her phone right after lunch, she found a text from Biff Townley.

I thought about what you said, Elise. And you were right. I have your money. Where should I send the check?

She didn't know whether to be pleased that he was finally coming through, angry that she'd had to tell him off to get him to pay up…or worried that maybe he couldn't really afford to give her the money back.

Pleased, she decided. Biff had borrowed that money over a year ago and he'd promised to return it to her within a month or two. It wasn't her problem how he'd finally come up with it.

So she texted back a thank-you and Jed's address. She'd had most of her bills and correspondence rerouted here. That way she didn't have to stop by her apartment every Sunday before making a run to the bank or whatever.

Plus, the way things were going between her and Jed now, she might never move back. She grinned like a fool at the thought.

Her phone beeped. Another text from Biff: I saw your boyfriend on NY at Night. The guy's really gone on you, huh?

I'm gone on him, too, so it's working out great.

They say he's a little bit crazy.

Elise scowled at the phone. Biff was way more annoying than she'd ever realized before. She replied, Yeah. In a very good way.

Ha, ha. I get why he's gone on you. You looked amazing at the wedding. Sexy. That bit of total squickiness was followed by a heart-eyes emoji that had Elise full-out gaping at her phone.

Biff Townley texting a move on her? That was just wrong.

What are you up to, Biff?

I told you at the wedding. I miss you. Meet me for coffee? It's been too long since we really talked.

Did you somehow not get that I'm with Jed now?

What? He doesn't let you see your old friends?

Where was this going? No place good. She texted back a final That was uncalled-for. You have the address. Send the check. Goodbye, Biff.

She hit Send and tossed the phone on the bed. If he came back with one more word of douche-baggery, she would block him and good riddance—even if he never gave her money back.

"Trust me?" Jack tried a reassuring smile. Sadika only stared at him, her incomparable face far too composed. "We have no choice. We have to jump."

Did she understand? Did she even hear him? He held those dazed eyes of hers for a count of five that they really couldn't afford. K's men were coming.

"No choice," he repeated, not happy with their chances. The river below ran cold and swift, ready to suck them under. But K's men would not be gentle, either. He wrapped her arms around his neck, lifted her and guided those long legs around his waist. "Hold on good and tight. Do not let go."

"Okay, what's the matter?" Jed watched Elise type the question and realized he'd failed to give the signal to stop. "Elise." Her fingers stopped moving. She assumed her waiting pose. It was a thing of beauty—her hands poised, shoulders relaxed. "We're taking a break."

She glanced up at him then. "Why? I think it's fine. Moving right along. What's not working for you?"

He looked down at her sweet upturned face. "It's you."

"Huh?"

"Something's bugging you. What?"

She gave him an eye roll and gestured at the screen. "Take a look. I don't think I missed a word you said."

"I know you didn't. You never do. But you were biting your lip. You even wrinkled your nose."

She laughed. "Wrinkled my nose?" She pressed her hand to her chest and faked a gasp. "No wonder you stopped me."

"You're trying really hard to blow me off. It's not working. Talk."

"Jed…" The woman could put a world of exasperation into the three little letters that made up his name.

"Come on." He held down his hand.

She eyed it warily. "Where?"

"Out to the catio. The sun is shining and your damn cat is always happy to see you." She laid her fingers in his and he pulled her up from the chair.

Outside, they sat on the sofa with the cat stretched out and purring on Elise's other side. She petted the big creature in long strokes, from his head to his tail. A smile curved her lips, but her eyes were far away.

"I'm waiting," he said.

Elise sagged back against the cushions. She *had* been distracted back there in the office. She kept thinking what a complete jerk Biff was.

And she'd kind of decided not to mention the texts to Jed. After all, she'd handled Biff. And Jed really was kind of a caveman. She had no idea how he'd react when he heard that Biff had put a move on her, even if it was only via text.

Jed hooked his big arm around her and pulled her closer. She settled her head on his shoulder. "Talk, Elise."

She gave in and told him. "I had a text from Biff Townley when I checked my phone at lunchtime."

Jed pressed his lips against her hair. "And?"

"He asked for an address so he could send me a check."

"So that's good news, then."

She sighed. "Yeah."

"Which doesn't explain why you were wrinkling your nose during the bridge scene."

"He pissed me off, okay?"

"How?"

She glanced up at Jed again. He was being wonderful and she was making him work for every smallest bit of information. She made up her mind. "Wait right here. I'll get my phone and show you."

He let her go without comment.

When she came back outside, Wigs was snuggled up close to him, purring louder than before.

She stopped at the sofa but she didn't sit down. "I'm going to show you these texts and you're *not* going to do anything about them."

He stared up at her, simultaneously lazy and predatory, the way Wigs sometimes watched the birds beyond the patio. If Jed had a tail, it would be twitching.

She added, "I've already handled the situation. There really is nothing for you to do."

He held out his hand. "Just give me the phone, Elise."

She dropped down next to him on the side Wigs wasn't already occupying, punched up the conversation in question and handed it over. He read it through quickly and passed the phone back to her.

"Well?" she demanded.

"The guy's a dirtball. It's not news—and you're right. You handled it. I promise not to hunt him down and punch his lights out. If I happen to run into him on the street, though, all bets are off."

"Thank you. I think."

He hooked his arm around her neck and drew her close to him again, pressing his nose to her cheek, breathing in, scenting her. "He's not worth biting your lip over."

"You don't get it."

"So explain it to me."

"I thought he was a basically good guy, okay? I used to consider him a dear friend. I would cook beautiful dinners for him and listen to him go on and on about how awful his wife was. And I would sympathize and top off his wineglass. Like *she* was the problem. I didn't even know Biff's wife, really, and I said a lot of bad things about her, and now I have to face the fact that she's probably the one I should have been feeling sorry for. I had my head up my ass for years, you know? And every time I have to face more evidence of my own past idiocy, it makes me want to scream."

He tightened his arm around her neck, pulling her close again so he could touch his warm lips to her ear.

His beard scruff tickled in the loveliest way. "Go ahead. Scream."

She elbowed him in the side. "Next you'll be giving me knives to throw."

"For that, there would have to be training." His low voice sent hot shivers racing across the surface of her skin. "That could be interesting, training you."

"Training me." She turned her head and kissed him, just a quick one, because she couldn't resist. "You make that sound really dirty."

He moved then, turning and rising in one seamless motion, his hand sliding down her arm to capture her wrist.

With a squeak of surprise, she found herself slung over his shoulder, blinking down at the patio stones. She hit him on the hard curve of his perfect butt because it was in easy range.

He grunted. "Do that again."

"I just might. And I shouldn't have to remind you that we have a page goal to meet."

"And we will. But first, I need to show you something up in my room."

"Let me guess. Your bed."

He didn't even bother to answer, just banded his arm around her dangling legs and headed for the French doors.

They met Deirdre on the way up the stairs. Elise realized she wasn't the least concerned that the housekeeper had finally witnessed the sight of Jed carrying her off to his lair.

Because, well, why shouldn't he carry her up to his room? She loved him and she was pretty sure he loved her, too, even if they hadn't actually talked about that yet. And come on, she *slept* in Jed's room. Deirdre had to have figured that out by now, anyway.

Bottom line: Elise was in love with the boss and she didn't care who knew it. She gave Deirdre a wave as they passed her. Deirdre grinned, nodded and continued down.

The next day, Elise got a letter and a big check in the mail. The envelope was creased, smudged and forwarded from her burned-down apartment on Central Street.

It wasn't from Biff. It was from her long-gone, struggling-artist ex-boyfriend, Sean. When she opened the envelope, she found a two-page handwritten letter and a check for twenty thousand dollars inside.

Her hands shaking only a little, she read,

Dear Elise,
I'm guessing you never expected to hear from me again—let alone for me to do the right thing and return the money you so generously invested in me. The hard truth is, I never planned to contact you again and I certainly never intended to give you back your money.

But it's been a long road for me. I have learned much about what's right and what isn't. And I have met someone special. Her name is Fiona. Fiona says that to walk in peace with the universe and realize my full potential as an artist, I must find a way to right every wrong I have perpetrated.

And let me tell you, Elise. That is a tall order...

A laugh burst from Elise right then. She was standing at the little built-in desk just off the kitchen area where Deirdre always left the mail. "Jed!" she called, and headed for the office where he'd remained while she'd walked the main floor during one of her five-minute breaks.

She found him leaning over her desk, studying the manuscript file she'd left open when she got up for her walk.

He rose to his height when she entered and she waved the check at him. "I just got a check for twenty thousand dollars and a letter from my ex-boyfriend, Sean. You have to read this…" Laughing, she went to him and held up the letter so they could read it together.

"Sean is a real piece of work," he said once they'd both reached the end.

"I sure knew how to pick 'em, didn't I?"

He sent her a wry glance. "At least you used the past tense when you said that."

"Of course I did. Because present company is definitely excluded—in fact, I think you must bring me good luck. If this check doesn't bounce, I've got my money back from Sean. And what I lent Biff is supposedly in the mail." She waved the letter. "Did you read the part where Sean says Fiona gave him the money to send to me?"

"Yeah, I noticed that."

She held up the check again. The account was in Sean's name and the signature was Sean's. "I really hope Fiona knows what she's doing. I kind of feel sorry for her."

"Don't." It was a command.

"But—"

"I mean it, Elise. He owes you the money. How he got

it to give it back to you isn't your problem. Plus, he says right in that letter that Fiona is 'a very wealthy woman.'"

"Right." She read from the letter. "'Fiona is a very wealthy woman and she's offered to support my art and help me get solid with the universe.'"

"Translation—Fiona is supporting him and also paying his debts, which is Fiona's choice, Elise, and not—"

"—my problem. I know, I heard you the first time." She thought it over a little more and then shrugged. "So okay, then. Fiona's on her own with Sean. Sunday, I'll put this check in the bank and in a week to ten days, I'll know if it's good or not."

He tipped up her chin and kissed the end of her nose. "That's my girl."

Saturday, the check from Biff arrived. And Sunday, Elise stopped off at the bank and deposited both checks.

After the bank, she went to her sister-in-law Addie's baby shower at Clara's house. Addie Kenwright Bravo had married Elise's brother James just last March. At the time of the wedding, Addie was already pregnant with the baby of her best friend, Brandon Hall, through artificial insemination. Brandon had died of cancer at the end of January. So technically, James was not the baby's father. But everyone in the Bravo family knew that James loved that unborn child as his own.

And they all loved Addie. She was small and spunky, independent and big-hearted, and today she was wearing a yellow dress printed with daisies. She looked like a walking ray of sunshine—or maybe a waddling one. A month from her due date, Addie seemed ready to pop.

They played baby-shower games: "baby sketch artist," "baby items in a bag" and "don't say baby." There was lunch and cake and champagne for anyone who wanted it. Addie opened a huge pile of baby gifts.

Later, Jody pulled Elise into a free corner of the kitchen and asked how she was doing.

"Terrific," Elise replied with enthusiasm. "Jed's an amazing guy and I'm happy, Jody. Really happy. I almost can't believe it. Two and a half months ago, my world was a total disaster. My love life was nonexistent, just like my bank balance. Now I have money in the bank and the greatest guy in the world thinks I'm the hottest thing around."

Jody beamed. "I saw you two at the wedding. Anyone could see he's crazy about you."

"It's mutual, believe me."

"You do have that glow."

"And I can't thank you and Clara enough. You put me to work, kept me busy and focused and made sure I didn't starve during the worst of it. And Nell... Don't tell her I said so. She thinks she knows everything. But I owe her large."

Jody put up a hand like a witness swearing an oath. "I will never say a word to her."

Elise laughed. "Whew."

"So, you'll be staying on as Jed's assistant, then?"

"God, no. I hate typing."

"But you're so good at it and Jed pays big money, right?"

"Money isn't everything—and yeah, it's easy for me to say, now I'm no longer destitute. I also happen to mean it. I am not typing one more word than I absolutely have to. Why doesn't anyone seem to understand that just because a person's good at something doesn't mean they're dying to spend their life doing it? As soon

as this book is done, so am I." She lowered her voice to
a confidential whisper. "But if it all works out the way
I'm hoping, I *will* be staying on with Jed."

Jody's smile was soft. "I love seeing you happy. And
it's about time." She held up her empty champagne flute.
"Don't move. I'm filling up my glass and then I have
something to propose to you."

Right on cue, Clara stepped up with a tray of full
ones. "More champagne, little sister?"

"You're a lifesaver." Jody switched out her empty
flute for a full one and they chatted with Clara for a
few minutes—about how great the party was, and how
big Clara's one-year-old, Kiera, had grown.

Then Clara moved off to share the bubbly with her
other guests and Elise picked up her conversation with
Jody where they'd left off. "What kind of proposal?"

"First, are you still thinking of opening Bravo Catering again?"

"I *am* opening Bravo Catering again. That was always
the plan. It was just that for a few really bleak months
there I had no clue how I would ever make it happen."

"Would you consider maybe going into partnership
with me?"

Elise got the loveliest rising feeling in her chest.
"Bloom and Bravo Catering, together?"

"Well, I mean before the fire, we did several weddings together, right? That went so well. And I liked
working with you when you were filling in at Bloom,
too. I think we make a great team. So I was wondering,
what if we formally combined forces? We could still
keep both companies, and look for a new, larger location, a shop where we would each have our own store,
but adjoining, you know? Two separate entrances, one

for Bravo Catering and one for Bloom, but we would design the space so the two shops kind of flow together. Food and flowers. I think it could be great."

Elise waved her hand in front of her face. "Jody. I think I'm going to cry."

"Good tears?"

"The best kind." Elise grabbed her sister and gave her a hug.

Jody hugged her right back, then took her by the shoulders to look in her eyes. "So you'll consider it?"

"Consider it? I love it. I'm in. And I'll have the money for it, no problem, thanks to Jed. But I'm working with him dawn to dusk on the book until he finishes the manuscript. I only have Sundays off and I need at least one day a week to run errands and decompress a little."

"I know. I get that."

"He's ahead of schedule, so maybe he'll be done early—sometime in October, if we get lucky. His deadline, though, is November first. I can't commit to anything until then. But I promise, Jody, from the first of November, I'm your partner."

Jody squealed in delight—and then clapped her hand over her mouth and shook her head, blushing. "Okay. I'm excited. Tell me, does it show?"

"Me, too. I really wasn't looking forward to being completely on my own."

"I know. I always envied you and Tracy, to have each other to count on. Now, *we'll* have each other. I'm so thrilled you said yes."

Elise got back home at a little after five.

She found Jed out on the catio with Wigs. "How are my guys?"

Jed patted the spot beside him on the sofa. She took it. He wrapped an arm around her and she snuggled close, resting her head on the hard bulge of his shoulder. He rubbed his scruffy chin against her hair and asked, "So how was Addie's baby shower?"

"You would have loved it," she teased.

A low, disbelieving sound rumbled up from his big chest. "Did you play those silly girly games —'pin the tail on the baby'? 'Bobbing for nipples'?"

"How do you even *know* about baby-shower games?"

"I'm a writer. I have to know a little bit about everything—plus, I went to a coed shower once, back when I was married to Carrie. The experience was one I would prefer never to repeat."

"Oh, you poor man." She patted his cheek.

"You need to kiss me and make it all better, wipe the memory of that terrible time from my conscious mind."

"I'm on it." And she kissed him, slowly and with a lot of tongue. "How's that?"

"I think I *might* be all right now."

"I'm so glad."

"But maybe you should kiss me once more, just to be sure."

With a happy laugh, she cradled his face and pressed her lips to his. When she lifted away, he tried to grab her close again. But she could not wait another minute to tell him about her conversation with Jody. She pushed at his chest. "I have news."

"About…?"

"I had a long talk with Jody."

He grinned. "You should see your face. Apparently, Jody had something really good to tell you."

"She did. She had an offer for me."

His arms loosened around her. "What kind of offer?"

She sat back against the cushions. "It's like this. As soon as the book is done, Jody and I are going into partnership together. We'll get a new space and combine her flower shop with my catering business." She kicked off her sandals and drew her legs up yoga-style. "It's a stroke of genius, perfect for both of us." A gleeful little laugh escaped her. "Jody suggested it and, well, I couldn't say yes fast enough. Not only will we do weddings together the way we were doing before I had to close down, we each get foot traffic from the other.

"I'm thinking I'll have a bakery area—great coffee and pastries, you know? I'll be open the same hours as Bloom. People come in to buy flowers and they can get a coffee and a muffin. Or they come for coffee and get tempted by Bloom. I can't wait to…" Her voice trailed off as the expression on his face finally registered.

He didn't look the least bit pleased to be hearing all this.

Chapter Eleven

You're not going into business with your sister, Jed thought but somehow had the presence of mind not to say. *I need you right here, working for me.*

This was bad. He should have had this out with her before she managed to go off and make a deal with Jody. But he'd thought he had more time—weeks yet—to create a workable plan, to come up with an offer so tempting she'd realize there was no way she could refuse.

What offer is that, exactly? mocked a knowing voice in his mind. *And what if she still refuses, no matter what you offer her?*

She'd never given him the slightest indication that she might change her mind and continue as his assistant after the book was done—except for that time on the plane to New York. But then he'd only *thought* she might stay on; he'd heard what he wanted to hear. She'd meant she would stay with *him*, not that she would keep typing his books.

And if he was any other man he would be telling himself he had to learn to accept her position on this.

But he wasn't just any guy. He had a certain process that worked for him and she was a big part of that process. She was not a cog in a wheel, easily replaceable.

Without her, the damn wheel didn't turn.

Well, you are going to need to replace her. Get over it and move on. The voice of reason in his head was calm. Logical. Right.

And he refused to listen to it.

That year after Anna left had been pure hell. He needed to find a way *not* to go through that again.

And if there was no way, if she was leaving no matter what once he finished *McCannon's Fall*, he damn well didn't want to know that now.

Now, the book had to come first. Having to accept her leaving would only mess with his mind and slow down his writing. That couldn't happen.

He would get to the end of the damn book and then find a way to convince Elise to keep working with him—so what if she had plans to work with her sister? Plans change.

And she was looking at him strangely now. "Jed. What is it?" She put her soft hand on his. "What's wrong?"

He ordered his expression to relax, even managed to form what for him passed as a smile. "Not a thing."

"But you seemed so—"

"There's nothing," he lied, turning his hand over, clasping her fingers, giving them a reassuring squeeze. "So. You and Jody, huh?"

She looked so serious now—because she knew him

better than anyone ever had before. She knew exactly
what was bothering him, which her next words made
painfully clear. "You said the day you hired me that if it
worked out with me, you weren't going to like it when I
left. I get that, I do. And I don't want to leave *you*—it's
just the job. Long-term, it's not for me."

"I understand. Don't worry. Everything's fine."

She wanted badly to believe him. He could see it in
those big dark eyes of hers. "You're sure?"

"Of course."

Elise *didn't* believe him.

He definitely had something on his mind that he
wasn't sharing. But she'd asked and encouraged—and
then prodded him for good measure. He didn't want to
get into it, whatever it was.

Well, okay. She would leave it alone until he was
ready to talk about it.

They went inside, had some dinner and watched a
movie in the media room downstairs. He took her to
bed and made smoking hot love to her.

That week, the book moved along at lightning speed.
Jed was really on a roll. At the rate he was writing, they
could be finished by the end of the month—a month
ahead of his final deadline. That would give him weeks
to go through it and clean it up before sending it on to
New York. He was pleased at his progress and he said so.

And when the workday was through, he was his
usual sexy, gruff self. By Friday, she'd all but forgotten
that something had been bothering him Sunday night.

A week and a day after Addie's baby shower, Elise
checked her bank balance online and found that both
Sean's and Biff's checks had cleared. Her nest egg was

growing by leaps and bounds. She called Jody and they agreed that Jody would keep her eye out for a workable location to lease—or to buy.

That week passed and the one after that. Jed was on the home stretch with *McCannon's Fall*, writing faster and better than ever, he said.

On the last Tuesday in September, Jody called during Elise's lunch break. She had news. The art gallery next to Bloom was closing immediately due to a family emergency. The gallery owner had three months left on her lease, but she wanted out now. Jody had already talked to the agent for the building. He said they would let the gallery owner out of the lease if Elise qualified to take it over. Elise could sign a contract for two years with an option to renew for another two. The agent also said Elise and Jody could open up the wall between the two shops as long as Elise signed a rider agreeing to make all the changes according to code and have the work properly inspected and approved—and to pay a nonrefundable deposit to rebuild the wall at the end of her tenancy.

Jody offered, "I'll pay to fix the wall for us if you put down the nonrefundable deposit."

"Sounds great to me. I've been through the gallery a couple of times. It's a nice space. I'll need to measure it, but I'm pretty sure I can put my kitchen in the back and a little bakery area with a counter and café tables in front."

At the rate Jed was writing, the rough draft could be done within the week. He typed his own rewrites, so he wouldn't need her for that. Maybe she would get lucky and be able to start working for herself again next month.

But even if he needed her right up until November

first, getting the shop next to Bloom for Bravo Catering was as good as it was going to get. Jody wouldn't have to shut down and reopen elsewhere and possibly lose customers in the process. They could build on what Jody already had.

"So are you saying we're going for it?" Jody asked.

"Oh, yeah. I'm in."

After she hung up with Jody, Elise called the agent for Jody's building. He agreed to meet with her on Thursday. Then she called her brother James. Addie's husband was the family lawyer. James said he would go with her to meet the agent.

That settled, Elise still had fifteen minutes left of her lunch break. Time enough to ask Jed for Thursday afternoon off.

She found him just where she expected him to be—in the office looking over the pages he'd written that morning.

He turned in the chair when she came in. "You're early. Eager to get back to work?" It was a joke. She always took the full hour at lunch to rest and recharge for the second half of the workday, which sometimes went past seven at night.

And why was her pulse suddenly racing and her stomach all queasy? All right, when he'd hired her she'd agreed to work all day, every day, six days a week. But surely he could spare her for a few hours on Thursday after more than three months of scrupulous adherence to his killer work schedule.

"Elise?" he prompted when she failed to say a word.

She had to make herself tell him and she hated how hard it was to do that. "I need Thursday afternoon off. The shop next door to Jody in the same building is becoming vacant on the first of the month and I'm going to take it. I need to deal with the owner's agent and get the paperwork going to make it happen."

Jed opened his mouth to remind her that she would be working for him on Thursday afternoon, that she knew very well what the job with him entailed when she took it.

That she damn well was not signing a lease on a space for a shop she was never going to open.

But he knew none of that would fly. She had a right to a day off now and then, no matter what unreasonable demands he'd forced her to agree to when he hired her. The book was a good two weeks ahead of schedule. And even if it hadn't been, his acting like a domineering ass wasn't going to help him convince her that she should stay on with him.

Uh-uh. To get her to stay, he needed to treat her right.

And also to stick with the plan—which was to do nothing until the book was done. So what if she rented a shop? He could pay the lease for her until another tenant came along and took it off her hands. It wasn't a big deal.

"We're ahead," she offered hopefully. "And I'll work Thursday evening if you need me." He rose from his desk and went to her, taking her by the shoulders, running his hands down her arms, linking his fingers with hers. She gazed up at him, apprehension in her eyes.

He squeezed her fingers. "Thursday afternoon is all yours."

Her sweet smile bloomed and she let out a sigh of obvious relief. "Wonderful. Thank you."

"I love it when you're properly grateful." He lowered his mouth to hers and banished all thoughts of her leaving from his mind.

* * *

Elise signed the lease for the shop next to Jody's that Thursday afternoon. She floated on air all the way back to Jed's house.

At dinner, she told him that Jody had already called Nell. Bravo Construction would open up the wall between their two shops and design an attractive iron gate they could close when one shop was open but not the other.

Jed seemed happy for her. He listened to her ramble on about where she might get her kitchen equipment at bargain prices and her vision for the bakery and how much she loved her family.

"The Bravos are really pulling together now," she told him proudly. "For years Nell and I couldn't stand each other and I thought Jody was a snake in the grass. We had all these jealousies, so many simmering resentments, you know? Because my father never could choose between their mother and my mother and essentially he had two families at the same time. We all felt cheated and we took it out on each other. But we've worked through it, united our family. Now, we're always finding reasons to get together. We *like* being together. Nell's got my back and I'd do just about anything for her—and Jody and I are business partners."

He brushed a touch across her hand. "I'm glad it's worked out so well with your family." He really did seem to mean it.

So why did she feel that something was off with him?

Let it go, she reminded herself. *He'll tell you when he's ready.* "So then—shall we work after dinner?"

He gave a low, sexy rumble of laughter. "I can think of better things than work to do after dinner."

They went upstairs early. He drew a bath and they shared it. She surrendered joyfully to the wonder of his big hands on her yearning body.

Had she ever been this happy?

No. Never.

After long months of worry and disappointment, she had everything: enough money, a new business she couldn't wait to make a big success—and most important of all, Jed.

She had love. Real love, deep and true. At last.

Now, if she could just get him to accept that she was moving on professionally...

A week and a day later, Jed got to the end of *McCannon's Fall*. They went out to dinner to celebrate.

The next day, she asked him if her work on the book was through. He evaded, said he had a few scenes that required serious reworking. He might need her for those.

Monday, he asked her to wait while he "organized the material." He went into his office and he didn't come out all day. That night, when she asked him again if he would need her, he said she should "keep herself available."

And in the morning, he did it again, went into his office to "pull things together" and didn't emerge for hours. When he did come out, he only said he was managing all right on his own "at the moment." He made himself two sandwiches, grabbed a bottle of water and disappeared into his office again.

That night at dinner, she'd had enough of waiting around all day for him to summon her when they both knew he wouldn't need a typist until he started the next book. "Can you just tell me the truth here? You really don't need me on this book anymore."

He took way too long to reply. And when he did, it was only to remind her of what they both already knew. "You're mine until November first. That was the deal."

"Yours. That's an interesting way of putting it."

He shot her a dark glance. "Figure of speech. You know what I mean."

"Yes, I do," she answered gently. "And I *am* yours as a matter of fact. I'm your girlfriend. Your lover. Your woman. All of the above. But as for being your assistant, you really don't need me for that anymore."

"We have an agreement. Until the first of November, *I'll* decide what I need you for."

She looked down at her full plate and realized she had no appetite. "Really?" she asked very softly. "You're going to play the big, bad hard-ass now?"

"November first," he repeated. "That was our deal."

"Jed—"

"I don't want to hear it."

For a moment, she just stared at him as the truth finally sank in: he refused to accept that she needed to move on.

Yep. Dinner for her was definitely over.

She rose, grabbed her plate, carried it to the kitchen and scraped the contents into the garbage bin under the sink. After giving her dish a quick rinse, she put it in the dishwasher and carefully shut the door.

Then she marched back to the table and stood behind her chair. Gripping the back of it, she tried to keep her voice even and calm. "I want to be with you. I think we have something good together. I love brainstorming your work with you. I'm happy to be your sounding board whenever you need one. But I don't want to type for a living. I don't know how to make myself any clearer on that point. I want you to admit that my part of this book is over. I want you to let me go."

He gave her a long, slow once-over. "Let you go," he repeated flatly.

She gripped the chair harder and tossed his own words back at him. "Figure of speech. You know what I mean."

He turned his gaze to his plate again and ate several bites of pork chop stuffing without saying a word. Just when she was considering grabbing her water glass and emptying it over his big, obstinate head, he looked up from his plate and into her eyes. "We need to talk." It was exactly what they needed. So why did she hate the sound of those words? "Sit down, Elise. Please?"

She yanked out the chair and dropped into it.

"I'm sorry," he said, his voice marginally gentler. "I just don't want to lose you."

"But you're not losing me. I'm not going anywhere."

"Yeah, you are. You're going to work with Jody. If you do that, I'm on the hunt for another assistant. And we both know how that's going to go."

She wanted to reach out, put her hand over his, to tell him she loved him and it would all work out. But would it? At the moment, she had her doubts. So she settled for repeating what she'd said way too many times already. "My leaving the job was always going to happen. That was our deal from the beginning. But I will still be here, still be with you, still be yours in the ways that really matter."

He shook his head. "You refuse to see it. You won't admit it. If you go to work with Jody, it *won't* be the way it is now. Until I find someone else I can work with, I'm going to be on edge. It's going to mess up what we have."

"You don't know that. You're in charge of your attitude and your behavior. If you can predict that you're going to act like an ass, then you can figure out a way to behave differently."

"It's not that easy."

"I never used the word *easy*, Jed. I only said that you don't have to ruin what we have because you're frustrated about work."

"Don't you get it?" He pushed the question out through clenched teeth. "I don't *want* another assistant. You're perfect for me in every way. I thought Anna was good, but you are a genius."

"Jed. It's just typing."

"No, it's not. It's everything. The way you listen. The stillness in you when there's a pause. The way you *know*. It's as though you're typing the words before I even say them."

"Thank you. I mean that. But it's just that I'm not intimidated by you, that's all. You'll find someone else who—"

"No, I won't. And I just don't understand why you'd rather be a shopkeeper than my writing partner."

A shopkeeper. She didn't like the way he'd said that, with a sneering curl to his lip and a grunt of disdain. She loved her work. What gave him the right to look down on it? She was seriously tempted to rise from her chair and walk out, just leave him alone with his half-eaten stuffed pork chop and his superior attitude.

But she loved him. So much. Enough to keep trying to get through to him. "Jed. Are you listening to yourself? First off, when it comes to your writing, I'm your assistant, not your partner and—"

"Wait." He put up a hand. "Stop right there."

She blinked and sucked in another calming breath. "Yes?"

"I do have an offer for you. I think it's a pretty good one."

"An offer?" Now he'd totally lost her. "An offer of what?"

"I'm up for contract. It's going to be a big one. If you stay, I'll bring you in as a co-author. You'll get thirty percent of the advance and royalties *and* your name on the next book right under mine."

Elise could only gape. She knew very well how huge it was for him to make her an offer like that. Was she tempted? It would be a *lot* of money. And prestige. She would be famous. Her throat clutched. "Oh, Jed…"

"You're worth it," he muttered gruffly. "Just say yes."

Say yes…

Except that she really *wasn't* tempted. Not at all. She wasn't tempted and it wouldn't be right. "It's not what I want, Jed."

Now he was the one gaping. "Do you have a clue how much money we're talking about?"

"A lot. I get that. But I'm not a writer, Jed. *You* are. And I don't want to be a writer any more than I want to be a typist. I want *you*." *I love you.* She almost said it, but she couldn't. Not now. Not when the world they'd created together in the past few glorious months seemed to be crumbling. "In the end, it wouldn't work for me, even if you paid me way more than you should, even if you put my name on your books. I'm exactly what you said. A shopkeeper, a party planner, a darn good cook.

I don't want to sit in an office day after day typing up stories. *You're* the storyteller. I want to help you and support you. But I have to have my own work and it's better that we face that now."

"I don't believe this." His eyes were green ice. "I offer you the moon and you say you don't want it."

She was losing him. She felt the loss as an ache in the pit of her stomach, an awful, increasing tightness in her chest. Still, she fought on. She tried to make him see. "It's not right, what you've offered me. It's a bribe, pure and simple, and I don't take bribes. You're shooting yourself in the foot over and over and wondering why you have trouble walking. I don't get why you're so blind, why you won't let yourself see it. You either need to stop being so rough on your assistants that you scare them off, or you need to find a different way. Like maybe figure out why you have this weird typing phobia, or try using speech recognition software."

"I do not have a typing phobia." He spoke so slowly, each word clearly enunciated, sharp as one of his knives. "I know how to type. I don't *want* to type. And I have zero interest in special software. That is not my process."

Oh, she could get good and snippy about now. *He* didn't want to type? Well, neither did she, and hadn't she made that excruciatingly clear?

Keep it together, her wiser self advised, though the hothead within had a whole bunch of not-so-nice things she could say.

No. She would not lose her temper. But damned if she would sit here and listen to him go on about his *process*, as if it was something sacred, something cast in stone.

"I have to say it, Jed. Your process isn't working for you."

"You don't know what you're talking about." It came out in a warning growl.

She refused to let him cow her. "I know a lot more than you're willing to give me credit for at the moment, that's for sure. I know that you're standing in your own way on so many levels. You're so much better than this *process* you keep going on about. We both know that you are. You're the man who held me so tenderly all those weeks ago, who listened without judging, who comforted me while I poured out my long, sad story of all the stupid mistakes I've made. You're the man who treats me like I'm beautiful and does it so well that I feel like a queen. The man who showed me how incredible sex could be, the man who flew me first class to New York City and gave me the time of my life there, the one who backed me up when Biff Townley tried to run a number on me again. You're the man who built Wigs his own catio—even though you claim you hate cats. Why do you think you have to scare everyone away? And why do you make writing your books more difficult than it has to be? Do you somehow think you don't deserve the amazing life you've built for yourself?"

"Enough." He said it way too quietly. She looked in his eyes and saw emptiness. He had shut her out, shut her down. And then he said the worst thing of all. "You should go."

Elise flinched as if he'd struck her.

And then the indignation flooded in. She longed to start shouting, to let him know exactly how destructive and stupid and wrong he was being. She needed to tell him off more than she wanted to draw her next breath.

It just felt so unreal. Impossible, that he would do this, that he would so curtly and coldly throw away all that they had.

On the heels of her fury came tears. They pushed at the back of her throat, begging her to let them fall. *I can't go. Don't make me go. I love you...*

Once again, she hovered on the verge of the big declaration.

But no. Tossing in words of love now wouldn't fix what he'd shattered here.

She gulped the tears back before a single one had a chance to dribble down her cheek. Yes, her heart was breaking. But she was angry, too—worse than angry. Furious. It was not a good time to proclaim undying love.

He was right. She had to go.

Chapter Twelve

An hour later, Elise tossed the last of her stuff in her car.

She went back in to get Wigs, knowing she would find him on the catio. As she went down the stairs, she could hear the driving beat of rock music coming from the workout room.

He isn't even going to come out and say goodbye. Traitorous tears tightened her throat again.

With a low hiss of fury, she gulped them back. She hoped he dropped a dumbbell on his foot, the big lunk.

Wigs sat on his catio, nose to the wire fence, watching several small brown birds, which flew off when she opened the French doors.

"Come on, sweetheart. Time to go."

Wigs remained at the fence, staring off toward the slowly darkening sky.

So she went over there, scooped him up and pressed her face to the warm ruff at his neck. "We are out of here. Now."

He purred for her. She found the low sound somewhat comforting as she carried him back through the house and out the door, pausing only to leave her house key and garage-door remote on the counter in the utility room.

The back stairway to her apartment still smelled of donuts. With Wigs in her arms, she paused on the first step.

And remembered...

Their first time. He'd set her on the kitchen counter and taken away all of her clothes. She'd been shy about the weight she'd put on from eating too many donuts.

And he'd said, "Thank God for donuts."

She'd wrinkled her nose at him, hadn't she? And asked, "What does that even mean?"

"It means the donuts look good on you and you should keep eating them," had been the reply.

Well, maybe she would just do that. Buy a whole box of donuts and eat every last one.

She wanted to kill him.

She wanted to get superdrunk, eat a dozen donuts and start auto-dialing his number.

Drunk dialing on donuts. Did it get any worse?

Forget the donuts for now. She went on up the stairs, sticking her key in the lock, pushing open the door.

Somehow, tonight, the place looked smaller and sadder than ever.

Just keep moving. Do what you have to do. You can have your crying jag later.

She brought everything in and set up Wigs with his box and his bowls, his activity center and his best buddy, the cleaning robot. As soon as she had the bowls filled with food and water, she called Nell.

Her sister had barely said "Hello?" before Elise felt the tears rising again.

"Nellie?" It was all she had to say.

"My God. What's happened?"

"Jed and I..."

"What? Tell me."

She gulped the tears back again. "It's over. That's all. It's over with Jed."

Nellie let out a string of very bad words. "I'll deal with him later. Right now, I'm coming over."

That sounded perfect to Elise. "Good. I'm going downstairs and getting donuts. And I think I have a bottle of tequila around here somewhere..."

Nell arrived fifteen minutes later. She brought Jody. And within the hour, all their other sisters—by blood, of the heart and through marriage—came, too. Clara came, and cousin Rory. And Carter's bride Paige. And Chloe, Quinn's wife. Even Addie, a week from her due date, drove in from the ranch where she lived with James. Addie's grandfather's girlfriend, Lola Dorset, came with her. Everybody brought something to contribute to what Elise proudly called her pity party.

They crowded around the dinky kitchen table, eating donuts and Cheetos, trail mix and Oreos, drinking coffee, tea, juice and soft drinks because Elise never did find the tequila and her sisters had enough sense not to bring liquor when a broken heart was involved.

Elise told them how much she loved Jed. She had no shame. Why should she? Jed had been a complete ass, but that didn't mean she'd stopped loving him. She told her sisters how she'd fallen and fallen and kept on fall-

ing until she was all the way in love with him. She also
told them that he'd offered her a fortune and her name
on his books if only she would stay on as his assistant.
"And when I said no, we had a big fight. I said some
really tough things to him. And then he told me to go."

Nell threatened to kill him in a gruesome, bloody
and painful way—after first removing his testicles. She
almost looked like she meant it. And that had everyone
laughing. They showered Elise in hugs and support,
passed her another chocolate-covered old-fashioned
and poured her a fresh cup of coffee.

It didn't heal her sad and torn-up heart, but it definitely helped.

And then Tracy called.

Her lifelong best friend said, "I had this feeling. I
was going to text and check on you—but then, I don't
know. I just had to call. Is everything all right?"

That brought a fresh flood of tears. Her sisters offered more hugs and tissues. She told Tracy everything,
that she was in love with a wonderful man who really
had no idea how wonderful he was. "Oh, and I'm in
partnership with Jody!" she added. She and Jody high-
fived across the table and she quickly told Tracy about
the upcoming reopening of Bravo Catering.

Tracy congratulated her on her new business venture.
"And about this thing with Jed. You're being noble and
sweet and not saying it. But I know you need me. I'm
coming home, at least for a few days. We can stay up
all night and tell each other everything."

But Elise wouldn't have it. "No way. You have a de-
gree to earn. I miss you and I always will, but I've got
backup." She smiled through her tears at her sisters

close around her. "I'll see you when you come home for Thanksgiving. We'll talk all night then."

Reluctantly, Tracy agreed.

Two days later, Elise got her final check from Jed. It was more than she expected—the entire amount she would have made had she stayed until the end of October.

A terse note came with it. *Don't argue about the amount. You deserve every penny.* She started to call him, but stopped in mid-dial.

He had taught her so much in their time together, not the least of which was her own worth. Yes, she'd said hard things to him. But they had been true things, spoken with love. And he'd sent her away for it.

A big check and a grumpy two-sentence note was hardly "I love you, Elise. Please forgive me."

So she didn't call. She cashed that check and moved on.

The next day Addie had her baby, a little boy they named Brandon after the baby's natural father, who had died far too young. Elise went to the hospital to meet the newest member of the family. She held the tiny boy in her arms and thought of Jed, wished he'd been there, sent a silent prayer to heaven that he was all right.

At least she had plenty to do. She kept busy working long hours with Jody at their expanded location, planning their social media campaign, ordering the equipment for her kitchen, getting it in and installed, hiring her sister-in-law Chloe to design the front area, to create a cozy little bakery, both beautiful and homey. There would be adorable crystal chandeliers, warm pink walls and cute iron tables with comfy padded chairs. And lots and lots of greenery, courtesy of Bloom.

She found that she was happy, mostly, her life back on track after a long string of setbacks. But her heart did ache. Nights were the toughest. Just her and Wigs alone in the darkness of her tiny apartment. She cuddled him close and longed for Jed, though she felt she couldn't reach out to him, that it wasn't for her to make that move.

She tried her best not to worry about him, all alone with no one to talk to.

Jed was not doing well.

At first, he pushed thoughts of Elise from his mind by burying himself in rewrites, working twenty-hour days, barely pausing to eat, let alone sleep. Ten nonstop days and nights after she left him, he sent *McCannon's Fall* off to Carl in New York.

Without the book to fill his mind, things got bad fast.

His bed was too big without her to hold on to. His fancy house was empty, the damn catio deserted. Sometimes, he thought he heard Wigs meowing. He would wander from room to room, knowing he would find nothing, driven to look for the fur ball, anyway.

After a week of that idiocy, he decided he needed to keep active. He worked out until every muscle jumped and quivered with exhaustion. He threw a lot of knives. He visited the shooting range.

On a Thursday, during the first snowstorm of the season, he took his Range Rover halfway up the mountain, where he and his father used to live.

Temperatures that day stayed well below freezing.

As if he cared how cold it was. He had good gear, rated for arctic conditions. When even the Range Rover could go no farther, he set the brake and got out into the driving snow. He found the trail he knew so well and climbed steadily upward, oblivious to the cold and the limited visibility.

The cabin was still there, locked up good and tight. The shed where his dad had stored their library of books hadn't fared as well. A tree limb had fallen on it, gone right through the roof. Jed felt some satisfaction that at least he'd emptied it out years ago and donated the books to the Justice Creek Library.

He stood on the rough steps that led up to the door and stared at the spot where he'd found Calvin Walsh's lifeless body all those years ago. That was a dark day, the day his father died, the day he saw for the first time that he was completely alone in the world.

It had been snowing that day, too. Tears freezing on his cold cheeks, he'd stared at the big man unmoving on the ground and wondered what he was going to do with himself now. He'd known peace and safety, companionship and mutual understanding with his father. It had always been the two of them, Calvin and Jedidiah, father and son, preparing for the end times, alone against the world.

How would he survive in the big, wide, corrupt, noisy world? He'd had no idea. But he had known that he wasn't staying on that mountain all alone. The end times hadn't come and he needed to learn how to live.

And he'd done that, hadn't he? He'd succeeded beyond his wildest imaginings. He was *the* Jed Walsh, a household name. He wrote the books people wanted to read and he made the big bucks.

But standing there on the steps of the one-room house where his father had raised him, staring at the empty, snowy ground where Calvin Walsh had fallen, he knew he'd gone nowhere.

He was as alone as he'd ever been—no. More so, now that he loved Elise. Now that he knew what it was to look in a woman's eyes and see everything, a full life, that strange thing called happiness, a future filled with laughter and tears, disagreements and compromises, with everything that made it all worthwhile.

The wind sang through the tall trees and the snow kept on falling, covering the rocky ground in pure, cold white. Jed turned and started back down the mountain.

That night and the next and the one after that, he woke in the darkest hours before dawn, disoriented. For a moment or two, he would wonder what was missing. And then he remembered: the woman he loved curled up in his arms. And that damn cat purring from the foot of the bed...

It took those three nights after he went up the mountain for him to finally accept what he needed to do. And it wasn't to find another assistant. He was finished with that. In his life as a writer, he'd found two women capable of putting up with him while he worked. Two women who understood him and took care of him and didn't take any of his crap. One had been like the mother he'd lost too soon.

The other was Elise.

After Elise, no one would stack up. There was no point in torturing even one more hapless keyboarder.

He needed another way. And what else was there for him to do but get going on that? He went into his office and sat down at his desk.

And after three more weeks of working like a madman, he was finally ready to go after what mattered most.

Jed knew where to find her. A few bills and circulars originally addressed to her apartment had shown up in his mailbox after she left and before she'd had them rerouted again. He'd sent that mail on to her—but not before making a note of where she lived.

On the Saturday before Thanksgiving, he got in the Range Rover and headed for Creekside Drive. He parked in the lot in back of her building and entered through the rear door. The smell of donuts hit him, along with a memory so perfect and sweet: Elise on the kitchen counter, shy, breathless and wonderfully soft. He'd never forget that night—or those little pink panties he'd torn off to get to her...

Longing almost doubled him over. He looked up the narrow stairs and didn't know if he could do it.

What if she couldn't forgive him? What if she'd simply moved on?

Didn't matter. He had no choice here. He couldn't go on without at least giving it a shot.

He gripped the banister and started climbing.

Hers was the first door on the right. He knocked.

Nothing. So he knocked again. Still no answer. He peered through the peephole, saw nothing and pictured her on the other side, refusing to answer, peering right back at him.

He tried the doorknob. Locked. He should call.

But he was afraid to call. What if she hung up on him? Surely she'd take pity on him and hear him out if he could only reach her face-to-face.

He went back down the stairs and out the door. Once in the car, he made himself call her.

The call went straight to voice mail. The answering message wasn't even her voice. "You have reached Elise Bravo and Bravo Catering. Please leave a message."

"Elise. I need to talk to you. Please call me back." He disconnected before he realized he hadn't left his name.

It had been almost two months since he'd sent her away.

Could she have forgotten what his voice sounded like in that time? Would she even know it was him?

She would, he realized, because she had his number programmed into her phone.

Didn't she?

He wasn't 100 percent sure...

God. He was pitiful. A hopeless case.

He started up the car and headed home—and somehow ended up on Central Street. And there it was, Bravo Catering, right next door to Bloom. He parked and went in. There were glass cases filled with wonderful-smelling muffins and cupcakes, greenery everywhere and old-timey crystal chandeliers overhead. Half the tables were occupied with smiling, muffin-eating customers. It was charming and well done.

"What can I get you today?" asked the pretty girl behind the counter.

"I want to speak with Elise."

"I'm sorry, you missed her. She's got a wedding today." A wedding? So soon? Didn't women take months and months to plan those? The girl behind the counter smoothed her pink apron. "Just let me take your name and number and—"

"No. It's okay. I'll...get in touch with her later." He turned and started for the door—but then, at the last minute, he pivoted and went under the wide interior arch to Bloom.

Jody turned from watering a fern as he approached. She didn't look especially happy to see him. "Jed Walsh." She marched over and plunked the watering can down on the register counter. "We all thought you died. You're lucky Nellie has restrained herself or you'd be missing a few vital body parts."

Okay, he was a douche. It wasn't news. "You can't possibly despise me as much as I do myself."

"Oh, but I can try. What is the *matter* with you?"

"A lot. Jody, I really need to see her."

Jody's mouth was a thin slash of complete refusal. "She's working."

"The girl in the bakery said she had a wedding..."

"Call her. Leave a message."

"I did. I forgot to leave my name. I... Come on, Jody. I know I don't deserve another chance with her, but give me a break here."

Jody stared at her watering can for an endless count of five, then turned on Jed again. "You want another chance?"

He held out both arms wide. "You are looking at a desperate man. Come on. Where is she?"

"Can't you just wait until—"

"I've waited too long already. Think about it. You'll know it's true. This shop—yours and hers." He gestured at the greenery around them, the bakery through the archway, all of it. Everything. "It's great. Well done. I get it. I know it's what she wants and I want her to have that. Whatever she wants. I know I ruined everything. Just give me a chance to make it right."

Jody eyed him sideways. "She took this wedding at the last minute. An old friend of ours got engaged at Halloween and wanted to have the big wedding *and* do it right away. Leesie's worked her butt off. If you mess it all up by making a scene..."

"No scenes. I swear to you. Just tell me where to find her."

* * *

The friend's wedding was in a farmhouse several miles out of town. Jed parked with the wedding guests, in an open field not far from the house. The snow from three weeks before had long since melted. It was a sunny day, mild for November. He walked up the wide driveway to the front door, where a white-haired lady greeted him, pinned a rosebud to the lapel of his jacket and kissed him on the cheek.

"You've just made it in time." She put a finger to her wrinkled lips. "Shh, now. They're all in the living room." She ushered him inside.

He went through a roomy foyer with a wide, flower-bedecked staircase leading up and on into the living room, where flowers were everywhere and the bride and the groom stood facing a guy in a clerical collar in front of a big brick fireplace.

The white chairs arranged in rows with an aisle down the middle were all occupied. Jed hung back near the arch to the foyer and watched two people he'd never seen before exchange their vows. They did look happy, he thought. And deeply in love.

He remained, staying out of the way as much as possible, through all of it—the picture-taking and the quick, expert switch from row seating for the ceremony to a buffet line and tables for the reception. A four-piece band set up in a corner and began playing dance music.

And Elise?

She was everywhere. She wore a pink cashmere sweater and one of those pencil skirts that clung to every lush, delicious curve. He wanted to duck into a closet and wait for her to walk by—just pop out, snatch her hand, haul her in there and start making up for all the time they'd lost.

But he didn't. He behaved himself. On the drive out here, he'd come up with a plan—not a very good one, true. But the best he could do given that he wasn't going home until he'd had a chance to talk with her. He would stay out of her way until the reception was over. He reasoned that as long as she didn't know he was here, he wouldn't be disrupting the party.

So he kept his eye out, ducking quickly out of sight whenever she got too close or looked as though she might glance his way. It wasn't easy, keeping her from spotting him. She was constantly on the move. She kept track of everything and yet at the same time, she didn't seem to be rushing or under any pressure. She was serene. Unruffled. Even bobbing and weaving to keep her from spotting him, he could see that this was her element.

And that had him worried all over again that he didn't have a chance with her now. Why would she ever come back to a man who'd tried to bully her into giving up the work she loved?

As the guests started filling plates at the buffet, the sweet older lady who'd greeted him at the door took his arm. "I've been trying to place you. Now, let me guess. You're Jerry's cousin Silas, aren't you?"

He made a vaguely agreeable sound that could have meant anything.

"I knew it." The old lady chuckled. "I'm Marlena. So lovely to finally meet you, Silas."

"Marlena, the pleasure is all mine."

She squeezed his arm. "A big man like you? You must be starving."

"Now that you mention it, that prime rib looks amazing." There was a guy in a chef's hat carving a giant, juicy-looking roast halfway down the buffet line.

Marlena let go of his arm and patted his back. "Well, get after it, Silas. And don't be a stranger, you hear me now? I know you and Jerry have had your disagreements, but family is family. Jerry speaks of you often. He misses you terribly."

By then, Jed was starting to feel a little guilty for letting the sweet old lady think he was someone he wasn't. He gave her another grunt of agreement and hit the buffet.

Once he had a plate piled high with prime rib and several mouthwatering sides, he chose a table in the corner, kind of out of the way, with a pillar to duck behind whenever Elise came too close. A couple of guys who were probably at least Marlena's age joined him. The food was delicious—no surprise there, given Elise's talents in the kitchen. And the company was great, too. The old guys, Mervin and Bob, were brothers, WWII vets who'd both been at the Battle of the Bulge. The three of them were talking brilliant military maneuvers through history when Jed smelled clean sheets and knew he was busted.

She was standing right behind him. Dear God, just the smell of her...

Longing coursed through him. She bent close and a loose curl of her hair brushed his cheek. He had to order his grasping hands not to reach back and grab her. "Outside," she whispered. "Now."

When he dared to turn his head, she was already headed for the door. He made his excuses to Bob and Mervin and hustled out after her.

She led him halfway to the field where the cars were parked. Then finally, she stopped and braced her hands on those fine, full hips. "I've seen the guest list. You're not on it."

He kept his arms at his sides, though every muscle yearned to reach for her. "I needed to talk to you. I was going to wait until the party was over, I swear to you I was."

Those coffee-brown eyes got softer—or was that just wishful thinking on his part? "It's not the time, Jed. I'm working."

"I know, but—"

"Look. If you'll call me tomorrow, we can meet, okay? We can talk."

Hope. He felt it now. A feather lightness in his chest, a burning in his brain. He only needed to grab her and kiss her, shove her in the Range Rover and drive away fast. Somehow, he kept himself from doing that. "Tomorrow? I'll call, you'll answer. You mean that?"

Her eyes were softer still. "I do."

His control broke. "Elise." He reached for her.

But she jumped back. "Not here. I mean it. Tomorrow. Please."

It took all the will he had, but he put a lid on it. "Tomorrow. Okay." And he made himself turn and head for his car.

He went back to his house.

But he couldn't stay there. He stopped the car in the garage—and then shifted into Reverse and backed it right out.

Where the hell to now?

He knew where: her place.

* * *

The back door onto the parking lot was locked when he got there. But he went around front, bought a glazed donut and ate it as he wandered down the hallway past the restrooms. The door at the end was unlocked.

Did he feel like a stalker?

Maybe a little.

Too bad. She'd said she would take his call tomorrow. He was only moving the time frame up a little. Nothing wrong with that. He polished off the donut and ducked into the men's room to rinse the sugar off his hands.

When he went back to the hallway, it remained deserted. He went on through the door at the end. Five steps more and he reached the stairs leading up to her apartment.

He went up and sat on the top step to wait.

An hour went by. And another. She still wasn't back.

Well, fine. He would wait all night if he had to.

Eventually, he leaned his head against the wall and closed his eyes. He must have dropped off because he woke up to the sound of a motorboat speeding toward him.

"Wigs. What the hell?" Wigs didn't answer, but the purring got louder. He pulled the cat onto his lap. "She's not going to like finding you out here with me."

Wigs reached up a hairy paw and gently patted his cheek. Jed stroked the thick orange fur. Eventually he leaned his head against the wall and went back to sleep.

The next time he woke, Elise was standing over him. The view was spectacular. But he tried his best to look regretful. "I'm sorry. I couldn't stay away—and I have no idea how this damn cat got out. I was sitting here minding my own business and suddenly he was in my lap."

She shook her head—at him. And at the cat in his lap, too. And then she said something wonderful. "Come on inside."

So he rose and carried Wigs into the one-room apartment. It wasn't fancy and it was much too small. Still, she'd made it cozy, with bright pictures on the walls and comfortable furniture attractively arranged.

"Homey," he said, and it was, because she was there.

She took the cat from him. He waited while she opened a can and filled one of the cat bowls. Wigs dug in. She washed her hands and dried them, took the pins from her hair and shook it out on her shoulders, at which point he realized he would pay half his next advance to be allowed to sift his fingers through the coffee-colored strands.

But first things first. He held up a memory stick.

When she eyed it with wariness, he quickly explained, "This is the first three chapters of my next book. I wrote it using voice recognition software—which I have to admit, has come a long way since the last time I tried it." Did she look doubtful? He couldn't really blame her. "I get that the last thing you want or need right now is an update on Jack McCannon. But still, I'm asking you to bring this up on your laptop. I need you to see that I really did it—I wrote sixty-three pages without terrorizing a single innocent assistant."

By then, those eyes had gone soft again and her beautiful mouth trembled. "I would love an update on Jack McCannon." She whipped the stick from his hand and opened the laptop that waited on the counter. "There's a beer in the fridge. Take another nap. Whatever. I'm going to need at least an hour. Maybe more..."

He did grab himself a beer. But sleeping? No freaking way. He sat on the sofa with Wigs draped along the back of it while she read the material through.

When she turned on her stool to meet his eyes at last, hers were suspiciously misty. "It's good. It's really good. I do have a few suggestions…"

He stood. "And I can't wait to hear them."

"But not right now." She sounded slightly breathless. Breathless was excellent.

"No. Not right now." He closed the short distance from the sofa to the counter. Gently, he guided a curl of hair behind her ear—and she let him. She even leaned a little into his hand. "I went to Bravo Catering today. It's beautiful, what you've done with the bakery. And the wedding? I wasn't even invited and I had a great time. The food was so good. And I watched you."

Did she seem disapproving? A little. He couldn't say he blamed her. She asked, "How long were you there?"

"I lurked for hours, ducking out of sight whenever you got near and I shamelessly pretended to be some guy named Silas."

She laughed. "What in the…? Silas?"

"Long story. Doesn't matter. What I mean is, you were doing what you love to do and you're really good at it and it shows." He caught her hand then, brought it to his lips and kissed it. "Elise, I was so wrong. I can't even count the ways."

Her eyes got misty. "Oh, yes you were. And I was so afraid, Jed. That you would never come for me." A tear escaped then. It left a shining trail as it slid down the velvety curve of her cheek.

He wiped it up with a finger and put it to his tongue—salty. And very sweet. "I couldn't come for you. Not until I knew what to do, how to move forward. And it's been bad, Elise. Now I've been with you, none of it makes much sense if you're not there."

"Oh, I know the feeling."

"I couldn't stand for you to see me like that, desperate and scared. Trapped in a bad place, afraid I would never find my way out."

"But Jed, you saw *me* like that the first morning I made you breakfast."

He ran the backs of his fingers down the side of her throat. Her skin was cool velvet. "I remember that day. You made me French toast. Best I ever tasted."

"And then I burst into tears and ran to my room and you followed me and listened to me pour out my sad tale of woe. You held me and comforted me and…well, you made it all better. I want to be the one who makes all better for you."

He caught her face between his hands, bent down and pressed a kiss against those lips he would never get enough of tasting. "You do make it all better for me."

"But you sent me away."

"I told you. I didn't want—"

"—me to see you like that. I heard you."

"And there's more," he admitted. "It gets worse. After you, there was no way I was having another person in my office sitting in your chair, typing my words for me. No one could compare, that's a simple fact. And then there was what you told me the day I asked you to leave, that I needed to get out of my own way, not be so hung up on my precious *process*. You were so right. Until I did change it up, until I proved to myself that I could make it happen on my own, there always would have been the danger that I would start in on you again, that I would try to manipulate you into typing my words for me, into saving my ass."

She laid her cool, soft hand against his cheek. "I have more faith in you than that."

"How can you? I did try to manipulate you. You told me repeatedly that you were done when the book was done and I refused to believe you." He shook his head and grumbled, "And I can't believe I'm confessing all this. I should keep my mouth shut. Quit while I'm ahead."

"Uh-uh. You should be honest with me. And you are." Her smile bloomed wide. "And I'm so glad. But I do need you to promise me that in the future, if things get bad for you, turning your back on what we have together won't be an option. In the bad times, you have to let me be there for you, no matter how tough it gets for you. That's part of what we are, part of you and me together."

He couldn't make that promise fast enough. "We have a deal. From now on, no matter how bad it gets, we're both staying. Nobody gets away. There's no escape. You're stuck with me."

"Good." She said it so easily, with no hesitation.

He stroked a hand down her hair. "How'd I get so lucky to have a chance with you?"

"Well, you did agree to pay me four thousand a week— and then there was that jetted tub." She was grinning.

And he couldn't let another minute go by without saying it. "I love you, Elise."

Color flooded her wonderful face. "And I love you, Jed."

Words rose in his throat and he let them spill out. "I want to marry you. I want a life with you…" What was he saying? He was babbling like an idiot. He should shut up. But the words just kept coming. "It's too early, right, to be asking you that? And there should be a ring. I know that. A ring with a diamond so big, you can't possibly say no. I've botched it. I can see that. I'm doing this all wrong and I—"

"Jed." She gazed up at him, surprisingly dewy-eyed after all his stupid blathering. "Yes."

The world spun to a stop. "I don't… I can't… Did you just say yes?"

She laughed then, full out and glorious. "Yes, Jed. Yes, yes, yes!"

That did it. He kissed her—a proper kiss. Slow and wet and deep. And then he scooped her up, carried her over to the bed in the corner and got to work undressing her. Once all her beautiful curves were bare for him, he got rid of his own clothes, as well.

They stood together, naked by the side of her bed. "Come home with me tonight, you and the fur ball."

"Yes, we'll come home with you."

"But first…" Taking her shoulders, he guided her down to sit on the edge of the bed. Then he kneeled at her feet. Looking up into her misty eyes, he saw the truth so very clearly. From the day his father died, nothing in the world had really made sense to him. There had been no one who claimed him, no one who felt like his own— not until now. "You're everything to me, Elise. I can't be- lieve I've found you at last, can't believe that you're here, that you said yes, that you're taking me back."

"I love you, Jed." She bent over him, close and then closer. He smelled her fresh scent, felt her breath in his hair, her soft fingers caressing his neck. She urged him up onto the bed with her and held him to her heart. He lost himself in the welcoming heat of her body.

Afterward, she fell asleep in his arms. He didn't want to wake her, so they ended up staying the night in her little apartment.

In the morning, she made him French toast for breakfast. Then she packed up her suitcases and gathered all the cat stuff together. He helped her carry everything down to the cars. She followed him home.

When they got there, before she even brought Wigs in, he took her hand and led her out the open garage door, around to the winding front walk and up the wide porch steps.

"Wait right here." He unlocked the door, stepped in just long enough to turn off the alarm and then stepped back out. She laughed as he swung her high in his arms and carried her over the threshold.

And then she kissed him. "I love you," she said, her dark eyes shining. "I'm so glad you came to get me, Jed. I'm so glad you've finally brought me home."

* * * * *

Watch for Darius Bravo's story
A BRAVO FOR CHRISTMAS
coming in December 2016
only from Mills & Boon Cherish.

MILLS & BOON®

Cherish™

EXPERIENCE THE ULTIMATE RUSH OF FALLING IN LOVE

A sneak peek at next month's titles...

In stores from 20th October 2016:

- **Christmas Baby for the Princess** – Barbara Wallace *and* **The Maverick's Holiday Surprise** – Karen Rose Smith
- **Greek Tycoon's Mistletoe Proposal** – Kandy Shepherd *and* **A Child Under His Tree** – Allison Leigh

In stores from 3rd November 2016:

- **The Billionaire's Prize** – Rebecca Winters *and* **The Rancher's Expectant Christmas** – Karen Templeton
- **The Earl's Snow-Kissed Proposal** – Nina Milne *and* **Callie's Christmas Wish** – Merline Lovelace

---

Just can't wait?

Buy our books online a month before they hit the shops!

www.millsandboon.co.uk

Also available as eBooks.

MILLS & BOON®

EXCLUSIVE EXCERPT

When Dea Caracciolo agrees to attend a sporting
event as tycoon Guido Rossano's date, sparks fly!

Read on for a sneak preview of
THE BILLIONAIRE'S PRIZE
the final instalment of Rebecca Winters'
thrilling Cherish trilogy
THE MONTINARI MARRIAGES

The dark blue short-sleeved dress with small red
poppies Dea was wearing hugged her figure, then flared
from the waist to the knee. With every step the material danced around her beautiful legs, imitating the
flounce of her hair she wore down the way he liked it.
Talk about his heart failing him!

"Dea—"

Her searching gaze fused with his. "I hope it's all
right." The slight tremor in her voice betrayed her fear
that she wasn't welcome. If she only knew...

"You've had an open invitation since we met."
Nodding his thanks to Mario, he put his arm around
her shoulders and drew her inside the suite.

He slid his hands in her hair. "You're the most
beautiful sight this man has ever seen." With uncon-
trolled hunger he lowered his mouth to hers and began
to devour her. Over the announcer's voice and the roar
of the crowd, he heard her little moans of pleasure as
their bodies merged and they drank deeply.

When she swayed in his arms, he half carried her over to the couch where they could give in to their frenzied needs. She smelled heavenly. One kiss grew into another until she became his entire world. He'd never known a feeling like this and lost track of time and place.

"Do you know what you do to me?" he whispered against her lips with feverish intensity.

"I came for the same reason."

Her admission pulled him all the way under. Once in a while the roar of the crowd filled the room, but that didn't stop him from twining his legs with hers. He desired a closeness they couldn't achieve as long as their clothes separated them.

"I want you, *bellissima*. I want you all night long. Do you understand what I'm saying?"

Don't miss
THE BILLIONAIRE'S PRIZE
by Rebecca Winters

Available November 2016

www.millsandboon.co.uk

MILLS & BOON®

Why shop at millsandboon.co.uk?

Each year, thousands of romance readers find their perfect read at millsandboon.co.uk. That's because we're passionate about bringing you the very best romantic fiction. Here are some of the advantages of shopping at www.millsandboon.co.uk:

* **Get new books first**—you'll be able to buy your favourite books one month before they hit the shops

* **Get exclusive discounts**—you'll also be able to buy our specially created monthly collections, with up to 50% off the RRP

* **Find your favourite authors**—latest news, interviews and new releases for all your favourite authors and series on our website, plus ideas for what to try next

* **Join in**—once you've bought your favourite books, don't forget to register with us to rate, review and join in the discussions

Visit **www.millsandboon.co.uk**
for all this and more today!